VILLARY

(Vieillerie—Fr.: old rubbish; old things; old-fashioned ideas)

J. Well Delozier

ISBN 978-0-692-95144-6
Publisher-Go-Joe! –Queen Creek, AZ
Library of Congress Card Control Number: 2017914631
Delozier, J. Wells
Villary / Delozier, J. Wells
Available Formats: eBook | Paperback distribution

ABOUT THE AUTHOR

J. Wells DeLozier was born in Memphis but grew to manhood in Nashville. He served eight years active duty in the U.S. Army, including two tours of duty in Germany in the 56th Field Artillery Brigade, the front-line in the Cold War (1975-1978 / 1979-1982). He received his Bachelor of Arts degree in English from (then) Memphis State University in 1986, then graduated summa cum laude from the last cycle of Lyndhurst Fellows at Memphis State U., 1988-1989. He is tri-lingual. He has taught English, German, and Journalism at various levels, but prefers accounting and public relations work. He has been married to the love of his life, the former Leah Anne Gorin of Nashville, since June of 1993. They live in the Metropolitan Phoenix, Arizona, area with their (rescue) dog and cat, and travel to Europe as often as possible. First published while attending school at Fort Sill, Oklahoma, <u>Villary</u> is his first novel.

I.

There was always—always something to worry about, wasn't there? And wasn't that more the *rule* now, as opposed to the exception? Christ, wasn't it always *something?!* He sat in his chair, the Yellow Rose of Texas, with its burnished armrests and velvet seat too wide by half a foot—sized *right* for a Texan, of course—glanced at the papers on his desk, stopped long enough to briefly admire the bronzed heads of Ronald Reagan and Audie Murphy used as paperweights, and pondered the latest challenge to his kingdom. So *when*, exactly, had it become somehow *insufficient* to be re-elected—to keep your seat in congress as the duly-elected representative of your constituents—just by beating a Democrat? When had *that* changed, and *why* hadn't someone told him? Is that why his more-elderly Republican friends referred to the good old days as the *good old days? What* did a fella' have to *do* to be guaranteed a little job-security—declare Martial Law, for Chrissakes?! He glared at the bust of his hero, Reagan, fire in his eyes.

"What do I *do*, Ronnie-baby?" he whispered apprehensively, hopeful of a sign from the great divinity himself. "You started this mess, so I took all my cues from you, brother-mine! Lord, if I move any further right I'm liable to go right on over the edge—but this fella' wants to primary your ol' pal Sid right back to the Lone Star state for *good* . . and I don't know what I did to deserve it!"

Sidney Villary, three-term member of the U.S. House of

1

Representatives, resigned to the coming storm, leaned back in the Yellow Rose and threw his pen on the desk, disgusted.

"Send me a *sign!*" he implored the bust, as though it held the inevitable cure. "Please, *please* . . send me a sign . . Can't you do that for your ol' pal, Sid? . ."

Had his parents been present to assess the damage—it was *never* a good idea to have either one around too close for too long—they'd have hemmed and hawed about this and that, grumbling here and there every now and then until, deciding that not only had nothing *changed* but that nothing was ever likely to, they'd have determined that when all was said and done their only child looked . . well, *moody*. To them he invariably appeared to be . . moody. Never happy, never sad, never elated, never blue, never *anything*, one way or the other. And *never*, God help them, with a woman. Just moody. "How such a *moody* young man ever got elected to congress I'll never know!" his mother cried election night at his first victory party, his father nodding in stoic agreement, like some sort of unaffected grim reaper . . only their *young man* knew better. He knew exactly what it was that had them so at odds with his campaign and victory—and it had nothing to do with his moodiness or demeanor.

For pity's sake, had he not always taken the tenet "Cleanliness is next to Godliness" to heart, even though a God-forsaken, liberal heathen had said it? Why wasn't that good enough? Next to his genuinely conservative politics, his young good looks, his freshness of appearance, his attention to detail concerning his clothes and haircut, his nails clipped and manicured—yes, his conservative *demeanor*—had served him well. Did he not sweep his soft black hair to the left, just like Cary Grant, his father's favorite actor (next to John Wayne, of course)? Was his seventy-four-and-a-half inches in height—

"the perfect height," according to his mother—somehow inadequate in his father's eyes, just because the old man was a few inches under six feet? The clear-blue eyes, the patrician nose, the beckoningly-thin lips, all set into a face that hid a five o'clock shadow beautifully—the thin, toned body of a former distance-runner—did *none* of this count for anything?! Had not every single one of these personal characteristics, in the shrewd lingo of his campaign manager, "contributed immeasurably" to his being elected in the first place? Were they worth *nothing?!* Moody, *hell!* How in the world could he ever smile about his immediate family, knowing full well that, come the holidays, he'd be raked over the coals like a pork tenderloin as he sliced into the Thanksgiving turkey? Moody? Did they really think he was that ignorant, *that* naïve about the real problem?

It had all been brought into focus yet again, for the *umpteenth* time, four months before as he turned the big *"4-0!"* Delivered in the familiar red, white, and blue Fedex envelope, his mother's birthday card seemed more like a funeral notice than congratulations. The card itself seemed innocent enough: its front cover had two Bassett hounds adorably photographed in such a manner that their noses seemed far and away their dominant feature, the caption overhead reading *'WE'VE SNIFFED-OUT A SPECIAL DAY APPROACHING!'* Inside the card he found five crisp hundred-dollar bills—as though he wasn't *really* knocking-down a hundred sixty thousand-plus per year—with **HAPPY BIRTHDAY!** in honest-to-god Burnt Siena block letters. Incredible! And then, of course, "We *love* you! Mom and Dad!" in his mother's handwriting at bottom. Nice enough, to be sure . . but it was the cover *and* his mother's handwritten message inside he'd surely remember best because, as usual,

3

both underscored the problem as only his parents could appreciate it. Two Bassett hounds? *Two?!* Yes, of course, two—for no one can be *really* happy unless paired with another, a reverse Janus of sorts, focused on each other and nothing else. Naturally, if he'd somehow missed the first innuendo—occasionally being smashed about the head and neck by a sledgehammer was *so* passe—there was the second, infinitely more subtle reminder, his mother's loving message inside the card, written in her beautiful longhand using black Indian ink—black being her symbolic color for shame and hopelessness, her sorrow and regret recorded for all time, finishing him off:

> "To my sweet, precious, incomplete boy! How I *pray* you shall find her! Your clock is ticking, dearest, and although you *appear* to be a babe-in-the-woods, we know better! Find her! We don't care if she's Mabel Loomis (just no Papists, okay?)! You shan't be whole until you do! We've renewed your subscription!"

Wow. Happy birthday, and then some. Just . . *terrific*. And stupid Sid, incalculably improved, and just when he thought a Wednesday couldn't *possibly* get any better! It was their actual, honest-to-goodness birthday present for number 40—the *real* gift. Yet another subscription to <u>Christian Singles</u>, Southwest Edition. Color glossies of dozens upon dozens of what he was forced to admit were some *very* attractive ladies indeed, allegedly Christians all, blondes, brunettes, redheads, most of whom were in their twenties, some in their thirties, even a select few in their forties and fifties (and why were *they* still single? he wondered), sent to his office every month, with love from mom and dad. Dozens of them, perhaps *hundreds* . . and only eighteen-hundred miles away from the District of Columbia, safe and sound in west Texas. *Gee.* If he wanted a '*hot*' date for the weekend with some lucky lass . . all he had to do was fly her halfway across country, pick her up at the airport, drive her to her hotel, drive to his place in Herndon to clean-up, return to her hotel to pick her up . . and then do whatever they liked. Ditto for Saturday night. *Yum.* And be sure to send her home Sunday afternoon, after church. *Cake.* And for God's sake, who the hell was Mabel Loomis?! Did she live anywhere within a thousand miles of D.C.? He promised himself he'd look further into young Miss Loomis as soon as he had the opportunity—whatever *year* that was.

His duty was simple, really. All he was required to do was perform his constituents' needs and desires on a daily basis from either his office or the House chambers; check his e-mails in case there was something he needed to take care of personally, either there in the district or back home; take important phone calls, <u>or</u> return them if he'd been elsewhere which, inexplicably, he usually had been; monitor his special work as a member of the House Committee on Foreign Relations, a post he felt especially qualified for having personally traveled as far west as El Paso, as far south as Brownsville, and as far east and north as the District of Columbia; have dinner on a semi-regular basis with the so-called party 'heavy-weights,' so he knew who they were and, more importantly, so *they* knew who *he* was and what he stood for, and that he was and would always be, through thick and thin, *one of them.*

Then there were his "other" duties, his unofficial duties, so important to the livelihood of any young congressman. These duties, if performed well enough, allowed Sid and his colleagues to "bring home the *bacon*," so to speak. Campaigning, naturally, had evolved into a 24-7 activity Sid fervently wished he could enhance through a voluntary, sacrificial avoidance of sleep; there were also infrequent trips to war zones to "check on the troops," which he so far had cleverly evaded by way too many visits to the border at the Rio Grande—never in the same spot *twice*, of course—thus using his full allocation of government-sponsored air-miles; public-relations work, so the folks back home would think he was actually voting the way *they* wanted instead of the way *he* wanted; attendance at various conservative fund-raisers, where he occasionally was invited to speak but more often than not listened as his older, more-experienced counterparts laid down the law; local trips to shops, or factories, or public schools, or whatever happened to be the current 'cause-*du-jour*,' most of which tended to agitate him because, no matter how noble or worthy that cause sounded, the *cure* invariably led to the need for *increased funding*, which he was sworn to oppose under any and all circumstances. Tight-fistedness *was*, after all, conservatism, plain and simple.

And, according to his parents, since he didn't have anything *else* to do, he could damn well afford to, if not actively *seek* one, at least keep his eye out for a wife.

"So what's the big deal anyway?" he asked them after his first political victory. "Why is it so important to have a *wife? . .*"

Their answers—for there were many—seemed as varied and distant as the stars in the sky.

"It just doesn't *look* right," said his father.

"A man in his mid-thirties *should* be married," his mother told him.

"Most congressmen are already married by the time they get to Washington, son."

"You need someone to help you day-to-day, son."

Um-*hmm*. Help me do *what*? And by the way, what's wrong with being a bachelor?

"The term *confirmed bachelor* has taken on . . different meanings now, son" she said tactfully.

"And just what is *that* supposed to mean?" he demanded, but his mother could only see fit to remain quiet, her dignity intact, eyes open wide, heart in her throat.

He glanced up to see his chief-of-staff, Regina Watts, standing silently in front of his desk, her eyes cast down at him; he hadn't even heard her come in. It had taken months and months but, at long last he'd decided that she was, all things considered, truly ideal in her position. Mixed Black and Hispanic, he knew the number of conservative congressmen who employed *that* particular combination in any capacity could be easily counted on one hand—with fingers left over! Six years his senior, a by-product of the 1968 Democratic National Convention held in Chicago, she had apparently been *born* mature, confident, efficient, capable, and intelligent, imbued with a natural sense of purpose and a curious, if carefully-disguised, streak of initiative. Since he was naturally suspicious of anyone who happened to be Black *or* Hispanic— and illogically much more distrusting of any such combination thereof—her interview had been nothing short of *seismic*: Sid and his trusted band of college cohorts were floored! She could type like the devil—her fingers *flew* across the keys, whether she busied herself looking at the boss, or the keyboard, the ceiling, or anything else—and turned out to be convincingly evasive when appropriate, tenaciously guarding her employer's privacy . She possessed the uncanny knack of both appearing to be on the dole and, literally in the same breath, pathologically averse to any suggestion of charity. She

7

was, in a word, *perfect*. After five years in Washington, congressman Villary found her talents indispensable . . and paid her accordingly. Whenever he momentarily drifted away, be it for work or family or something else, it was typically Regina who brought him back to reality. She was not pretty, much less beautiful—her few extra pounds settled in her seat—but she was strangely attractive, and strove to stay that way by jogging daily along the river in Georgetown.

"So," he greeted her askance. "How much trouble am I in today? .."

"You need to spend *less* time worrying about your parents and how *they* want you to live and *more* time thinking about this spending bill and *how* you're going to justify turning it down, okay? . . Just remember . . *mucho travajo, poco dinero!* . . okay?"

"Yeah, okay . . but that doesn't tell me what my morning or afternoon looks like . ."

"Morning will be spent at Berclair Public School, remember? . . you'll be dropping by their campus completely unannounced—we didn't tell them you were coming until a week ago, remember?—and, you'll be so happy to be there you're staying for lunch with the administration . . right? . ."

"If you say so," he nodded meekly. A curious shadow of fear suddenly washing over his features, his eyes betrayed a fleeting concern. "Gina? . . Have I been to this school before? .."

"Ye-e-s-s . . three years ago . ."

"Do I know anyone there?"

"*Most* of them, ye-e-s-s . ."

This seemed to temporarily placate his concerns—until he remembered a possible down-side to visiting any school anywhere at any time.

8

"God, do I *have* to speak with the kids? . ."

"What difference does *that* make?"

"Well, I'll tell you," he said. He swung his legs into the air until they landed on the front left edge of his desk, one leg over the other at the ankle, his favorite position. "The kids—unlike the adults—will tell you if there are problems that need addressing. The adults, usually in the administration, will tell you what they think you wanna' *hear*—never underestimate the amount or variety of information a bureaucrat, *any* bureaucrat . . will carefully *avoid* telling a politician. Same goes for a visit to an air base or army post: the folks in charge will do just about anything to hide a problem—including taking someone off-post, if need be. Officers *only*, you know? . . Well, school folks are the same—you'll grow old and die before you hear about a problem from an educator! What you'll hear and see is the scores and stats they've improvised to prove they're doing a wonderful job—but the kids? They'll let you know what's going on, which means you've gotta' *do* something about it! I've often wondered what they'd do with administrative personnel were it not for the existence of schools . .'

"At any rate, have we anything pressing this after? . ."

"You'll be on the hill with Perkins, Chandler, and Cahill—working on that emergency cash outlay for the Poseidon Group—you know, the drillers on the Atlantic seaboard who want to bring their work a little closer into the Outer Banks and Norfolk? . ."

He began nodding, the trouble from the week before burned into his brain like a hot branding-iron, then added "I don't suppose there's anything of *substance* . . from the Warrington group I need to know about today? . ."

"Nothing yet," she grinned, turning to leave. "But . . it's still

9

morning."

Good lord, wasn't it always *something?* Turning away the threat from, of all places, the *right* would by necessity require a long, drawn-out, relatively-dull, excruciatingly-painful experience requiring Sid and his henchmen to get, as they put it, *down-and-dirty* to emerge victorious. This much he accepted as a given. Denny Warrington was certainly no fool, and his organization was staffed by very capable people almost as dedicated as Denny himself: young, bright, organized, and now . . ambitious! And what the hell was this whole '*challenge*' concept anyway? Where was the victory in Warrington, a typically mild-mannered if ruthless conservative, suddenly announcing to the world that he sat to the *right* of an incumbent conservative who was already so far right the <u>Washington</u> <u>Post</u> caustically referred to him as "Congressman *Bormann?*" But give credit where it was due, Sid freely admitted, ol' Denny sure had a set of *huevos*: how many politicians had the guts to publicly announce their decision to oppose the construction of a fence on the Texas-Mexico border, *unless* . . it was both electrified *and* had concertina-wire running across the top? And just *how* had the state senator arrived at such a grand solution? *Because*, Denny smiled into the camera, getting caught in such a painful exsanguination would not only physically prevent illegal entry into the United States—it would also psychologically *scar* other Hispanics considering a crossing in the future! And this, announced during a live television interview in the territory of a state senator whose constituency was becoming exponentially richer in Hispanic voters by the day?! What in the name of *Gawd A'mighty* was he trying to do? Protect the illegal Hispanics already inside Texas from the screaming, starving multitudes still trying to swim across the Rio Grande to steal jobs Hispanics had *already stolen* from Americans, thus protecting his illegal constituents' cash-flow—thus securing their votes?! *Ahh!* Perhaps, as some colleagues secretly suggested, it was just a publicity stunt: R.C. (Rumor-Central), Sid's long-time inside intelligence source in Austin, had mentioned the possibility that Denny's PR agency, in fabricating its first political TV commercial, had gone all-out on its initial foray into big-time state sweepstakes: they'd contracted to stage a re-creation of the infamous conflict at the Alamo—only with a slight twist. *This* time, Border Patrol agents would fire BAR's and AR-15's into a chaotic mass of fleeing Hispanic men, women, *and* children from atop the fence-line already built close to Laredo—a real barn-burner, the amount of blood spilled and ammo expended would remind folks of Sam Peckinpah's <u>The Wild Bunch</u> in sheer violence—concluding in the message "<u>State Senator Denny Warrington's Immigration Reform Bill,</u>" spread across the television screen in large, bright vermilion letters. R.C. mentioned that no one would actually be *shot and killed*, of course . . unless the film crew somehow got *really* lucky, so chances of a lawsuit were slim and none . . but there it was for all to see. Yes, *sir*, no question about it: Denny Brom Warrington had a pair! My, *my*, the neo-cons, skinheads, criminals, and other members of the lunatic- fringe would have Denny in Washington in a jiffy if Sid and his considerable forces didn't take this arrogant, obtrusive threat seriously. His inner-circle of friends and advisors? The few and the faithful? The Dream-team? No way in hell they'd be gathered in Herndon before Friday night, and more likely early Saturday afternoon, to formulate a workable strategy of containment, espionage, and dirty tricks in an attempt to

11

derail the danger before it became too lethal. Cas Turley was stuck in *Munich*, for Chrissakes, and couldn't untangle himself before late Friday afternoon, which would put him into BWI or Dulles, he couldn't be sure which, around *nine*—and who the hell wanted to plot strategy all night after a trip across the pond? No, a *fun* weekend was summarily out of the question—even if Friday night proved a bust, he figured, and the ceremonial night of bowling with his congressional comrades was scheduled for Thursday at 7:00, and he *would . be . there*, of course. Which—*if* he wanted to throw back a few cocktails and catch a game at Pandora's Box—left only that very evening and nothing else until the following week. The pleasant thought occurred that, were he to telephone his parents in west Texas right out of the blue and establish his priorities, to express how very busy he was in D.C. to them, to somehow make them understand how utterly impossible it was for him to instigate a romantic involvement with any female on the *planet*, much less one of west Texas's finest—and then further explain that, like W.C. Fields, he liked his children boiled *or* fried and, hence, might *not* make a loving, doting father after all—well, the rest of his day might seem brighter but, they being resourceful folks, what might *they* do in retaliation? Christ, it was always *something*, wasn't it?!

Swinging his feet off the desk he quickly tapped a few buttons on the computer and his government e-mail, pre-screened then forwarded by Regina *and* Julie *and* Carmen—it was critical, no . . *vital* . . that messages of a disturbing or annoying nature be placed into the "junk file"—how else was he to be faithful to his supporters and simultaneously give his detractors the impression he was concerned about their thoughts and problems, no matter *how* ridiculous?—spread across his laptop. Force of habit sending him scanning top to bottom, his eyes stopped on a familiar, friendly name; there was always time to read words of encouragement from so bright and honest a patriot.

My dear Congressman:

I was so pleased to receive your letter of the 11th and to know matters are progressing so very steadily on such a wide array of concerns, the same concerns that you and I and so many millions of loyal, patriotic Americans are fighting for every single day. Your news of the progress on drilling rights and properties off the coast, east of Corpus Christi and Padre Island, was especially gratifying in view of my son's enormous investment in the future of not only Texas, but the country, as well. Our family prays for your good health every single day, my dear boy, every single day. Your concern about being [primaried] by that jack-ass Denny Warrington is, in my humble opinion, unwarranted at this time. His stances on immigration, taxes, abortion rights, and size-of-government are virtually identical to your own, and his incredible proposal to transfer Fort Hood to a point seventy miles west-southwest of San Angelo is just that: *in*-credible! A more un-godly man I cannot imagine. I'm rather convinced that Consuela Garcia, their candidate-in-waiting, shall be your real test; aside from integrity, truth, facts, and honor, she has little going for her . . *and*, her religious affiliation needs no explanation.

At a time when the socialist front in Washington wants to increase taxes on hard-working Americans—not to mention increases in funding for public education, food stamps, various and

sundry 'social' programs, infrastructure (whatever the hell *that* is), and the general bulk of the Federal government, *all* of which are anti-individualistic measures—with a commensurate

reduction in sacred military spending, of course—it's refreshing to know you and your loyal compatriots are pushing for *increased* military spending, and your group's proposal for a usage tax on food stamps and these other so-called 'safety-net' programs is nothing short of genius. We really couldn't be happier!

In the unlikely event Warrington gains substantial political ground on you and, later on, Mrs. Garcia, please know my family, friends, business associates, and political allies stand ready to not only support you through the roughest seas, but also to bring upon them enough *heat* to make this global-warming hoax seem like an ice-cream cake factory! My very best wishes always, Sidney!

Your friend,
Reverend Hugh Beauchamp
Pastor, the Pentecostal Church
in Christ's Name

Plucking a tissue from the box on his desk, the better to prevent the tears welling in his eyes from cascading down his cheeks—was there *anything* more un-manly?—he recalled his last visit to Hugh's church when, after being allowed to personally address the assembled multitude, so many ladies, both young and old, had gathered round when he finished, some to shake his hand, some to say thank-you, and some to just exist in the glow of his love . . three of whom, emotionally agitated by the enormity of the occasion, fainted dead away. He didn't even mind Hugh referring to him as *Sidney*, which he detested; the right reverend never, *ever*, broached the subject of wives, or women, or the Washington night-life, or anything of the sort. If only his parents would follow suit . . .

Jotting down a reminder on a Post-It! note to call Hugh's son, Jeremiah, his old college chum and present-day oil-drilling entrepreneur, he needed a progress report on the newer, more-resilient drill-bits they were experimenting with sixty miles out to knock through to the "gushers" they knew were waiting for them. *Salary*—especially a six-figure number like his—was all well and good, but there was nothing like independent wealth to make the day go by. Besides . . nothing good ever lasted. . *forever!*

II.

His mood had already fouled the anticipation of comfortable, relaxed consumption of alcohol and baseball-watching in a decidedly impersonal setting, though Pandora's Box was its usual rollicking self by the time he strolled in at half past eight. Damned shame, too, he told himself, for the day had started so well. The administration at the Berclair Public School had appeared pleasantly stunned to see a congressman—and, lord, such a *handsome* congressman, at that—within its walls that morning. Duke Wayne would have been proud and pleased with their individual and collective performances, he felt sure. Even the students forced to spend the day away from their regular classes, found inside a room marked "I.S.S.," hadn't tried to take a shot at him—whether it was because he was a congressman in a suit or because the principal and two SWAT-team members accompanied him he wasn't sure—but *not* being shot-at was always a good thing. The cafeteria visit had proved interesting, as well. So many of his detractors had complained about the gigantic hunger problem plaguing inner-city American kids that he'd finally taken notice—it was, ostensibly, one of the reasons he made visits to schools like Berclair—but whenever he looked up from his food he observed students with trays of pizza, candy bars, and chocolate milk. The student body at this particular secondary school, as a whole, primarily leaned toward the *heavy* side and, unless his memory had completely failed him, student obesity was more the *norm* than the exception, which only confused him. When he innocently inquired about their physical-education classes he soon regretted opening his mouth: the *funding*, it was reported, was more friendly to the acquisition of computers than anything even remotely related to phys-ed teachers and sports equipment, neither of which existed at Berclair. Funding, it *seemed*, allowed one or the other, but *not* both, according to Elizabeth Banson, the forty-ish principal Villary remembered from his previous visit. He found her attractive, confident, reasonably honest, and absolutely dedicated to the progress and well-being of her students; if she was concerned by their lack of physical activity and subsequent excess baggage, it was never expressed—but it bothered Sid enormously. The students' collective physical condition begged certain unavoidable questions no one seemed inclined to ask. What did so much extra weight accumulated by the teenage years portend for the future? Was computer proficiency actually a reasonable sacrifice for excess fat gathered around the heart, promoting a premature death? Moreover, what were the odds these students would ever play college sports and enter the NFL or NBA without high school sports? *Most* importantly, what about locker-room shenanigans, whereby the strong could overpower the weak, as nature intended—using the most traditional methods, of course—like towel-popping sissies on the ass and hurling selected bodies into the showers for their first clean-up since their Uncle Maury died the previous February? In his mind, this uniquely All-American rite-of-passage had been completely circumvented because students needed to train their fingers to fly across computer keyboards like Van Cliburn at the piano—*except* that hardly anyone would be as great as Van at *any* damned thing (for after all, Van was, first and foremost, a *Texan*).

17

"Oh, but there's an easy *cure* to the problem," a mid-twenties teacher spoke-up, her monumental epiphany illuminating the lunch table. "Increase funding, and have *both!*"

The red cabbage souring in his stomach at her words, the remainder of his lunch was spent silently observing the students, faculty members sitting alongside, and the policemen stationed at the doorways in case of an emergency. And it had been such a pleasant visit, too . . up to that point. Increase funding. Spend *more* money. Sell our grandchildren down the river. *Or,* perhaps buy them a carton of chocolate milk (why in hell didn't I ever have a chance to buy chocolate milk in *my* school?!) and sit them down in front of a computer to watch them gradually assume the shape of a *basketball* or, if they got lucky, merely a football. Pardon me, young lady, but are you familiar with the term *recession?* That's what happens when cash and investments and tax revenues and *funding* dry-up and blow away! Jesus H. *Christ,* it was always something, wasn't it?

The afternoon had proved only marginally better. As he took his traditional stool at one end of the bar, a casual nod of the head telling the veteran bartender he was ready for his usual, he recalled the pain of 3:30 P.M.: the EPA wanted to inspect the Poseidon Group's long-range plans in the Atlantic *again* before they'd sign-off on it. Son-of-a-*bitch!* Those sorry bastards would want to know if an oyster had ever received a blow-job from a shrimp before it could be served as someone's *dinner,* for Chrissakes! His friend and colleague, the honorable David Fallum, the nineteen-term veteran from Idaho, had really summed-up the situation with the agency more eloquently than anyone, and nobody, but *nobody,* had dared challenge him. "Name one founding father, just *one* . . Federalist, Whig, Tory, Democrat, Republican—whatever you

18

like," Fallum gleefully challenged his opponents, "who ever mentioned the *possibility* of such an agency . . and I'll shut-up!" Well . . *that* had taken them by surprise, the best part being that all the pansy-ass tree-huggers were rendered speechless! Oh, *sure*, there'd been complaints about time-involvements and combustion engines and the industrial-age and century misplacements—the usual liberal *crap*—but Fallum had ruled the day, no question. The other side had nothing to say. *Nothing*. If Sid and his colleagues hadn't known better they'd have sworn the other side couldn't say or spell the word *profit*. And what was so difficult, so very incomprehensible, about the concept of making money first, then tackling everything else *later?!* Even if the clowns who invented the term *'endangered species'* were right—if global warming was real, medical care for all Americans was necessary, educational funding needed increasing, and the Pentagon was over-funded—yes, even if women thought Chuck Norris's hair was more *gray* than blonde!—wasn't there money to be made by overcoming these problems, and wasn't free enterprise the preferred method of change for the better? It was enough to make a grown man *drink*.

His second bourbon had just arrived when he spotted her sitting at the bar directly across from him, blocking one view of the Nationals game. Only thirty seconds before she hadn't been there—but there she was, nonetheless, right out of the blue. Naturally, it was imperative that he ignore her: in his world of national and international intrigue, where the rigors of clear thinking absolutely demanded his undivided attention, to be distracted by anything as fleeting and egocentric as a female—well, it was not only bad form . . it just wasn't allowed! *Period*. So, too, his parents could only be trusted . . up to a point! Who could say when they might choose to arrange a chance-encounter with a husband-hunting, dinner-cooking, shirt-washing, house-cleaning — lord, *child-bearing* — young beauty from the Lone Star state?! And so very *many* to choose from, too?! Jesus, his mother and father could occasionally be so . . well, unutterably heartless! If only he'd spotted his challenges sooner . . he might have had time to shoot them before they arrived! If only . .

Careful, Sidney, he told himself. *Careful.* For Chrissakes, don't let her know you've seen her! Got to keep your mind clear! *Clear*, damn it! *No* distractions! Danger . . lurks . . *everywhere!*

His second bourbon summarily hurled down like a blazing fastball, he nodded for another, his senses aroused to the ever-present specter of potential disaster, eyes distractedly focused on the lonely form seated a mere three hundred inches away, her head turned sideways-right to accommodate the arrival of her first Guinness. Predictably victorious in his herculean efforts to ignore her, he couldn't have noticed the fact that every other man at the bar — and at least *some* of the women, too — had their eyes on this woman in the plain white dress . . just as *he did*. She sat alone, apparently content with her solitude and, quite aware she was shamefully, even criminally distracting, obviously felt comfortably resigned to being ogled as a matter of routine. Most men she'd met had struggled mightily to take in the richness of her beauty with their infantile glances: it was like attempting to dignify a Picasso or Matisse with a shrug. But Congressman Sidney Villary from Texas's 38th district wasn't most men: he decided almost instantly that her appeal began with her hair. Parted in the middle, the large, coal-black waves cascaded away from her lofty forehead in thick, rich tendrils, the sides of her neck completely covered in its fullness, the tips extending at least three to four inches beneath her neck in back, her ears plainly visible, the striking contrast of raven glory and sheer-white linen stunning in its primal magnetism. And that was only the *beginning*. To say she was "attractive" was to say a Rolls-Royce was a car: she was *breathtaking!* The shimmering blue eyes, her most enchanting feature, sang a song of perpetual melancholy, seemingly on the verge of tears, ready to burst into sorrow at a moment's notice . . yet strangely strong and optimistic. Her nose, large without being *too* large, but exquisitely shaped and contoured, provided the perfect symmetry to the eyes above, overly-large and luminous, and the mouth below, the flawless, indulgent lips painted scarlet beckoning an endlessly-complex involvement. All set inside a shape magnificently formed of eggshell-white skin with peach-rose highlights, her jawline tapering elegantly to its logical conclusion, an excellence so very delicate Da Vinci would have wept. The slightest hint of a grin swept across her features when she grabbed the Guinness, half its contents gone only seconds later when she set the bottle back on the bar. Villary thought he detected the whisper of an Hispanic heritage in her face when she smiled, but couldn't be sure from such a distance . . not that it mattered a fig; there were elections to be won, laws that needed passing, weaponry to be purchased, people who needed encouragement and, for some, discouragement. *Women?* He simply didn't have time for them.

Which didn't seem to matter one bit when, having carelessly thrown back the latest shot of Wild   Turkey, he caught her staring right at him, almost as though he was some sort of sleazy 1950's monster from a Hollywood 'B' movie. He turned away to watch the game on a big-screen set to his right and, motioning to the barkeep for another sip, couldn't help notice the Guinness bottle was now empty, its owner out of her seat, nowhere to be seen.

"You're Congressman Villary from Texas, aren't you?"

The vision from across the bar stood next to him now, no hint of a Spanish heritage in her face or voice; on the contrary, her question literally reeked of the liberal, eastern establishment, her accent a New England or upstate New York derivative. Could a young, dedicated public servant from west Texas not trust *anyone* anymore?!

"So . . how long have you known my parents? . ."

She thanked the barkeep for her second Guinness, took a healthy draft and said "Your *parents?!*"

"Never mind . . what's a young woman from Italy doing in a place like this? . ."

"Surrey . . I just wondered if you keep your hair in place like that with *lacquer* . . or is that some new kind of polyurethane? . ."

There was something vaguely . . interesting about this woman, he decided, although he'd never been one with the ability to pinpoint the precise causes of any misfortune that befell him, professional or otherwise. Was she a plant for Denny Warrington? Some other enemy? There was never, ever a viable excuse for bad manners, though, regardless of someone's motives.

"You seem nervous about developments in the Gulf of Mexico . . but I want to thank you for your support and your vote . . so how long have you lived in west Texas, anyway? . ."

"Tyson's Corner," she said, still enjoying her stout. "Were I to run my hand across the front of your hair, would it bleed? . . or just *stick* to it, like cotton candy? . ."

"A *militant*," he said admiringly, the inexplicable warmth in his throat rapidly descending into his gut with the rest of the bourbon. Out of the corner of his eye he saw that his beloved

22

Nationals now   led the Astros, 3-1. "*So* . . been a baseball fan all your life? . ."

"Soccer . . I just thought it'd be a kick to see what the untouchable Mr. Villary looked like up-close. And you know what? In person you strongly resemble your pictures—except that you don't *really* look like someone who hails from the state of Texas . ."

"How incredibly observant you are! And how unobtrusively *accurate*, as well! . . Truth is, the only hailing in Texas is normally found during a squall, or perhaps a thunderstorm—though it's my understanding the *best* hailing is done in Oklahoma, during the spring . . since I drive my own car I don't hail much here at all—wait! I most humbly apologize: I *do* . . taxi down the runway occasionally, but I try to limit that to airport visits *only*, I'm afraid . . *So* . . how long have you been assigned to the Canadian Consulate? . ."

"British Embassy," she smiled easily, the tail-end of her second Guinness headed the way of the dinosaur. The bartender, an astute, experienced bar-and-stools type and seasoned raconteur named Max, had her next stout on the wood before she could order, just to see her lovely face aglow; that—and a smidgen of cash—was all he needed before retiring. "I believe a coral snake from west Texas has announced his intention to run for public office, congressman . . care to comment on that? . ."

"So it *is* true," he said lucidly. His fifth bourbon had brought the evening's conspiracy into sharper focus, a picture so clear there could be no mistake—and wasn't that just like them? His parents, in a fit of frustration and transparent desperation, had located an *extremely attractive* west-Texas female, sent her to school to speak the kind of formal English not even King George VI could manage, educated her in the

23

politics of the Lone Star state, and planted her in the nation's capital like a giant redwood tree to be 'cultivated' by a hard-working, deeply patriotic, unwaveringly-conservative congressman for the singularly despicable, entirely self-serving, unflinchingly-selfish purpose of someday producing . . lord, *grandchildren*. And here he sat, an oversized boat jammed-up the proverbial tributary with no visible means of propulsion . . cast upon the heap. Why else would a young stranger of the so-called 'fairer' sex   strike-up a conversation, other than to gloat that his life had, just *lately*, taken a turn for the more arduous? And why else would she be so very . . *agreeable*—unless there was some kind of ulterior motive involved? Worst of all, neither of *them* was even remotely interested in discussing retirement scenarios as they sat in west Texas, secure in their wealth and their abject smarminess, allegedly dedicated to the furthering of their only child's political career. Yeah, *sure*. What a wagon-load of pure, unadulterated horse-feathers. The danger was here, and the danger was *now*. Only one thing left to do: he'd have to sharpen-up even *more!* Index finger out, the Wild Turkey arrived *tout de suite*. "That particular coral snake, verily, is a viper of another strain, is he not? . ."

"Elapid . . and, it's my understanding he'll wiggle up to your favorite side—that being your *right* side, of course—to mount his challenge . . so tell me . . will you allow him sufficient room to maneuver between you and that barren wall, quickly squeezing through just enough to say he'd played? . . Or will you willingly permit a slower, smoother entry into the game, letting him feel his way around comfortably until, agitated to a fault, he self-detonates, suddenly splattered about the playing field, utterly spent by the campaign, his defeat assured, your latest triumph already in the bag from start to finish, victoriously intense in its climactic arrival? . ."

"It's not my way to vanquish anything virtually in the blink of an eye. It's bad form, you see. Better if the onslaught is a steady, more gradual conquering of the . . *district* in question because, even if the area to be taken is precious, a longer, more drawn-out approach seems more agreeable to all parties involved—even when a snake is in the mix, if one cuts off its head too quickly—well, the body may remain intact, but the fangs are still dangerous, you know . ."

Her Guinness dried-up as the last swallow of bourbon drifted down to its final resting place.

"But I don't suppose," he said, his eyes narrowing in the light, "there are any snakes wallowing about *your* house? . ."

"*Condo.*" Without taking her eyes away from him she reached inside her purse, found her car keys and pulled them out. "I've heard enough. My place is closer . . can you follow me? . ."

Dropping several bills onto the bar-top, he paused for a moment to enjoy her form inside the linen cloth of the dress before following a few feet behind her, escorting her outside to her car before heading for his sedan. As an afterthought he stopped next to his car, pulled out his billfold and ran his fingers across an interior portion of the soft leather, the familiar feel of the concave circle inside the raised border as satisfying as running into an old friend. *Ah*, security! As he followed her late-model Volvo off the lot the thought never occurred to glance back at the bar patrons who watched them leave together and, even now, observed the goddess and the luckiest man on the planet roll merrily away from the Wednesday evening gathering at Pandora's Box.

When he finished sipping his second bourbon, lounged comfortably on her sofa, she led him by the hand into her

25

bedroom while he prayed to his lord and savior to please, *please* not let his heart fail him in this, his finest hour.

"Churchill was British, wasn't he?" he half-inquired—it was more a statement of fact than anything —and she grinned affectionately when he said he'd always admired the old rascal. Better to let her think he'd been completely fooled by his parents' bold conspiracy—more *fun* that way, too, all the way round—but when she first kissed him he simply forgot about everything . . everything, that is, *except* being alone with her.

Sometime after eleven, when he confirmed for what had to be the hundredth time that women, after all, were unquestionably the most delicious, most mouth-watering substance known to mankind—and that his present company was undoubtedly the best of the *best* and that, in being drained of his seed, his mind temporarily cast away in the most pleasurable manner imaginable, his parents' saving grace being that their choice of a partner-in-crime could arguably be considered their finest achievement, *next to their son*, there was much to be thankful for. But then, there was always something to be thankful for. Protectively cradling the adorable woman in his arms—did her repeated imploring of the holy father, "Oh god Oh god Oh GOD!" while *in flagrante* merely define her ideas of pleasure, her Christian sense of responsibility, or perhaps *both?*—the thought that remaining single for the rest of his natural life *might not* be his best move momentarily lodged itself inside his head at the exact moment she settled herself more deeply into the safety of her lover. The scent of lilac and lemon, the same aroma he'd fallen asleep with the thousand nights of his childhood, wafted into every corner of her home—even into the bathroom a few minutes later where he first noticed his security, his latex pal on so many other occasions had, for the very first time, so miserably failed him. His blunder, his defeat so complete—he sat and stared transfixed at the enormity of what would undeniably become his eventual undoing. God, the pain and anxiety, the very *shock* of such an unenviable sight felt *massive*, but in a way . . it figured, too: Godfrey-Daniel, it was always *something*, wasn't it?!

"Mmmm . . .Charlotte?" he whispered into the darkness of her bedroom, barely able to speak for terror, hand over his heart . . just in case the precious muscle stopped beating, " . . we need to *talk* . ."

III.

"No, I will *not*, under any circumstances, agree to anything that requires my presence in the state of Texas for Memorial Day weekend" he shouted into his cellphone. Face turning pale, hands clammy, forehead bathed in sweat from the assault on the other end, Sid felt as if he was hanging from a rope by his thumbs. Eying the assembled multitude gathered round the dining room table, his political brain-trust sitting quietly in abject sympathy, all four advisors keenly aware of the inhumane pressure now being heartlessly applied to their champion, war-stricken faces of deepest concern with furrowed brows, the congressman sat upright in his seat, his posture the very epitome of perfection as he courageously endured salvo after salvo of venom, waiting patiently for the battle to end. "I don't care if Ken Attleman flies into Houston ten times a *day* . . he only does that because he's a stupid, lazy fruitcake who consistently abuses his right to return home to consult with his so-called *constituents*, most of whom are either headed to prison or just becoming eligible for parole . . . Well, *he's* a blockhead, too, and if the president wants to place his trust with a first-grader, that's his privilege . . Now, why in *hell* would I want to do a thing like *that?!* . . Listen, I'm backed-up into a wall here, busy trying to reduce the illegal *bulk* of the federal government and protect our great country from Mexicals, health-care Marxists, professional spendthrifts, murderous pediatricians, anyone who might oppose or obstruct lawful gerrymandering, pacifists, and communists

28

attempting to increase taxes on the poor wealthy! I don't have *time* to examine every piece of mail I get with a fine-tooth comb because I'm more concerned with military appropriations, okay? . . Yes, I *will* consider flying home to Texas for the Fourth—especially if Willie's playing in Dallas . . *Yes*, for pity's sake, I *am* keeping my back straight, mother! . . I love you, too! Okay, best to dad, good-bye!"

He closed his cellphone and laid it aside, head shaking with eyes closed tight, his world-class migraine yet to be dealt with. He eyed his advisors, his guilt and embarrassment too evident.

"Sorry about that, y'all . ."

"Are you okay?" said Cas Turley, a rare tone of genuine concern in his Texas drawl. "I've known your mama a long time, Sid—and she can be a *tough* ol' broad—'specially when it comes to them *grand*-kids!"

At the first sound of 'grand-kids,' Dow Pettigrew, his advisor on abortion, health-care, and global-warming hoaxes, half asleep in his chair to Sid's left, sat up wide-eyed and peered long and hard at his dear friend and employer, muttering under his breath *"Jesus H. Christ,* Sid, you've got grandchildren?!"

"No, D.P., you *know* I don't have any grandchildren because I don't have any *children,* and according to my parents *that's* the biggest problem facing our country today—the fact that their only son, the honorable Sidney Hunt Villary of Texas, has somehow managed *not* to provide them with their rightful due, namely, a houseful of grand-kids they can bounce on their knees and spoil rotten! If a French damn muslim blew-up a nuc-u-lar weapon in Austin, *that* . . would be our *next-biggest* problem . ."

"Well, then . . . okay," Pettigrew said cautiously. It was still difficult, after all those years, to know whether his friend Sid was being serious or, like he'd done so many times when they were kids, was actually pulling his leg. Then there was the 'other' problem: unlike his friend, who had perfect hair and plenty of it, Dow's hairline had receded dramatically over the years and Pettigrew, never a big smash with the ladies in the first place, had suffered accordingly. "Oh, and while I'm thinking about it, remember those 'murdering pediatricians' you mentioned to your mom? . . I believe those are actually *osteopaths* who've come so unglued after being shot-at inside those abortion clinics, Sid, asking for protection and what-not . ."

"And they can *keep* asking for all I care! Hell, if they'd just go look for some kinda' honorable work—like the army or navy—nobody'd be shootin' at 'em, the stupid sons o' bitches! *Now then* . . anyone have anything else before we get back to business? . ."

"I 'preciate what you did for my cousin Melvin, boss," Lynch Bohannon said from the end of the table. Sitting to Cas Turley's immediate right, all present knew Lynch didn't embarrass too easily, but now his temples assumed a distinctly reddish hue, swelling out then shrinking in with a curious regularity, a sure sign his humility had taken a beating. "There's no way in the *world* he coulda' known that merchandise was hot! . ."

"As long as he's more careful in the future, *that's* the main thing," he reminded him. "That ol' boy he was partnering with—I believe you said his name was Pickett?—did Melvin ever say if this Pickett character had any business dealings with those Hispanic brothers, trading car parts and such? . ."

Bohannon's eyes closed in utter humiliation, the ugly truth almost too much to bear, chin resting on his chest, head hung in shame. There was no place to hide.

"Yes, with *both* of them—and *another* Hispanic family, too," he quietly allowed.

The other four shook their heads in calm regret, arms folded on the tabletop in silent unity, for when one of them was taken advantage of, everyone felt the pain. If only I could let the rest of the country see what's happening in Texas, thought Sid, good Christians everywhere—even the two or three found in the *northeast*—might learn a thing or two from their brethren in the southwest, fighting the good fight on the front lines, all aimed at future relief.

"Remember this episode with the cousin, okay, Cas? . . We don't want any surprises down the road, and who knows? . . Maybe this unfortunate instance can work to our benefit someday and, even if it doesn't, it's always a good idea, *always* . . to know exactly who you're dealing with. Right? *Right!* This, my friends, is the slippery slope all those smart-ass liberals kid us about, but now there's eleven million of them here *illegally* and I'll be *damned* if I'm gonna' roll over and pretend they're *not!* They're here, for Chrissake! And what the hell do we owe them—citizenship? Because they were clever enough to cross an unprotected border after we told them to stay out?! Why don't we just make Mexico the fifty-first *state* and make the joke complete, huh? . . Now . . who wants to discuss the touchy subject of Denny Warrington and what we're going to do about him? . ."

"I'd like to *shoot* that son-of-a-bitch!" offered Cas Turley.

"So would I," agreed Sid, "but with this 'DNA' bullshit the liberals have cooked-up they'd nail us inside a week, so we've gotta' come up with a strategy to keep his sorry ass down in San Vicente where it belongs . . Now . . Cas has already determined that what we're dealing with here is *perception*: we know Warrington isn't any more conservative than anyone else—least of all *me*—but if he can convince enough weak-minded, weak-hearted Audie Murphy wannabes that *his* stand on the Mexicals is somehow an improvement over my position—well, we've all seen what a little propaganda can do if it's applied correctly, haven't we? . . Cas, you remember when Albert Cuthbert accused me of cruelty three years ago just because I put a rattler inside my girlfriend's locker in the sixth grade? *Jesus*, trying to sully my reputation twenty-six years *after the fact?!* . . True, it did *not* work, but we were forced to scramble our asses off, locate Susan Beeson in *Seattle*, for Chrissakes, and have her announce to the friggin' *world* it had all been in fun . . cost us a few thousand, too . . Anyway, as I see it, we have *got* to make sure as few people as possible switch-over to Denny's side and, whether or not it's fact or fiction, our butts have to be *perceived* . . as the true conservative choice in the upcoming race! Otherwise, we get handed permanent one-way tickets back to the Lone Star state after a pansy-ass *six years* in the nation's capital, a disgrace of epic proportions I don't even want to *think* about! Anything less than thirty or forty years is, of *course*, entirely unacceptable! . . Thoughts? . . Comments? . ."

"I've been thinking about that little prick ever since I flew in from Frankfurt last night and I suspect that, like everyone else, Denny has a skeleton or two, or *ten* . . in his closet!" beamed Cas Turley, his Aryan blood evidently stirred-up by the sadistic gleam in his eye. "We *all* have a skeleton or two . . the difference being that we're not running for public office like he is, and *our* candidate, thank God for small favors, is squeaky-clean. So, realistically, what can he do? Well, his options are limited . . if he wants to come after us on the immigration issue—and that *appears* to be his main thrust, believe it or not—his end run can only consist of something a tiny bit more

32

coarse and vulgar than what we've proposed, namely, that after all the adjustments are made, the wall is finished, the machine-gun towers are erected and manned, and the official warnings have been extended to the affected governors south of the river—the diplomats, *too*, lest we forget—*his* position might very well be that all we lack to render the adjustments a complete, unqualified success . . is a body-count!"

"That *asshole!*" Lynch Bohannon cried suddenly from Turley's right, cutting him off. "That is absolutely fucking *brilliant!* . . I don't suppose we could adopt that policy first for ourselves and cut his legs out from under him at the knees, could we? . ."

"Not so fast, Lynch, not so fast," warned Cas, his right hand in the air palm-out. "This is the old two-sided coin if I ever saw it. It's dangerous as *hell*, is what it is! The *upside* is that the body-count option would likely emerge a winner with most o' the menfolk, which is unfortunate, but before we go wringing our hands in defeat . . just imagine, if you will, the effect on the female voters in our district when the cameras begin to show the bodies of mothers and their children face-down on the ground, their corpses riddled with bullets from an American machine-gun! I'm telling you right *now* . . those could be the bodies of convicted felons or child molesters, or God knows *what*—but just a few weeks of *that* and the women of Texas would rise as one and demand *immediate* action—and it would not be pretty when they did! . ."

"So where does that leave us?"

"Well, Sid, I'll tell you where . . as I'm sure you've all heard me say before, Warrington isn't the sharpest saw in the hardware store, *but* . . his inner circle is comprised of at least two or three fairly-shrewd characters, one of whom I know personally, and he's certainly no fool. Therefore, I suggest we watch them *attempt* to attack you from the right and take their chances. In the meantime, my contacts in Baden-Wurttemburg will initiate communications with the embassy here in D.C., something along the lines of, ohhh, *'we're searching for the Warrington family of Texas that helped so many communists escape the fatherland after Kristall-Nacht, then volunteered to fight the Nazi horde for Comrade Stalin'* . . something along those lines, with a healthy dose of anti-Fascist history — totally, completely *fabricated*, of course, but, as you so accurately point out, it's not the truth that counts, or even the *lies*, for that matter, but the *perception*, and I want loyal Texans everywhere to know Denny can be pretty much bamboozled effortlessly, just in case they *really* think he'd be a good fit in Washington . ."

"So . . even if he's spic 'n span, he *appears* to be a dyed-in-the-wool socialist?" Sid grinned in pure admiration. "God-*damn*, I like that! . ." His attention suddenly shifting left to his domestic guru, he said "Whatcha' think about *that*, D.P.? . ."

"As bodacious a plan as any I've heard lately," smiled Pettigrew, who sat directly across the table from Turley, "as long as there's *no chance on earth* any shenanigans can be directly or indirectly traced to *you* . ."

"No chance at *all*," Turley swore confidently. "A DNA-sniffing *bloodhound* couldn't trace it any further than his nose, and even if he *could* . . the trail would vanish like a fart in a forest fire!"

"Any other threats, Cas . . real or imagined? . ."

"Well, boss, you just never know about those things," he cautiously admitted, "because none of us can see into the future . . I'm thinking Denny might, just *might*, question the legitimacy of you being on the Foreign Relations Committee in light of the fact that you've never left America for any reason whatsoever. Mind you, I'm not saying he *will* . . but, he might.

Of course, your tenacity concerning unnecessary spending, both here and abroad, doesn't make you a very good target for Warrington or anyone else attacking you from the right. One, you were *appointed* to the committee; two, the spending you helped authorize helped create two *thousand* service-related positions where none existed before; three, a full three hundred of those jobs—*fifteen* percent—went to minorities, and that doesn't factor-in the number of women and handicapped employees! That said, Denny will more than likely claim—rightly or wrongly, who knows?—the verdict on this one won't be realized for another ten or fifteen years, *minimum*—that the money you helped authorize to assist the freedom-loving peoples of Iraq and Afghanistan inadvertently helped to create a sufficient number of traumatic, combat-related injuries to eventually cost this country's treasury somewhere in the neighborhood of five to six *trillion* dollars, give or take a few hundred billion here and there—and that all we got in return was a hundred thousand civilian casualties in Iraq, and even *fewer* in Afghanistan . . and I fully realize that sounds *bad*, and five or six trillion *is* a lot of money, but the fact is that, if he's going to claim that . . he also has to *prove* it, or he looks like a whimpering, simpering, whiney-ass kid! . ."

"*Traumatic!*" howled Sid Villary, undisguised contempt in his voice. "*Trillions! Eventually! Combat-related! Inadvertently! Authorize! Sufficient!* He's going to criticize *me?!* Just because there was no truth to what any of us said and a couple of camel-jockeys ended up losing a finger or toe?! Then he's a *picky, petty-ass* son-of-a-bitch and it'll be a pleasure beating his *ass* in a primary election! . . Who's next? . ."

"The Senate Appropriations Committee still wants to cut the Pentagon's budget between forty and *seventy* billion dollars, Sid, and every liberal in both houses is getting behind it," Lynch Bohannon warned ominously, groans of shock and disgust emanating from the assemblage. "The *one* damned thing that's kept us free for over two hundred years, and they're willing to hurl entire weapons programs underneath the proverbial bus, and I *don't* like it! . ."

"And just what do the idiot-liberals think would be a wiser expenditure of public finds? . . I suppose they prefer to fund *more* so-called 'free meals' . . that you and I pay for? Maybe another hundred billion so every child in America can not only have their own computer, but also have fifty or so video games with it—to increase their modern-world skill-set? . . Should we just admit that our country consists mostly of drug addicts and legalize every illegal narcotic known to mankind? . . Perhaps we should also take every single convicted murderer in the land and set them free to murder *again* . . because they didn't get as many birthday cakes as they wanted when they were kids, and now they have childhood *cake 'n icing* issues? . . What this country really *needs* . . is a five-hundred-pound mulatto woman sitting on her fat ass in a Chicago ghetto with nine children from nine different fathers telling everyone else how to stay slim and trim in order to get the most out of life! . . *Jesus*, what the hell is wrong with people anyway, Lynch?! . ."

"I spoke with Blythe Campbell, and Dan McFaddon *personally* and was informed their number one priority is funding for *infrastructure* projects across the country . . When I pressed them as to their idea of what constituted infrastructure, they hemmed and hawed about the usual shit—you know, the 'powergrid,' bridges, highways and overpasses that are known to be dangerous . . They seem to think the   increased employment from construction jobs will more than offset the costs of paying cash for these badly-needed improvements . ."

"And I'm supposed to *fall* for that shit?"

"All you have to do is turn your back on your friends at the Pentagon," interrupted Pettigrew, a fresh bottle of lemonade clutched in his hand, "so that your liberal friends can better understand the terms *'treason'* and *'jerk-off'* and *'surrender'* . ."

"They already understand those terms very well," the congressman pointed out, "because those are the words they *live* by—those three and a few others. Besides, I don't *have* any liberal friends! Come to think of it, the only friends liberals have are . . *other* liberals! Dow, these idiots have been talking about infrastructure since Everett Dirksen first got to the senate, and you're my homeland guy. Now, I know you'll probably find this distasteful, but I want you to dig into this 'infrastructure' crap to see what you can come up with; what I mean is, I want to know *exactly* what it is they keep harping about because it's almost become a goddamn *religion* with them, you know? . . Maybe we can use it as leverage a little further on down the road, but what I suspect you'll find is that there are hundreds—and perhaps *thousands*—of bridges and overpasses that are, in fact, in desperate need of repair. What is invariably lost in this discussion—and what no left-thinking, tree-hugging pink-o wants to mention, by some bizarre twist-of-fate—is that, had the construction been performed by competent architects and engineers in the first place, as opposed to those infiltrating, underhanded, godless, communistic, union-loving malcontents with last names like Karzov, Kowalski, and Klein, we very likely wouldn't have to fix them *now!* Of course, I could be wrong—dead wrong, in fact, but if I'm *right* . . then their need for funding can be used as leverage to buy military hardware we cannot survive without! . . Lynch, does the Committee for Military Progress and Smaller Government have any idea who's behind this push to destroy the military-industrial complex? . ."

"They're not quite sure at this point, Sid . . as Ben Smith explained it you never really know exactly *who* wants to do *what* with the liberals because they hide their true motives behind rhetoric and stale platitudes meant to throw us off the scent . . but as near as they can tell, it's—and I'm really glad you're sitting in that chair, boss—it's our old pals, Dolores Flanagan and Irma Schatz . ."

The blood draining from his face, eyes glazing-over in furious disbelief, his beloved fountain pen from college dropped onto the table with a loud crack, the molten lava deep inside boiling hard into an historic eruption: well . . and speaking of *traitors* . . .

"*Flanagan and Schatz!*" he roared. "What a goddamn *surprise!* . . The 'Philby-and-Burgess' of the senate, no less! Pray tell, were they any further left, it'd be so much easier for all concerned to station them *inside* the Kremlin—that way they could cast their votes every time the Poliburo cabled the KGB about a security matter! And just *which* weapons systems do these two fine Russian patriots want to get rid of, Lynch? . ."

Bohannon, enjoying his moment in the limelight, took a long draft of coffee and cleared his throat, checked his paperwork for the fourth time, then proceeded.

"I don't want to upset you unnecessarily, boss, but it appears the first item up for cancellation is the next aircraft carrier . ."

Their congressman, employer, inspiration, and hero could only sit and stare expressionless at Bohannon. Having already exploded, his blood pressure right through the roof, it seemed the right time to extend an olive branch to the other side in a gesture of goodwill, reconciliation, and friendship for, as he often said, nothing good or constructive could ever come from enmity and overt hostility.

"*So* . . the senate wants to scuttle plans for the next Nimitz-class carrier, do they? . . the *same* carrier named after our former Defense Secretary and fellow Texan, Marshall Tallant, a patriot and American of the finest caliber? . . As though Fiji, Tahiti, and New Zealand should just defend *themselves* from Chinese expansionism, the colonialist *bastards*? . . I must say, that's a *terrific* plan—if you don't mind

turning your back to your friends and allies while you let chance and fool-*luck* determine your foreign policy . . and, it seems especially timely in this new age of world-wide terrorism perpetrated so very beautifully by the followers of that most serene and peaceful prophet, Mohammed . . Lynch, would you mind terribly delivering a message to those two fine ladies . . . making extra-certain they know it's from *me* . . and no one else? . ."

"Not at all," Lynch said expectantly. "I'll make doubly sure they get it . ."

"*Good* . . then please tell those two-dollar Russian *prostitutes* from Moscow that their plan to destroy American military power, beginning with their charming, systematic dismantling of the navy, may very well find a receptive audience in our socialistic *senate*, where legends are born every time they break wind . . but in the house—the same house comprised of American patriots like myself—*my* house—their plan, no matter *how* they might dress it in leftist fashion straight from Paris, will be dead-on-arrival . . Tell them their plan is such that, were they to somehow plant *their* master, Comrade Khadbroskova, inside the oval office, it couldn't possibly be more . . *distasteful*. Yes, tell them as calmly and nicely as possible . . that their plan just *won't work* today, or tomorrow, or next week — or next *year!* . . And let them know I appreciate their concern that San Diego harbor will become too crowded with naval vessels, but that the *house* . . has already taken steps to alleviate this problem . . Can you do that for me, Lynch? . . *Good!* Now then . . what other suicidal proposals have they had the audacity to mention? . ."

"They just want to completely halt the production of tanks and APC's, cancel the Air Force's newest fighter jet with advanced Stealth technology, reduce the number of service members by roughly a quarter-million, and postpone the development of the latest generation of self-propelled artillery pieces to replace our outdated, antique guns we used in the Gulf War in the early 90's . ."

"Is that *all?*"

"Probably *not* . . it's just all we know about so *far* . ."

"Are you *sure* they didn't mention the conversions of West Point and Annapolis to their latest idea on educational innovations, 'Centers for Spanish-Speaking Abortionists'? . ."

"Not *yet*, they haven't," Bohannon said to gentle snickering, "but, in time? . ."

The congressman took a long, satisfactory drink from his ceramic cup with the burnt-sienna elephant emblazoned on the side, the merry pachyderm grinning at a briefcase filled with what most anyone might guess was American cash in large denominations. Substantial proposals like the ones he'd just heard required substantial answers, that much was sure; a mere 'blanket' response seemed wholly inadequate and, in a way, disrespectful, and there was never, *ever* a good excuse for bad manners — especially from a Texan.

"Alright then, Lynch . . here are my responses to their fiscal proposals as concerns the United States military . . To their proposal of constructing no more armored vehicles of any

40

kind? . . *No.* To their suggestion of scrapping an improved fleet of Stealth aircraft? . . *No.* To their target of reducing the size of military manpower by a seemingly modest two-hundred-fifty-thousand? . . *No.* As for the notion that the new self-propelled artillery systems need to be postponed—and let me be *clear* here, gentlemen—in liberal-speak the word 'postponed' is best translated as 'out-of-sight, out-of-mind'—those systems would be tested and fielded at Fort Sill, Oklahoma, and that's *damn* close to our beloved state of Texas! And, that's my good friend Logan Seddle's congressional district—my answer has to be *no!* You got that, Lynch? . . My answers to their proposals are: no, no, no, *and* no! . . And when you *tell* 'em . . always begin with a respectful greeting, like 'With all *due* respect, ladies' . . and *then* you can cut and slash and disfigure to your heart's content, okay?"

"Understood, boss," he nodded emphatically, then added "Do we have time to discuss what Dan Masters from the NRA is thinking of doing next year? . ."

"Not today, we don't . . I'm more concerned with this ridiculous, liberal-induced, commie-inspired campaign to be waged by the honorable Mr. Warrington—that back-stabbing *sumbitch!*" Sid grinned shrewdly, as if he wasn't sure to take the threat seriously or not. "Anyway, whatever Masters is up to I'm sure will be in the best interest of loyal Americans everywhere, so I'm not gonna' worry about *him* anytime soon, I promise you . . Now . . D.P.? . ."

Sid turned slowly to his left where Dow Pettigrew shifted nervously in his seat, his lemonade only a memory now, throat awash in finest sand. Waiting to speak had only made things worse: since he hadn't seen Warrington's bid for public office until it fell on top of him, his anxiety level had risen exponentially in less than a week. Job security had been

41

loaned to someone else . . . indefinitely.

"You're my point-man on domestic issues," Sid continued calmly, his tone unexpectedly matter-of-fact, which served to calm his restless assistant, "and Denny's war-room is most definitely a domestic attack on *all* of us, so your work may be the most important until primary-time has come and gone, so . . give us a quick synopsis of what we might be up against on the home front, the better for every one of us to prep for these next roughly three months—until we can send his dead ass *home* . ."

A bit more reassured now, D.P. nodded his grateful acknowledgment, cast a final, cursory glance at his notes, and began his report by saying "Well, we all know how current-events in Texas—and the country, too, as a whole—are always in a state of *flux* . . especially during election-time when an occasional statement taken out of context, or misstatement about a particular issue, or some seemingly *innocent* mistake can, depending on the circumstances, make you or *break* you, right? . . We have also come to understand how the *verbal* blunder—whereby the obviously damaging, even stupid-sounding utterance of *today* can, only four to six weeks later— re-emerge as a statement of sheer brilliance, even *prophecy*, due to unforeseen developments. My news, therefore, is both good and bad . . as it *usually* is . .'

"The *good* news first, okay? . . We have a distinctly built-in advantage in that our candidate is the incumbent . . this is always—*always*—a position of strength. So, too, we have the advantage of backing a man of honor, a man of his convictions, and by that I mean we support a man who's managed to stay out of trouble. You see, there are *no* scandals to deal with, no . . real questions as to his moral integrity and, at least to the best of our knowledge, no skeletons in his closet—or anywhere *else*,

42

for that matter, so, yes . . our candidate is *clean*. Therefore, the moral 'high ground' is ours, unless we carelessly toss it away and voluntarily surrender it which, to be sure, isn't very likely, is it? . ."

Scandal. Moral integrity. Skeletons in the closet. High ground. Surrender. Convictions. *Scandal?!* Sid's focus suddenly shifted into reverse, racing back to events of Wednesday night at Pandora's Box and early Thursday morning in a condo in Tyson's Corner. No scandal *there*—only the intertwining of two really *lovely* people in every possible embrace known to humanity, the female of whom was arguably the single most-attractive woman he'd ever laid eyes on. As a purely lovemaking endeavor, it had been the experience of a lifetime: no memory, recent or distant, had felt *sweeter*, no thought held more dear. In a sense, he considered the whole affair to be. . life-altering!

"On the global-warming front," Pettigrew continued dutifully, "there really isn't enough difference between our stance and theirs to shake a stick at . . I took a fairly extended look online at their set of '*principles*,' as they call them, and they're obviously the work of Warrington's campaign manager, Mr. Dudley Thomas, whom most of us know . . Now, I'm not saying Dudley's *predictable*, because he really isn't, but if their global-warming stance was any more similar to ours, I'd say they copied us and let it go at that . . They feel that the Environmental Protection Agency was established *not* to protect America from unscrupulous businessmen bent on making as large a stack of cash as possible without regard to damage done to the land, water, air, or people, but as a safeguard against those elements of the natural environment that might harm the country, assuming guilt invariably assigned to a particular business and /or owner, without due

43

process. This is a virtual mirror-image of our stance, the major difference being—and this is pure *semantics*, gentlemen—that the EPA, in our opinion, could . . and *should* . . be held liable for monetary damages in the event their claim, or claims, are proved *wrong*. Dudley's men make no mention of this, but so what? It's a dead issue, at any rate . .'

"As for the so-called *scientific community* the liberals keep touting, the voodoo witch-doctors who claim that cattle are the greatest contributor to global-warming? . . Each camp categorically denies any and all claims without absolute, irrefutable *proof*, and evidential proof, at that! And as far as 'clean-coal' being some kind of conservative conspiracy to keep poisoning America is concerned? . . The nuc-u-lar power enthusiasts have yet to demonstrate to anyone that the debacle at Three Mile Island will not—*not*—be repeated should we convert to primarily reactor-generated power . . Dudley Thomas and his cohorts aren't fools either, having pushed the proverbial envelope a bit further by publicly posing the obvious question, to wit: 'If reactor-power is, indeed, the wave of the future, why does the present *not* bear that out?' . . What our everyday, mediocre, run-of-the-mill *liberal* fails to understand in this mess is that, in being forced to reduce carbon-dioxide emissions in conjunction with CCS, or *carbon capture and storage* technologies, a formidable array of for-profit companies have been created by both savvy entrepreneurs seeking new cash-cows *and* government-sponsored 'inventors,' for lack of a better word, attempting to maximize improvements developed for the sole purpose of providing cleaner air! . . It would seem their major complaint is that someone, somewhere, *somehow*—is turning a profit! . . *However*, as there are always options to any problem, their options are severely limited in this instance. We can stop using coal *entirely* to power our electrical grid—the downside being forced to determine which *forty percent* of the country no longer wants electrical power . . *Or*, we can, for better or worse, construct more nuc-u-lar power plants, cross our fingers, and hope our luck holds out at least until the tremors commence and subside beneath us . ."

Tremors, *indeed*, Sid remembered fondly. After their third go-round, when Charlotte collapsed onto him headfirst, succeeded incrementally by feet, then arms, then legs and, finally, midsection, she rolled over onto her back, nestled next to him after a few moments and grabbed his right hand, grinning mischievously. "Feel *that!*" she cooed sweetly, her eyes gushing with pride and wonder as she guided his hand to her lustrous black thicket of pubic hair, careful to place his fingers atop her mons. Muscles underneath, rhythmically expanding and contracting with their glorious workout, rose and fell in the splendid *song of two*, their implacable journey toward well-earned rest commenced, his hand rising and falling in unison. *Tremors galore!*

"Okay, D.P., so far, so good . . What can you tell us on the health-care front? . ."

"Another area of virtual *non*-contention, fellas' . . nobody in either camp wants universal health coverage for *every* Texan— put it another way, our respective positions emphasize the need for quality health-care for *native-born* Texans, okay?—in this way, resident aliens, both legal and otherwise, can continue to receive *their* medical care through ER's across the state, much the same way they do in Mexico. This serves a dual purpose: one, no one can accuse only Sid and the rest of us of insensitivity towards the medical needs of our Hispanic population and, *two*, the profit margins of the trauma docs are enhanced—*plus*, the bill now circulating through our state senate, which is gaining momentum literally with the passing of each day, to allow public hospitals the right to confiscate personal properties of those in legitimate debt to them, *if they are proven to be illegals* . . should become law by the middle of football season, roughly mid-October. And what does our boy Denny have to say about all this? . . Hell, it's *his bill*, for Chrissakes! What we need to understand about this is . . *here* is a real opportunity to get a leg-*up* on Denny and his pals! All we're proposing—through our friends in Austin, of course—is that any public, or *private*, hospital corporation be allowed to do the same! Gentlemen, this is a win-win on top of a win-win! Neither Denny nor any of his henchmen can very well complain about his own bill being enhanced and improved in the name of increased commerce!'

"*Now* . . we need to talk about the so-called 'morning-*after*' pill," he said, his tone dramatically altered to reinforce the inherent depravity of the subject. Eyeballing each and every member gathered round the table with a decidedly grave expression, he continued after a quick pause, an edge of alarm in his voice. "There exists . . in our beloved state of Texas . . an element of the population that believes making this 'morning-after' pill widely available on demand is the proper, even the *ethical* thing to do. Determining what percentage of our district is actually in *favor* of this proposal is an extremely 'iffy' task and must be handled delicately, but everyone here is more than vaguely familiar with blatantly terroristic, overtly *homicidal* young women who casually consider themselves capable of making life-and-death decisions without the benefit of proper deliberation. This hasn't *always* been the case, of course, but we also know that the more illegal women who successfully cross the river equals a proportionately higher percentage of *tramps and sluts* in the general female population and, frankly, at this point, there's not a whole lot we can do about it. I, for one, will never raise my hand in favor of murdering the unborn, and I'll be *damned* if I'll sit idly by while others *do* . . Right-thinking men everywhere know that in Texas, if there's any killing to be done, it'll be done by duly-appointed men who are required to execute condemned citizens in accordance with the rules of law and the *will* . . of the people of the Lone Star state. Furthermore, if this morning-after pill becomes available on-demand, that's just an invitation to the weak-minded, morally non-existent females of Texas to go out at night and walk the streets, get drunk and smoke pot and have unprotected, pleasurable *sex* . . with virtually any yahoo she happens to meet . . Now, I'm *not* saying that every red-blooded Texan is a veritable pillar of strength, incapable of taking advantage of the so-called *'fairer'* sex when the occasion presents itself—who among us hasn't been tempted at some point?—but if the thinking, *conscientious* men and women in government fail to take the bull by the horns, who does that leave to protect the innocent? . . The *liberal?!* Hah! Those sons-of-bitches are the *champions* of extra-marital sex! They've actually convinced themselves that taking personal responsibility for their own actions is *wrong!* It's always someone else's fault, their childhood was awful, they ate too many hot dogs, we've *all* heard it, haven't we!? Therefore . . it is *our* contention that the morning-after pill be controlled and dispensed to those select few it was originally designed for . . That means it *cannot* be made available over-the-counter at *all*, but has to be prescribed by a licensed physician from the state of Texas. *Period*. As for those who for whatever reason, disapprove of our position? Well . . you can dislike it all you want, but if you want

to commit murder against any person in this, our state, with a *pill?* . . Sorry, you'll just have to carry your ass to *another* state! . .'

"Wouldn't it be *fantastic* if we could prove that Warrington and his ilk are really in favor of this pill being widely available? . . They're *not*, of course, but if it was possible to make it *appear* as though they *are*, that by itself would probably be enough to destroy their hardline stance on immigration 'cause they'd be catering to society's misfits and malcontents—the very *same* elements they're so zealously dedicated to keeping *out!* Hah!"

The haunting vision of his dependable latex *amigo*, inexplicably split wide open at the precise location its greatest strength was required, forced itself into Sid's unconscious as he sat attentively absorbing his friend's wisdom. The unfortunate reckoning of the otherwise *perfect* night and, as undeniably devastating as it had been, the entire experience with the young embassy employee had been superior to any in college . . or anything *since*. Still, there was the mistake itself to be dealt with: '*Charlotte? . . we need to talk.*' And deal with it they certainly had. What a godsend he'd allowed himself to be seduced by a woman of maturity and common sense, a woman who, much like her latest conquest, was intelligent enough to take reasonable precautions! Thank you, *Jesus*, thank you so *much*, because the complications might eventually prove to be . . *unspeakable!*

"Pardon me, Dow," interrupted Cas Turley, ever the polite gentleman from Tyler, "but you said this 'morning-after' pill should only be used by a select few it was specifically created for—or words to that effect . . Right? . ."

"Yes, sir . ."

"Well, I certainly don't mean to sound stupid or ig'-nant, but just *who* . . who was this pill meant to be used by? . .

48

Doctors? . ."

"But don't you see, Cas, *that's* the main problem: no one in a position of knowledge or authority—whether it be doctors, lawyers, nurses, politicians, *hell*, the manufacturers their *own* selves—has stood up and said the first damn *word* about its proper applications! . . *Sure*, some doctors claim there's no moral dilemma to speak of, but just as many, if not *more*, say the opposite," Dow explained as best he could, for he had right *and* truth on his side. "What I know is *this*: all these life-threatening, life-*ending* pills seem to come from France—and we already know what *their* priorities are, don't we?—those traitorous *bastards!*—but what we do *not* have . . is a general consensus-of-opinion, one way or the other. So . . how do we fill this void? Why, the same way we always *have* and always *will*: the right honorable, upright, and right-*thinking* men of Texas shall lead the way . . and make the correct determination for their *selves!* . ."

"Goddamn *right!*" echoed Lynch Bohannon, his right fist dramatically pounding the table's surface, for who in their right mind could argue with the common-sense approach? "Like anyone else could *ever* make the right decision . ."

"Excellent work, D.P., truly *excellent!*" cried the now-enthusiastic congressman from west Texas, congratulating his long-time friend and ally with an affectionate pat on the shoulder. "That seems to cover any health-care questions *nicely* . . Now . . we need you to educate us *properly* . . on the constantly-evolving situation with abortion-rights and any potential problems we might incur with the challenge from the honorable Mr. Warrington . ."

This time Pettigrew took a deep breath, hesitating briefly to consider how best to begin before proceeding. Clearing his throat, he replaced the top sheet of paper sitting in front of him with another sheet from underneath, tapping it perfunctorily while gathering his thoughts.

"I've given this one a great deal of thought, which isn't necessarily true for the other matters, and I've decided there is, at least, the *potential* for a common sort of misconception on the part of the public in regard to our respective positions concerning not only the general *availability* of abortions, but also regarding specific conditions under which abortions are *warranted* . . As you all know, it has *long* been our position that abortions should not be allowed under *any* . . but the most dire circumstances. Real

person-hood begins at the moment of conception—*not* at twenty-four weeks, *not* at twenty weeks, *not* at sixteen, *nor* at twelve, eight, four, nor *two* . . neither is one week acceptable, nor one *day*, truth be known . . In this particular matter, our respective camps are in utter agreement—but then, it's not as simple as that, is it? . .'

"There is, of course, the matter of precisely *when* it should be allowed, and there's more agreement between our two camps than disagreement here, *but* . . I personally question the wisdom of certain of their exceptions—not *because* I disagree with them, but because I think they will, in the long run, foul themselves imprudently . . We have vowed to permit the procedure only in the instance that the mother's life is in clear and present danger. Further, it has always been our position that only through the complete agreement of a minimum of three licensed physicians can the threat to the mother's life be accurately verified. We make no exceptions in the case of rape or incest—*zero*—and in this respect, the Warrington camp is in full accordance with our position again . . *However* . . they have made it known that they are open to the possibility of— are you *ready* for this?—*abortion-on-demand* if the offending

50

party just happens to be of a different race . ."

As the rasping, surly noise of insufficient oxygen being sucked-in rolled around the table in stunned, bewildered awe—the only exception being to Pettigrew's immediate left— the speaker stopped long enough to gauge their individual reactions. Even the congressman seemed stupefied: invariably the poster-boy for good posture, thanks to his mother's incessant harping, Sid now rested his head in his right palm, his right arm resting on the table from shoulder to elbow. Cas Turley tilted his head right to stare at the speaker, as though what he'd just heard couldn't possibly be what he just heard. Lynch Bohannon's mouth dropped open sufficiently to place an egg inside it or, if one was careful, maybe a grapefruit. But to D.P.'s left not a single sound could be heard, the silence steady and deafening.

"Now, fellas', I *know* what you're thinking," he began again, "but I think it's important we not jump to conclusions here . . Yes, I freely admit that, on the surface, their position *sounds like* political suicide . . but I want you to stop and consider *every* angle . . before you write-off Denny Warrington . ."

"That's *insanity!*" Bohannon cried gleefully. "Why, the NAACP'll assassinate his stupid ass—and if they don't, some Mexican cousin in a drug cartel *will!*"

"Exactly" D.P. grinned deviously, "*except* that . . in case of rape or incest—or in case of rape *and* incest—how in the world is *anyone* going to prove *anything* illegal ever happened *anyway*—without waiting eight and a half or nine months for the resultant child to be born *full-term,* so that a verifiable determination can be made?! . . *unless* . . you're lucky enough to have an offending party with an I.Q. of thirty stand-up in a genuine moment of insanity and shout 'I did it! *I* did it! It was *me,* your honor!' . . Now . . *gentlemen* . . I humbly suggest,

51

again, that you consider every angle here before you rush to judgment on this one . . Believe me, I thought long and hard about the ramifications of abortion-on-demand under these particular circumstances: the immediate, completely *logical* reaction to such a system would be the female victim first accusing her attacker . . then being forced to wait a little in excess of eight *months* to prove her accusation by delivering a child she almost certainly did *not want* in the first place?! . . *That*, Lynch, really *is* . . insanity! But, consider the obvious alternative, if you will . ."

"Which is? . ."

"All she has to do is wait a month and a half or two months until she's confirmed pregnant, have the abortion, then run DNA tests to see what's what . . then his sorry ass goes to prison, where it *belongs*, justice is served, and everybody's happy . . *simple* . ."

Cas Turley shook his head in disbelief.

"And just who in hell would favor such a fucked-up system? . ."

"Oh, the usual suspects, Cas . . Let me see now . . there's the Prison Guards Association, for one . . they supported *you* last time, Sid, with votes *and* cash . . then there's that tiny-ass group called the Texas Bar Association, and *they* seem to like the idea, too . . of course, you have the women's groups who've endorsed it—you know, NOW, the Dallas Garden Club, the West Texas Ladies Auxiliary . . shall I continue? . ."

"No, I catch your drift, loud and clear," Sid nodded, hardly enthusiastic about developments. Then he grinned and said "You know something? . . That's the *shrewdest* damn thing I ever heard of—but you're absolutely correct in assuming that, should Denny and his boys actually *endorse* this plan, their share of the ultra-conservative vote could suffer a sizable hit . ."

"That's what *I'm* thinking, boss," agreed Pettigrew, "and for somebody attempting to attack you from your *right* . . that's an *extremely* risky proposition, and one I personally wouldn't take . ."

"But what if they *do* . . endorse this plan for real?" said Lynch.

"Let 'em! We can't very well wait for them to endorse the plan and then endorse it ourselves without looking like schmucks . . We couldn't stop them anyway, so we'll just keep tabs on their progress, fine-tune as necessary, and continue to march. I'm absolutely convinced that, for every vote they wrangle away from us on this particular issue, they'll *lose* another for being in the pocket of a man who turned his back on a core-conservative issue—in this case, Denny Warrington . . I maintain we're better-off doing nothing, letting *them* take the lumps when the arms start twirling round, but fighting for all we're worth when the time is right . ."

"I'm inclined to agree with you, D.P.," said Villary, "and not just because I'm the one who'll have to return home this summer to campaign . . I'd much rather *watch* the fight develop than start the fight and have nowhere to turn in the event things start headin' south . . The good folks of Texas already know that '*new*' and '*better*' don't always go hand-in-hand, so I'll be happy to stay on the sidelines—at least for a little while—and let someone else bring the thunder. The bottom line is, I defy *anyone* to tell me abortion-on-demand—*hang* the circumstances—is a conservative value! For Chrissakes, it sounds more like something Consuela Garcia might be willing to support, and we all know how conservative that socialist creature is, don't we! . . And think about *this*: if a young lady wants to spend time with a member

of another race, I'd be the last person to stand in her way—
everyone has the right to pick and choose as they see fit, and
the fact that I personally disapprove of whoring has nothing
to do with it—but if she gets *careless* and subsequently decides
to murder her own child, just because her calculations
happened to go awry—*oh, I've made a terrible mistake!*—she's
not going to correct her mistake by killing that which she
helped to create! . . What was it you called these fine women,
D.P.? . . *tramps and sluts?* . . well, there it is . . God put women
on this earth to bear our fruit—by *God*, that's how we call it in
Texas!—and bear our fruit they shall! . . *Now*, D.P. . . whatta'
we got on the availability of abortions that we need to
cover? . ."

"Well, now, this is a much, *much* easier patch of ground
we're dealing with here," said Pettigrew, his time in the
spotlight drawing to a close, "much less complicated and
much more straightforward . . Conventional wisdom basically
says that it's too *damned easy* to get an abortion in the state of
Texas . . there are simply too many clinics . ."

"Too damned *easy!*" echoed Lynch Bohannon, fist dropping
to the tabletop again.

"And those . . *gentlemen* . . in the Warrington camp? What
are *their* views on availability? . ."

"Basically, the same . . their stance is that abortion clinics are
like *Mexicans*: there's just too damned many of them!"

"Too *damned* many!" nodded Lynch.

"And what is Mr. Stract and our friends in the legislature
attempting to do with this enormous, long-standing
problem? . ."

"Their proposal originally called for the eventual
establishment of two abortion clinics, one in El Paso, the other
in Texarkana, to be staffed by not only licensed physicians, but

by physicians' assistants, psychologists, and representatives from most Protestant denominations—even *priests* from the Roman Catholic faith! . . this, of course, to proceed once these other so-called '*clinics*' are deemed unsanitary, unprofessional, and unbecoming to the welfare of the state of Texas, and are subsequently shut-down to

help reduce the number of sexually-transmitted diseases . ."

"Seems reasonable," Sid nodded approvingly—no one made mention of Muslims, Hindis, Sikhs, or Buddhists. "Those cities are easily within a thousand miles of each other, so nobody should have to travel more than a day's drive—day and a half, *tops!*—to receive services . . anything else? . ."

"I hate to say it, but it didn't take very long for the professional agitators to begin raising a ruckus . . the first general area to cry 'Foul!'—predictably enough—was the Laredo-Brownsville region, followed less than a week later by trouble-makers from Amarillo—with *both* areas claiming they'd been excised completely from the loop! . . Unfortunately, instead of their hollerin' being squashed, it just got louder until Dwight and them had to add two more clinics to the deal, so now, at long last, the latest proposal authorizes a total of *four* . ."

"Goddamned trouble-makers!" Lynch muttered under his breath.

"Wait *just* one minute!" cried Sid Villary, right index finger pointing toward the ceiling, his traditional sign of displeasure. "I want to make sure I understand this new development completely . . Okay, so there'll be a clinic in Amarillo and another one in . . Laredo, or *Brownsville?!* . ."

"Oh, Laredo, of course," smiled Pettigrew, like it was common knowledge.

"Thank *God!* . . for a second there I thought we were in real trouble . . There are probably a hundred thousand street-walkers in Matamoros, a few hundred feet across the Rio Grande—every one of them a *virgin*, naturally—and all of them willing to swim the river in case they need a little medical assistance should we put the clinic in Brownsville . . *whew*, thank God for small favors! . . and what, pray tell, do the Warrington people think about *that?* . ."

"Well, their hands are tied, too . . they don't want folks angry with them any more than we do, so they're willing to let the legislature work its magic and let the cow-chips fall where they may which, realistically, is about all any of us can hope for . ."

"If this gets pushed through, do we receive any residual damage?"

"*Hell*, no!—if anything, it might actually help us, if we support it in the right way . ."

"Well, *alright* then!—and we appreciate all your fine work, too, D.P. . . Sounds like you didn't leave any stone unturned on this one and, considering we've never been attacked by one of our *own* until now that's likely the way we'll have to play it until this thing's over and done with . .'

"*Now* . . Mister *Shaw*," Sid Villary said quietly, a distinct undertone of reverence and respect in his voice, his focus shifting to Dow Pettigrew's left to properly address the esteemed fourth member of his advisory group. "Your complete and utter silence, both disturbing and thunderous, is even greater than normal . . and I can hardly guess why . . Pray enlighten us in any manner you deem appropriate, as we anxiously await your perceptive observations . ."

The little man anchoring the far-left table corner, a full generation older than Villary, saw three more sets of eyes swing his way at mere mention of his last name. Leopold

Wilson Shaw—"L.W." to virtually everyone, for he was said to despise his first name to such an extent that anyone who used it, inadvertently or otherwise, for any purpose, in his presence, would *not* be spoken to again until Mr. Shaw obtained an apology *in writing*—and it was generally accepted knowledge in Washington that incurring his wrath was a politician's surest method of accomplishing involuntary retirement. Shaw's demeanor, always calm and unassuming, carried the weight of one who'd weathered storms far in excess of the norm: thin-lipped, the nose above so small and delicate it appeared to have been placed there only because it was compulsory, his cold blue eyes revealed a depth of acumen few ever hoped to achieve and even fewer realized. The baby-fine hair, straight and thin and ever-fashioned in a Princeton-cut, had turned mostly gray at the temples and, to a lesser degree, atop his brilliant head, the top half of which was noticeably larger in circumference, lending the somewhat disquieting notion that he suffered from some sort of nebulous brain fever. That Sid Villary referred to him as *Mister Shaw* rather than "L.W." was nothing more than a sign of respect and admiration for a man with too many victories to count.

"It's my custom never to underestimate my opponent," he began, his voice low but soft and firm, "and it has never failed me. Deception has the unfortunate consequence of taking an individual only so far before the ruse turns the tables on its perpetrator, at which time the proverbial torrent of invective washes away everything in its path—even that which was never intended to be swept from its foundation. Once this process begins it is impossible to reverse its course, therefore one caught in the middle of the onslaught, having initiated the battle in the first place, perishes early and painfully. I've told

57

anyone patient enough to listen that the ancient scourge of hypocrisy, first practiced by the Greeks in several of their theatrical productions, has the capacity to annihilate even the best-intended of men and women, and I've repeated this lesson often in more locations than I can recall and still . . the true believers, convinced of their moral superiority without any basis in fact—for how can one judge another by a set of rules unbeknownst to the other party?—place their faith in artificial altars erected to that most holy of holies, the sacred covenant of thou art inferior and wholly different, and therefore undeniably unworthy. My invitations to seize the loftiest plateau, to share and recommend it to all who might benefit from it, to maintain it without ambition or acknowledgment, to nurture it with as many good works as possible, and to never relinquish it, invariably go unheeded. And so I feel it's my sacred obligation, my duty as a human being, to advise certain other members of my species as to their responsibilities to other members of the flock, and in this I do not intend only a select few to be instructed as to their political, economic, social, spiritual, and emotional properties as some may think desirable, but to all members—all—in order that they might spread a substantial measure of good through it. And therefore, since I make no pretenses about possessing the fine qualities of a doctor of theology, hear me well when I say I take no pleasure in being correct at his being mistaken. Any wisdom gained by my words is as old as dust, but in this bizarre age of technologically explosive growth, it seems even more appropriate. For you see, to be *technically* correct is not enough. To be technically correct and nothing more is *never* enough. This is true for the simple fact that, in dealing with human beings, one must know how to speak correctly to another human being, no matter how technologically advanced or remedial the other might be. The human being who has learned to covet—which is generally perceived as a major character flaw—has also inadvertently learned what it means to hold something dear and to think in terms of that which is precious, and is therefore capable of feeling loss. This is a human being in full. This person will guard his freedom of choice as tenaciously as his life, for life without choice, for the rational being, is no life at all. We may very well think we have someone cornered in order to make him do our bidding, but the use of force or coercion will at some juncture return to haunt the aggressor, and that at the most inopportune moment imaginable, so be very, very careful when applying pressure. It is my considered opinion that your plans covered here are, in aggregate and microcosmic terms, foundationally solid and reasonable, but I would remind you all to beware of the fluctuations that occur almost without rippling the water. The only matter in this life that I am absolutely, one hundred percent sure of is that what we believe and see and think and know will *change*. Everything—*everything*—will change. It may not come quickly, which makes it virtually impossible to identify and acknowledge, but it will arrive anyway, unannounced and unloved. So the organization whose foresight extends no further than the end of its nose will morph into a sordid kind of anachronism, to be vanquished by those who are stronger, more determined, and willing to at least envision things as they *could* be rather than settle for things as they *are*. And so in your dealings with those around you as the campaigns progress through the summer and fall, keep your ears tuned to the winds of change. If for any reason you doubt this particular piece of counsel I would ask you to consider this: six months ago you had no challenge from any other conservative in the state's primary election. None. *Zero.* Is that true today? . ."

Having listened attentively to everyone's words and then spoken his mind, L.W. Shaw rose from his seat, gracefully sliding his chair into its rightful place beneath the table. Sid Villary, his countenance perceptibly lifted by his elder's sage wisdom, rose in stark admiration as his other three advisors sat contemplating the great man's guidance.

"Thank you for allowing me to be part of your grand plan for continued success," said Shaw.

"Oh, *no, no,* L.W.!" grinned Villary, his head shaking in heartfelt gratitude as his right hand grasped the other's in a warm embrace. "It is *we* who thank *you,* sir!"

Pettigrew, Bohannon, and Cas Turley jumped to their feet to shake hands, each in his turn stepping forward to address the elder statesman as 'Mister Shaw' before watching their employer and benefactor escort the esteemed gentleman to the front door.

"Safe-home, L.W.," he called after him, real affection in his voice, "for I couldn't replace *you* in a

hundred years! . ."

Villary's eyes searched those of his friends: when he again took his seat at the head of the table their collective expressions presented a curious amalgam of uncertainty. Unquestionably, words from a man of unparalleled integrity, a true patriot possessed of a piercing sagacity, had been heard by all . . but had all present been able to grasp their significance?

"Tell me, Lynch . . what did *you* take from L.W.'s advice? . ."

"I'm convinced that, in the mind of L.W. Shaw, we'd better not forget that in politics it's every man for himself, but that as we go forward we should dance with the partner what brung us! . ."

"Nicely put, Lynch," he smiled, the other's interpretation settling comfortably inside his head. Glancing left he said "D.P.? . . hear anything important? . ."

"Well, I'll tell you *one* thing—I'm damn glad he's on *our* side, 'cause I'd hate to go up against someone like that on *any* dang battleground! . . What I think he was trying to say, in his modest terminology, is that if we know what's good for us, we'll be ready to adjust, and adjust, and adjust, and adjust *again*, if need be—that being the most reliable strategy for meeting this primary challenge head-on . . Oh, and one *more* thing: he gave us fair warning that Denny Warrington is a *genuine* challenge, and an opponent *not* to be taken lightly either! . ."

"Loud and clear on that one!" Cas Turley jumped-in, more than ready to share his thoughts. "I remember L.W.'s first statement best, when he said his habit of never underestimating his enemy had always worked well for him . . Now, I might be wrong, but I don't think him beginning with that particular statement was any *accident*, fellas' . . And if you don't mind, I'd like to share a few words of wisdom I learned from one of *the* smartest men I ever met—my *father* : 'He who prepares first . . prepares *best!*' . . and I'm reasonably sure the honorable L.W. Shaw would agree with that, too."

"Hear, hear!" Sid Villary saluted, his water goblet held high. Each raised their respective cups in deference to the approaching conflict, taking their rightful sips as one.

"So what are your thoughts, boss?" Turley continued, his natural curiosity roused. "We work for *you* alone."

"Well, fellas,' the first thought I'll share with you is this: L.W. Shaw has likely *forgotten* more shit than I'll ever *know*, so we're probably going to conduct ourselves in the manner he so

61

artfully prescribed," he began thoughtfully. "We're facing a crossroads in our political convictions, and I'm convinced our enemies—and I'm referring to our liberal brethren across the aisle here—would like nothing better than to see us scurry down the wrong road to conservative perdition, whereby opening our borders to international riff-raff, the proliferation of the welfare state, personal irresponsibility, universal health care, the unlimited expansion of the federal government, open whoring, and the cowardly betrayal of our sovereign right to defend ourselves is not only *accepted*, but is shoved down our collective throats like so much bad medicine! But let me tell you something here and now: *none* of that insanity is going to happen, gentlemen! . . And *how* can we stop it? . .'

"By simply *refusing* to let it happen in the first place, that's how! . . and here's my official position on the high points of today's discussions . . Global warming? . . it's a hoax and a sham, period! So today's weather events are super-violent, huh? . . Well, pardon me all to *hell*, but even as a little boy of *seven* I remember my folks talking about a cluster of tornadoes that converged on Wichita Falls in April of '79, killing I don't know how many people and destroying a coupla' *thousand* homes before fading away, so I don't wanna' hear about, quote, '*bad weather*' . . And as for health-care? . . yeah, I'm all in favor of people having health care—just as long as they can *pay* for it! . . If you're in our country illegally and you get sick, but can't afford to see a doctor? . . *Tough shit!* . . Go back to Mexico and munch some more peppers or somethin'! . . As for the mindless bimbos and tarts who think nothing about sleeping with complete strangers, then seem surprised six weeks later when they get a little nauseous? . . and *then* think it's okay to murder their child, as though their condition is someone *else's* fault? . . I have bad news for them too! Mindless, careless *pleasure* has a price, to my way of thinking, and since there is virtually universal agreement that women were put on this earth to grow our progeny—at least in *Texas* they were, my friends!—*that* is what shall happen, in full accordance with God's law! If they really want an abortion, I'll do all I can to help them get to *France*, where morals have been stuck in the gutter for centuries! . .'

"Now, Cas . . I realize I said we didn't have time to discuss plans the NRA has drafted for introduction next year, but you tell Dan Masters his friend and fellow patriot, Sidney Hunt Villary, is *already* pro-active on this one, and by that I mean their proposal to make it mandatory that home-grown Texans—'home-grown' being a euphemism for white Anglo-Saxon Protestant, mind you—that all home-grown Texans be required to own at least one firearm per household will meet with stiff resistance from minority groups all over the state who stand to lose countless millions of dollars—not to mention probably *hundreds* of lives—in botched car-jackings, burglaries, hold-ups, muggings, and armed robberies by patriotic, gun-wielding Texans who don't mind defending themselves . . but that it will find a friendly reception in the legislature. In my view, anyone killed in the process of committing an act of violence against another Texan saves the Lone Star state untold funds in housing, feeding, prosecuting, and executing the prisoner. The law's the law, plain and simple . .'

"As for those commie-loving pacifists in the senate . . their grand plan to quadruple the size of the federal government will fall on deaf ears in the house, Cas, just as sure as I'm sitting here in front of you . . Myself and my fellow conservatives, in a valiant effort to save our country, will actually *shrink* the size of government by expanding defense-spending as we dismantle the departments of Education, Housing and Urban Development, the EPA, and whatever *else* we believe we can get away with. We simply don't *need* the Education Department because our educational system, contrary to what the pansy-ass *liberals* claim, is in great shape! We didn't just *happen* to place eighteenth among other industrialized countries of the world by accident, you know! . . Let the slope-heads place first in math, science, and engineering—we're still number one in God-and-country, houses of worship, military spending, and number of college football stadiums—and those are the ones that count! . . And don't even get me started on housing and urban America . . If it wasn't for the disgraceful shape they're in we'd all be better off, but we've poured money into social programs for over half a century, and what have we got to show for it? . . not a goddamn thing worth mentioning, except maybe runaway crime, and in Texas that's considered a *bad* thing! . .'

"The Muslim scourge has to be met head-on on a continuing basis whenever and wherever it rears its despicable head. Therefore, we're introducing legislation to fund continued operations in the middle-east on a case-by-case basis and, since it appears the various factions of the Muslim religion, in fact, *despise* each other, we're willing to sit back and observe the slaughter. *However*, should one faction clearly gain the upper hand and threaten to win outright, thus prematurely *ending* their sacred conflict, we're also willing to assist the faction that needs our assistance *most* in an effort to continue the fight because the increased business to our weapons-producing sector would be immediately enhanced. We have to face a few facts here: war is just good business— always has been, always will be—and it's our job as conservatives to make sure the proper side wins. As conservative Christians it's our job to ensure that *non-*Christians, fighting for what they erroneously believe, have every weapon possible at their disposal in order to wage justifiable warfare against their own kind . .'

"Denny and his criminals are going to do whatever they're going to do, no matter what, and we can't stop them, but what we *can* do, at least as far as immigration reform goes, is make sure it doesn't *appear* as though he's even capable of going to our right, and if they *try* it—and I wouldn't put it past you that they *will*—we, in turn, might suggest that their ulterior, *hidden* agenda involves making Mexico our fifty-first state, with the predictable result that the welfare state *doubles* in size overnight!—and when they complain that we've gone too far over the edge of decency, we'll completely *ignore* them as we repeat the accusation a thousand times! . . and *then* . . we'll see who wins and loses—the bottom line being that nobody, but *nobody* . . is going to get away with primarying *us!* . .'

"Any questions, gentlemen?"

"Is it correct to assume," Dow Pettigrew began, "that when I look into this . . *infrastructure* garbage and discover that there *might*, in fact, be a little something to it, you'll *consider* limited corrective cash funding—as long as certain criteria are met? . ."

"That is *affirmative*, my friend—as long as the specific criteria includes the absence of preferential treatment given to any contractor bidding on government-funded work . ."

"In other words, minority and non-Christian entities need *not* apply . . right?"

"I think you put that rather *well*, D.P.," he said, a mischievous twinkle in his eye. Business concluded, their primary burdens established and placed squarely on their collective shoulders, the congressman grinned and said "This session is officially ended! . . Anyone care for a beer or a nice shot o' bourbon? . ."

IV.

Monday mornings invigorated the third-term congressman from the Lone Star state's thirty-eighth district. Where others saw the week's first workday as the worst possible development, Sidney Hunt Villary, relaxed and refreshed from his weekend's peaceful reflections, conversations with the folks back home, and the timely arrival of Sunday morning worship services that served so very many worthy causes, his view of the brand-new week inevitably aroused his most admirable personal characteristics of service, loyalty, and faithfulness. His unbridled enthusiasm on Monday mornings spilled over to his staff, as they typically arrived for work a few minutes early and, unless their boss had some kind of extraordinary matter to attend to, the kind that kept him away from the office, stayed late. Monday evenings, his designated late-night, they invariably stayed longer than required on the mere chance he might find their services useful — and this long after most offices had emptied out. These lucky ladies adored him: under no circumstances, he told them early-on in their respective employments, were they to work on weekends after having put in a solid week at the office! People needed their weekends for family, friends, sports, church, travel, or whatever else they might want to do, and when the week was over late Friday afternoons, more than a few employees in other offices jealously observed the ladies waving good-bye to one another, promising to meet again three days hence. They *loved* him: he meant what he said, and said what he meant!

"Your man Dow has called *already*!" Regina greeted him as he strolled through his office doors that Monday morning in June, her eyes wide in alarm, office phone to her ear, free hand covering the receiver, "and this is your mother, and she *says* it's important! Line two . ."

"I'll take it in my office," he whispered, whisking-by without breaking stride. Bumping open his office door with his briefcase, he sauntered in, dropped it on top of a desk already cluttered with more paperwork than he liked and, dropping comfortably onto the Yellow Rose, his gaze coming to rest on his bust of Reagan sitting atop a short stack of <u>Mad</u> magazines, he grabbed his desk-phone and jabbed the flashing white button. "Hey, *mom!* . ."

"Well-*well*, looks like I called just at the right time!" came the familiar, lofty-pitched voice from west Texas. "And how's my precious little boy today? . ."

Ignoring the affectionate reference to his size—he hadn't really been her *little* boy in over thirty years now—he said "Your precious boy is busier than an infantry commander in a firefight with a field full of Commies! . . How's everything at home? . ."

"We're good, too, son. We were just wondering if you'd firmed-up plans to be here for the Fourth because we've spoken to Dow twice in the last few days, and he said he didn't know when you were headed home either. You know, he's got a *bus-load* of campaign stops for you to make over the next seven or eight weeks, and Denny Warrington's already been here in town *twice* this month, so we were all getting a little concerned about not seeing you . ."

"I've just been busy, that's all, especially with that immigration-reform committee stalled on the question of increased manpower for the Border Patrol . ."

"Well, you're still coming home, aren't you? . ."

"Of *course*, I'm still coming home, mother—how on earth would I be able to run effectively for re-election without being there to physically connect with my constituents?!" he explained, his voice almost imperceptibly tinged with frustration at such a ridiculous question until, disappointed with his own impatience, he reminded himself that she was, after all, his mother. He glanced at his calendar from McElroy's Bar, confirmed the day and date and said "I'll be flying-in on Thursday the third at 2:51 P.M., a day *early*, okay? . . and I won't be headed back here until the following Sunday-week, the thirteenth, so I'll be home for a total of ten days . . Then I'll be back on Friday the twenty-fifth to shake some more hands and apply as much pressure as I can to that rascal, Denny Warrington, okay? . ."

"He stopped-by to see me when he was here earlier this week, son," she chortled, evidently pleased with the unexpected attention. "He remarked that I look as young as his Evelyn . ."

The son-of-a-*bitch!*

"He's always been a thoughtful person, mom . ."

"He stopped to talk with us just after church let out Wednesday evening . . said he didn't want to visit his old stompin' grounds without stopping to pay his respects . ."

Je-sus *Christ!*

"I've never had anything but the highest respect for Denny Warrington, of course . ."

"We invited him in for a bite of dinner, son . . we knew if you'd been here you'd probably have done the same thing . . he seemed so lonely and, you know, *lost* without his family . ."

"Was there anything else I could do for you, mother? . ."

"There's a big barbecue dinner—in your honor—the night

69

you fly-in at Highland Hills, and a huge rally the afternoon of the Fourth at the Civic Center . . by the way, do you remember Meg Adkins? . ."

Meg Adkins? Are you *kidding?* One of your best friends *forever*—who was caught with her pants down, literally, cheating on her husband, the biggest connoisseur of bourbon in the entire county, while he lay in a hospital bed recovering from emergency gall-bladder surgery? And she actually managed to talk her way out of it successfully? *Yes*, I seem to vaguely recall *something* about her . .

"Is that a rhetorical question, mother? . ."

"Her daughter, Sabrina, who's *never* been married?—has been living in France and England for the past nine years, and is thirty-six, but looks *twenty*-six? . . She'll be here for the holidays and would very much like to see you know *who!* . ."

"All right, mother," he said resignedly, for what sense did it make to fight her on priority number-one? "I'll introduce her to Dow—but he already *has* a wife! . ."

"You know *exactly* what I'm talking about, Sidney! . . Oh, and your father is *really* enjoying his beautiful Father's Day shotgun! . . He sends his love . . call us this weekend, okay—and we'll be looking for you on Thursday, the third—and don't forget about Sabrina Adkins, okay? . ."

"No, mother, I won't forget, I promise . . Bye, for now! . ."

He laid the phone in its cradle and sank listlessly into the Yellow Rose. Just *great*: what he needed to do *now*, according to the Gospel of Saint Joan Villary-Still-Without-Grandchildren, was return home to campaign for the first real primary election he'd ever faced and, since it was apparently a given he'd be both successful *and* desperate not to waste all his spare time while busy campaigning, strike-up a hasty romance with a woman he hadn't seen since she was, what, *fourteen?!*—fall in love, get married, and provide her a grandchild by the following Easter. *Cake.* For Chrissakes, he couldn't even remember what she looked like! Sabrina's mother, Meg, and father, Albert, both seemed overweight and jowly, if memory served, and had the extra, added attraction of being relatively *short.* Albert Adkins, in addition to being the resident expert on the manufacture and quality of various bourbons, had always reminded him of the actor who portrayed the rotund character of Friar Tuck in an old Errol Flynn movie about Robin Hood. When he envisioned what any daughter of that particular marriage might look like he experienced stabbing pains in his temples. He sat up straight, peeked at his watch and, finally noticing his bust of Audie Murphy had tumbled over on its face, set it aright and grabbed the phone again, punching-in the familiar numbers.

"Talk to me, D.P. . ."

"Things are heating-up P.D.Q. down here, boss . . Between you being stuck up *there* and Denny spending most of his time campaigning *here*, I'm guessing he's gained some ground on you, but it's impossible to know how much . . What I can tell you for sure is that his immigration-reform commercials have almost *certainly* garnered him some of the Hispanic vote, what with him sitting down to dinner with a Mexican family before they all head outside to smash that pinata all over God's creation—not to mention what's *inside* that goddamn thing! . ."

"I haven't seen that one . . what's inside?"

"WARRINGTON FOR CONGRESS buttons, for Chrissakes! . . The commercial ends with Denny and the entire *family* of nine wearing these goddamn buttons, smiling and shaking hands like they're old friends, and Denny's got the *baby* in his arms! . . First time I saw it, it made me sick—I blew Velma's chicken casserole all over the back yard! . . I'm not

71

worried, mind you, 'cause that never helps, but I *am* concerned, and you won't be here for another week and a half? . ."

"Don't worry 'bout a thing, D.P.," he said as he sketched the figure of a human being onto a sheet of copy paper with a red-leaded pencil, his blood pressure beginning to rise at a snail's pace. "I'm just glad he's running a clean campaign because when the public gets wind of trickery, lies, and deceit, everybody loses . . We need to leave the smear tactics and mud-slinging to Consuela Garcia and her band of cut-throat liberals . . the public doesn't expect conservatives—*any* conservatives—to run for office using gutter-tactics, and we're not going to allow ourselves *or* Denny Warrington and his wolf- pack to ruin it for our fellow conservative patriots in Texas and the rest of the country . . You be sure to let Dudley Thomas and his boys know *exactly* . . what our position is on this, if you happen to run into him . . by the way, I don't suppose anyone calls Mr. Thomas '*Dud*' for short, do they? . ."

"Not that I'm aware of," said Pettigrew, "but it's an idea. You want me to research it with Lynch and see what we come up with? . ."

"Nah . . we got bigger fish to fry, and I'm not real sure where that damned frying-pan is right now . . Did you know there's a barbecue dinner for me next Thursday evenin' at the country club, complete with me making a quick campaign speech? . ."

"Better late than never, I always say . ."

"I can't get home before then, goddamnit!" he said, his blood pressure rising with each passing second. He sketched two eyes, a nose, and an oversized mouth onto the face of his paper figure, adding straw-like hair as an afterthought, congressman Cezanne, before scratching the letters '*D W*' onto the forehead of his masterpiece. "These hearings on immigration-reform are serious business, D.P., don't I get any credit for taking care of the folks back home? . . What the hell do I have to *do* up here to gain a little leverage, for Chrissakes?! . . Declare war on Mexico?! . ."

"Now boss, don't get all in a huff. There *are* some good signs down here, too . ."

"Well, *talk* to me! . ."

"The <u>Green Valley *Ledger*</u> has endorsed your candidacy for the first time, for starters . ."

"Why didn't they endorse me *last* time? . ."

"Not enough cash is my best guess—not that their left-leaning, socialist publisher would've ever in hell put his weight behind *you*, of all people—but he died last November and his daughter took over the reins, and she's a horse of a different color . . A much, *much* more reasonable type on a bad day than her pappy ever was on a good one, I sat down with her for a little while, went over the issues with her, stated our positions as clearly and quickly as I could, listened to her concerns and recommendations and told her we shared a lot— a *lot*—of the very same concerns she *and* her readers care about and, at the end of our talk, we shook hands, she promised to do all she can to assist in your re-election, and I left with the endorsement . ."

"Um-*hmm*," he hummed, his tone noticeably more upbeat. He sketched shoes and socks onto his paper figure with the red pencil, adding a pair of blue jeans complete with belt and buckle, the rendering beginning to assume a definite shape and fashion. "So . . how much did we give her? . ."

"Twenty-five hundred . . she said it'd come in handy when vacation rolled around . ."

"You trust her?"

"Sure . . why shouldn't I? She not only endorsed your

candidacy in an editorial two days later—one I'm sure Denny and his boys found *really* disheartening—her staff went to the trouble to compose an issue-by-issue comparison of you two, seven items in all, with you winning all seven!—she also failed to say even one good thing about France during our entire conversation.."

"Okay.. when I'm home next week remind me to pay her a personal visit, alright?.. Mom tells me you've scheduled a thousand and one campaign stops for week-after-next—I believe she said it was a 'butt-load,' or bus-load, or something—and would you believe she's already got me set-up with the daughter of one of her best friends?!.. Do you remember anything at *all* about a girl named Sabrina Adkins?.."

"Alright, boss, I see *three* different issues here," said D.P. "One, I absolutely approve of you paying a 'thank-you' visit to the _Ledger_—the personal touch of the district's esteemed representative in the   nation's capital is always appreciated, and she'll be delighted to see you!.. Two, your dear mother must've said 'bus-load' of campaign stops—I can't even imagine her saying '*butt*-load' in reference to *anything*—and she's right, you'll be an extremely busy fellow while you're home ..Three, why on earth would I *ever* be surprised your mother has managed to entangle you socially with a female?.. *Sid*, when it comes to your future in politics, your future as a husband and father, and, of paramount importance, your future as a provider of *grand*-children, *when* are you going to accept the fact that your parents—and especially your *mother*—don't play anything but *hardball?!* .. and wishing it would just go away *isn't* going to make it go away!.. Relax a little when you get home, *enjoy* yourself at the barbecue, pound the flesh a little after your speech at the Civic Center, everyone'll be *glad* to see you— you're their *congressman*, Sid! . . and here's a special tip for you: it probably wouldn't hurt to be seen with a female on your arm! That way, *other* females tend to keep a respectable distance—three's a *crowd*, you know— since you're ostensibly working anyway, what's the harm in west Texans seeing you cavorting through the crowd with a west Texas gal in tow? . . makes perfect sense to *me* . . And since you asked if I happen to recall anything about Sabrina Adkins, it's my sad duty to inform you that, unless my memory of women has turned completely to *shit*, the last time yours truly saw her was about ten years ago, and that luscious figure, and that willowy blonde hair, and those Hollywood legs of hers, *and* . . that lovely face . . had no effect on me whatsoever . ."

"*No?!* . . and why's that?"

"Because Velma was with me, why do you *think?* . ."

"Oh . . you think she looks okay, huh? . ."

"If I was another *woman*, Sabrina would be my basic nightmare, yes . ."

"Okay, I'll give it some serious thought, but I think you should know that—well, according to my mother, Sabrina's been living overseas for most of her adult life . . in *France*, Dow, and I don't know if that's such a good thing! I mean, what if she's been in with the wrong crowd? . ."

"I don't care if she's been playing nappy-time with Chairman Mao's nasty *corpse*, Sid! . . I mean, for Chrissakes, nobody in west Texas is going to have any idea what she's been up to—not you, not me, not even Denny Warrington! Nobody . . so what difference does it make? . ."

"Okay, okay," he said, letting-go a bit. His human figure drawing project now sported a shirt with hinged flaps over the pockets, its right arm and hand extended downward to the blue jeans' front zipper, which was unzipped and open. "Got anything else for me? . ."

"*Well* . . not really—except I've managed to place an operative inside the Warrington for Congress headquarters . ."

The red pencil dropped suddenly onto the desktop, its handler frozen in motion, his head cocked right, the desk-phone pressed more firmly against his disbelieving ear, his top half now sitting at full attention within the Yellow Rose, senses awakened as if they'd been the frozen turf, now thawed and bountiful, primed for planting.

"Uhh, could you let me have that again, D.P.? . ."

"That is correct, sir," Dow Pettigrew happily confirmed on his end. "The Sid Villary-for-Congress re-election campaign has a—now *how* should I put it?—a private detective, of sorts, inside our enemy's headquarters, monitoring day-to-day operations, reporting all pertinent details on a nightly basis, assisting the opposition whenever it's convenient, and sabotaging records, telephone calls, volunteer efforts, fund-raising activities, and whatever else his supervisor thinks is a safe, secure target at that particular time and place . ."

"D.P., there is no way I can endorse, accept, authorize, condone, approve, excuse, tolerate, support, or otherwise affirm such a dastardly . . *breach* of political etiquette and trust as this abjectly covert, despicable, unfortunate . . turn of events . . He must be—is it a *he* or a *she*? . ."

"He!"

"He must be terminated before the contemptible stain of disgrace swallows us *all* it its inimitable humiliation!" he cried with a solemnity bordering on grief, his red pencil working overtime now, the paper figure's right hand now clutching the most diminutive of phalli, the slotted handle of a butcher knife embedded blade-first into the paper figure's bleeding chest.

"*No* chance of him being traced to our campaign coffers? . ."

"*None* whatsoever, I'm afraid . ."

"Very well . . please ensure that this . . *interloper* has left the dangerous confines of their organization no later than the last Friday before the primary election, understood? . ."

"I understand *completely* . ."

"Good work! . . and call me with an update this afternoon on my cell, okay? . ."

He sat back comfortably in the Yellow Rose, mind racing with the possibilities his trip home to west Texas might present, the unsettling vision of Sabrina Adkins, as D.P. described her, disturbing his Monday morning routine. Furtively checking two separate social networks on his desktop, his supposed quarry surely found on one of them, he came away empty-handed; thoughts of his one-time interlude with the lovely Charlotte less than six weeks old, fading more and more with each passing day, his thoughts turned to his experience in church the morning before. He wondered how many women he met there knew who he was . . or whether *any* of them knew. He attended services at three different locations. Rotating week-to-week, he attended services at a relatively out-of-the-way chapel located in Fairfax, another larger church in Reston, and a Unitarian church in Vienna, but never felt sure if women peered at him because he was pleasing to the eye, or because they knew he was a congressman, or perhaps because they instinctively sensed he was a force to be reckoned with. He attended services in

Reston that Sunday and the place was packed . . but there was one young lady who'd stood out. Dark-haired, oval-faced, and honey-tanned, she was more than pretty and sat towards the front a good sixty or seventy feet away, but a blind beggar would have spotted her in her orange sundress. More importantly, she'd spotted him, too. The congressman's Sunday 'best' was good, indeed: thousand-dollar suit, Armani shirt, Italian loafers, and Neiman's silk tie . . but what was it she'd really *seen?* Had he been pleasing to her eye? Had she thought he was a force to be reckoned with, as a major 'dude'? Did she have any notion at all he was a congressman? Or was it the fourth option this time—*that* option, the one he never discussed with *anyone*—because it was the single most frightening threat to his present *and* future happiness, his personal Achilles heel, the most colossal fear he possessed?

It was an apparition without form or substance—it was absolutely *nothing*, really, and had someone asked him what its most appropriate technical name might be—say, a psychiatrist or church minister—he would have been at a complete loss to describe or explain it, for how can one explain away that which he himself cannot fathom? To this point in his life he felt it had left him alone, which scared the hell out of him. Sidney H. Villary, born and reared in Texas, was mortally afraid that, when the occasion arrived that his future wife stood in front of him—that they would meet and marry was an absolute given, for that was the key to the grand plan—he either wouldn't recognize that he had, indeed, met the woman of his dreams or, *worse*, she would for some inexplicable reason look right *through* him like he didn't exist, as though he had no existence worth mentioning. That he might not recognize her was bad enough: she'd merely meet someone else, fall in love, and get married, in which case the woman meant for him all along would spend the rest of her life with another man, namely, the *wrong* man. The mere thought she might look right through him—that she'd look directly at him, but see *nothing*—formed goose-bumps on his arms, an accompanying chill shuddering down his spine. Why might this absurd possibility ever manifest itself? He had no idea. She might see him as a heartless bastard, or maybe a political junkie already married to his career, or perhaps the sort of man no woman in her right mind could trust; she might look upon him as one would gaze upon a plague victim, equal parts pity, terror, and repulsion. Truth was, it might be *anything*: whether it was true or not, fair or unfair, right or wrong . . didn't matter. This fear never completely abandoned him, as he was one of the most eligible bachelors around: the striking-looking brunette in church had seen him staring at her, admiring her, and she'd smiled at him—but what had it really meant? Anything? Had she looked right through him and, once services were finished, forgotten him before she got to her car? Would he see her again? Did it matter, one way or the other?

He again saw the eminent vision of Charlotte: brunette and intelligent, vivacious and soft, young and fragrant, tall and lean, lovely and delicious, sultry and British. Oh, what a night it had been! What had *she* seen in him?

The workmen had first appeared the week before on a Tuesday. They hadn't sounded British or even faintly European when they spoke, but Marigold Godwin, a twenty-nine-year veteran of the Foreign Stenographer and Cypher pool and, in her own estimation, nobody's fool, thought she knew better. The taller one—he identified himself as 'Charlie' and did most of the talking that first day—laid the work-order in front of her, declared himself one of the *official* representatives of the Haskins Contracting Company, promised to stay out of everyone's way as much as possible, and calmly proceeded to the corner of the embassy lobby with his co-worker to inspect the faulty ceiling and its water stain.

79

Charlie looked *and* sounded like every other American craftsman it had been her dubious privilege to meet: coarse and rough, with an acute need to shave and wash his clothes, for pity's sake, and do you think it would kill you if I was to hit you with a bar of *soap?* The work-order looked genuine enough, signed by the familiar pens of Doddy Kenworthy, the British Embassy's elder maintenance supervisor, Roger Breen, the comptroller, and Francis Dill-Finchum, the Deputy-Attache for Culture and Defense; the signatures were the real thing, of course, for the simple reason that, unlike most anything written by a Yank, the British names, as signed, were clearly *legible*.

The shorter of the two workmen, a curious sort who seemed contentedly bemused by everything life had to offer and answered to the unlikely name of '*Danger*,' brought in the first ladder, stationed it beneath the water stain and, without ever taking his eyes from the ceiling, carefully scaled the metal steps until the twenty-foot ceiling was no more than a foot from his head. The water stain, roughly football-shaped with a diameter of approximately four and a half feet lengthwise, was situated a good five or six feet from the lobby's east wall, but no closer than twenty-five feet from the lobby's front wall, with nothing hindering the workmen due to the open space in that location. Marigold Godwin, after observing these two for mere moments, rather than minutes or hours, decided they were about her age or a little younger—they might actually *appear* to be fifty, and maybe a year or two less, were they to ever locate a razor and can of shave cream, but who knew?— and she could see them to her left and behind her just by turning slightly, her eyes shifting suspiciously. Should the pattern of American 'workmanship' she'd grown accustomed to hold true to form, these two latest Yanks—could it possibly be a coincidence that 'Yank' and 'Yahoo' sounded so *very* similar?—would more than likely determine the precise problem, *sort of*, set about repairing the damage with a highly elastic, thickly-padded, jumbo-sized, state-of-the-art band-aid, and scurry away to the next job well before the arrival of that grand American labor tradition, *lunch*. Blimey, they were Yanks, all right.

But then, just before eleven that Tuesday morning, everything changed: the 'Yanks' had become something *else* entirely and, as the work-week progressed, by Friday became what Doddy Kenworthy scathingly referred to as 'damned *unaccommodating*, really!' It began with Charlie's admission that, due to circumstances beyond anyone's control, the problem was bigger and more complex than anyone had realized—plaster-of-Paris being more antiquated and difficult to work with than commercial-grade, five-eighths inch, fire-rated sheetrock, and that by a *long* shot. More and different equipment would undoubtedly be required, as ladders were no longer adequate for such a job, and they'd have to return to Virginia to their warehouse to find it.

"But don't worry yourself any," Charlie told Miss Godwin, "we'll be back! . ."

And with that the two craftsmen grabbed their work-gloves and flashlights, the eighteen-foot ladders—for now there were two of them—still opened-out and ready for use in their same positions directly beneath the water stain, and disappeared through the embassy's front doors, the one called *Danger* still with that bemused expression of bewildered satisfaction.

It was Wednesday morning that Marigold Godwin first became suspicious that the Haskins Company craftsmen weren't actually American at all, that despite appearances to the contrary they were secretly British or, due to their extraordinary affinity for maintaining four and five-day-old beards, either Belgian, Dutch, or French, and had just been in America so long that now they spoke a sort of *pretend* English most any first-grader would be jealous of. When she arrived for work at half past eight Charlie and Danger were nowhere in sight. Neither had they returned Tuesday afternoon after Charlie promised to, although after much discussion about the matter with Doddy and Fiona Rodland, Roger Breen's secretary, it was finally determined that in telling Miss Godwin their intentions, Charlie hadn't volunteered exactly *when* that would be. Doddy, their stodgy yet beloved maintenance foreman, shrugged it off, but Marigold Godwin's internal radar had already begun telling her there was an Irishman homesteading inside Windsor Castle. Workers arrive at their job-site, discover they're not properly-equipped for the task at hand, then depart for the ostensible purpose of obtaining the proper equipment with a promise to return, only they somehow fail to come back, and the very next morning refuse to materialize *again?* How *very* British, decided Marigold Godwin, how extremely *European!* And how *unlike* the crazy Americans, for the Yanks were notorious for 'half-assing' the job, as Doddy liked to put it—merely patching a hole when *plugging* it would work far better, thus cutting a sixteen-hour repair to merely *six* so the men can race to the next money-maker, the patched hole in dire need of attention the following year. It was just the American *way*, and its methodology was diametrically opposed to the English/European model, which she found infuriating: a one-week road-repair project would more often than not become a one-*month* road-repair, either in London or Manchester or the continent, it really didn't matter—and this ceiling-repair project was beginning to assume all the nasty characteristics of

82

the latter.

Her radar in fine working condition when Charlie and Danger sauntered-in unannounced at half-past ten, she greeted them with a smile, and in her very best short, crisp English said "Well-well . . *look* who's here . . Would one of you kind gentlemen please tell me if either of you . . is an *American? . .*"

The two craftsmen, unaware of potential recriminations for not being more punctual, eyed each other in mock suspicion until Charlie grinned and said "I grew-up in Covington, Kentucky, across the river from Cincinnati . ."

"I'm from Pittsburgh, ma'am," Danger said politely, "do you know where that is? . ."

"Yes, I do," she said, but when they stood idly by for just a few seconds, Danger seemingly more lost than usual, she said "It's okay, *loves* . . we just wondered . ."

In short order they proceeded to bring their new equipment inside , metal scaffolding and the thickest sort of lumber anyone in the embassy had seen in quite a while, wood both very stout in its solidity yet approximately a foot wide, which the craftsmen laid atop the scaffolding frames until the elevated system reached about thirteen feet from the floor. Setting about their project with renewed enthusiasm, it proved no time at all before granular particles and occasional chunks of plaster began tumbling down onto the canvas drop-cloth they'd spread below. Shortly before the lunch hour arrived Charlie and Danger were temporarily rendered speechless by the appearance of Fiona Rodland: quietly emerging from Roger Breen's office, dressed in a form-fitting fuchsia outfit that emphasized her enviable figure, the black Comptroller's secretary, born and raised in Northampton, not too far from Shakespeare's ancestral home, crossed the lobby to Marigold Godwin's desk and in a refined, very British accent said "We're tasked to cover the hotel expenses of Sir Nigel when he arrives next week on his visit representing the Academy of St Martin-in-the-Fields . . Can you please let myself or Mister Breen know when the tab arrives so I can take care of it, Marigold? . ."

Then the two British ladies glanced at their curious American craftsmen standing fifteen feet above them and, in seeing they stood thunderstruck by the voice of the thirty-year-old Fiona, mouths agape, Danger as utterly perplexed as Miss Godwin had ever seen him, each woman giggled when Fiona casually crossed the lobby again, stopping at the Comptroller's office door to look up at them one last time before saying "*In*-hale, *ex*-hale . . *In*-hale,*ex*- hale . ." Then she was gone!

Thursday and Friday embassy life arrived on schedule, but without pause in what was now the ongoing ceiling-repair project. That Friday morning, the fourth day of work witnessed the unexpected arrival of a third craftsman, a younger laborer who identified himself as 'Barry,' who proceeded to take his rather oversized electrical cutters and masonry auger up inside the ceiling-hole Charlie and Danger fashioned the day before. The ensuing roar had proved deafening to the point that neither Fiona, nor any other embassy employee, dared venture outside their office, Marigold Godwin relocating her desk, chair, and telephone to the embassy's west wing, the front doors now temporarily closed to the public until the workmen could finish. Doddy Kenworthy, informed as to what they found and what it would require to fix it that Thursday afternoon, hauled himself up the scaffolding for a personal look, shook his head resignedly when he saw it and climbed back down; it would

84

sound like "London being bombed by the Luftwaffe again!" he announced, and he didn't like it 'worth a damn,' but saw nothing to be gained by postponing the inevitable.

Another steamy Monday in Washington, D.C., had arrived. The official start of summer had come and gone over the weekend, three million people in the D.C. area were already busy preparing for what promised to be a wonderful Fourth-of-July weekend—the further away from the district the better, all things considered—and the unflinchingly irritating noise of the British Embassy ceiling-repair job entered its fifth dreadful day. Closing office doors had been helpful, of course, but the sound of metal being split in half by infinitely more-resilient metal, coupled with the incessant '*puka-puka*' of plaster being shredded away, made for an intensely edgy return to work. Barry, the twenty-something master of metal-cleaving, hadn't helped the situation much when he discovered the Haskins Company wasn't actually performing the first, but the *second* repair to that exact same section of the ceiling, the first having been done in 1871 by a decidedly British firm, Pendleby's Amalgams. No one had ever accused young Barry of diplomacy—nor would they—after the episode with Doddy and Marigold Godwin that Monday morning.

"Miss Godwin, after viewing that plaster up-close last Friday I finally figured-out what the problem was," he told her that morning during his first cigarette break. She stopped her work long enough to cast the young know-it-all a scurrilous leer, waiting for the earth-shattering news of the ceiling while she busied herself imagining what a large, bulbous wad of bubble-gum might do for his ponytail. "The problem with *this* ceiling is that it's been repaired before . ."

Doddy Kenworthy, his demeanor already fouled by having been inside the embassy during the majority of the plaster and metal demolition, walked-up behind Miss Godwin as young Barry revealed his secret.

"That's correct, my good man," Doddy agreed, "it was repaired the first time a little over six years after the end of your Civil War . ."

"Yeah . . and it's a masterpiece of shoddy workmanship," Barry added authoritatively, "which is why we're having to fix it *now* . ."

"Young man," said Doddy, Marigold Godwin with an expectant eye on her maintenance foreman, "the repairs were performed when none of us were around to inspect them — so nobody here can really say anything accurate about anything . . What I *can* tell you is that the work was approved by a gentleman named Ulysses Grant — and that he authorized the best ceiling firm in four states to carefully reconstruct the original molds, because he mandated that it appear as *new* . ."

"I see," said young Barry, cigarette smoke curling out of his nostrils. "It seems really odd then, that the firm would send such careless maladroits to do the work . ."

"For heaven's sake!" cried Miss Godwin, her patience wearing thin. "The repairs were done over a *hundred forty years ago!* . ."

"That's correct," said young Barry, "and had they been done by competent American artisans, this ceiling might've lasted *another* hundred forty! . ."

Only the timely intervention of Charlie, the project foreman, who stuck his head through the door to announce the official end of everyone's cigarette break, managed to save young Barry from having the normally tranquil hands of Doddy Kenworthy wrapped securely around his smug, arrogant throat. By lunchtime the incident had been more or less forgotten, but not before Kenworthy secured Charlie's promise to keep young Barry, their accomplished metal-jockey with the tact and subtlety of a reticulate python, away from Miss Godwin at all costs. So upset was she with the 'big-mouthed, mush-brained' Barry that, rather than remain at her station through the morning without respite, her established custom, she departed at a quarter 'til eleven for a "few minutes away, and a *strong* cup of tea."

At 2:15 that afternoon the three Haskins employees took their mid-afternoon break, as usual, their never-ending ceiling project placed on a much-appreciated, if temporary, hold as the echo of their grimy disturbance died away. Embassy staff, alerted to the deafening silence, had by now adopted the practice of waiting until the incredible din was immobilized for that now-precious fifteen minutes before racing from office to office with anything that required a physical signature or dispersal. Sixteen minutes after two the door to the Deputy-Attache's office swung open and the somewhat tall, raven-haired secretary, Charlotte Tillstrom, dashed into the lobby with a quarter-inch of paperwork clutched in her left hand. Swiftly negotiating her way through the lobby's open area, her right hand sweeping furiously to and fro all round in a vain attempt to keep the dust from clinging, she disappeared through the narrow hallway leading to the ambassador's office and kitchen in back, the click-clack of her high heels fading as she went. The three craftsmen, sitting on the floor with backs resting on the lobby wall, sat silent yet attentive, utterly captivated as she crossed the lobby and vanished into the darkness of the hallway.

"Did you see *that!?*" Danger whispered excitedly, throat suddenly dry, eyes wide with awe.

"I'm in *love!*" young Barry swooned dreamily, a rare smile illuminating his face.

Eleven minutes later they again heard the click-clack of her heels as she approached from the same hallway. Not one of the three noticed her paperwork was gone when she reappeared; all three noticed her creamy English skin, the perfect make-up, and locks of darkest night, but only Charlie noticed her canary blouse and sand-colored outfit. For only the briefest moment her eyes met theirs as she started the trek back across the lobby towards the safety and security of the Deputy's office. Young Barry felt motivated to say something suave, sophisticated, and understated, something so delightfully cute no woman could possibly resist, something subtle and charming, along the lines of . . he had no idea what! Charlotte stopped suddenly in mid-stride directly in front of their line-of-sight and, standing no more than fifteen feet from their work-boots, involuntarily clutched her mid-section. As her head dropped to observe her hand attempting to cover the mysterious rumbling from within, her mouth opened a little, then a little more, and when she turned her head left and saw the craftsmen watching her, she started to speak of her discomfort but was instantly sidetracked by the sight of her lunch of salad with croutons and lentil soup quite unexpectedly spraying out of her mouth.

"Good *lord!*" cried young Barry as the three scrambled to assist her, "we're not as bad as all *that*, are we now?! . ."

V.

Cas Turley arrived at his Alexandria office Tuesday morning in a cloudburst so torrential and sweet it evoked memories of Krung Thep in September and October, the cooling swirls of wind turning the Chesapeake Bay area into a moist-towelette on its way up the coast to Philly, New York, and Boston. Standing under his umbrella, the downpour slapping its droplets onto its surface like a thunder of drums, he saw himself in southeast Asia once again, over thirty-five years in the past. Near impossible to remain completely dry during the monsoon months but relatively comfortable after the swelter of February through May, Krung Thep had changed remarkably through the ages and no longer maintained any vestige of the primitive fort it had once been. Climbing into a *jinricki* for the ride to the river, a flagon of *anak* strapped to the side of his burly chest, he'd float for a mile or two upstream before directing the boatman into a canal of his acquaintance to locate a riverside cafe, the clientele of whom knew an American when they saw one and didn't mind. Otherwise, he might settle for a visit downtown, complete with an extended stopover in the House of 1,000 Colors, a carton of American cigarettes in tow. Ah, those were the *days!*

Hardly had he put aside his umbrella and windbreaker when the land-line lit-up, his agitated employer from across the river on the other end: Sid Villary sounded worried, though why was anyone's guess.

"What's up, boss? . ."

"I have it on good authority from west Texas that the honorable Mr. Warrington is planning to air a TV commercial claiming yours truly has done *nothing* for the Hispanic population of the Lone Star state—nothing at *all!* . . The nerve of the son-of-a-bitch! If that was true, how'd I ever get seventy-six percent of the Hispanic vote?! . ."

"Uh, *twenty*-six percent, boss . ."

"Whatever . . I need for you to tell me *now* about all the good things I've done for those people, Cas, so we can formulate a message of our own, but *not* as a response to any lies or half-truths or insinuations the Warrington camp might make—you know, so the wet-backs know we care about *them* and not just their votes! . ."

"Actually, I'd planned to ignore the Warrington threat with the Hispanics, Sid . . it's so much more the general election in November against Connie Garcia that counts with that voting-block. I mean, how do you think that's gonna' play with the folks back home who supported you in the past and want to vote for you again this time around? . . If they see Denny getting most of the attention from friends of the Pope, do you really see that as a *bad* thing? . ."

"No, not really," he admitted, blood pressure dropping closer to the normal range, "but for me to do and say nary a word is almost like conceding that group of voters to someone else—namely, *Denny*, in this case—and no one can tell me there aren't conservative Hispanics out there, Cas, that's not being realistic at all . . hell, there are *dozens* of 'em! . ."

"Tell you what, boss . . why don't you let me call Diego Quintanilla to see if he'd be willing to make a commercial with you to be shown before *and after* the primary? . ."

Following an extended silence on his end, Sid said "Uhh, *question* . ."

"Shoot."

"Who in the name of God is Diego Quintanilla?! . ."

"Oh, you *know!*" cried Turley, a little exasperated now. "You arranged for Diego's company to be general contractor for the new airport in Apache County around four years ago . . and the work crews ended-up being over eighty percent Hispanic? . ."

"I *do* seem to remember that airport job, yeah . . but why in *hell* did I ever agree to give the whole thing to this Quintanilla fella'? . ."

"There were really two reasons . . Diego's company was one of two that bid on the job, and the other guy's name was Mahmoud Khalil Al-Kill-All-o-You, or something, and you swore there was no way *he'd* ever get it! . . Also, number two, you thought Diego's wife was a stunner . ."

"Oooh! *Now* I remember: *Carmelita!* She *was* a stunner, and probably still *is!* By all means, see if you can arrange another meeting when I'm home next month! . . I'd *love* to see her again—I mean *them*, excuse me . . She actually let me swill some tequila off her navel, Cas!—don't know if she ever told Diego or not . . And you know, strangely enough, I even remember that other guy who bid on that airport job . . Mahmoud, yeah, and he always wore the strangest outfits, like he lived in the wild west of Billy the Kid or something . . claimed he was my brother in a previous life, remember? . . Wanted to build Apache County an airport, then go on tour as the fastest gun in the west, but his wife had other plans for him . . Did she ever manage to have him committed? . ."

"Beats me . . I lost track of him after that, tell the truth . ."

"So what do I do about this *alleged* perception that I do nothing for my Hispanic constituents, Cas? . . What can I do that I haven't already done for them, for Chrissakes?! . . I've

91

long made my position clear, that if an illegal joins the military and gets killed in the line of duty defending our great country, that illegal *automatically* becomes a legal citizen of the United States! . . and it was yours truly that introduced legislation making it illegal for any border agent—any agent *at all*—to shoot illegals while they're in the process of eating a taco, enchilada, burrito, tamale, *or* chimichanga! . . I supported legislation outlawing a nuisance tax on low-riders! . . I also supported legislation making it mandatory that *any* lawn-service company offer its Hispanic employees—legal or illegal—health insurance—*minus* any kind of abortion assistance, of course—at the *same* price as its non-Hispanic employees—plus a modest ten percent! . . I actively support granting *pardons* to any Mexical son-of-a-bitch who took part in the murders of William Barrett Travis, Jim Bowie, and even congressman Davy Crockett of Tennessee, at the siege of the Alamo . . *and*, even though he wasn't a *real* Texan—even though he only made movies *inside* our borders, but never actually held Texan citizenship—I supported, and I *continue* to support, any and all efforts to make John Wayne an honorary citizen of the Lone Star state! . . Now tell the truth, Cas, what the hell *else* can I do for them that I haven't already done? . ."

Turley turned around at his desk and depressed the *ON* button to his coffeemaker, paused long enough to pull a cigarette from his shirt pocket, then went through five drawers in the desk before finding a pack of matches.

"If you were ever to be successful in making the Duke an honorary citizen of Texas," he said reverently, "that would in all likelihood go down in the books as your crowning achievement . ."

"Four different shots I've given it, all without success, the last one from up here through Dwight two years ago," Sid lamented. Thinking back to his first miserable winter in D.C., when as a freshman legislator virtually no one knew or cared who he was—not that anyone knew or cared who he was *now*, because just about everyone had at some point misspelled his last name—he arrived convinced his would be, at most, a four-year stay, only two short terms to make a difference, and then he'd return home, satisfied he'd made his mark. Then someone else could give it a shot. "But I'll keep trying until I *do*, I promise . ."

"I had a short-short convo with Heywood O'Rourke yesterday . ."

It had always struck Cas as strange that, with a seemingly simple statement of fact, a lousy ten or twelve words—*lord*, it wasn't even a complex sentence, much less one of those compound-complex humdingers—he could command his employer's complete, undivided attention . . and, predictably, he had it now. O'Rourke was the travel-master for both houses of congress.

"And what did my buddy Heywood have to say, pray tell? . ."

"Only that the fact-finding mission to eastern Europe is scheduled to depart the Wednesday-week after Labor Day . ."

"From which committees?"

"Oh, the usual suspects . . Commerce . . Trade . . Foreign Relations . ."

The increasingly familiar anvil of dread settling into the congressman's stomach at the news, he managed to say "Why on *earth* did you call O'Rourke?"

"I didn't . . he called *me* . ."

"Oh . . Cas?"

"What?"

"I'm scared *shitless!* . ."

"Of what? . . *What* are you talking about, Sid? . . there's no reason for you to be scared of anything," he said, peering round at the half-full coffee pot. Come on, baby, *come on!* Got to get the blood pumping. "You're the best candidate in the race, for starters, and everybody knows it! You have me on your side, and Dow, and Lynch—*and* L.W., and that's a combination nobody can tear asunder! . . Look, you're as conservative as 'conservative' can possibly be, and while that may not play well in most of California, it plays *great* in Texas! . . Sid, your positions *are* your essence: you're concerned about decay from within, like any good conservative . . you unequivocally support the NRA . . you're properly concerned about the growing power of the federal government . . you support the military with all your heart, you know *damn* well we spend too much money, and you're as pro-life as anyone I've ever known . . I'm telling you, there's nothing to sweat here—*nothing*—and Denny Warrington can *say* whatever he likes—he can *claim* you're a flaming liberal—he can *swear* you're a closet-pacifist—but I don't care, and neither should you, and you know why? Because *none* of it's true, and it's impossible to prove a bald-faced lie! . . can't be *done!* . . So take a deep breath, do whatever it is you need to do for Texas and the nation, as you see fit, and go home next week and knock 'em *dead*, okay?! . ."

"Maybe you're right . ."

"Whaddaya' mean *maybe?* . . I *know* I'm right!"

"You know what'd make me feel better? . ."

"What's that?"

"Something . . *monstrous* to put this thing away . . something solid and unbeatable! . ."

"I'm not sure I follow you there . . solid and *unbeatable?!* . ."

"I'm talking about something so intensely solid . . so

94

monstrously unbeatable . . that it removes *any* doubt as to the eventual outcome of the primary election!" cried Sid Villary, the vision of his dismantling of the Warrington engine now first and foremost in his thoughts. With so many people he cared-for so completely dependent upon him to succeed—his office staff, political team, like-minded allies in Austin, fellow conservatives in the house and senate, and the good and decent Christian folks back home—nothing less than decisive victory was now acceptable. His fear, the anxiety of the unknown, had summarily vanished! "It can come from either camp, you see . . Cas, if it comes from *our* side it has to be something so favorable to us that Warrington drowns in our positive liquids . . conversely, if it comes from *their* side it's got to be something so dreadful, so very *distasteful*, that the public turns on him, casting him down a sinner of the worst order . . And I'm fully aware that our best possible scenario would be for us to experience something wondrously beneficial while something equally catastrophic occurs to ruin their chances, but . . I'm not so naïve as to believe that'll happen, so . . . one or the other would do the trick, I think . . Your thoughts, Mr. Turley? . ."

"Well, *yeah*, boss, that'd be terrific—*if* it ever happened, naturally—but I still think your wisest path is the shortest one . . just take care of business like you always do and everything'll be *fine*—but in the meantime we can always pray for divine guidance and intervention . . After all, a little faith can go a *long* way . ."

"I'll tell you, Cas . . after speaking with you I feel a hundred percent better! . . You know what else? . . I can't really explain *why* I feel this way, because God didn't want us to know every little damn thing—but I have every faith that something enormous, something *monumental*—is headed our way . .And

95

it'll get here in plenty of time to secure my re-election! . ."

Turley, an optimist of the first order, loyal patron of the cause and protector emeritus of the status quo, signed-off and poured himself a large cup of joe, cream and a smidgen of raw sugar duly stirred-in—the U.S. Air Force, like the other branches, couldn't always guarantee you'd get your coffee the way you wanted it—and settled into his chair. Maybe something monumental *was* on their horizon, but who could say? In the interim there was the problem of the pending mission to Europe: O'Rourke hadn't specified exactly *which* countries were on the list, "eastern Europe" being a rather general term for a widespread area, but Cas had a pretty good idea. The former Yugoslavia was a given, true, but where else? Hungary? Romania? The Czech Republic? *Lord*, he thought, if you truly love me, let them go to *Prague!* And maybe Sid hadn't had the time nor the inclination to discuss the journey, but that certainly didn't mean it would miraculously get canceled. No, *this* time the boss would almost surely be required to be a part of the mission team . . but, departure was still over two months away, so there was an abundance of time to prepare. On a lighter note, was it possible some kind of good fortune lay right around the corner for the primary campaign? Had Sidney Hunt Villary truly lodged his faith in the proper place?

"God, I hope so," Cas Turley murmured to no one.

The return phone call that Tuesday morning had come more quickly than expected at half past nine— a lucky break, thought Charlotte . . and the news was even better.

"We're booked solid, like I said," reiterated the office manager, a capable lady in her mid-thirties, gifted in the art of medical concern, "but after what I heard on your message from earlier this morning, the doctor wants to see you at two-thirty . . can you make it?"

"I'll be there," she said.

Upon her arrival in Washington two years earlier she'd first rented an apartment in the District, then purchased a car and moved across the Potomac to Tyson's Corner, a fair distance from work, but close to the Capital Beltway and convenient to malls, dress shops, and a fairly good selection of pubs. Young and in demonstrably excellent health, locating a competent physician hadn't been any sort of priority, but embassy veterans, including Miss Marigold Godwin, recommended she at least begin her search as the medical *systems* of the respective countries were vastly different. A bit confused as to *type* of doctor desired, at length she wisely chose an internist and carefully perused the list of preferred candidates available through the network. She found seven within three miles of her condo, sixteen within five   miles, some in groups, others practicing alone, and knowing virtually nothing about American medical training selected an internist a scant two miles from her front door. Only when her birth-control pill prescription timed-out did she seek services from her new, as yet sight-unseen, doctor.

Charlotte liked her immediately. A Minnesota native, Dr. Pat Scheckleburg earned her M.D. in Charlottesville before tackling an internship at U.C.L.A. and an "eye-*opener* of a residency" split between Manhattan's Bellevue and VA Hospitals, blissfully claiming no preference for one experience over the other. The Greater Washington, D.C. area exercised an almost predictable gravitational pull on the young internist when selecting a practice site: an enormous pool of potential patients, a veritable kaleidoscope of interesting clientele, limitless in range, and a relatively short drive to the hills

97

around Charlottesville, it was the literally-perfect situation to set-up shop. Only five years Charlotte's senior, Pat Scheckleburg remained, in her own words, "technically single," sharing a rather large house in Chantilly with her friend, Chester, a pediatric oncologist and chess junkie. When Charlotte inquired as to her doctor's hobbies, the green-eyed, red-headed Dr. Pat quickly replied "Oh, jumping out of airplanes!"

Departing the embassy at 1:50 P.M. she encountered slow traffic until she crossed the river, no fewer than three new construction zones with their trademark orange-and-white barrels clogging the already narrow thoroughfares, but arrived at the doctor's office at 2:24. Grateful for a shorter-than-expected waiting-room visit, a white-clad staff member ushered her into a patient room at 2:40, weighed her, took blood-pressure and temp readings, then told her the doctor would check-in with her shortly, the door closing silently when she left.

"Charlotte Tillstrom, what on earth is going on with *you?*" said Pat Scheckleburg when she stepped through the doorway, her freckled smile betraying a residual fatigue. The two women shook hands, then sat across from each other for their chat.

"I'm afraid I got sick at work yesterday afternoon," she said, her Sussex accent very much in evidence. "Just an hour or two after lunch, and I don't know if it was the salad I ate, or the heat, or the construction, or *what*, really . ."

"Might've been the food . . you never can say about salad, especially in the summer months . . have anything else? . ."

"Only the lentil soup afterward, which was delicious, but then, everything they serve is *scrumptious*—and their desserts are simply heavenly! . ."

98

"Did you have dessert, too? . ."

"Oh, heavens *no!* . . if I ate just one, I'd eat *ten*, and my size-nine clothes would quickly become size eighteen, or *twenty*, and I *like* my size-nine outfits, really I do! . ."

"So you've eaten there more than once or twice, I take it? . ."

"Several times, yes—and never got sick once . ."

"Okay . . let's assume for the moment it wasn't your lunch . . You mentioned the heat a minute ago, and that's something you and I have never discussed . . is the heat and humidity a concern for you here in the Chesapeake region? . ."

"*Well* . . it would be foolhardy to claim southern England is as warm as it is *here* . . this is my third summer in Washington, and it is most certainly *hotter*, but . . the heat hasn't bothered me so far . . I just thought, maybe it was heat-*related* . ."

"It may very well *be*, Charlotte," said Dr. Scheckleburg, her pen scribbling notes inside a medical chart, "but I'm thinking along the lines of something *else*, at this point . . Mind you, I'm not saying it couldn't be heat-related or possible food-poisoning—it could be either *one*—but I'd want to eliminate a few other, more likely possibilities before I looked at either one of those again . . *Now* . . you also mentioned 'construction' as a possible culprit . . Is it road construction, or something of the sort? . ."

"No—but that it were," she said. She shook her head resignedly and added "It's inside the embassy, and there's just *no escaping it!* . ."

"Tell me about this . ."

"It's *dreadful*, is what it is! . . There's a leak in the ceiling in the lobby . . Mr. Kenworthy thought it a minor repair, one or two days at most, but they've been in there more than a week now . . there were just two of them working at first, but now there's *three*, and it's the most *horrible* racket imaginable . . The

99

dust, of course, is the worst part . ."

"The dust . ."

"The dust is *everywhere*, Dr. Scheckleburg . . there's no place to hide from it . . It's a plaster ceiling, you see, and the dust created inside that hole in the ceiling covers everything, and I mean *everything!* . . We shut our office doors, but when we come to work the next morning there's a thin layer of dust on our desks, on the chairs, inside the bathrooms, the floors — *everywhere!* . . They *cannot* finish that job soon enough to suit anyone inside the embassy! . ."

"These workers you mentioned . . Did they provide masks for the embassy employees and, if so, is everyone using them? . ."

"*Masks?*"

"Like the ones I wear sometimes," said Dr. Scheckleburg. She rose from her seat, opened a wall-mounted cabinet, and pulled out a white surgical face-mask. "Like this one? . ."

"They haven't given us anything like that to put on . ."

With fire in her narrowed green eyes and muted rage in her voice, an incredulous, astounded Pat Scheckleburg looked up from the medical chart and said "Do you mean to tell me that these morons came into the British Embassy, ripped a hole in the ceiling, creating a cloud of particulate dust, then *failed to provide protective masks for embassy employees?!* . . Is *that* what you're telling me, Charlotte? . ."

"Well . . *they* wear them, of course . . otherwise they'd get sick, too, I guess . ."

"They ought to be *crucified!*" the doctor said in a voice ripe with fury. She wrote a few more notes onto the medical chart, dotted an "i" with an emphatic stab of her pen and said "No wonder you're sick . . who wouldn't be in an environment like *that?!* . . I don't suppose you know what their company name is? . ."

"No—but I can find out tomorrow . . it's 'Harbin,' or 'Harkin,' or something . ."

"When you leave today I'd greatly appreciate it if you'd take some masks with you . . that way you have one, and the other embassy personnel *also* have one . ."

"If you like, certainly . . So you think it's the dust-cloud inside the lobby what set me a-tumble? . ."

Dr. Scheckleburg stopped writing and set the chart in her lap, saying "I think it's at least the major culprit here, yes . . you're fever-free, and you exhibit no outward signs of infection. Naturally, there *are* a couple of nasty bugs making their rounds now—the usual summer fare, intestinal flu strains for the most part, one or two with fevers—but even if you already had any of those symptoms before the embassy work began, the dust would only make matters worse, *not* better, so we need to improve the situation there *first* . . And another thing: being British, I don't know how familiar you are with American law, but we take careless air-pollution violations *very* seriously, and this company, whoever it is, will wish to God they'd done better by the time I get through with them! . . How are you feeling today? . ."

"Better than I felt yesterday . ."

"Glad to hear it—but I want you to call me immediately if you start feeling weak again. I'd also like a urine sample, if you don't mind, to rule out the presence of E. coli or some other bacterial invasion, okay? . . just let Greta know how many masks you need . ."

Then a curious thing happened: when they stood, Dr. Scheckleburg first noticed how much shorter she stood than her patient as she gave her an affectionate pat on the back, a gesture of sympathy for her temporary malady—and

101

Charlotte wasn't even wearing *heels!*

"You're about five-*nine? . .*"

"Just a hair under a hundred seventy-five centimeters, yes," smiled Charlotte.

"You wear it well . ."

She turned to leave but paused to give Charlotte's mauve dress and sandals the once-over.

"*Love* your outfit! . ."

Lynch Bohannon, suspicious by nature, embarrassingly pro-military, wholly comfortable within a chain-of-command, and armed by habit, seemed to feel the tingling of non-specific doubt whenever forced into a phone conversation with someone he didn't know or, worse, didn't *trust*, which was just about everyone. Conversely, being able to distinguish the person on the other end as either friend or foe, trusted colleague or otherwise, allowed his competitive juices to flow warmer, whether it be football, advanced weaponry, or politics. The voice on the other end of the line that Tuesday afternoon sounded vaguely familiar; not exactly a voice from his past, the sing-song pattern of speech, the ironic tone inflected, indicated a short acquaintance from . . *what?! Where?!* All newspaper types, of course, could *never* be trusted under any circumstances, due to the fact that they were born troublemakers.

"Is this Newt Franklin from the <u>Hastings Gazette</u>?" he finally ventured.

"Been a long time, Lynch! . ."

"Not long enough . . how you? . ."

"Oh, you know . . . we paper-folks just wanna' get at the truth, whether it helps or hurts! . ."

"Uh-huh—especially if it *hurts,* anyway . . I'm still keeping my eye out for that newspaper editor who *helps*, Newt . . a year or two ago somebody thought they found one frozen in the ice of Siberia, but when they dug 'im up it turned out to be a large pile of petrified *mammoth-shit!* . . So why you callin' me?—the <u>Gazette</u> got no use for someone who deals in *facts* . ."

"Oh, we just got a whiff—just a *trace*, mind you, hardly a hint at all, Lynch—from over Odessa-way . . that your boy, Sidney, helped a young lady acquire an abortion year before last . . know anything about that? . ."

"That's a *goddamned lie!*" Bohannon, always a promoter of handling sticky situations with kid-gloves, gently roared into the phone, his oversized fingers reaching clumsily inside his top desk-drawer for a stomach mint. "And listen *carefully*, Newt, because I don't like to repeat myself: anyone—anyone *at all*—who claims such a ridiculous story is *true* . . is a *goddamn liar* himself! . ."

"May I please quote you on that last remark, Lynch? . ."

"A goddamn liar!" he repeated hoarsely as he bit into an antacid tablet. "And *NO*, you can't quote me on *anything*, understand? . . you vultures are all alike, every one of you! . ."

"Now, Lynch, ol' buddy, I'm *confused* here," came the soft, calm, slightly ironic voice on the other end, "because I've got names, dates, addresses, whys and wherefores—hell, I got the whole nine *yards* right in front o' me—and I'm not sure what to do with it . . I was really hoping and praying you could help me out here . . I'm *sure* this young, unmarried woman from Texas was in danger of losing her life—I fully realize how susceptible twenty-year-old women are to *ill*-health, of course—and I think it was a wonderful gesture on the part of Congressman Villary to assist with the actual abortion . . uh, *arrangements*, he being so concerned and all with women's abortion rights—I confess my surprise at his candor and concern for the young lady in question, she being the daughter of one of the biggest liberals in the state of Texas, but I suspect you're not interested in any of that either . . I guess this means Mr. Villary is truly one o' them—what is it they call 'em?—*compassionate* conservatives?! . . what should I do with all these sworn affidavits provided by the good folks from around Odessa? . ."

"I *know* who the 'good folks' from Odessa are, Newt—and they can shove it up their ass! . ."

"I take it that's a *No comment!* . . right? . ."

"You can shove it up *your* ass, too! . ."

"Oh, well, that *does* alter the dynamic somewhat . . okay, *when* did you discover, if you don't mind my asking, that Congressman Villary was the *father* . of the aborted child? . ."

"You blood-sucking *asshole!* Nobody in their right mind would ever believe Sidney Villary had any part in this *bullshit* story! . . If you choose to print this crap and suffer the consequences, that's strictly your business, Newt, so I'd advise you to be very careful—*very* careful, indeed—committing libel against a congressman can have devastating effects on one's wallet—*pocketbook* in your case, I suppose—though I'm sure you have insurance . ."

"Alright, Lynch," said the voice on the other end, "jus' trying to help . . but I think you should know somebody's planning to use this information in my hands for a television commercial in the very near future . . and it won't look good for your boy . ."

"Refresh my memory, Newt . . *who* was it the <u>Gazette</u> endorsed for president last time? . . was it Khrushchev or Brezhnev? . . or maybe Kosygin? . . I just can't remember . ."

"Don't forget we had this conversation, Lynch . . if your boss asks me about it, I'm not going to lie for you . . let's get together and have a drink sometime—you *animal!* . ."

Bohannon slammed the phone into its cradle, steam rising from his scalp: freedom-of-the-press was, in his opinion, vastly overrated due to the overwhelming preponderance of scum-bags in the business. Newt Franklin was the same gullible malcontent who'd secretly 'exposed" the existence of the super-revolutionary fringe group "Friends of Josef Mengele" in Ft. Worth—only to later discover the group was a complete fabrication of Dwight Stract and his conservative PAC in Austin; Franklin, properly embarrassed and identified as the dunderhead he was, had wanted to get even ever since. Bohannon mulled over Newt's message once or twice, laughed the entire conversation away, then reconsidered. Was it even *remotely* possible the stupid son-of-a-bitch had something? He'd sounded so uncharacteristically *confident,* even smug, and that just wasn't like Newt. He pressed the intercom.

"Yes, sir? . ."

"Carmen, is the boss still here?"

"No, sir, he left about an hour ago to meet somebody over at State . ."

"Okay . . thanks."

Grabbing his cell he punched-in the numbers and waited.

"Talk to me," Sidney Villary said on his end.

"Are you by any chance sitting down, boss? . ."

VI.

The young man circled the block twice, his eyes focused straight ahead at the oncoming traffic, and faithfully checked his rear-view mirror every ten to twelve seconds, per his specific instructions, and again every time he took a corner, his vision barely registering the existence of the silver Camry parked on Broad Street directly across from the Woodland Bowling Alley. Finishing the second go-round he sped north past the Taco Grande, pulled into the Pickle's Shell Station and Convenience Store, walked inside and bought a pack of smokes so that both employees had a good, solid gander at him, then headed north again until he was two miles past the city limit before turning around. He checked his watch: 8:36, and the sun was setting to his right as he headed south back into town. The girl who sold him the cigarettes was young, Hispanic, attractive, had a nice rack, and seemed glad to see such a handsome young gentleman walk inside—'Mirna' was emblazoned on her nametag. Well, Mirna, baby . . . another time, perhaps?

The delightful descent of dusk providing natural cover now, he slowed to twenty-five and again circled the block twice, the silver Camry still sitting unattended on Broad, not even a whisper of anyone having followed him. Pulling into the bowling alley's gigantic lot he counted the cars and trucks parked there by row, up one and down the other as he slowly drove by each vehicle at no discernible speed, league night providing an especially bountiful cache of rides. *Seventy-three!*

Parking his red super-charged Yugo in between a full-sized black BMW and navy-blue F-150, he stayed in the shadows of the elms on the lot's south side until reaching the sidewalk and, eyes hurriedly scrutinizing the traffic flow, zipped across Broad Street to the waiting rental. Eyes again hastily sweeping the street, he depressed the electronic opener and climbed in. Ten minutes later, after sitting like a bowl of pudding behind the wheel—his instructions had been *very* explicit, and for *this* kind of money he was taking no chances—he slowly pulled away from the curb, easily blending into the traffic flow before turning right, then right a second time two miles further down.

Fortunato Avenue was quiet at 9:13 that evening. He enjoyed driving past the upscale homes and condos of Laurel Valley Estates with their expansive front lawns, fences both practical and aesthetically pleasing, and asphalt driveways often poured in an arc from one side of a property to the other. He drove past number 9789 twice and, detecting nothing that might indicate a source of potential trouble, pulled into the driveway with recessed bluish-white lighting, the split-level ranch home a hulking shadow in the dim starlight. Shutting the car door as quietly as possible, he trotted toward the entrance, a motion detector suddenly illuminating the immediate area with a blinding incandescence as he leaped over the two front steps, the massive front door opening to reveal the balding figure of Dow Pettigrew, his new boss and benefactor.

"Any problems getting here?" he said, waving the young man inside with a suspicious glance around his front yard.

"Didn't see a *soul!*" the young man answered happily as he pulled the precious DVD from his jacket pocket and handed it over. "They gave Dudley Thomas three of these . . one was for Denny himself, one for Dudley, and one for Miss Martha, but both Dudley and Miss Martha left their copies sitting out on their desks, so I grabbed hers after everybody left and headed this way as fast as I could . . Hope I'm not too late . ."

"Not at all, Tommy . . you did fine . ."

Pettigrew examined the disc marked *Security Level III, 1 July*, rambled leisurely into the kitchen and poured himself a tumbler-full of Scotch, flipped the disc over for a cursory look and smiled, a deviously-malicious gleam in his eye. Yes, things were going to work out just *fine*: he had the enemy's prized TV commercial in his hands a full six days before it was set to be aired and, as much as he tried to avoid self-adulation, it was still difficult not to feel anything but enormous pride and satisfaction at such a significant coup. Reaching into a cabinet drawer, he pulled out an envelope marked 'Tommy Burke' and placed it into the grateful youngster's hand.

"Next week's pay a couple days early, alright? . . would you like a Coke or somethin'? . ."

"No, I'm good, thanks . ."

Pettigrew led Tommy into a short hallway before stopping to shout "Velma? . . we'll be in the rec-room if you need anything" behind him, then proceeded past a half-bath with washer and dryer before stepping into a large, carpeted room with a door leading out into the side-yard. A pool table to their right dominated that half of the room's space, the front portion to their left occupied with a leather couch and three overstuffed chairs, the far wall facing them covered by an expensive component system with massive JBL speakers, the likes of which the younger man had never seen. The plasma set and DVD player were situated in the center-top of the entertainment rack, a buffed and polished mahogany that matched the paneling, DVD's, older VHS tapes, and a few hundred CD's pushed into compartments here and there, a smattering of old cassette tapes lingering about.

"You haven't seen this, right?" said Dow as he moved toward the DVD player.

"No, sir, I haven't," said Tommy, who busied himself by opening the envelope with his name on it, only to discover six one-hundred-dollar bills inside. He peered inside and plucked the bills out for a closer look as they seemed real enough but, at the same time, *unreal*: the numerals '100' were in all four corners like before, but they were small, plain and, like the rest of the bill's front, colorless. Benjamin Franklin's head, so large and dominating on the hundred-dollar bills he was used to seeing, was about half its normal size and perhaps *smaller*, the rendition of his head complete with shoulders and colonial attire set inside an oval-shaped, grayish ellipse, but with a *vertical* major axis, as though it had been turned sideways. The back side, more colorful by far, was still only green and white, with a fine artist's representation of Philadelphia's Independence Hall, trees surrounding it, completely dominant in the center. He ran his fingers through his blondish hair as he turned the bills over and over, everything apparently in order *if*, in fact, the bills were genuine; they were in various states of quality, some being fairly new, some old but, in general terms, mostly soft and flimsy, and all were signed *Robert B Anderson, Secretary of the Treasury* on the bill's front surface.

"Are these *real?*" he said casually as he dropped into a chair.

"Sure," said Dow Pettigrew as he slid the critical disc into the DVD player, "they're just *old*, is all . . twenty-five years ago, those were the only hundreds in circulation . ."

Adjusting a potentiometer next to an interior door, the lights dimmed to a comfortable darkness as the congressman's domestic advisor took a seat on the brown leather couch,

Scotch in hand, to assess the opposition's professionalism, strategy, and marketing savvy in advertising. If it was anything at all like the last clown who'd challenged Sid Villary there was little to worry about: the opposition's man had seemed so stiff he resembled a gigantic cardboard figurine, a breathing, talking prank who could barely spit his message out, much less make sense.

The TV screen turned bright blue before fading to the patriotic red, white, and blue of the stars and stripes, Denny Warrington's colorized picture superimposed onto the flag, an orchestra and choir heard in the background beginning with "O beau-tiful . . For spa-cious skies . . For amber waves of grain . ."

The strangely-soothing voice of the speaker, who Pettigrew believed sounded remarkably like Tony Manowitz, a well-known Dallas television personality who'd done work for every Sidney-Villary-for-Congress campaign thus far, began calmly reciting the Warrington message. Shrewdly devised by Dudley Thomas and his boys, the would-be successors to congressman Sidney Hunt Villary, it seemed a first-class effort—but Sid and his henchmen weren't about to just *go away*.

" . .State Senator Denny Warrington, a life-long Texan and resident of San Felipe, first elected to the state senate in 2006, a *true* conservative's conservative, has served not only his constituents, but *all* Texans, with a courage and honor only a native-born Texan can possibly appreciate, and *now* . . he wants to serve you in the nation's *capital! . ."*

"And he has all the pre-requisite qualifications . . of a gen-u-*ine* Texas rattlesnake," sneered Dow, eyes fixed to the screen. "Let's see, there's greed, avarice, ambition, disloyalty, stupidity, clumsiness, and sloth—*and*, he's a back-stabber! . ."

" . .Married to his childhood sweetheart, Evelyn," the speaker continued, the screen now filled with Denny, his wife, and two pre-teen daughters sitting at their dinner table talking about whatever it was they happened to be talking about—the classic contrived shot that everyone works so very diligently to *not* look so unmistakably contrived—"for fourteen wonderful years, and the father of two lovely daughters, it's easy to see why *family values* are so incredibly important . . to Denny Warrington . ."

"Denny's wife is unbelievably *hot!*" cried Tommy Burke, eyes popping out of his head.

"Yes, Evelyn's a good-looking woman, and sweet, too," he admitted, the Scotch now working its intended magic, "and, as such, she is definitive proof yet *again* . . that a woman's love is just as likely to fall upon a *turd*, as a rose . ."

" . . But there are forces at work in this country," continued the narrator, the second verse of *America , the Beautiful* still heard in the background, "that strive every day to threaten the health and well-being of our children, our schools, our retired people, our great state of Texas, and our way of life . ."

"Yes, there *are!*" agreed a smiling, chuckling Dow, his Scotch held high in salute, "and we call 'em *liberals*, and *Mexicans*, and *fudge-packers*, and *tree-huggers*, and *muslins*, and they're all Communist sons-of-*bitches!* . ."

Suddenly there appeared on the screen the man himself, Denny Warrington, in all his radiant glory, perched in front of the state capital building in Austin, three-piece suit from Saks and all the trimmings, haircut short and starkly-conservative with a slight crown on top that likely sounded like a struck golf ball when it hit the pillow at night . . and, he was loaded for *Griz*.

"Anyone who's lived in Texas for any amount of time at all

knows who I am . . Even better, anyone who's lived in Texas for any amount of time at all knows exactly what I stand for," Denny began, his message right on target. "But there are members of congress from right here in our great state of Texas who would say one thing and turn right around and *do* *another!* I cannot, and will not . . stand idly by and do nothing when the people of our great state are being misled and bamboozled by a fellow Texan! . ."

At this point in the proceedings Denny Warrington disappeared completely from the screen in favor of a recent camera shot of Congressman Sidney Villary's congressional office door, the word '*Sidney'* and the letter '*H.'* clearly visible, but not the last name . . and Denny was far from finished.

"What' this now?" said Dow Pettigrew, his curiosity finally aroused.

"One of the best-known *so-called* conservatives of this state . . claims to be *pro*-life and deeply *anti*-abortion," continued the voice of Denny Warrington—but the screen now displayed images of Sidney Villary, congressman from west Texas, shaking hands with a well-known, urban, Texas liberal—and not just *any* Texas liberal, but a *black* Texas liberal who was married to an Hispanic woman. "This *anti*-abortion congressman, however, not only *assisted* an infamous liberal from San Antonio in obtaining an abortion for his twenty-year-old daughter, but also helped to *locate* the abortion clinic to perform the legal murder of a child! . ."

By now the commercial had also displayed a fairly recent picture of a young, pretty woman of about twenty, followed by another, more damning photograph of what was clearly a Planned Parenthood office. And Denny was *still* talking.

"I've been asked to investigate the possibility this congressman assisted in the child's murder because he is the

112

child's *father*," Denny's voice continued solemnly.

"*WHAT?!*" exploded Pettigrew, completely off the sofa now, his mind reeling from the sheer girth of such an excessive, wholly untrue, completely outrageous charge.

"Texas—and *Texans*—will *not* stand for double-talk and back-stabbing representatives in their congressional contingents! . ."

"You lying, low-life son-of-a-*bitch!*" Pettigrew howled, livid. "You've gone a million miles beyond the *pale* on this one, Denny-boy! . ."

"A vote for Denny Warrington is a vote to restore Christian decency not only in Texas, but in the halls of congress!" Denny vowed, standing on-screen in front of the state capital again. "Some of our congressmen simply cannot support family values because they *have no family to value!* I'm Denny Warrington, and I approve this message, because Texas, and our great country, deserve *better! . ."*

The stars and stripes once again filled the TV screen in living color, the patriotic image of Denny superimposed at center, hand over his heart, 'DENNY WARRINGTON FOR CONGRESS' in bright-red lettering stretched across the top of the screen as the orchestra and choir concluded with "And crown . . thy good, with bro-therhood, From sea . . to . . shi . . ning . . *sea!*"

Dow Pettigrew sat motionless on his couch, rendered completely speechless, mouth agape in abject horror, the shock of what he'd just seen too excessive, too vulgar to be quickly absorbed. Even his Scotch didn't taste right.

"What about that oldest *daughter?!*" cried Tommy Burke. "She's hot, *too!*"

"To hell with the daughter, for Chrissakes!" snapped Pettigrew, his wits finally restored. The blatant enormity of

113

what had to be a bald-faced lie—it *had* to be a lie, what else could it possibly *be?*—the sheer *bulk* of such a trumped-up, phony, disingenuous, genuinely hateful prevarication was tantamount to a declaration of political warfare, down and unspeakably *dirty*—gloves *off*, fangs bared, pistols locked and loaded. So *that* was how Dudley Thomas and his mangy pack of curs wanted to play it, eh? Did Dudley not realize two could play that game?

"Boss? . .When did Congressman Villary arrange for that girl's abortion anyway? . ."

"Tommy, for heaven's sake . . *shut-up for a second!*" he warned him, his right hand palm down, fingers spread open in 'attack' configuration as his mind whirled round and round in tormented anguish until he saw the longed-for opening appear, the bolted gate suddenly pushed ajar just enough for light to pass through the golden slit. "I'm trying to think, okay? . ."

Pensive to a fault, the barely audible sound of the air conditioning unit outside switching itself on the only distraction now, his face betrayed neither humor nor patience as the gate swung open a little wider now. His response to the intentionally misleading, openly-libelous defamation of Warrington's ad slowly formed itself until the corners of his mouth registered the slightest upward movement, his plan of attack concrete-solid in his mind.

"Sorry I dug my teeth into ya' like that, but that's a pretty upsetting piece o' work there," he said with a shrug, his half-smile letting the bewildered lad know everything was alright. "So tell me . . you're taking this disc back to their headquarters tonight, right? . ."

"It'll be sitting on her desk just the way she left it this afternoon," grinned Tommy, "and *nobody'll* know it was ever gone . ."

"Good work, Mr. Burke, *good* work, indeed," said a rejuvenated Dow Pettigrew, his hand wrapped around what remained of his Scotch, which was beginning to taste like its old self again. "Now *here's* what I want you to do tomorrow and Friday . ."

The letter sent to the office of Congressman Sidney H. Villary made no mention of anything along the lines of "If it *pleases* you," or "If you don't *mind*," or even "If the spirit eventually *strikes* you." Signed by no less a personage than Heywood O'Rourke, then sent by special courier and signed-for by Regina Watts, it read "You are requested to report to either Walter Reed Army Hospital, Bethesda Medical Center, or Fort Meade, Maryland, no later than . . ." A job obviously well-suited to the special talents of Cas Turley, Sid telephoned him immediately to have his name dropped from the official roll of office-holders who needed inoculations prior to departure to Frankfurt and points beyond. It was the *points beyond* that made the difference: when Cas inquired as to specific cities and countries listed on the itinerary his heart sank when he heard 'Bucharest' and 'Budapest,' for any visit to Romania and Hungary required all the usual shots, plus a few more exotic numbers a trip to Germany or the Czech Republic didn't. Please, *please* get Heywood off my back, Sid begged him; it's imperative I stay here and campaign—I really *don't* have time to spare to go nation-hopping in Europe in late summer!

"You don't understand, boss," Cas explained as tactfully as possible. "When the letter reads 'You are *requested* to report' . . it's not really an invitation to be accepted or refused like a dance-party invite . .In fact, no one is *asking* anything—they are telling you in no uncertain terms to report, and there's

115

nothing I or anyone else can do about it . ."

Christ on a cross! thought Sid Villary. It was always *something,* wasn't it?!

Receiving no better treatment from the house majority whip, Dobrey Hollins of Louisiana, who advised him to "grow-up, find a pair of *balls,* and march your ass over to Walter Reed," Sid informed Lynch Bohannon and the girls he'd be out-of-pocket that afternoon and, after a short, animated conversation with Lynch, decided that Dobrey had more than likely steered him in the right direction, generally speaking. It was all a question of how best one received his medicine and, in this particular instance, Lynch had personal experience to draw upon.

"*Fuck* Walter Reed and Bethesda—if it was me, I'd go to Ft. Meade," said Bohannon.

"Why?"

"Jesus, Sid, I hate needles—*hate* 'em!" he winced, a frosty shudder descending down his spine. "I mean, I don't even like a tetanus *booster,* for Chrissakes! . . What's so great about a little shaft of metal sinking an inch into your arm, anyway? . . not a damn thing, *that's* what! . .'

"When I entered the navy they gave us our shots with the *gun,* Sid . . I dunno' how you feel about this—needles or the gun, what the hell's the difference?—but I'd rather be shot by the damn *gun* than get stuck by all them damn needles, any day o' the week! . ."

Villary, whose skin had begun to assume a ghostly pallor as he listened to talk of needles, had always *liked* guns, and for all the right reasons: they were fun to shoot, if you hit your target it didn't move much afterward and, best of all, nobody ever gave you a ration of *shit* when you had a gun in your hands! But now a trusted colleague was telling him it was better . . to

116

get shot with a *gun?!* What the *hell?!*

"Tell me about this fabulous gun, Lynch . ."

"No needles within a *mile*, my man! . . they just take this gun—it looks kinda' like a spray nozzle on the end of a garden hose?—and they put it right up against your upper arm and, after making sure you're ready, they squeeze the trigger and this sudden bolt of air shoots inside your arm carrying this medicine with it, see? . . It feels like somebody giving you a love-tap on the arm, and it *does* hurt, *but* . . not for long . . So . . ask yourself this: would I rather get inoculated with the *gun* . . or do I want seven or eight different needles sticking me like I'm a pin-cushion? . ."

Not really wanting either, Sid managed to mumble "I see what you mean," although he didn't.

"Just be very careful not to *move* while they're giving you the gun treatment," warned Lynch, "because that would cause *big* problems . ."

"How so?"

"I remember well when we started basic training and they gave us our shots with the gun . . they warned us ahead of time *not* to jerk away when getting the shots—but you always get these smart-ass over-achievers who don't listen, and their arms got ripped open by the force of the gun—then, even the *stupid* ones figured-out they had to be still while getting their shots, so . . if you want the needle treatment, by all means go to Bethesda or Walter Reed . . if you'd rather have the gun— and I personally would drive a couple hundred *miles* outta' my way to have it—head for Ft. Meade . . yeah, it's a little further—but it's worth it . ."

No matter which military post or base he happened to be visiting, regardless of its location, the fact that the security personnel invariably saluted him always struck him sideways:

sure, it was terrific to be recognized as someone of genuine importance, and Sid enjoyed it . . but wasn't it also true that the military, whether people supported them or not, made every other American's life *possible?* Surely even their detractors—the ones who claimed America's fighting men and women were little more than homicidal maniacs—realized that, without the military's existence, their civilian lives of personal and professional achievement and comfort were nothing more than *toast?* Sid Villary, in his capacity as a U.S. citizen, typically felt he should be saluting *them* instead of the other way round: they certainly made *his* life possible.

When security personnel spotted his congressional license plate as he rolled through the front gate of Ft. Meade early that afternoon they snapped to attention, saluting with a practiced crispness that matched their uniforms. He slowed to a crawl, stuck his head into the brilliant sunshine, and gave the best return salute he knew how, saying "You guys are *my* heroes!" before driving on through—and he meant every word of it.

Twenty minutes later he found himself sitting inside a chamber so immense he thought a 747 could be dragged inside with room to spare, though it wasn't nearly as large as it seemed. A bit on the clean and sterile side, the requisite pictures of the president and secretary of defense adorning the pastel-green walls, nothing indicated the chamber was used for anything but pushing through groups of overseas-bound service people. He cast a wary eye across the chamber to the opposite wall where several thick, black cables of perhaps twenty feet in length were mounted roughly three feet apart, the cable-heads fashioned more or less as Lynch Bohannon had described, extremely sturdy brass-colored metal with a trigger and a tiny hole in the flat surface of the nozzle. When the doctor strode in, Sid was busy on his cellphone, as usual, giving instructions to Regina regarding his whereabouts and contact numbers in Texas for his trip home, now only eight days away. He signed-off, turned the phone's volume down to nothing and dropped it into his shirt pocket, the better to give his undivided attention to the task at hand.

"Hi, I'm Dr. Kelley," said the fresh-faced young man dressed in white, who Sid guessed was about ten or twelve years his junior. They shook hands and, though the doctor hardly seemed a veteran of any real medical experience, Sid had the distinct impression the kid knew exactly what he was doing. He managed a wan, nervous, apprehensive smile.

"I don't suppose you're from Texas? . ."

The 'kid' grinned playfully and said "Close . . Enid, Oklahoma, actually . ."

"Cowboy *U*.?" Sid asked hopefully.

"U of *Sooner!*" said the fresh-face, his grin even bigger now.

"Oh, my . . this *is* going to be tough . ."

"Not at all . . you came to the right place," said Dr. Kelley as an even younger-looking nurse with dark-blonde hair and calm demeanor appeared next to him, a plastic bottle of liquid in her hand. "*Good*, Amy, you brought the magic potion with you . . I took a reasonably careful look at your shot records, congressman, and while you're woefully deficient in some areas, it's not an *entirely* bleak picture we're dealing with here . . the worst part of it is the fact that, because you're going to Romania—not to mention the other stops along the way— we're going to have to give you a hepatitis-*A* vaccine due to the dangers in the water supply there—that in addition to the other vaccines, of course . ."

Swallowing hard, he managed to whisper "How many *total*, Doc? . ."

"Six with the gun, plus an oral version of a cholera vaccine, and you'll be all set . . Of course, you can split this in two if you like—three today, then come back sometime in the next ten days for the last three—it's really up to you, as we're here for your convenience, but it's not uncommon for someone to take all six bumps, then drive home and take it easy for the rest of the day with a light regimen of fluids . . totally up to you, sir . ."

"Any real danger if I took all six in one fell swoop? . ."

"*Well* . . I'm not going to stand here and tell you there's no risk taking all six at the same time because there *is*, though it's certainly not a life-or-death situation as far as the medical side of things is concerned," the 'kid' explained. "What we typically see is someone—usually a teenager or someone in their very early twenties just entering service—attempting to take all six or seven at once and, for any number of reasons, fainting as they get to number five or six, but that's a much more frequent occurrence using needles instead of the guns by far . . I *do* remember one young man passing-out standing up after only *three* bumps from the gun, *but* . ." And here the youngster in the whites stopped and grinned, adding playfully "Of course, he wasn't from Oklahoma, *so* . ."

"Yeah, I read you loud and clear, Doc . ."

"Like I said, whatever you think is best is what we'll do, sir . ."

Sid thought it over a moment before saying "Hell . . let's just do it and be done with it . ."

"That's the spirit! . . just don't pull away as I squeeze the trigger, okay? . ."

And then they started. Dr. Kelley led him across the chamber to the cables, nurse Amy with them every step of the way with her bottle of fluid. Sid removed his dress shirt and folded it over a nearby chair while Kelley checked his respective cables and applied electrical power to the system, which sprang to life with a low-pitched, steady hum easily spoken over.

"You stop me any time you like if you have a question, if you feel inexplicably faint, or for any other reason you might have," the white-clad 'kid' told him reassuringly. Sid nodded that he understood, so the doctor said "We'll begin with the dengue-fever vaccine first . ."

He swabbed Sid's left upper arm with an alcohol-soaked cotton ball, pressed the nozzle of the second cable from the right firmly against the arm, then carefully squeezed the trigger as Sid looked away in the opposite direction.

"Ready?"

Whompa!

As Lynch had foretold, the sensation felt similar to one of his childhood buddies unexpectedly 'goosing' him with the knuckle of the middle finger in a fist, uncomfortable without being acutely painful; when he ventured to look at what happened all he saw was a tiny red dot surrounded by perhaps an inch of subtly rising flesh, the natural reaction to having his skin pierced violently by a sudden jolt of air. On the plus side, there was no sign of flesh ripped apart by the gun.

"Not *bad*," he said, evidently relieved at the ease of the procedure.

"Let's continue then," suggested Dr. Kelley.

Whompa! Whompa! Whompa! Three more inoculations, one after the other in alternating limbs, right, left, right, guarding against hepatitis, encephalitis, and malaria. Congressman Villary doing fine with the entire program, shuffling his feet to a minor two-step of his own imagining with each successive

121

bump of his arms, each bump bringing him one step closer to the finish line. Left arm for the third and *last* time, cotton alcohol swab, and it's time for the old *bird-flu* vaccine. Good to go and . .

Whompa! Mister Villary, how about a quick ingestion of something *tasty* . . to keep you hydrated, your throat wet and comfortable, and your electrolytes flowing free and easy—no, nothing *bourbon*-flavored, you understand, but tasty as compared to powdered milk or prune juice? Umm, down the hatch! Okay now, right arm one *final* time for the dreaded *yellow* fever, eh? Cotton swab? Check! Medical gun? Check! Upper right arm? Check! Here we go . .

Whompa!

"Well *done*, congressman," said Dr. Kelley.

"And a very *stylish* conclusion, I must say," added nurse Amy.

Smiling, twirling round and round in celebration, the challenge met and now triumphant, three little red dots on each upper arm, a simply fantastic resolution to the ever-present dilemma of how best to mystically appear in some European capital without benefit of modern medical protection, third-term congressman Sidney H. Villary from Texas twirled clockwise again, stopped, exhaled, and crumpled in a heap like a deflated, abused accordion at the doctor's feet, out cold.

"Oh, *my!*" said Kelley, stooping to take a look.

"*Oops!*" added nurse Amy. "Maybe *not* so stylish . ."

"Good *lord*, Charlotte!" Marigold Godwin said to her anemic-looking co-worker when she returned from lunch. "You're as white as a *ghost* . ."

"I'm not feeling the best, Marigold," she said, the embassy's

122

side door closing behind her. "I was sick this morning, but I'm a little better now . ."

"Your doctor's office called while you were gone . . I set the note on your desk . ."

"Thank you, ever so . ."

'HAVE YOUR TEST RESULTS' the note read. ' . . COME SEE ME END OF DAY . . . IF ANY PROBLEM PLEASE CALL . . .' Dr. Pat!

Greta, Dr. Scheckleburg's chief assistant, the lone occupant of the front office when Charlotte arrived at 4:57 that afternoon, a 'worrier' in the grand tradition of nursing who usually appeared to be busy and *was*, gave her an uncharacteristic smile as she signed-in at the window.

"I'll let Dr. Scheckleburg know you're here, Charlotte . ."

The extraordinary absence of bustle and noise a peculiar distraction—the echoes of the pounding and sawing on the embassy ceiling still shattering her sense of calm—she'd barely had a chance to take a seat in the waiting room before the diminutive form of Dr. Scheckleburg appeared in the doorway leading to the patient rooms, a grin of smug satisfaction on her normally expressionless face when she said "C'mon, young lady . . we need to *talk!* . ."

"We've discovered an acute progesterone shortage in your system," she said solemnly after they'd taken seats in her office, the better to mask her true purposes, "and that, coupled with an acute *deficiency* of estrogen, has brought us to our present situation, I'm afraid—it's a complete medical *failure* of the worst sort—but at least we know the source of your discomfort and, even *better*, there's a name for it, *and* . . we know how to treat it! . ."

"*Blimey!*" she said, a little worried still, yet strangely relieved. "What's it called? . ."

123

"Well," the doctor hedged matter-of-factly, "over here we call it *morning sickness* . ."

"Oh, morning sickness," Charlotte repeated blandly, the message temporarily missing its intended target until the greater, more-accurate implication revealed itself, the patient's eyes slowly enlarging, becoming round as half-dollars when she said "Oh, my *God*—morning sickness?!"

"You're pregnant, Charlotte, *yes* . . and I pray you're happy with it . ."

In the space of a long moment it seemed to her that she and a doctor and a friend—a *good* friend, of course, for news of a historic, life-altering nature should only be shared with someone dear and utterly trustworthy—were engaged in intimate conversation, just the *three* of them—except that when her eyes searched the area there were only *two*, just she and the doctor, because her best friend, Helen, was in London. Her visit to the office was now, officially, a blur. Incapable of lucid thought, a thousand notions arriving in a flash of light and just as suddenly departing in like manner, the questions of a lifetime's dreams slowly coming into focus . . but which ones were most important now?

"How long? . ."

"Oh, I'm guessing about six weeks, give or take . . Sound about right? . ."

Finding no comfort in the knowledge of who the father had to be—and little enough comfort that he was the sole possibility—she stopped to calculate the time passed since her visit to Pandora's Box. Let's *see*, she thought hungrily, it was the . . first *Wednesday* past Mother's Day, which was the eleventh, so there remained twenty days of May, minus the *three*, of course . . plus the twenty-five here in June, and today happens to be a Wednesday, too, so-o-o . .

124

"Good *lord!*" she cried, the problem solved, "it was six weeks ago *tonight* .."

"You're kidding!?"

"It *has* to be, Dr. Pat—he's the only man I've been with this *year*—it couldn't possibly be anyone else .. but him .."

"Wonderful! .. You're still seeing him? .."

"God, *no*, not him," she said emphatically. "Too much danger there, I suppose .."

"Danger? . . *Really?* . . You mean he's a contract-killer or something?" the doctor suggested. "Is this the sort of man you're afraid to be around, Charlotte?"

"Oh, no, nothing like that," she said, smiling for the first time since she arrived, "he's just in a very sensitive position, that's all . . He's American, and a fairly well-known politician—and I'm not *sure*, but I think he may be up for re-election this year .."

"Oh—he's *married?!*" said Dr. Pat, acknowledging an even greater complication.

"No, *single*—and I'm sure that's the way he'd like to keep it! .. The fact is .. I haven't seen or talked with him since that night, and I don't know if it's because he doesn't want to see me again, or if he's simply too busy right now—or maybe *both* .. I just don't know .."

"Charlotte? .. For any number of reasons, I can't believe any man who saw you could *ever* forget you!—you're stunning-looking, your British accent is adorable, and you're one of the finest people I know .. I don't know what the circumstances happen to be for your political friend, of course, but I hope you understand my questions regarding *your* circumstances I only ask because, one, you're my patient, and two, there are *two* of you now, not just one, so . . When you said there was too much *danger* with this guy, I had this nightmare vision of a

125

mafia hit-man running berserk through a crowd, taking random shots at unsuspecting bystanders—but if he's a public office-holder I'm reasonably sure he's just busy. That said, naturally he's *got* to be made aware of the situation, and there are certain matters I need to cover with you since I'm your primary-care physician . . Do you have any questions before we begin? . ."

VII.

It had really been *incredibly* thoughtful and considerate of Dr. Kelley and nurse Amy to assume personal responsibility for ensuring their V.I.P.—very impatient politician—arrived home safely that evening. Congressman Villary appreciated what he considered the needless attention he received: didn't *everyone* taking all the inoculations in one fell swoop unceremoniously pass-out standing up, thus giving themselves a good whack on the head from the concrete floor below? Occasionally, one simply had to *man-up!* The two hours rest on his back at Ft. Meade hadn't hurt—just as their LOB (lack-of-bourbon) hadn't *helped*—and the ride home to Herndon in Dr. Kelley's Audi, nurse Amy following in the congressman's vehicle, had proved uneventful and pleasant. They'd stuck around long enough to see he was safe, reasonably sound, and more or less pain-free before climbing into the Audi for the ride back to Maryland, Dr. Kelley wise beyond his years in not mentioning anything about Oklahoma. The Lor-Tab Sid took at bedtime, after behaving admirably in drinking only the tiniest amount of bourbon that evening—he'd tossed it down in two swallows, but sensed another might be overtly stupid—eased him into a good night's sleep, the vision of a dark-haired beauty he'd met some weeks ago contentedly capturing his dreams.

Waking at six-thirty the next morning had been tragic. His head throbbed, his upper arms were killing him, and for once he didn't feel like jumping out of bed to go to work. Willing himself into the kitchen he started a pot of coffee, greedily swallowed three aspirin, then left Regina a message on his office answering machine before stumbling into the shower. What the hot water couldn't accomplish the coffee sufficed for as the throbbing slowly subsided, his aching arms still sore but firmly attached, the combination enabling him to slide in behind the wheel for the nightmare drive into D.C. a few minutes before eight. 'You'll *earn* everything you achieve today,' he told himself. Thursday, his favorite workday, had long proved invaluable as the best time to reflect on what degree of progress had been made that week, a gauge to measure achievements both realized and yet to come, with the weekend on the horizon; so far, it had been a blue-ribbon period, no question. The medical debacle aside, the cluster of inoculations had certainly been an intimidating roadblock, but they'd been overcome; plans for his trip home and campaign swing had firmed-up nicely; talks concerning beefing-up the overall number of Border Patrol agents had progressed more than he'd believed possible only a week or two prior; and Sabrina Adkins, who he hadn't even *seen* in half a lifetime but was reputed to be nicely assembled, wanted to see him and, perhaps, become better-acquainted. Well . . as the Mexicals liked to say, *O-lay!* Today's number one task was to discuss whatever it was that had Dow Pettigrew *so upset* he'd left messages at the office, at his home, and at his parents' home in west Texas, the result of which had been yet another shaky, mournful conversation with his mother as his head waited patiently for the throbbing to diminish the night before. Mother? . . if I promise to marry Sabrina Adkins and mystically present you and dad with *triplets* next summer, would *that* get you off my back for a while?

"Oh, my *God!*" Regina Watts whispered breathlessly when he walked through the door, head shaking in sympathy. "I had no *idea* . . I'm so sorry . ."

"Great to see you, too, Queenie!" he said in passing, striding quickly past his three office ladies as he loped toward his office door, stopping only after crossing the threshold: the Yellow Rose, God bless it, had never looked so good! Eight minutes later when line three lit up, the incessant ringing grating on his frayed nerves a bit more than usual, he waited until Julie's voice gently erupted through the intercom with "It's Dow!" to pull himself away from the soft, velvet luxury of his golden comfort.

"Mister *Pettigrew* . ."

"Are you alive?"

"Of course, I'm alive—I'm also *sore* in a few places I'd prefer not to be sore in . ."

"One of your girls told me you—her exact words?—'He looks like *shit!*' I believe is how she put it—did you faint and crack your head open?! . ."

"Yes and no, my friend, yes and no . . Yes, I passed out but, *no,* I didn't crack my head open—though it took a pretty sizable hit on the right side . . It only *feels* like it's split open, if it makes you feel any better—and for Chrissakes, *don't* tell my folks, okay? . ."

"Wouldn't dream of it . . You want me to call later when you're feeling better? . ."

"No, talk to me . ."

"I've seen the commercial Denny and Dud Thomas are running, beginning July first in west Texas, and he's gunning for you on abortion now . . *in addition to* the immigration side of things, so it's getting hotter here by the week, Sid . ."

"That's what I heard . . I understand there's a chance I impregnated Quentin and America Hanson's daughter, Octavia, then arranged for her to have an abortion so the

129

Hansons wouldn't get dragged into it? . . Am I close? . ."

After almost ten seconds of stunned silence, Dow finally said "How in God's name did you know *that?!* . . I mean, I just found out about it last night and it made me sick . . damn-near lost a glassful of single-malt in the process! . . Why am I always the *last* one to hear this shit?! . ."

"D.P., if that's the best they can do, we've got nothing to worry about . . The fact is, I *did* help Quentin and America obtain an abortion for Octavia . . it's absolutely *true* . . but what those idiots are insinuating *isn't*: all I did was ask a friend in Lubbock who they might send her to so she could receive a safe and sterile procedure after she was date-raped — in *southern California*, for Chrissakes — so if that's how they want to come after me, let 'em . . Also, I only agreed to do this after their state senator in Houston, or wherever the hell he's from, called the office and complained I wouldn't do a favor for a U.S. Army hero, namely Quentin, when the truth is I didn't know about it . . I would never, *ever* turn down a veteran's request for assistance, I don't care a fig for party affiliation, and everybody knows it . .

They're just trying to make something out of nothing . ."

"Then should I proceed with my plans to somehow . . *compromise* the quality of their ad? . . 'cause unless you tell me to hold off, I've already taken steps to — shall we say *neutralize?* — any perceived benefit Denny might receive from running such a half-baked collection of lies, half-truths, innuendo, and omissions . . and I'm doing it in such a way as to cast doubts about the veracity of his candidacy . ."

"Is there anything that might hurt Evelyn and the kids? . ."

"Absolutely *not!* . . I would *never* . ."

"Then you can either deny their charges, providing hard evidence that proves beyond a doubt that I'm clear of any and all wrongdoing," he said, his bust of Ronald Reagan smiling his benign approval from atop the desk, "or you can take steps to rectify the situation using the tried-and-true, original Dow-Pettigrew-Takes-No-Prisoners method which, I'm sure, is just as effective and a lot more fun . ."

"I must say, you're taking all this rather more sedately than I would be . . I figured you'd hit the ceiling when you heard what a sneaky, under-handed, sinful, non-Christian way they were coming after you, so my hat's off to you . ."

"D.P., we must always—*always*—take the high road in our dealings with everyone—not just our political enemies and the minorities who would tear down every vestige of the life we've created through our lord and savior, Jesus Christ, but *everyone*—Catholics, Jews, Muslins, Mexicals, and snake-charmers alike," he said, piously eyeballing the cross that adorned each office wall, the secret that would never allow his electoral defeat. "*Even* the G.G.C. qualifies on this one, you know . ."

"The G.G.C.?! . ."

Sid paused momentarily—as their champion and spiritual leader it was his sacred duty to be kind and benevolent, enlightening and generous, understanding and charitable—even *ground*-breaking, in the greatest sense of the word—when no one else gave it a second thought.

"The *Godless Gay Community*? . ."

"Oh . . *yeah*, I suppose so . ."

"Remember, we're *all* God's children—although in his eyes I'm sure the devout and truly faithful are more worthy than the God-awful, but that's a discussion better saved for another occasion . . Now . . are we clear on tactics and strategy? . . Is there any question as to what we're allowed and *not*-allowed to do? . . 'cause if there *is* . . we need to establish reasonable

131

parameters so there's zero chance of ethics violations—I am *not* capable of enduring another sermon from my dear mother and father about what a fine, upstanding citizen and *family-man* my opponent is, that sorry son-of-a-*bitch!*—oh, and if you happen to run into Evelyn and the kids, please tell 'em I love 'em and that they're in my thoughts and prayers *always*, okay?.."

No one could accuse Sidney Villary of taking his obligations lightly. Poring over his project to once and for all establish a history of Audie Murphy as a lifelong member in good standing of the eastern Texas Pentecostal faith, a personal favor to the Reverend Hugh Beauchamp, he felt more than ever the grand tidings that Thursdays typically brought, musing from time to time about the possibility of transplanting Ronald Reagan from his ancestral home in Illinois to his future native roots in west Texas. The so-called "insurmountable *hurdles*" the liberals were so fond of quoting, which was actually little more than obstructionism cloaked in the thin disguise of both rhetoric and overt communism, had never amounted to a hill of beans—and *pinto* beans fixed Texas-style, at that. One of Sid's all-time favorite professors, an American History buff whose lineage included a distant relative named Joseph Goebbels, had once told him that history was nothing more than a "collection of *lies*," to be re-written and re-established at the whim of anyone with the guts to mount the challenge. Defeats could be transformed into victories, skirmishes could become major military campaigns, a thousand casualties could become merely a *hundred* .. if the proper person was creating fiction rather than facts, simply to establish a personal truth. *Facts* were worthless anyway. How best to re-locate Reagan a thousand miles from the mid-west to the Texas-west? There had to be a way, and *that* was an indisputable fact.

He'd just verified Murphy's baptism at the age of nine months in the First Pentecostal Church of the Divine Ascension in Farmersville, Texas, March 22, 1926—Murphy wasn't *really* an Irish name like it sounded—at least, not in the *new* reality, it wasn't—and anybody who claimed otherwise at any time in the future was a goddamned *liar!*—and recorded the holy event in Chapter One of the Personal History, entitled "His Immaculate Conception and First Two Years as a Christian." As an afterthought he placed a small arrowhead pointing upwards between the words "a" and "Christian" and inserted the word "Devout": literally anyone could be a Christian, but only an *exceptional* person like Audie Murphy could be classified as a "Devout Christian." He'd also read somewhere that World War I's most-famous hero, Sergeant Alvin York, had also been a member of the Pentecostal faith for practically his entire life. A coincidence? Not too damned likely, thought Sid Villary, that two of America's greatest military heroes just *happened* to be members of the same faith but, simply because it was always *something*, there would inevitably be the detractors of all that was holy, claiming that God and fate and courage and inevitability had nothing to do with it—like Heaven and earth were an *accident*. Let them open their big, stupid mouths, he thought: they were the same idiots who claimed you couldn't weigh the earth because you didn't have a big-enough *scale!*

"Congressman Villary? . ."

It was Regina Watts on the intercom, and she rarely, if *ever*, used the contraption.

"Yes, Regina? . ."

"There's a young lady here to see you, sir . ."

133

"Give me thirty and I'll be with you . ."

Now he sat uncomfortably in the Yellow Rose, only moderately startled at his parents' audacity. '*So,*' he thought contemptuously, 'you two couldn't wait one little more *week* for me to fly home, eh?! . .' *Mother Mayhem,* it was always *something* with those two would-be grandparents, wasn't it? The very idea—sending a young, undoubtedly attractive young female from west Texas who was planning on visiting the D.C. area *anyway* into the capital for the sole purpose of paying a personal visit to the young (eligible), upstanding (as yet uncommitted), God-fearing (child-averse), right-thinking, capable congressman (bachelor) from the Lone Star state— well, this wouldn't be the *first* time they'd done it . . and probably wouldn't be their last attempt either. *Not* a problem, though, for he had the "rebuttal and non-involvement" clause down to an absolute science: *great* to meet you, *thanks* for stopping by, *wonderful* of you to be so thoughtful, *got* to work right through my lunch hour, *must* be in the chamber all afternoon (morning) . . oh, and *don't forget to vote!* My, but those two in west Texas had a rude, *rude* awakening in store when he got them alone at the barbecue dinner at the country club! Well . . time to say *"hello!"* and be done with it . .

What struck him as so profoundly extraordinary, he would later recall in his initial contacts with his analyst, was the inestimable quality of Regina's expression when he opened his office door and saw her gazing up at that spectacular face, for it was his chief-of-staff's peculiarly playful grin he noticed first. He'd never seen her in such a state. Of course, she'd never been introduced to Charlotte Tillstrom—had never laid eyes on her, really—but pleasantly surprised she was, nonetheless. From that point on, in the congressman's humble opinion, until that second meeting with the British beauty had concluded, the other-worldly experience would become increasingly *bizarre*—it was the precise adjective he used in his first session on the couch to describe his present dilemma, Dr. Milner would remind him, and should invariably be remembered in that particular context. Dressed in a light-gray pinstripe outfit and plum blouse that highlighted her narrow waist, the stranger dazzled.

"Hello, Sidney," she said pleasantly to her wide-eyed, unsuspecting acquaintance.

"I just *love* your accent!" Regina gushed exuberantly, her smile refusing to retreat.

"Charlotte!?"

Everyone in the front office—Carmen and Julie eagerly sharing Regina's curiosity about their elegant new stranger—then witnessed their employer, hero, and champion do something they had not only never before seen him do, but thought likely they'd *never* see. Like two impassioned lovers reunited after a years-long hiatus, he stepped forward and took her in an unmistakably loving embrace, his expression of pleasure and unmitigated joy superior to anything audible. Lynch Bohannon, entirely unaccustomed to such scenes, opened his office door, saw the embrace, gasped audibly, then disappeared from whence he surfaced, utterly aghast, Sidney Villary never having seen him. Evidently overjoyed to see her again, the congressman made introductions with smiles all round, unceremoniously inviting her inside his inner realm, her hand in his as they disappeared into his office.

"I'm *overwhelmed* to see you, Charlotte!" he said as he settled her into his most comfortable chair. "I know you may not believe this . . but I think about you all the time . . In fact, I dreamed about you just last night while recovering from a small shock to my system yesterday afternoon . . can't say *why* exactly, but I did . . Maybe it was the pain-killer playing tricks with my head or something . . or maybe it's just that I haven't seen you in—hmm, let me *see*—"

"Six weeks and a day . ."

"My, has it been that long?" he said. But he knew in his heart that it had been because his thoughts told him it had been even *longer*, which prompted him to blush shamefully at his negligent inattention. Taking up his accustomed position in the Yellow Rose, he peered longingly across his desk to drink in her sumptuousness; absorbed by the visual treasure, all thoughts of his trip home, campaigning for re-election, and the very challenge from his political right long-vanished into thin air with her presence, he smiled and said "I want to apologize for my incredibly bone-headed behavior. I should've called or tried to communicate with you in some way, and I want very much for you to know it's *not* you—it's just that I'm in a fight for my political life, which I'm not really accustomed to . . so please, *please* . . forgive me . ."

"Have you decided why you dreamed about me? . . Perhaps you foresaw my visit today . ."

"No, I didn't," he said at length, "and I may never know . . but the important thing is, you're here *now*, you look radiant, and I'm delighted to see you! . ."

"*Are* you?" she said pointedly, though she heard nothing in his tone that spoke otherwise. "I'd have thought you'd be a bit *on edge* . . seeing me standing in your business office for no apparent reason . . other than the fact that we met, got along rather *splendidly* for one memorable night in mid-May and, save for your little . . *malfunction* towards midnight, had a good enough time to at least ring me, *but* . . I never heard from you, of course, and wondered what I'd done to put you off so . . it crossed my mind that perhaps you . . just didn't care

136

for my company, or found me *lacking* in some respect, that Isomehow . . couldn't measure-up to a Texas congressman's *standards*, whatever they might be—and I stay pretty busy myself so, after three or four weeks I *assumed* you were done with me and never wanted to see me again . ."

"Well . . like I said, it's not you, it's *me*—and the notion that you're not up to my *standards* never entered my mind—I should think kings and emperors would find you good enough, and then some . . I'd also like to think your being here is a personal way of saying you'd like to hear from me, or that you'd like to know me better, or something of the sort—once all this crazy campaigning is over and done with, of course . ."

"Up until yesterday I hadn't given it much thought . . like most singles, I protect my privacy and desire nothing more from my friends than honesty and trust—with a healthy dose of *decency* tossed in for symmetrical purposes, naturally—and I follow affairs of the heart in *much* the same way . . Some men are worthy, others not so much, and should a good one come along, that's terrific—if not, then I'm still waiting, I suppose. And I *like* my independence—I really *do*, and I'm loathe to give it up—but circumstances change, sometimes as a matter of course, often unexpectedly, and one must do the best she can," she said. Her lustrous blue eyes, moist and oversized, focused on his when she shifted forward in her seat and said "I'm having trouble deciding whether this visit is unexpected or more in tune with the natural course of events . ."

"So you *do* want to get to know me better?" he said innocently.

"It's not so much *want* as it is *need*, I'm afraid," she said ruefully. "I really *need* to get to know you better . ."

Still unable to divine her meaning, he eyed her cautiously and said "I'm not quite sure I follow you there, Charlotte . . is

137

there something you need me to do for you in my official capacity as a United States congressman? . ."

"Not as a congressman, no," she said quietly, "only as a *man*, Sidney . ."

Not minding that she called him 'Sidney,' a luxury precious few of his acquaintances were allowed, he sat comfortably in the Yellow Rose, idly pondering the forces of the universe that, irrevocably smiling down upon him, had brought her to him, his utter, complete trust in providence holding unshakeable dominion over his life. 'Not as a congressman, but as a man,' he imagined she repeated, 'as a man, as a man, as a *man*, Sidney!' Suddenly he sat upright, his senses abruptly alerted to what had up until then been a remote possibility of calamity, maintained at a distance thousands of miles away, thrust inside his office like a knife into butter, past his business desk adorned with Ronald Reagan and Audie Murphy, disrespectfully shoved in his face like so much foul-tasting medicine.

"*Charlotte?!* . ." he began to say before his voice failed him.

"It would seem *your* malfunction that evening was merely the most visible one," she said by way of explanation, "but apparently not the *only* one . ."

The exquisite memory of their first encounter came rushing back: it had unquestionably been the single most satisfying evening of the year, a torrent of heat and passion white-hot at its glorious epiphany, embers of smoldering affection still present when he pulled her close for the tranquil ride to sleep. Now it had returned not as before, but as a raging, vengeful harbinger bent on his political end, a ravenous monster unknown to him, but kindled and nourished by those forces arrayed against him for the purpose of bringing about his utter and complete destruction, for reasons he could only hypothesize. It was, for all intents and purposes, the *end*. He wished he could somehow identify some facet of her lovely gaze that might reveal hateful avarice, but his vision seemed as that of a blind man.

"Please don't look at me like that," she pleaded, mistrust and suspicion too easily spotted in any man. "I certainly didn't *plan* it . . my pills have always worked before . ."

"Not *always*, it would appear," he said frostily, the conspiracy manifesting itself before his very eyes. "Your reasons for being here are now painfully evident . . did you have a *particular* dollar amount in mind, or will you simply return to your political friends triumphant, knowing my career has been thrown to the proverbial wolves? . ."

Charlotte, predictably puzzled at such an unexpected question, could only lay an arm on his desk-front and manage a weak "Excuse me? . ."

"How *much?*" he demanded earnestly. "This shakedown you and your political allies have so carefully perpetrated can have only one of two possible payoffs, at most—either my resignation or a fantastic amount of cash to keep quiet . ." He leaned forward in the Yellow Rose, placed both hands atop his desk one over the other and rested his chin on them, a mere three and a half or four feet separating them. " . . So . . *which* is it? . ."

"My political *allies?!*" she repeated incredulously. "Have you forgotten that I'm *British?!* . . that my only allegiance is to the *Queen?!*"

Mulling this over momentarily—true, it *did* seem unlikely the British Prime Minister or another member of the British government would conspire against him—he quickly concluded there had to be an even more seditious, *more* under-handed, entirely *evil* force at work now—one so devious it made the acrimonious feelings between Sherlock Holmes and Professor Moriarty look like the detective and mathematician were lifelong pals.

"So . . you *are* working in cahoots with my parents! . ."

"What on *earth* are you talking about?!" she cried, at a complete loss to comprehend anything he'd suggested. "I came here to discuss my pregnancy, which you, unfortunately, had a hand in—so to speak! As for your *parents?* . . I wouldn't recognize them if they were standing in front of me right this *second*—so get a grip, forget this conspiracy business, and talk with me like an adult about whether or not we are going to have this *child*, okay?! . ."

"How can you be so sure it's *mine*, Charlotte? . . I've known you for six weeks, and out of that entire time period we've spent exactly nine and a half hours together in a single evening . . I've no way of knowing how many men you've been with this year, *who* they are, *why* you picked each other, or anything *else*, so I hope you'll forgive me if I'm just a little bit *curious* . ."

"You know, Sidney . . that's the *first* logical thing you've said since I arrived," she pointed-out while retreating from his desk, preferring the comfort of the chair, "and your question, being perfectly legitimate, deserves an answer, so I'll tell you . . *You*, sir, are the one and *only* man who's spent the night in my bed this year—I personally don't feel any great urge to go out at night and find *anyone* for any purpose—in fact, you're the only man I've been with in nearly eleven months, so my best guess is that, *yes*, you had a hand in this most *dreadful* business and, as such, you are intricately involved in the decision-making process. That said, I'd like to ask *you* something—if you don't mind . ."

"What's that?" he said warily.

140

"You see me sitting before you in much the same way you saw me the first time—perched on a stool at the Box, enjoying a Guinness?—and you apparently liked what you saw *then* because you made love to me three times—*three!*—before you left the next morning . . I can only assume my appearance today is highly-similar to my appearance that night . . so tell me . . do I *really* look like the kind of girl who *needs* to prostitute herself to get along in this world? . . Or might you give me the benefit of the doubt and surmise that I'm very intelligent, *extremely* selective about the men I spend time with, am attractive enough to pick and choose whomever I *please*, and would rather *die* . . than willingly be used to injure or harm *anyone?* . ."

Congressman Sidney H. Villary of west Texas took a long moment to consider the question. Serious situations required solemn, no-nonsense consideration—and his present set of circumstances seemed about as serious as any he was likely to ever have, a dilemma of gigantic proportions. In a rare moment of candor, he admitted to himself he held real feelings for her and didn't want to upset her needlessly. What other answer could he give?

"I've never met anyone," he began, his voice slow and steady, "who reminded me *less* of a prostitute than yourself, Charlotte . ."

"Well, it's about *time* you were making some sense of all this!"

"Charlotte? . . You *must* know this comes as quite a shock to me! . . There is *no way* I was expecting *this*, for Chrissakes! . . I'm still recovering from my inoculations-fever they gave me yesterday, and now *this* on top of it?! . . *and* my re-election campaign is fixing to shift into high gear? . . Could it possibly be any *worse?!* . ."

141

"You can't honestly believe this was *intentional*, can you?!" she fumed, the color in her cheeks darkening in anger. "I mean, for all I know you could be a child molester, or *worse* — congressman or *no* congressman . . I hardly know anything about you, really, and given the choice, I'd rather have a child with someone I know and *trust* than someone who might or might *not* even be a decent human being, Sidney . ."

"You could give me a little more credit than *that* . ."

"Do I assume correctly then . . that you have no interest in marrying me or raising a child together? . . . I'm well aware of your reputation as the 'most-*single*, most-*eligible*, and *most-determined-to-stay- single* member of congress . . Therefore, am I correct in assuming you want me to *abort* our child? . ."

"Oh, *God*, don't do *that!*" he gasped, terrified.

"Then you do *not* . . want me to abort this child?" she said, a bit perplexed.

"Absolutely *not!*" he said, his primary campaign foremost in his mind.

"Then you're actually considering having this child with me as your . .*wife?!* . ."

"Absolutely *not!*" he cried, the haunting vision of his desperate parents obscuring his view. Chiding him for not being married was easy for *them*, but in their case, talk was cheap: neither of them had ever had to address the assembled multitude, run a campaign, or serve their constituents fifteen hundred miles away. Were the shoe on the other foot they wouldn't have time for a wife and kids *either*.

"Oh, I *see*," she said at length, the picture becoming clearer now, "you want me to have the child, but you want no part of *me*, is that it? . ."

"Absolutely *not!*" he said, his options running headlong towards ground-zero.

142

"Then do you just want me to have the child and then . . *abandon it*, or put it up for adoption—then have myself disappear from the face of the *earth?! . .*"

"Of course not!"

"Let me get this straight then," she said, her available choices having completely run out. "You don't want me to abort our child, and you *don't* want to marry me . . so you want the child, but you don't want me to have any part of having the child . . is *that* what you're telling me? . ."

"Isn't there a way," he began cautiously, "you could *give* the pregnancy to someone else? . ."

Rendered temporarily speechless, Charlotte sat and stared at him as though his eyes had suddenly morphed into one gigantic orb centered in his forehead.

"What do you mean '*Give* it to someone else,' Sidney?!" she said finally, the very embodiment of bewilderment.

"Don't women have the ability to give their pregnancy to another woman?" he said, not even a hint of humor or malice in his voice. "Some of my colleagues were talking about this very thing just last week . ."

"Your . . '*colleagues*,' as you call them . . they don't happen to live in a comic strip, do they? . ."

"I beg your pardon? . ."

"Because if you or any of your *colleagues* seriously think a woman can *give* a pregnancy to another woman," she continued, "you're living in a world I've never seen or heard of, where fairies and elves make the rules, pigs *fly*—first-class, of course, why would they want it any other way?—and hungry people stand around sucking their thumbs without any rational notion of reality, wondering where their next imaginary meal is coming from! . ."

"Charlotte, these are *congressmen* from the United States of

America I'm talking about here, *not* some group of deranged idiots discussing impossibilities! . . We are educated, literate adults who receive the same scientific information as everyone else and draw conclusions based on the best evidence available . . We are *not* the quacks and whack-os the media claims we are! . ."

"Scientific information?!" she repeated in disbelief. "From *who*? The seven *dwarfs?!* I can't believe I'm having this conversation! . . A woman can*not* give her pregnancy to another—neither can she *loan* her pregnancy to another woman for a week or two—and please tell your . . *colleagues* that *renting* a pregnancy is illegal in every state . . and they should know that! . . after all, aren't these the same*educated* adults who establish your laws? Don't they enact the laws everyone must live with? Good *God!* How on earth do they dress themselves in the morning?! . . And who empties their *napkins?! . ."

"I'm not going to sit here and argue with you over semantics," he said finally, the stress from Ft. Meade an oppressive weight on his frame, arms aching under the blows from the gun. "Upsetting you, of all people, was the last thing on my mind, and I can see I've upset you, so let's start over one day next week, shall we? . . About all I want to know is what you'd like to do about this, Charlotte—you haven't said a single word about what *you* want—and you need to . ."

"Well . . I don't know, really . . I came here thinking this might make you happy, and it's only made you belligerent . . Instead of being supportive you've been combative and suspicious, and that's not the sort of environment I'd want any child of mine to have to endure . . I can say with absolute certainty that the child belongs to you and me, and no one else, and that if you'd prefer a paternity test to establish the undeniable identity of the child's father, you're more than welcome to waste your money . . Your professional career seems oddly inhabited by gnomes and leprechauns, the sort of nuts and flakes best-suited for psychiatric work—but only as the *subjects*, not the experts, of course—and your notions of what women are and are *not* capable of sounds like it comes right out of a script for *Star Trek* or *The Twilight Zone*, not anything from the real world," she said calmly. Rising from her chair unexpectedly, she looked him in the eye and said "Frankly, I wouldn't mind having a daughter or son I could call my own, but I'm not convinced any child being reared in a single-parent household is a good idea . . I was hoping for more than what I got *here*—that much I can tell you unequivocally . ."

Rising from the Yellow Rose at the same time his guest stood up, he said "I'm confused with this entire ordeal, Charlotte . . I want only to feel better than I do now, and I want you to know that you're not in this alone—and that you have my full support no matter what you choose to do . ."

When he walked her to the door she turned and said "I was led to believe that Americans—and especially senators and congressmen—were exceptional people . . but after talking with you, I'm inclined to believe they're nothing more than a pack of ignorant, insignificant *morons* . ." Then she opened the door for herself and departed, leaving him standing alone and slightly forlorn in his office doorway to muse at length about providence, fate, a spectacular evening at Pandora's Box, and the cruelties of human existence.

No one had mentioned a single word about 'alcohol' and 'Thursday evening' in the same breath during or after his Wednesday afternoon adventure at Ft. Meade: not Dr. Kelley, not nurse Amy—not a living soul. "Congressman Villary? . . there's really little future in mixing pain medication and alcohol, even for a larger man like yourself," Dr. Kelley warned him the evening before, "and codeine, being an opiate, tends to dull the senses so, as much as it pains me to say it, I strongly advise you to lay *off* your favorite spirits until the codeine is out of your system . ."

"Why mention it at all?" he'd asked. "What the hell do you care? . ."

"Human nature," the youngster answered, like that was the solution to all life's problems. "I don't trust anyone who's without vice—it runs contrary to the smidgen of experience I have—and you don't smoke—kudos for *that* one—and the fruit of the vine is too damn *sweet* to give-up, so . . for this one night only . . please refrain . ."

But now it was Thursday evening, it had developed into the Borneo-Thursday-from-Hell at work, two or three loose ends had been left uncharacteristically dangling in the breeze, destined to be ripped away to travel an unsteady course to lands beyond if someone wasn't careful, and Sid hadn't taken any codeine in twenty-four hours; all bets were off. It was now time for some serious soul-searching, sans safety net. The afternoon had effortlessly withered away to nothing and, despite his best intentions to accomplish goals set that very morning, the day had ended a miserable failure. However, his staff—Lynch Bohannon notwithstanding—had enjoyed their best day at work in months. The mere sight of Charlotte Tillstrom visiting their office had turned their day upside-down, with but one hardly discernible, unfortunate side-effect: the greater their collective joy, the greater his sense of guilt.

Regina Watts started it, of course. As it was her preference not to use the intercom except very occasionally, the better to

146

deliver personal service to her employer, she entered the inner realm fifteen minutes after her return from lunch, the boss hard at it all the while.

"What else can I say but *Wow!?*" she grinned down at him from the front of his desk.

Comfortably smothered inside the Yellow Rose, he stopped work and glanced up.

"Wow? . ."

"Yes, *Wow*, and *Wow* again! I don't know where you found *her*, but let me be the first in the office to offer my sincere congratulations on a job well-done! . ."

"We're just friends," he said, returning to his work, hoping she'd do the same.

"Yeah, just *friends!*" she chuckled, head nodding at the great denier. "The sort of friend one keeps close-by for the rest of one's *life*—if he's smart! . ."

When he ventured out into the main office, Julie's desk to the right and front, next to the main entry, Carmen's to the right and recessed between Regina's desk to his left and Bohannon's office on the far right, it was more of the same, only not nearly as ostentatious. He'd barely poked his head through the door when he saw Julie poring over her paperwork as usual—except this time she didn't look up to see him outside his office and immediately return to her work. This time she looked up, noticed him peeking out, and promptly dropped her paperwork to sit and stare at him with her "I *love* my boss!" expression of pride and joy, the quintessential happy-camper.

"What?" he said . . though it was easy enough to guess.

"You know *what!* . . and don't stand there and *pretend* you have no idea what I'm talking about! . ." Delivered in a tone of mock-anger, followed by a very quiet, very restrained "Not easy to say who scored best on *that* one . ."

Carmen, who operated as though her very existence depended upon being mistaken for a perpetual-motion machine, sat complacently at her computer, stealing glances at him through her soft brown   eyes, fingers zipping across the keyboard much faster than anyone could keep up with. Only the corners of her mouth betrayed her amusement.

"Well, Carmen? . ."

His communications specialist never pulled her eyes away from the keyboard for longer than a half-second, sighing heavily as she spoke over the general hum of the office: "De gustibus non disputandum *est!* . ."

"And *what*, prithee, does that translate-to in west Texas-yahoo lingo, my dear? . ."

"It means there's really no explaining someone's personal taste, that it's not worth arguing about," she explained, her expression unchanged as she spoke, until the hint of her smile gave way to a more favorable approval. " . . But I must say . . she is clearly—*clearly*—a cut-*above*, and we are all pleased and very proud of you . ."

Sure, they liked her; of *course*, they liked her! But what of the ones who really *counted*: what would Cas Turley think? He'd been married and divorced and seemed quite content being on his own, especially when he was in Europe: in Germany, Italy, and France he spent time with women who would drop whatever they happened to be doing when he called, just to spend time with him. Lynch Bohannon? As comfortable with the guys as he was with his wife, he loved Theresa, and she was a strong, supportive female—but she knew when to disappear and never sought the limelight. Of course, Dow Pettigrew had always believed Sid's bachelor status was a natural draw for a number of reasons, though his

Velma was a wagon-load of fun and even more devious and sneaky than Dow, if that was possible. And what of L.W. Shaw? Yes, he was married but, except for his parents, no one Sid knew had ever laid eyes on her, much less received her counsel. As the same bleak scenarios repeatedly raced through his mind, his favorite glass began the evening at home with bourbon and water on ice, then bourbon and water *only* a few glassfuls later, ultimately digressing to bourbon alone. And wasn't that the way it always ended-up, for Chrissakes? Was there no way *out?*

If Charlotte were to abort our child, thought he, I'd no longer have to worry about the various and sundry duties of a father, which would for years and years detract my time and energy from where it rightly belongs: my *work*. This would be fine, *except that* . . if anyone discovered it had been my child and I knew and approved of the medical procedure, it would make the crucifixion of Jesus Christ look like a round of golf. Danger level? Incredibly high, so forget it! . . Man, do I need a drink!

If she carried the child to full term, gave birth, but decided she wanted no part of me offering any kind of assistance, save perhaps monetary, that would allow me to focus on my work with virtually no external pressures. This would be fine, *except that* . . if anyone discovered it was my child and asked why I took no responsibility—even if I claimed the mother had requested I stay away—the publicity would be devastating. Danger level? Exorbitantly high, so forget it! . . I have *got* to find myself a drink!

If I married her and she brought the child to full term and subsequent delivery, my life as a congressman would be split between my duties as a father and my ultimate duties to my many loyal constituents. This would be fine, *except that* . . my effectiveness as a conservative, right-minded congressman would take an unavoidable hit in the kisser, my attention-span reduced to tapioca-mush, my allegiances skewered like a smoked sausage. Danger level? Unbelievably high, so forget it! . . Holy *shit*, what do I have to do to get a *drink?!*

Fixing himself a light zombie, sipping slowly as he meandered from room to room in the rental house, the stereo blaring *"Luckenbach, Texas"* loud enough to be heard a few miles south of the Rio Grande, it seemed crystal clear that, barring some unforeseen miracle, his congressional career was beginning to unravel. *Why* seemed unimportant. The Computer Age, he reckoned, had certainly helped bring about his professional demise: were it not for the fact that someone hopelessly wedged into a one-and-a-half-floor elevator in eastern Absurdistan could, upon reaching full hopelessness, die from blunt-force trauma on impact after mindlessly jumping fourteen feet to his death — the *real* kicker being that his only friend in the world, Namirufskiposs, caught the suicide in full color and immediately launched it viral — there remained the remote possibility that a congressman-induced pregnancy could remain what it was and should ever be: a private matter. Failing the "but-for" test was the surest signal of doom known to mankind, so what chance did anyone in a position of responsibility really have of keeping a secret child a secret? Two-thirds the way through his cocktail he detected the foulest-tasting, most hideously-annoying substance he'd ever encountered and, upon closer inspection, determined that his tongue was touching the floor, inadvertently sampling his maid's pine-based floor cleaner. Pulling himself together, he crawled to his sofa, carefully placed his head on a cushion and opened his private box containing others' business cards. Not finding a name or address that made any sense — and this after a fastidious search revealed nothing he considered of any real value—he lurched to the other side of the coffee table, opened the drawer on all fours and with considerable difficulty liberated the phone book from its cavernous prison. Lucidity, like competence, seemed a fleeting commodity.

"P-H-Y," he enunciated unsteadily, "got to find P-H-Y . ."

Sliding his fingers through a half-inch of yellow pages before stopping to look, he grabbed a second half-inch and stopped again, then howled his displeasure as he turned the pages the other direction, stopping every few pages until he stumbled across the letter "P." Laughing nervously at his hard-won triumph, his head hit the yellow pages in the 'Pawnbrokers' section and flopped right, the rest of his body quickly following.

VIII.

The offices of Dr. Edison Milner and Dr. Basia Lee Holcomb, located on the fifteenth floor in the fashionably upscale Columbia Heights Professional Building in Georgetown, reminded the weary congressman of his pediatrician's malodorous digs from thirty-something years before: gloomy without trying to be, unintentionally sterile in its décor, the perfect sort of place to establish an outlet for creative anachronisms. The magazines, on the other hand, were qualitatively outstanding, as the June 22 editions of <u>The New Yorker</u>, <u>Time</u>, and <u>Newsweek</u>, as well as recent editions of <u>Psychology Today</u>, <u>Jungian</u>, and <u>Mindful Pleasures</u> lay about, waiting for a taker. Sid thought it the quietest waiting room he'd ever seen; the patients sitting about, perhaps more keenly aware of their surroundings than in most doctor's offices, were likewise silent. He got the distinct impression that all of them—each and every one—felt grateful to be there, troubled yet hopeful, admittedly confused, but well on the road to recovery. He hoped so. No outward manifestations of leprosy or lupus here: all the maledictions surrounding him today were the more or less 'invisible' type, subject to adjustment over an extended period of time—or so he'd been told. His fellow patients seemed an austere if interesting collection, too. Another gentleman, perhaps ten years older than he, with a shrewdly-thin mustache and premature silver hair, busied himself with a hand-held computer, though Sid couldn't be sure of the make and model. A rather elegant woman dressed in a stylish, dark-red outfit—he guessed her at about his age and would have been astounded to discover she was pushing seventy-five—enjoyed perusing a month-old copy of <u>Cosmo</u>, pausing to smirk at an article or cartoon every now and then. The youngest present, a young man of perhaps twenty-five, chose to humor himself by reading absolutely nothing, opting to shift his gaze left and right through slit-thin eyes—this when he wasn't chuckling at something above him on the wall to his front-left, which to anyone who happened to look was a print of a very colorful, shade-rich Monet. And, there was the redhead: with a heaviness around her eyes so mournful-looking it felt strangely painful to look directly at her, her thirty years carried as though they were sixty, she was nonetheless strikingly handsome, her lofty cheekbones and thick, voluptuous lips salvaging the mute savagery of her myopic orbs, the rest of her looking more thirty-ish than sixty-ish.

Realizing he was likely low man on the office totem pole, Villary grabbed a sports mag, gave the assembled field a quick once-over—are any of you lovely people by any *chance* from the great state of Texas?—and settled into a chair to wait his turn. One by one the others disappeared: the lady in the dark-red reading <u>Cosmo</u> first, followed by the young man with the shifty eyes. Before the redhead was called-in, two more patients arrived for their sessions. When they called Sid for his initial meeting with Dr. Milner all four had gone, the elder gent disappearing through the door on the right barely five minutes before.

"I'm Edison Milner," he introduced himself, and he shook hands with the congressman. Rather tall and about Sid's age, he combed his light-brown hair straight back, with mustache and sideburns and, on the whole, seemed appropriately distinguished-looking. When they entered the doctor's inner sanctum, a light-filled, non-threatening office of mostly open space adorned with only a desk and chair, another chair and matching couch in front, and the doctor indicated the chaise for his guest, Sid hesitated and searched for another seat.

"First time on the couch?" said Dr. Milner.

"No . . I have one at home, too . ."

"I'm sorry," laughed Milner, "I think you might've misunderstood me . . It's an old-enough phrase, I suppose . . I was just asking if this is your first time with an analyst? . ."

Sid slowly took his seat on the couch, nodding that it was. The mounted prints resembled the one in the waiting room — all color, light, and shade, a la *Monsieur Claude*, though Villary couldn't have identified the artist had his life depended on it. Dr. Milner, busying himself with pen and notepad, noticed his patient's attention riveted to the prints.

"I've found Monet's works have a calming effect on most folks," he explained without looking up, "and calm and quiet is how we like it here, you see . . let's us concentrate on our work . . I'm convinced that, were I to display a print of <u>Guernica</u> instead, some of my patients might become airborne—you know, through the windows?—and from the fifteenth floor the landing might be a bit . . *rough*—and that just wouldn't do at all, would it? . ."

"No, I suppose not," agreed Sid, though he wasn't quite sure if the doctor was serious or not. Too nervous to relax by a hefty margin, he eyed the couch's pillowed end suspiciously, the notion that his first visit might very well be either his *last*, or that the idea of calling for the appointment in the first place had been a horrible miscalculation. But, right or wrong, there he was, a fish summarily ejected from the pond, seeking strength and courage. Not blessed with the best eyesight, he

154

could only see the school names on the professional placards adorning the wall behind the desk, the adjoining signatures and smaller print a troublesome blur: 'Cornell University,' 'The University of Oregon,' and 'University of Pennsylvania,' schools and locations he found uninteresting, at best. "Doctor? . . do you know who I *am*? . ."

"I most certainly *do* . . you're my newest patient, Mr. Villary—has kind of a *French* ring to it, eh?—and, you are also a fairly-well-known member of the House of Representatives from the state of . . *Oklahoma*, I believe? . ."

"*Texas!*" Sid barked, cringing twice in a span of a few seconds, first at the sound of 'French,' then again at 'Oklahoma.' "I'm a proud member of the conservative delegation from the Lone Star state . . "

"Yes . . well . . would you mind very much telling me how you happened to get my name and number? . . as opposed to someone *else's*? . . I'm hardly the lone psychiatrist in this area, I can assure you, so I always inquire as to whether someone has recommended me . . Is that the case? . ."

Villary swallowed hard, his throat dry, head still a little out of kilter from the night before when he'd tried to drain the Potomac River of its entire contents, finally saying "When I awoke this morning on my living room *floor* . . I turned to the page marked 'Psychiatrists' in the yellow pages, closed my thundering eyes and poked my finger onto the left page—and it was *your* name I hit . Pretty scientific, huh? . ."

"Well-done! . .Well-done, indeed! . . Alright then, why don't you stretch out on the couch there—you'll find it's really *very* comfortable—and catch me up on events in your life . ."

"Events in my life?!" cried Villary, on the defensive before the doctor had a chance to take his seat. "Why the hell do you want me to tell you about events in my not-so-great-life, for

Chrissakes?! . . .Isn't it bad enough that I'm *here*, and that my life is disintegrating right in front of me, that I feel cornered and betrayed—that my *life*, as I know it, will soon be coming to an *end!?*—is that not enough to suit you, *doc-tor?* . ."

Without saying a word Dr. Milner walked to his desk, opened the top right drawer and pulled-out a plastic pill-bottle, removed a small, round tablet before replacing it inside the drawer, then disappeared through a door in the rear of his office, re-emerging moments later with a bottle of water. He offered them to Sidney H. Villary, congressman, without a word.

"What's this?" he said, still sitting on the couch.

"It's called 'diazepam,' and it'll help you calm down a little so you can tell me what's putting so much pressure on you . . because unless you accept the fact that I'm here to *help* you, you're not about to make even an inch of progress . . Not a very *trusting* soul, are you? . . Frankly, Mr. Villary, you're a bundle of nerves, you're suspicious of me and you don't even *know* me, it sounds like you had the kind of Thursday evening best reserved for a college frat-party on game-day, and you sit here agitated as a washing machine and tell me your life is *over?* . . Now . . you can either take this, relax a little and tell me what's bothering you, or you can continue to feel the way you feel now—so take this and we'll get *started*, okay? . ."

Sid reluctantly obeyed, but didn't move a muscle from his sitting position: lying flat on his back in the presence of a complete stranger in an unfamiliar setting for dubious purposes had never been part of his repertoire. Taking pills wasn't high on his list of priorities either.

"Do I *have* to lie down?" he said, ever the suspicious malcontent. "I'd rather stay sitting up, if you don't mind . ."

"Suit yourself . . I just want you comfortable so you might

156

speak more easily . ." The doctor took his seat adjacent to the couch, an expensive pen in his right hand, notebook in his lap. "You'll find there's really not much you *have* to do while you're here, congressman—it's *your* money . ."

"I'm dying to know something, doctor—and it has nothing to do with the reason I'm here . ."

"What's that? . ."

"Are you named after the guy with the light bulb? . ."

"Actually, *no* . . my parents named me after a rock group popular at the time of my birth—one of their favorites, obviously—and for as long as I can remember I've been grateful it wasn't something that sounded completely idiotic," he said with a hint of a smile. "My older brother is named after my father—Crassus Jacob Milner, Jr.--and I'm even *more* grateful he got stuck with it instead of me . . Do you come from a large family? . ."

"No, I'm an only child," said the new patient, "named after my father's younger brother, Sidney, who died in the crash of a navy fighter jet, and my grandfather on my mother's side, Hunt Lawrence Stevens, who died fairly young before I had a chance to know him . . I've always felt as though my parents should have had at least one more child, you know? . . just a brother or sister to play with, although there were always friends and neighbors around aplenty—yeah, I was lucky in that regard . . still, had there been a second child . . maybe they could've taken some of their focus off me, even if it was for just a little while . . no such luck, though . ."

"Sounds like that's caused problems for you, congressman . . has it? . ."

"Nothing I couldn't manage . . can't say I had a horrible childhood, 'cause I didn't . . it's just that there's this enormous importance about the Villary *name*—my Uncle Sid died before

157

he could settle down and raise a family, which left my dad and his two sisters—so now I'm the only male with the family name, and that's put a lot o' pressure on me . . My folks think producing a male heir is the single most pressing issue our country faces today, just ahead of national security, military spending, and the deficit, and my turning forty—which I erroneously believed would be cause for a grand celebration— turned into an occasion for family grieving because I still hadn't had the good sense to get married and have kids! . . I know what I'm about to tell you may sound utterly ridiculous, but if you were to approach any member of my extended family—*not* just my mom and dad, mind you—cousins, aunts, uncles, *anybody!*—and ask them point-blank what they think of their most famous family member, do you think a single damned *one* of them would mention the fact that I'm a member of congress? . . or that I've performed more personal favors than I can *remember?* . . or mention the fact that I personally lobbied for cuts in federal funding for abortions? . . Do you think any of them would mention any of *those?* . . No, not a snowball's chance in hell! What you'd hear is something along the lines of . . '*Who?* . . Sidney? . . ah, there's a good lad, I suppose—although he *has* let the family down where it really *matters!*' . . At this point, doctor, anything less than a wife and four kids by next Christmas is a disaster of *epic* proportions! . . and the worst part of it, Dr. Milner? . . the worst part of it is the fact that they neither understand what I'm up against here in Washington, nor do they care *a rat's ass!* . . I see it every day in my work, every *damned* day, and I don't want to be put into a situation like that, and no one seems to give a good *goddamn* that I'm at least *trying* to do the job I was elected to *do! . ."*

"Can you explain to me, congressman, exactly *what* it is you see in your work every day? . ."

158

Sid opened his mouth to answer but was sidetracked by the sight of Dr. Milner sitting in his chair—a nice, upholstered number, very comfortable-looking, not the equal of the Yellow Rose by a long shot, but nice, nonetheless—with his shoes *off*, cast aside like so much chaff, and he sat happily sock-footed to enable the occasional massaging of the feet by means of a modified cross-country skiing motion, fabric-to-fabric, socks-to-carpet. He hadn't made a sound doing it. Dr. Milner observed himself being observed at ground level by his curious patient.

"It really helps when your feet are as flat as mine," he explained.

"Do you mind if I take my shoes off and lie down? . . I've really had an *extremely* stressful week and I think it's starting to catch up to me? . ."

"I'm surprised I didn't think of that . . when you feel like you're ready to talk about it . . . tell me what it is you see every day in your work that bothers you so . ."

"It's what everyone *else* has to contend with—everyone except *me*, is what I mean to say—and it infuriates me because it affects my output, and I don't appreciate it one bit," he began once more, one loafer slipped off by the tip of the other before it, too, fell to the carpet. Swinging his legs up to rest on the couch, his head fell comfortably onto the pillow at the other end, his eyes closing in the sweet solace the soothing texture of the couch provided. Keeping them shut he remained motionless for almost two full minutes before they popped open again to scan the room for signs anything had changed during his brief respite. Once satisfied everything was as it should be, he continued. "You need to understand how very difficult it is to discuss important matters with a colleague whose mind is occupied by thoughts of what he has

159

to *buy* on his way home from work, or what his wife is likely to think if her biggest pet peeve is ignored, or where they have to go tonight and what time they're supposed to be there and why it's so important to make an appearance—there was a fellow member of the Foreign Relations Committee who couldn't make up his mind *what* to bring home for dinner one night—why dinner became *his* responsibility is anyone's guess, but that's another story—and when I suggested rotisserie chicken as one reasonably healthy, yet delicious alternative, you know what he told me? . . 'Lord, I can't bring *chicken* home—my mother-in-law would *kill* me!' . . like grilled chicken had suddenly turned into arsenic, you know? . . I couldn't believe he had to organize dinner by process-of-elimination, for one thing, and to think he was forced to consider how his *mother-in-law* might react were he to commit the mortal sin of bringing home something other than rib-eyes or T-bones, or whatever the hell it is she likes? . . I say to *hell* with his mother-in-law!—his wife, too, if she's cut from the same cloth!—oh, and he couldn't bring chicken home because it was too *ethnic*—I don't even know what the hell that *means*, for Chrissakes! How can a grilled chicken be too ethnic? . . Do chickens have different *nationalities* now, or some shit?! . . Must our country become embroiled in the battle of the *hens?!* . . How the hell are we supposed to get anything *done* if we're constantly barraged by petty-ass *bullshit* we have no control over? . . How can a member of the Congress of the United States ever get anything accomplished if he's consumed about *where* to spend the weekend doing *what* with *whom?* . . And *this* is how my parents want me to live, Dr. Milner: they want me to be just as *inefficient* as everyone else—'just settle down with a wife and kids, Sidney, that's *all!'*—and I *don't* want to do it! . .'

160

"And another thing . . they think it's perfectly alright to introduce me to all manner of single women every time I go home—like there are *zero* single women in D.C.?—and now I'm right in the middle of kicking-off my re-election campaign, which means I'll be as busy as a liberal prostitute at a Communist Porno Convention until the votes are in and counted, okay? . . and what are *their* plans for me when I return home next Thursday? . . My dear mother has already got me paired-off with the daughter of the town *vixen*, I'm afraid, because I'm not *really* running for re-election . . you see, my visit home, in her eyes, is nothing more than a social event designed to run as many women as possible in front of me in the hope I'll become weak and abysmally domestic in some kind of bizarre, overnight-transformation ritual! . . I'll fall head-over-heels in love with some west Texas gal, utterly bent on giving my mother just as many grandchildren as she wants—ten or twenty would do *nicely*—and live happily ever after in some kind of Washington, D.C. fantasy-land of mom's creation, thank you *so* much! . . Doctor? . . do you have any notion of what I *dream* about from time to time? . ."

"What's that? . ."

"I return home in a wheelchair, and I'm being pushed through the airport by someone I've hired to dress-up in a doctor's white surgical smock . . my mother and father are there to meet me, of course, and just before they come into range I carefully place an ice bag—the hospital variety, naturally, because I don't want to have to do this *again*—the ice bag is in my lap, okay? . . And I begin moaning this quiet, subdued, *incessant* dirge of woe because, as I relate the horror-story to my folks, it very slowly dawns on them that what has happened to their little forty-year-old boy is called a *vasectomy*, and there were complications no one could've *foreseen* because

161

of the unusual *bulk* of the affected parts, and that I'm black-and-blue and in unimaginable pain as a result of the procedure which has, *by the way*, left me completely sterile with *no* chance of reversal, and it shouldn't even happen to a *dog*, much less a conservative congressman from the great state of Texas who, after all, was only trying to do his part *not* to over-populate the world with drape-apes, a sacrifice like no other . . And the priceless expressions on their faces when I give them the good news that, not only have they never *had* grandchildren, but never *will!* . . ah, but then I wake-up and realize that not only would I never do such a horrendous thing to myself *or* them, I haven't even managed to say why I'm not suing for malpractice when anyone else *would* . . So it amounts to an empty threat, you see, for my brain still hasn't figured-out how to end it successfully—for *me*, that is—maybe marry and have a flock of kids . . but only *after they're gone!* . .'

"Can you see how terribly unfair it is for them to expect me, their *only* child, to marry and have a veritable *houseful* of kids—their grandchildren, naturally—after they, in their infinite wisdom, stopped at one and *only* one? . . though there was never any problem with normal concerns, like money or home? . . I mean, how selfish is *that?!* . . To tell you the truth, a part of me wants to get married and have about, oh, four children—all *girls*, just to spite them *and* ruin any chance of continuation of the name, at which point I can rightfully say 'Well, mom and dad . . I've given it that old college try four separate times and all I have to show for it is, oh, four future *weddings* . . sorry about that!' . . I simply don't think it's fair for them to expect me to do something they themselves were irrevocably *opposed* to, and since I first won my seat in the House the pressure has steadily mounted to a fever-pitch. Once I was here, their rationale became '*Son?* . . You're making plenty of money now—more than enough to support a wife and family—why not go ahead and get married, then settle down with a family?' . . Well, excuse the hell out of me, but the last time I looked men and women were getting married because they fell in love first—*then* decided to raise a family when they thought the time was right—and maybe I'm just terribly old-fashioned, but that seems like a pretty good plan . . Besides, if the only consideration is cash, what kept *them* from having more children? . . It's painful for me to admit to something else here, and that's the fact that my mother keeps throwing single, highly-available, and typically *lovely* women in my path because I once told her that, even though I'd known and dated literally *dozens* of women in college and beyond, I hadn't met the *right* one yet so, in a way, her habit of introducing me to women is my fault—so much so, in fact, that I've toyed with the idea of finding a regular girlfriend I can introduce to the folks, spend some time with and have a few laughs—but not be any more serious about than a high-school chum. The only thing keeping me from actually doing this is the certain knowledge that, the longer I know this as-yet *nebulous* woman and the better we get to know each other, the more *time* I'll end-up spending with her which, in turn, takes my focus away from where it needs to be, the same as a *wife* would, so I'm right back where I started! . .'

"Not too long ago they thought they had me, that their most recent and well-thought-out reason for my settling-down was not only the '*common sense*' approach, but was also virtually impossible to disprove—and this time it was my *father* who approached me, which is rare! . . 'You know, son,' he said, 'if you keep holding out for the *perfect* woman, you'll never find her because she doesn't exist. I love your mother with all my heart, and always will, but if we hadn't met I'm sure I

163

would've found someone else.' And you know something? . . when he told me that, I knew my answer would break their hearts. I've *never* looked for the perfect woman . . truth be told, I personally believe there are dozens, maybe *hundreds* of women out there I could be happy with, and I just haven't met her. It seems to me the notion that everyone has their one and only true love is simply a *crock* . . If that were true, nobody would ever marry because it's illogical to assume you'd ever run into your ideal mate—your chances would be *slim* and *none* . . of course, they *were* heartbroken when I told them, just like I knew they *would* be, and I hope you don't misunderstand me when I say I haven't met the right one. I've met several women I liked *very* much—just none I wanted to marry, that's all . ."

"What would you say if I suggested that you secretly *loathe* your parents because they were too selfish to give you a brother or sister?" said Dr. Milner. "It's the rare human being who feels no resentment towards a mother and father for *something*, you know—like us, they make mistakes, just like their parents made mistakes, and *their* parents before *them*. How would you describe your relationship with them in one word? . ."

After considering his answer for the larger part of a full minute, eyes narrowed to more easily formulate an honest reply, he finally said *"Respectful* . ."

"Respectful?! . . I hope you don't mind my saying so, but that strikes me as something of a surprise. Would you mind very much explaining why you chose that particular expression?   ."
"No, not at all. I say it because it's *true* . . sure, we have our ups and downs—maybe even more *downs* than *ups*—but I love them dearly . . Would I have been happier with a sibling or

two? Yes, probably, but I realized a long, *long* time ago that it wasn't my call, which leaves me pretty much in the middle of nowhere . . And I *do* respect them—for all they are and for all they've done for me, which is a great deal . . I never wanted for *anything*. I always had not only what I needed, but what my egocentric little heart *thought* I wanted to make me happy which, more often than not, didn't measure-up . . Whenever I hear someone tell someone *else* how happy he or she will make the other one, I cringe with fear and physically shudder at the actual *impossibility* of such a promise! . . I could be dead *wrong* concerning what I'm about to tell you—it sure wouldn't be the *first* time I was wrong about something!—but it occurs to me that people are simply incapable of making anyone or anything *happy*, regardless of how hard they try—about the best we can hope for is that we find someone who is *already* happy, then figure-out a way *not* to ruin it for them . . Dr. Milner, I know a couple who met in college in Austin, fell madly in love almost from the first moment they met, and got married when he graduated a year ahead of her and, good *lord*, were they *crazy* about each other! Every aspect of their relationship—and I mean *everything!*—was almost too good to be true: their respective outlooks on life, two-as-*one* in the eyes of their lord and savior, good families on either side, promising careers in law and nursing—even volcanic sex that was mutually satisfying and enjoyable—the perfect union of two lovely people—or so it would seem . . but it was not to be. Over a period of months and years she came to realize that, no matter how hard she tried to please him, whether it was food, or the house, or sex, or whatever, he was *never* happy, and when she finally confronted him about her worst fears he was honest enough to admit that he'd been unhappy for as long as he could remember, that he was dissatisfied and unhappy by

165

nature, and that nothing was likely to change him . . So it would seem that perhaps he made *her* happy for a while, but she couldn't return the favor due to an inherent weakness on his part, and it's not a question of whose *fault* it might have been . . *'fault'* had nothing to do with it, it's just the way things played-out . . And *yes*, I respect my parents because they've always been there for each other *and* me . . It doesn't mean they're perfect, or that we don't have our differences—given half the chance, they can be rather infuriating, at times—but seeing how devoted they are to one another gives me hope. You see, Dr. Milner, despite my claims to the contrary, if I meet the right girl, I'll gladly marry her and pray for the best . . and she'll need to know that I take my work seriously, and that when I need to be gone to take care of work-related concerns, I won't be around much until it's finished, and that's just the way it is . . Were you to ask my mom and dad why I'm not married yet, I'd give odds they'd claim it was me attempting to get even with them for forcing a life of loneliness on me, but it's not true . . I've lived alone in Herndon for over five years now, and haven't had so much as a roommate for almost fifteen years . . I enjoy my solitude—but I entertain some, too, and go out with friends—and, believe it or *not*, occasionally I enjoy female companionship . ."

"In other words," said Dr. Milner, translating what he heard so that both might accept what had been spoken, "you're not in this to punish your mother and father at all. Rather, in terms of seeking-out and finding your significant-other, you lack the time, the drive and, for lack of better terminology, the *luck* one sometimes deems necessary to achieve such a tricky arrangement . . Am I close? . ."

"I think that describes my situation nicely . . . "

"Your observations about human behavior—specifically

166

that, regardless of what people think they're capable of doing for others, promises of that nature tend to remain *unfulfilled*—reveal an insight I'd have thought peculiar in a man such as yourself—but then, I suppose, a sitting congressman would do *well* to nurture the ability to 'read between the lines,' so to speak—maybe he can remain a congressman a little *longer* that way. I'm only hypothesizing, of course, but I'm betting this isn't your first term in the House . ."

"No, my third," said a relaxed, restful Sidney Villary, his agitation somewhat smoothed-out now, "and I'd like to continue what I've started—at least for another term or two . ."

"Sure you would . . but you have another election to win so, for better or worse, your return to Texas next week is critical. A good visit home could turn out to be really *helpful*, no doubt . . but you said your mother has already set the wheels in motion for a bit of socializing, so maybe you're a bit apprehensive about how much you can get accomplished in the time you're there—*especially* if you have to busy yourself with matters inherently distracting . . Are you, in fact, worried? . ."

"I'm worried about a multitude of challenges, Dr. Milner . . the first and most pressing of which is the fact that I have not one, but *two* elections to win before I can return to my seat in congress . . I'm being challenged from the right by someone I once believed was my friend and supporter, who now believes he should be in Washington instead of me . . If I win that round I'll still be challenged by a left-wing, communistic Hispanic woman hell-bent on my removal from office so that the liberal traitors in this country can make Mexico the fifty-*first* state! . . then the government can pay for abortions in Mexico City, the people on welfare can have enchiladas anytime they like, and we can disband the military to put our

167

liberal citizens on the 'honor' system—in *Guadalajara!* . . But I'm here to make sure *none* of that happens, you know? . ."

"Then I take it you're not overly-concerned with women at present, or satisfying your parents' desire to provide them with grandchildren anytime soon? . ."

"Actually," Sid admitted ruefully, "that's not entirely, one-hundred-percent *true*, as fate would have it—at least, not as true as I'd like it to be . ."

"*Which* part—giving them grand-kids, or concerning yourself with women? . ."

Before he could answer, the room's serene tranquility was interrupted by the singular, soft chiming of a bell emanating from the direction of the window. Peering round to discover the source of the music coming from behind him, he saw the same nondescript office, spare and unassuming in its simplicity, except that now he saw a small green light glowing atop a contraption sitting on the desk. Only four or five inches in height and rather odd-looking, the contraption appeared to be about three inches wide at the base, narrowing to no more than two inches at top, with a series of silvery-metal bars perhaps a third of an inch wide mounted in diminishing lengths, bottom-to-top, roughly fourteen or fifteen in number, to a brown wooden frame in a stair-step pattern. For reasons he couldn't quite fathom, save the fact that his strength had waned during and after the ordeal at Ft. Meade and hadn't been fully restored yet, he hadn't noticed the curious device sitting atop the doctor's desk until now. He had no idea what it was.

"A gift from my wife," smiled Dr. Milner, the puzzled expression on his patient's face too obvious to ignore. "She, like myself, has a soft-spot for miniature instruments and stumbled across this charming little glockenspiel-timer in a little shop down close to Roanoke . . It comes in very handy, as it turns out, because occasionally I'll lose track of time elapsed, lost in the particulars of a patient's situation . . so we've just been informed your initial visiting period has expired. I want to apologize for the rather *abbreviated* visit this time—I didn't actually have any spare office hours today, but my appointments lady said you sounded so out-of-kilter she thought it best to at least have you come in for what we call the *introductory* session—and I'm glad you *did*, congressman Villary. So feel free to answer that last question before we call a halt to today's proceedings and, *if* you're inclined to, schedule you for another visit—at *your* convenience, of course . . I realize how incredibly busy you must be in the best of times, but with an election or two in the offing and your visit home, I'm sure that squeezes you somewhat . .Would you care to return for a second visit? . ."

"Yes, I think I *would*," he said almost without thinking, his mind drifting away to the business so near at hand, the approaching campaign and travel, the challenges he had to face directly to avoid the humiliation of electoral defeat. There would be other challenges, as well: if there was an advantage to having a personal challenge in league with a political threat, he hadn't found it yet. And what of Miss Tillstrom? What would he do? What *could* he do? To think that problem would somehow take care of itself was a fool's errand: how had something so wonderful become so horrendous? "Dr. Milner? . . we need to meet again, I'm afraid . . There are a number of issues we need to discuss at length . . I need to focus on the primary election back home, but there are situations here in D.C. that could conceivably turn into obstacles, and that's the very last thing I need right now . ."

"Would you like to come back for another session when you

return from home, or sooner? . ."

"Sooner, *please* . . this really can't wait two weeks . ."

"Okay," said Dr. Milner, still busy scribbling on his notepad. With a few taps of his finger his next week's appointments magically appeared on his new iPad. "Since you're flying out on Thursday the third, just ask Gloria to have you back in here Wednesday afternoon at three for a full session, if that doesn't create a conflict with your scheduling, and we'll see what we can do for you then . ."

Rising from the couch unexpectedly refreshed, Sidney H. Villary, third-term congressman from west Texas, shook hands with his new analyst and, gearing-up for the political fight of his young career, half-jokingly said "If you happen to know *anyone* from my district in the Lone Star state—anyone at *all*—please tell them their congressman *loves* them, will work *hard* for them . . and would very much appreciate their *vote* . ."

The sweet prospect of a newly-arrived weekend in northern Virginia was vastly improved by the acquisition of a fresh bottle of bourbon, preferably one and a half liter's worth or larger, and in this there existed no room for discussion. It was just a basic *truth*, like the greatness of Texas, the evil of liberals, and the courage of conservatism. Besides, his arms still ached—what better way to erase the discomfort than by imbibing some liquid Novocaine? Three long weeks would pass before he spent another full weekend in the nation's capital: better to make the most of it. An impromptu stop at a Falls Church convenience store netted him a six-pack of Guinness, though if someone asked him why he'd bought it he would have been at a complete loss to explain it. He didn't drink stout and didn't know anyone who *did*. The first cocktail, the bourbon, ice, and water mixed perfectly before his suit-coat came off, proved medicinal: the residual ache in his upper arms melted away, the crick in his neck from a night spent passed-out on the living-room carpet loosened its iron-grip on his nape, and the rumbling in his alcohol-tempered stomach subsided to a bearable murmur. Ordering-out steak and potato, his still-lucid thoughts turned to conditions back home: even as he enjoyed the ninety-proof elixir, he knew Dow Pettigrew was busy alleviating the possibility of any last-minute surprises the upstart, traitorous Warrington camp might be brewing. There was a solid sense of security in having such a capable, dedicated team surrounding him, safely shielding him from all political woes past and present. Worry? That solved nothing and helped even less; at length he decided his fretting and anxiety was baseless, that everything was rolling along just *fine*.

A few minutes after eight, the strip-sirloin and 'loaded' baked potato nestled inside his now-contented belly, the local and national news played-out on the giant screen in fair and balanced fashion, the familiar sound of Mozart's Symphony Number 40 in G-minor—known to Sid only as his cellphone ringing—erupted inside his shirt pocket. His face lit-up when he saw the number: *ah, Mister Pettigrew,* right on time!

"Lay it on me, baby, and don't leave out a *thing!* . ."

"I have some interesting news, boss . ."

"Is it extremely interesting . . or just moderately interesting? . ."

"Well, truth be told, I'm not *sure* which," admitted Dow, "but it's something I just got wind of this morning, and I wish I could say I understand it and know why they did it, but I don't . . *However,* I've got my usual spies checking-up on the details, such as they are, and they've promised me something no later than midnight, so I'll know something *definitive* by

171

then, but until that time let me just say that there's been a change-in-plans for the Warrington campaign television commercial *blitz*—originally scheduled for this coming Monday or Tuesday evening . ."

Enjoying this tidbit of information—truth or gossip, it didn't matter—Villary said "I don't suppose you're about to tell me we got galactically-*lucky* . . and that Denny and his minions had to cancel the commercials due to lack of funds, or something equally *righteous? . .*"

"No, they didn't *cancel* . . but they did *postpone* the supposed slaughter until Thursday evening, July third—I just don't know why . ."

"The day I get home, huh? . . *well* . . that is interesting but, like you, I don't understand it . . I have to wonder if there's some kind of connection, though . . some ulterior motive on their part—like maybe waiting until I'm actually inside Texas to begin their lies, half-truths, and innuendo in an attempt to embarrass me . . any thoughts along those lines? . ."

"I don't know what in hell it would be, if *that's* what they're after," said Pettigrew. "You've been very careful to make sure your life in Washington is an open book to the folks back home, Sid, and west Texans *like* the fact that you do that! . . Not only do you publish a monthly newsletter of events in the nation's capital, but your office puts it online for everyone to see at their leisure—so *nobody* can accuse you of not communicating with your constituents—I wish they'd try some underhanded *shit* like that, just so we could kick 'em in the ass! . ."

"What about my trip to eastern Europe in September? . . hear anything? . ."

"Everybody seems to know you're going . . they're just not exactly sure *why*, is all . . There seems to be some question as to the specific purposes of the trip, which turns out to be something of a double-edged sword . . on the one hand, when the suggestion is made that you're going over to see who qualifies for more *financial* assistance, all we get is sour faces . . But when we suggest the trip is more concerned with military hardware sales and maintenance packages to fight the Commie *threat* . . all we see is *smiles!*—and lots of 'em, at that! . ."

"Commie threat?!" Sid repeated, a bit confused. "*What* Commie threat?! . . There *is* no 'Commie' threat—there hasn't been one in over twenty years! . ."

"I know, I *know* . . but everybody knows what a bunch of atheistic *bastards* the Commies are—they simply do *not* believe in Jesus Christ, so they are the *enemy*—*and*, that's what we're selling, so this is a visit to those countries that hate the Commie *hordes* and want to buy weaponry to *kill* the sons-of-bitches!—the fact that there's money to be made from weapons systems is totally irrelevant—we're killing Commies for *Christ*, and that, my friend, is selling like *hotcakes!* . ."

"So do we straighten 'em out as to our real purposes, or leave 'em guessing? . ."

"What better opportunity to settle matters once and for all than while you're *home*, Sid? . . and what better source to hear it from than the *man* himself?—the campaign is the perfect chance to establish, re-establish, and re-establish *again* . . exactly what you stand for, what you would like to see happen, and what you will *make* happen while in D.C. . ."

"Still picking me up at Lubbock International in the after, right? . ."

"Don't worry, I'll be there—and when I find out what this TV-commercial deal is all about, I'll get back to you . . you want your folks at the airport? . ."

173

"You do, and that'll be the *last* thing you ever do for me . ."

"*Right!* . . Out here!—oh, and Velma says she can't wait to see you!"

For ten minutes he sat in the minor comfort of his living room recliner—it was *minor* comfort as compared to the Yellow Rose—meditating on the significance of his visit to west Texas, what he needed to achieve while inside its friendly borders, who he *needed* to see as opposed to who he *wanted* to see—they were almost never the same—and the more his plans solidified, the more convinced he became that the strategy worked through by his stalwart lieutenants—Cas, D.P., Lynch and, most of all, L.W. Shaw—was the correct path to follow, the more his thoughts turned to Charlotte Tillstrom. At last, surrendering to impulses simultaneously prurient yet innocent, he searched his wallet until he discovered the thin strip of white paper she'd given him that wondrous night in May. He punched-in the numbers and waited.

"Hello, *Charlotte?* . . Good evening . . *Yes*, this is Sid, how'd you know? . ."

IX.

The Denny-Warrington-for-Congress headquarters had been a virtual beehive of activity the entire day, Dudley Thomas's 6:00 P.M. daily *wrap-up* little more than an admission that Tuesday, July first, had begun in confusion, progressing to chaos just before noon, culminating in sheer pandemonium a few minutes after three. In his kindest terms, it had been a day like no other: Murphy's Law had taken dead aim at the campaign and scored a resounding bull's-eye. Had the screw-ups been anything but completely explicable he would have *sworn* somebody was intentionally sabotaging the campaign machinery—a series of mistakes like these simply couldn't occur without a little "outside" assistance.

But they had, nonetheless!

The campaign-button debacle that morning had started-off the new month on the wrong foot. Four boxes of buttons were delivered at 9:00 A.M. sharp. Volunteers enthusiastically tearing into the boxes, it didn't take long to discover one *tiny* mistake: one boxful of the white-background buttons had been correctly emblazoned with red letters spelling-out "DENNY 4 D.C.!"—but the other three had the same solid-white buttons with *nothing* on them. Thomas was predictably furious, but also realized the work had been performed by an out-of-town firm, not the locals: it was simply an honest mistake. One of the volunteers, a witness to Dudley's hasty phone call to the offending party, wondered if he'd left *scorch-marks* on the other end of the line.

Lunch, a catered extravaganza of Texas-style barbecue, potato salad, baked beans, and iced tea, with pecan and apple pies for dessert, enough food to feed a small army (though there were only thirty-four present), arrived at 11:30. A film crew had set-up an hour earlier to record Denny and his support staff standing in front of campaign headquarters, a segment of a commercial to be first-shown starting the coming holiday weekend, with Denny at his humble best, faithfully extolling the conservative line about his desire to represent *all* the people of his district. Of the thirty-four present, thirty-two were white, one Hispanic, and one black. Someone suggested a properly-attired Muslim — decked in an Armani *robe*, silk tie, Joseph Abboud suit over the robe, Italian sandals, preferably Prada, with white socks, and silk jockey-strap with pink daisies on the cup — would prove a valuable addition . . . and was promptly escorted out of the building. When the assembled staff and volunteers took their places, shortest in front, tallest in back, and the cameras started to roll, the trouble began. Denny reached the half-way point of his beautifully-prepared spiel when a second-floor window fell out, frame and all, crashing to the ground only three feet behind the taller volunteers in back, the glass shattering into thousands of tiny shards at everyone's feet.

The second try was only marginally better. While most everyone dashed inside headquarters to load a plate with their favorite lunch goodies, Dudley Thomas commandeered a clean-up squad to take care of the window, paying cash money to bystanders interested in making a quick buck. At 11:58 A.M. the second attempt ensued, cursed almost from the moment it began: with cameras rolling, Denny cruising through the proceedings with his message of hope, patriotism, and glory, staff and volunteers all aglow with the promise of the future, a crow flying overhead dropped a hefty wad of avian refuse, hitting Dudley Thomas in his sternum like an atom bomb. Seconds later, in a twisted bit of irony that just about everyone managed to let fly-by undetected, the downtown air-raid sirens, scheduled for their usual first-of-the-month dry runs at high noon, commenced full blast right on time, the din of which completely drowned-out everything the candidate had left to say.

"You have *got* to laugh!" chuckled a genuinely-amused Denny Warrington, " 'cause if you didn't, you'd go crazy . ."

Dudley Thomas, the least-amused man on the street, retreated to his home to change shirts while his lieutenant and second-in-command, Barbara Sue, put everyone on temporary furlough to finish lunch while the camera crew, spooked by the atypical run of bad luck, debated whether or not to throw in the towel. Determined to see their task through to its bitter end, the crew decided to give it a third and final shot, with the understanding that if anything went awry, the seven-man recording team—producer, director, cameraman, and four technicians—would leave and return the next day. Warrington, in a display of loyalty, insisted everyone wait for Dudley's triumphant return before the third and final try proceeded—and this at a cool rate of forty dollars per *minute*. Volunteers were cleaning-up after lunch when the campaign manager returned, jeans, cowboy boots, and ten-gallon hat gone the way of the wooly mammoth, replaced by a navy-blue suit he'd purchased tailor-made many years before in Hong Kong. Twenty-three years removed from his navy days, Dudley Thomas hadn't gained an *ounce*.

"Let 'er *rip!*" he cried when everyone was reassembled, and the cameras rolled a third time.

Fifteen seconds in, everything was perfect. When they hit

the half-way mark at thirty seconds all systems were *go*, and they were headed home. At forty-five seconds, Denny barely finished with his pitch, it was still a jewel. There remained only the wrap-up.

"I'm state senator Denny Warrington, and I *approve* this message . . because Americans—and *Texans*, in particular— have lost their taste for big government and empty promises! . ."

As the phrase "big government" left the candidate's lips, a female volunteer in the front row, behind him and to his left in plain sight, fainted in the midday heat and humidity, swooning slightly forward with her eyes closed as her legs folded, her body meeting the concrete sidewalk with a resounding *slap*.

"Oh, come *on!*" yelped Denny, and who could blame him? Three up, three down, and the team's director, a thirty-ish type with John Lennon specs and hair to match, gave the rest of his crew the *Deguello* signal across the throat.

The final blow arrived at 2:49 when the eight land-line telephones went dead, campaign volunteers cut-off in mid-sentence frantically pushing buttons for other lines . . none of which worked. Dudley Thomas, unshakeable in his resolve, the consummate professional and chief practitioner of operating calmly during stressful times, took it philosophically.

"*Goddamn it*, that sorry son-of-a-bitch guaranteed me we wouldn't have any trouble operating inside his building!" he bellowed in front of everyone, the wide-eyed volunteers strangely horrified yet encouraged by the outburst. "I wonder how the sorry *bastard* will react when I stop payment on the July rent check! . ."

By half past five the repairman from the C.W.A. had isolated the problem, removed the suspect wiring, then replaced it with wiring actually manufactured *post*-World War II, explaining that the old material, as unlikely as it seemed, had apparently been attacked by hungry squirrels and was still in relatively good working order.

"Don't underestimate the little critters," he warned good-naturedly, "they're smart as can be, but they'll eat almost *anything*—wood, paper, plastic, tape . . and coated *wire* . ."

And when Dudley gave his customary six o'clock message of thanks, cheer, and camaraderie, steam venting from every pore, he emphasized the absolute necessity of vigilance at all times, "especially you volunteers because, whether you know it or not, all of you would be extremely valuable targets for the Villary people—you carry privileged information that the enemy could easily exploit to their own evil purposes, so be *extra* careful." One volunteer particularly enamored with the pep-talk, Tommy Burke, inquired about carrying the misfortune of their day to the Villary camp; who else but their spies, he argued, could possibly have arranged for so many '*accidents*' in such a short period of time? No less a personage than Denny Warrington himself interceded at this point: it was categorically *un*-wise, he said, to reduce the political conflict to the level of trench-warfare without irrefutable proof the other side had a hand in it. A political "eye-for-an-eye" might be a valid tactical theory in certain cases, he admitted, but then the inevitable mud-slinging and rhetoric would predictably sink each campaign to the gutter, thus discouraging friend and foe alike; better for everyone if the *high road* was maintained. Tommy Burke, agent *extraordinaire*, basking in the glow of faithful service, nodded his understanding.

A few minutes before seven the director of the recording crew stopped by to pay a personal visit, expressing his regret so many unlikely mishaps had occurred in the process of trying to prepare a sixty-second television spot due for airing the holiday weekend, which was now mere days away. Denny and Dudley Thomas, never shy about accepting an extemporaneous dinner offer, departed with the director, Hurst, leaving Barbara Sue in charge again, this time with only skeleton staff and four volunteers to make campaign calls and answer the phones. A half-hour later she took a call from Dudley, spoke for less than a half-minute, and hung up.

"Tommy Burke? . . you still here? . . "I'm here, Barbara Sue!" he cried from the phone line. He sprang to his feet and stood next to her at attention, waiting for instructions.

"Mr. Thomas just called and wants you to retrieve a DVD from Wannamaker's down on South Second," she said. Handing him a thin slip of paper, she was careful to place it inside his palm and gently close his fingers over it. "Don't *lose* that, understand? . . It's the only way you can get your hands on that DVD! You're not to go anywhere else either—just there and straight back, ya' *hear?* . . This is a very important item here, so there can't be any screw-ups like we had with the camera crew, okay?! . . Now *git*, and call me once you've got the disc! . . Any questions, young man? . ."

"No, *ma'am!* . . I understand perfectly!"

The headquarters building had hardly faded from sight in his rear-view mirror before he plucked his cellphone from his shirt pocket, carefully punched-in the numbers while he steered through town, and waited.

"*Hey, T.C.!* . . Can you meet me in twenty minutes at the corner of South Fourth and W.B. Travis with your magic machine? . . Have I got the cash? . . Heyy, what's my name?! . . I got you covered over, under, sideways, *and* . . I got your *back!* . . Yeah, twenty, twenty-five tops . . Yeah, I'm in my ride . .

okay, see you there! .."

The empty parking lot of Hollis Drugstore at the corner of South Fourth and W.B. Travis had but a lone car when Tommy Burke pulled in; the windshield of the late-model Mustang convertible reflected the brilliance of the setting sun as Karl 'Top-Cat' Levesque leaned against the driver's door gazing south, away from the light, cigarette wedged between his index and 'bird' fingers like a movie star.

"T.C.!"

"Mister Burke—the man with the *plan!*"

He handed the sleeve-jacketed DVD to his business associate through his car window, grinned and said "Is this easy money, or *what?!* .."

"Give me two and a half minutes, okay? .."

'T.C.' Levesque opened his car door and leaned-in across the driver's seat. The machine, two wires running from the lower dashboard into its base, sat in the front passenger seat. It reminded Tommy of an old VHS player, about four inches high and a foot long, and perhaps ten inches front to back, with three sets of LED's running horizontally across the front. When its master fed the disc into the slot, the machine didn't make even the slightest sound. T.C. pushed a button, then two more simultaneously, pulled himself out of the car and leaned against his Mustang, a crafty smile dominating his features. "It'll be ready in a minute or two .."

"What do you call that thing anyway, T.C. . . . it must have a name .."

"Oh, it has several names . . some call it a memory duplication machine . . some call it a ROM identifier-and-enhancer . . still others call it *illegal* . . but it's really just a copier . . and it comes in *real* handy sometimes, don't it? .."

"And tonight is one o' those times . . I 'preciate the quick service—my buyer will appreciate it even *more!* . ."

The subdued, barely audible tone of a muffled *ding* from inside the Mustang and a soft, blue light flashing on and off on the far upper corner of the machine alerted T.C. He leaned across the driver's seat again, grabbed the original disc, retrieved the copy, and handed both to Tommy, who reached into his right shirt pocket to pull out a single piece of folded paper.

"Could I interest you in a little Ben Franklin *action?* . ."

"Brother *mine!*" saluted T.C. Levesque, and they high-fived right hands together with a resounding smack. "A pleasure doin' business with you! . ."

"We'll do it again soon, I swear we will!" grinned Tommy Burke as he started to pull away. "Until that time, T.C. . . . until that *time!* . ."

When he hit the divided four-lane and accelerated, he pulled out his cellphone again and punched-in the numbers. A voice on the other end said "Um-hmmm? . ."

"I got another one for you, sir . . if you want it tonight I can have it to you by eleven . ."

"I've come to expect no less, Mr. Burke," said Dow Pettigrew. "I suppose we'll see you around *eleven* then . ."

Sidney Villary's subsequent visit to Dr. Milner's office was as different from the first as coffee and Beaujolais. The deep-seated anxiety of finding and employing an analyst, by itself a confirmation that matters were getting a little out of hand, had darkened an otherwise sunny Friday in D.C. the week before, and the negative stigma of the session itself had certainly felt palpable enough. But that wasn't even *close* to being the worst part: if anyone—*anyone*—discovered a congressman was seeing a psychiatrist, the resultant publicity would devastate

182

any political future he might covet. The media, alerted to a potential bonanza, would flood the various outlets with the good news, and even if the enhanced scrutiny exonerated the target in question, the mere *idea* that some form of mental process was somehow skewed had already ruined more careers than Sid cared to think about. Discretion was absolutely *vital!*

No one recognized his rental car, the only thing he felt absolutely sure of. And, strangely enough, he didn't feel a bit of the apprehension that had paralyzed him so the Friday before when he'd sat stone-faced in the waiting room, terrified of faceless specters waiting to pounce on him like starved leopards. All professional personnel in the doctor's office observed strict confidentiality rules, thank *God* for small favors, and when he breezed through the doorway the only face he saw was the same face he'd seen the Friday before, waiting to check him in.

"I take it you're still homeward-bound tomorrow, or has that changed since we last spoke?" said Dr. Milner, seated in his chair as usual, notebook and pen at the ready.

Sid sat comfortably on the couch and pondered the political sway of his benefactor seated not five feet away: he didn't seem threatening at all. Why did he feel threatened?

"I can hardly wait to climb on the plane," he said truthfully. "I wouldn't call it an *escape*, exactly . . but I suppose there are several unrelated factors urging me to get out of town for a while . ."

"Like what?"

"Oh, the election, of course . . but family and friends, too . . speeches to make, hands to shake, and babies to kiss . . and my west Texas social-life, of course . ."

"Oh, that's *right*," Milner recalled. "Your mother as

matchmaker . . you must be fairly worried about seeing this woman she's arranged for you to spend time with while you're home for the holidays . ."

"Not nearly as much as the woman I'm leaving behind *here*, I can tell you! . ."

Dr. Milner stopped writing, looked up at the congressman, and frowned.

"Woman you're leaving *here?!* . . Would you care to elaborate on that? . ."

"Not really," he said emphatically, the notion ironically amusing yet cruelly ominous. He lay as before now, head on the pillowed end, legs and torso spread comfortably the length of the good doctor's couch, shoes off, hands folded complacently atop his midsection, the ideal configuration for a long, friendly chat. "She's really of no significance to me whatsoever . . the fact that she might eventually prove to be part of my political and personal ruination is pretty much beside the point . . The worst part, I suppose, is that I'm completely powerless to change it . . except for that, she's a complete non-entity, unworthy of serious consideration . ."

"Perhaps it would help if you told me a little bit about her . ."

"Like *what?* . ."

"Anything you'd like to share, really—though I'll tell you now that the *nature* of your relationship is of paramount importance . . I don't know if she's someone you met at church, or if she's a colleague, or a former professor—I know *nothing* of her, so anything you share with me will be both informative and helpful in guiding me as to how best to approach the puzzling aspects of your situation . ."

"Oh . . well, I guess you could say I . . she's employed at the . . she's British, you see, and when I stop to think about the special relationship between our two countries, I . . Dr. Milner,

I hope you'll excuse me, but I really don't know where to start . ."

"Start at the *beginning*, of course," he suggested wisely as he again scribbled in his notebook, "for it appears to me this young lady has beguiled you to some degree. At this point I'm guessing your relationship is, for lack of a better term, a *romantic* one . . and they can be *very* tricky, indeed, so you might start by telling me where you met her . ."

"Alright, then . . the first time I ever laid eyes on her was at a bar not far from Tyson's Corner called Pandora's Box," Sid started to explain, but at first mention of the name Dr. Milner lowered his pen and paper and laughed softly to himself. "Uhhh, did I say something *funny*, doc? . ."

"Forgive me, congressman . . an unfortunate *faux pas* on my part . . please continue . ."

"I'd stopped in to catch the Nationals game and throw back a whiskey or two on my way home that night . . I'd already begun feeling the stress of the primary battle facing me, but hadn't really had the opportunity of meeting with my advisers to plot our strategy for the campaign, so I was feeling a little vulnerable—you see, it's a terrible, terrible thing to know you have a real battle staring you in the face and *not* have a battle-plan—anyway, there I was sitting at the bar, comfy as can be in a familiar place with the Nationals on the screen, minding my own business—and I probably hadn't been there over a half-hour when she suddenly materialized on the other side of the bar . . No doubt in my mind I'd been watching the game and didn't see her come in, but there she was, and there was no way *anybody* in the bar could've *not noticed* her presence . . I spotted her just as the bartender put the first bottle of Guinness in front of her, but then I noticed I wasn't the only one distracted by her . . Jesus, *everybody* was staring at her—

185

men, women—who knows, but if there were any gay men inside the place at the time, I'd bet even money *they* were staring at her, too! . . Well, I finally turned back to the game, but it was impossible to keep my eyes off her, and she ordered more Guinness, and—*man*, you should see her drink stout!—she drinks it like a man, only *faster!*—I thought I caught her looking right at me a couple times, but I'd had a few bourbons by then and thought I was just '*seeing*' things, you know? . . Believe me when I tell you I wasn't looking for *anything* that night: I think I've already explained my feelings about permanent attachments, so when I turned around from the game and found her standing right next to me with her Guinness . . You see, she wore down my defenses by approaching me first, which I wasn't expecting, then became dazzled by my position, or hair, or clothes, or *something*, and then she . . then she . ."

He shrugged as he lay on the couch, as though the inevitability of what happened next wasn't anyone's responsibility. He remembered being on the beach in southeast Texas during spring break while an undergrad in the mid 90's; no one ever took responsibility for what happened under those circumstances either—though many a family, love affair, and divorce began the exact same way. Who could say, with any kind of dependable authority, the number or strength of the individual storms one encountered on the way to a successful conclusion to *anything*?

"Take your time, congressman . ."

"She told me she lived closer to the club than I did . . so I should follow *her* . ."

"And did you?"

"Did I *what*? . ."

"Did you do as she asked? . . Did you follow her home? . ."

186

Sidney Villary closed his melancholy eyes and said "Yes, of *course* I followed her home . . I mean, come *on*, it's not like I had a choice . ."

Dr. Milner said "I'm afraid I don't follow you there . . You could have said something along the lines of '*no*,' or maybe '*not* tonight, I have a headache,' or perhaps 'my *wife* wouldn't understand,' . . but you make it sound like you were somehow *incapable* of turning her down—that you couldn't say *no* to a complete stranger? . ."

"You just don't understand what I was dealing with, doc . . when she looks at you with those doe-eyes, and those eyes *beg* you to do their bidding . . there's no such thing as '*No!*' . . What I'm telling you is . . there wasn't a single man in that whole place who could've turned her away—those eyes of hers are so full of unrestrained *longing*, so unremitting in their desire to make you do what *they* want you to do—there's no way a normal man could resist her—a weak man, poor bastard, would be as putty—and even a strong man would find himself inexplicably grinning like an idiot at the prospect of spending time with her . . It's almost impossible to explain, Dr. Milner, because it actually defies logic," he half-muttered intelligibly, mystified by the dynamics of his own dilemma, "and I know this may sound like sour grapes on my part, but it's *not* intended to be . . but in a way . . I wish I hadn't been so wildly attracted to her, because *that's* the precise point where the trouble started! . . If it hadn't been for the fact that she saw me and *liked* what she saw—in conjunction with the inescapable fact that I saw *her* and liked what *I* saw—*none* of this would've happened, and my life would still be *manageable!* . . Jesus, if, If, *IF!* . . I'm telling you, the whole thing's driving me *crazy!* . ."

"I see . . Am I correct in assuming this young lady from the

187

British Isles is attractive? . ."

Resigned to his fate, Sid remained motionless, muttering "Understatement of the *month* . ."

"Then would it be too much for me to ask if you've allowed yourself—against your nature and well-thought-out intentions, of course—to fall *in love* with this woman? . ."

"Hell, *no*, I haven't fallen in love with her!" he protested. "I've never fallen in love with *anyone*, and she, of all people, is certainly included on *that* list! . . The very *idea* of falling in love makes me want to pitch lunch! . . Christ, what if my *parents* heard this shit?! . ."

"Oh, I see," said an amused Dr. Milner, "so you *don't* love this woman from Great Britain . . this woman with the '*doe*' eyes, as you call them, who can for all intents and purposes make you do anything she wants you to do, simply by *looking at you* in a certain way. Tell me something then . . do you consider yourself a *strong* man, congressman? . ."

"Well, *naturally* I consider myself a strong man because I *am* a strong man . . I'm a United States congressman from west Texas, for Chrissakes, I was *born* strong! . . I have physical strength because I take good care of myself . . I have mental strength because I limit myself to the pursuit of choice, high-quality bourbon, and nothing else—no drugs or pills or powder, or any of *that* crap!—and I possess emotional strength because I try never to let my personal feelings affect my decision-making—I owe the people who elected me, and I'm bound to make *damn* sure they receive their money's worth! . . and, I have massive spiritual strength—*massive*—because I believe in my lord and savior, Jesus Christ, the son of God . . yes, *sir* . . I am a strong man . ."

"Then I'm beginning to think we've got a classic *love-hate* relationship developing here . . You claim to be a strong man,

188

and I've no reason to doubt you—and you yourself told me a few minutes ago that a strong man would grin at the idea of spending time with this woman from Britain—yet you are neither grinning nor spending time with her because, in *your* words, when you first saw her, your trouble began. Now . . I'm not trying to hamstring you here, but what exactly is the source of the *trouble* with this woman you do *not* love and don't want anything to do with? . ."

"I *never* said I didn't want anything to do with her—I just said I didn't *love* her . ."

"How does that make you feel? . ."

"How does *what* make me feel? . ."

"You admitted you're attracted to her, and you apparently enjoyed her company on the, what, *only* occasion you've been with her, so it would seem—"

"I've been with her *twice!*" interrupted Sid, like there was a galactic difference between one and two, "but you're right, we haven't spent a whole lot of time together . ."

"A thought occurs to me," said Dr. Milner. He stopped taking written notes and dropped the pad into his lap, his attention diverted solely to his patient. "How long have you *known* this woman you've only been with twice? . ."

"Well, let's see . . we met the week after Mother's day, I believe . . yes, it was before Memorial Day weekend, so it was around the middle of May . . why? . ."

"So you've known her about six or seven weeks then? . ."

"Yes, give or take . . so? . ."

"And in that six or seven-week period you've been with her a grand total of . . *two* times?! . . My *point*, congressman, is that my experience tells me that when a man and woman are attracted to each other they typically want to spend as much time together as possible and, even if there are obstacles, they

189

invariably find a way to do just *that*. I simply find it interesting that you and she *didn't*, and I have to wonder about that . ."

"Our schedules didn't allow it, that's all," he said with a shrug. "I'm busy with more fires than I can keep up with, what with a trip to Europe in September, the ongoing fights over immigration, abortion rights, out-of-control government spending, and everything else dear to the hearts of my constituents—*and* I have a campaign to conduct, more travel between here and Texas than I care to think about, plus the pressure from my parents to marry the first woman who winks at me, and I'm going to be there in west Texas at their mercy, God *help* me?—and that's just *my* side of things! . . Charlotte has her own life, Dr. Milner, and stays pretty busy, too . . She has her work at the embassy and, poor thing, she's three thousand miles from her family and friends . . we spent the one night together and then went our separate ways, and it's *not* that I didn't want to see her again . . I'm just *busy*, incredibly so, and so is she . . I *like* her very much—probably more than what's good for me—but I don't know if we'd ever have seen each other again if she hadn't stopped by my office last week . . and good *Lord*, you should've seen the looks on my office staff's faces! . . Princess Di, God rest her soul, couldn't have received a better reception . ."

"She stopped by your *office!*" said Dr. Milner, his notepad and pen back in business.

"I introduced her to my office staff . . the girls in my office were favorably impressed, to say the least . . One or two of them said they were *proud* of me—like I'd brought home the biggest fish or something. I also suspect they're of the mind I've finally met the woman of my dreams—although I haven't, of course . ."

"How did that make you feel, seeing her in your office all of a sudden? . ."

"I'll tell you *exactly* how it made me feel: she was the very *last* person I expected to see when I   opened my office door, but there she was, all butter and sugar poured into business clothes—like that could somehow disguise the fact that, on the standard scale of one-to-ten, she's an *eleven*—and I walked right over to her and hugged her close to me! I was absolutely *elated* to see her! It would be impossible to accurately describe how I felt when I wrapped my arms around her . . I was petrified she'd never want to see me again after ignoring her for six weeks but, like I said, we're both busy and it's no one's fault we hadn't seen one another again . . It took some doing, but we finally got that straightened-out the last time we were together, and I think she feels better about *us*, you know? . . I know *I* do . . That office visit was fairly rough, though . . she let me have it pretty good, and I probably deserved it . ."

"Hold it . . *hold* it . . You're telling me that, after you hugged her and told her—well, what *did* you tell her after you hugged her? . ."

"I told her I was extremely happy to see her—*overjoyed*, really . ."

"And then afterward everything suddenly turned . . *sour?* . . I don't understand . ."

"Well, she hadn't felt the best last week, what with the morning sickness and all, and not having anything for it and not knowing what to take to feel better, and the stress of finding out . ."

Dr. Milner's notepad and pen fell into his lap, his head up in the blink of an eye, eyes wide with what the congressman perceived as shock, or maybe fear, when he said "*Morning sickness?!* . ."

"Yes, morning sickness," he repeated. "She's about seven

weeks gone . ."

"So this woman is *pregnant* by you, congressman?! . ."

"That seems such a *strong* term, 'pregnant' . ." said Sidney Villary, like there was a convenient way of expressing the fact without the unfortunate reality. "And she claims it's *mine* . ."

"I see . . Do you have any reason to doubt her claim? . ."

"Not really, no . . She seems like the type of person who would never lie about anything—and sure wouldn't lie about *that* . . truth is, she's probably one of the most trustworthy people I've ever met, so what she says is almost certainly the truth . ."

"Why didn't you tell me this before?" said Milner.

"I told you from the get-go she was trouble . . What did you *think* I meant? . ."

"The only information at my disposal, *Mister* Villary . . is what *you* tell me!" Dr. Milner asserted in as brisk a tone as possible. "I'm glad you finally saw fit to share the *source* of the 'trouble,' as you so diplomatically put it, but at this point I'm convinced you somehow believe this is all some sort of conspiratorial *mistake* on her part. Let me also impart a bit of knowledge here . . and feel free to take it or leave it, as you see fit, but the fact is, pregnancy is an extremely straightforward matter—there is no *half*-pregnant, or *semi*-pregnant, or anything of the kind. So if she is, indeed, with child, I'd love to know how all this makes you feel . ."

Congressman Sidney Hunt Villary of west Texas laid supine on the doctor's couch pondering the ways of providence, as he was prone to do from time to time. Feeling as though the forces arrayed against him were closing-in for the kill, his defensive position growing progressively weaker by the hour, he quietly said "My life as I know it, the life I have now and would love to have kept for as long as possible, is effectively

192

ended . . No matter which angle I approach my situation from, the answer is always the same: I am simply done for . ."

Dr. Milner, his annoyance abated somewhat by his patient's admission of futility, calmly said "I can easily understand why you might feel a degree of stress in correlation to her condition, particularly in view of what you told me in our first session regarding your colleagues and their respective families, your own views on marriage and children—not to mention the residual difficulties with your *parents*—but to think a woman you're admittedly fond of is ruining your political career? . . I'm having difficulty making the same connection, so if you don't mind explaining it to me in some detail—and the *more* detail, the better—perhaps I can better comprehend the somewhat *dour* take on your *non*-future in Washington, D.C. . ."

"I can't help coming back to the fact that . . had we *not* been attracted to each other, none of this trouble would have happened, and my political future—and I know full well there are no promises in politics, no guarantees of anything except having to fight for everything you believe in, every single day you wake-up—but at least I wouldn't have as *many* threats to my position in the Texas delegation as I do now . . Dr. Milner, do you not have any *idea* what I've done to myself? . . I've stepped into a Texas-size cow-patty and continued to march right through the goddamn field like it wasn't there, spreading the scent and the filth as I go, *that's* what I've done, and I can seek the understanding and benevolence of those who asked me for the very same empathy and kindness, *begged* me for it like it was the secret of life and death . . but, I can't expect to receive it . . oh, *no*, that's the one thing beyond my grasp . . because in my superior way of thinking, in my determination to get things done right or not at all . . I turned them *down*—

refused them for a political principle and a proper share of the *vote*—and now the tables have turned and I should be *forced* to beg for mercy . . but I've got a surprise for them, because I *won't!* . . and if, despite my best efforts to conceal the reality of my circumstances, someone discovers the truth and the news spreads across the wire services, thus sealing my political death, at least I'll be able to say I fought for what I *believe!* . .'

"I must also prepare myself for the very real possibility that Charlotte will not only *have* the child—against my wishes, of course—but that she'll prefer to raise the child by herself, without any interference from me . . That frees me to pursue what I do best, but I say again, I'd prefer she not have the child in the first place . . We talked things over this past weekend and she's leaning toward taking the pregnancy full-term, while I volunteered to arrange for the termination itself, any fees, and whatever assistance she requires . ."

"You'd prefer *not* to father this particular child then?" said the doctor, furiously scribbling in his notepad, his question more a statement of fact. "Which would require—unless I'm missing something enormous here—that she have an abortion, would it not? . ."

"That's correct . ."

"*Aaahhhh!*" sighed the doctor. He laid his pen and notepad on the chair next to his, alongside his iPad, and regarded his patient with eyes grown shrewd from years of experience dealing with every level and aspect of humanity. His expression, non-judgmental yet piercing, serious but curiously winsome, revealed a mere trace of an opinion. "Your dilemma is frighteningly clear, and for once I can honestly say . . I'm *glad* it's not me! . . Before we proceed any further, can you tell me if this woman has entertained any notions about what life as the wife of a conservative congressman might entail?—or has that conversation not taken place? . ."

"That particular conversation has *not* taken place, nor *should* it!" Villary said firmly. "I made my position clear regarding that particular subject, and Charlotte was wise enough not to press it any further . . in any conversation between equals, the ground-rules have to be established first . . *then* the particulars can be discussed by both parties . . it's the only way . ."

"Be serious, congressman: *who*, exactly, are the 'equals' here? . ."

"What do you mean, *who? . .* we're only discussing two people, right? . ."

"*Equals!?*You and *her?!* Are you *kidding?!* Have you any idea how incredibly *frightened* she must feel, a resident alien in a foreign country, impregnated by a congressman in the United States House of Representatives, in the national seat of government, Washington, D.C.?! . . And you do *not*, under any circumstances, want anything to do with the child *you* fathered on top of that?! Equals?! After being *bullied* like that?! Is *that* what you really think? . ."

Quiet for a long moment before venturing to speak, Villary finally said "I hadn't quite thought of it in those terms, no . . but can't you see where I have much, *much* more to lose than she does? . . Can you not see that the stakes are considerably higher for me than for her? . . that I have an enormous amount of pressure laid at my feet as a direct result of this sole indiscretion? . ."

"Oh, I'll give you credit for *that*, yes. You've managed to wedge yourself nicely between the proverbial solid venue and a bit of igneous, as it were—but I have serious reservations about your chances of extricating yourself from your predicament. You've got too many shotguns aimed in your direction, and it only takes one solid shell to achieve irreparable damage . . But what *really* makes this an impossible situation for you is the fact that you are ready, willing, and able—even *eager*—to sacrifice the life of a human being and the well-being of what I have to assume is a good and decent human being—and a very pretty one, at that!—to protect and lengthen the political career of another! Yes, congressman, a single slip-up of any kind—the media gets hold of the mother-to-be, your political *opponent* discovers what's going on, the champion of all anti-abortion activists pays to have his own child aborted, the protector of persons from their very *conception* sells out, British national strong-armed into aborting her child to preserve political career of congressional father—*anything at all*—and you're so much *toast!* You wouldn't have to worry about your political career anymore because you wouldn't *have* one! Neither would you need to worry about your parents for the foreseeable future, because if *they* discover what happened they'd *disown* you as they correctly accuse you of murdering their precious, long-awaited grandchild! . . My, *yes*, congressman—you've got a brilliant future in politics! . ."

"No one ever said it'd be easy . . and it never dawned on me how vulnerable she might feel . . But now you can understand why I believe my career as a politician is over . . you basically said the same thing yourself . . 'Too many guns aimed at me,' remember? . . Sounds like you don't have too much faith in my chances of winning re-election . ."

"No, it's not that . . I don't have much faith in you *surviving* long enough to win re-election . ."

"I'm not sure you're familiar with what it takes to ensure a solid, long-lasting career in politics, Dr. Milner," he said, no hint of arrogance in his tone.

"I couldn't care less about your politics," said the doctor. He tossed the pen and notepad next to his iPad and sat with hands folded on his lap. "When I mentioned survival, I wasn't referring to your career in politics . . I was referring to your career as a *human being* . ."

When the chime sounded sixteen minutes later, their session officially ended by the miniature glockenspiel, and the doctor and congressman shook hands in parting, the doctor more convinced than ever about the desperate need for tolerance, forbearance, and benevolent consideration in all matters human—the congressman temporarily refocused toward the future requirements his friend and lover might encounter along her way, divine providence relegated to a secondary position of significance for the time-being—neither man felt as sure they would meet again as before . . . one because his faith in the other felt ill-founded and misplaced, the other because it was just human nature to at least attempt to find the easiest way out, which invariably meant putting the self above all else. Congressman Sidney H. Villary, the more religious man, hoped the doctor would continue to grow a thriving practice, while the doctor, the more spiritual of the two, prayed his patient would ultimately, in spite of himself, find a measure of peace.

Dudley Thomas had known his lieutenant and confidante, Barbara Sue, for the better part of twenty-two years: aside from the fact that she was bright, efficient, and loyal, she possessed one overriding characteristic he'd always found useful—better than virtually anyone else of his acquaintance, she could keep a *secret*. Spanning their years together, it translated into the safest sort of teamwork imaginable. In conspiratorial terms, two parts working in tandem as one were vastly superior to the 'lone cowboy' concept; in brainstorming activities, two completely trusting minds produced measurably better results than separate attempts; and for investigative purposes, where discretion was the most critical component in the discovery process, two operating as one almost without exception emerged successful, and anyone who'd known them a fair amount of time admired their work as a pair.

When Dudley arrived at campaign headquarters late that Wednesday morning, pausing on the sidewalk long enough to admire the new window installed on the second floor, he strolled inside and immediately began an impromptu inspection of the six campaign rooms, stepping inside both men's and women's bathrooms for a quick glance around before taking a seat at his desk, Barbara Sue on the phone at her desk barely eight feet away.

"Care to take any bets on our office machines exploding before the day's out?!" he grinned   maliciously when she hung up.

She rapped her knuckles four times on the wooden desktop, the apparent universal cure to mischievous, evil spirits.

"No, I wouldn't . ."

"What time did he leave for Abilene? . ."

"Right after the film crew left . . Everything went off without a hitch, too, just perfect . . what a difference a day makes sometimes . ."

He opened his top-left drawer, saw his .357 nestled snugly inside its holster, checked the box of hollow-points for signs of tampering and said "Tell me about last night . ."

"I sent him down to Wannamaker's to pick it up, just like you said, and according to our little device . . . he went straight there and came straight back—no side-trips anywhere else, no six-pack bought and consumed while he was behind the wheel, no dilly-dallying with the girls at any of the fast-food places—nothing!—and the DVD was as pristine as I expected it to be, brand-new and not a thing outta' place . ."

"Nothing suspicious at all, then . ."

"The only thing that caught my attention was his second stop: he'd just left Wannamaker's and gone a few blocks—he couldn't have been more than a third of a mile from the store—and he stopped for about three or four minutes, then continued on his way and came straight back," she said complacently, "but he never turned-off the designated route between here and there . ."

Dudley's piercing eyes narrowed, his interest piqued.

"What street was he on when he pulled over, Sue? . ."

"W.B. Travis, right where he was supposed to be . . course, I didn't want to seem too nosy when he got back, so I asked him if everything went okay and he said 'yeah,' except that he'd had to pull over to put some air in a tire, which explains why he stopped for three or four minutes . . one of the girls on the phones last night asked him if he was still having tire problems, too, so where does *that* leave us? . . the whole thing's got me flustered . ."

Thomas sat pensively in his chair, his veteran eyes focusing on nothing in particular until he swiveled round to gaze through the east-facing front glass at the sunny day outside. The early July sun, hot and steamy in west Texas from mid-morning to sundown, sat directly overhead now, baking and wilting everything in its path. He turned to face her again.

"And what's his contributory status now? . ."

"See, that's *another* thing . . Tommy's in the number three overall slot in contributions, so the boy's been getting us some decent coin, no question . . If he's turned around to the other side he's got a *very* peculiar way of showing it—but I still don't

199

doubt for a second that you're onto something there . . it's just that putting our hands on some *evidence* is proving a lot tougher than we thought, Dudley—and if we get rid of a contributing volunteer without cause, what does *that* say about us? . ."

Fingers interlaced behind his head in support, he said "Wouldn't it be *great* if we could figure out a way to see all the words floating through cyberspace? . ."

"If you think being able to see the gibberish my three girls and my son come up with when they're running their mouths on their cellphones is worth your time, knock yourself out . . Personally? . . I can live without it . ."

"Okay, maybe not *all* the words . . but wouldn't it be wonderful if you could somehow find a way to focus on a particular conversation being conducted through cyberspace? . . Maybe it's a market no one's thought to exploit yet, but imagine yourself being able to walk inside a communications center, dropping a few dollars into a machine and then designating a certain phone number to be monitored at that precise moment, at which point you not only get to see *what's* being said, but also get to know *who's* saying *what* on the other end . ."

"I'm not sure about the communications center or the machine," observed Barbara Sue, "but the covert listening devices are a reality and business is probably better than anyone wants it to be . . it's called *eavesdropping*, and it's illegal as hell . ."

"You know what I mean . ."

"If you've got something up your sleeve, would you mind sharing it with me? . ."

"When's Tommy due in today?"

"Three-thirty, why? . ."

"And how many more are here with him this evening? . . She glanced at her desktop, the roster lying face-up on the right-hand side.

"Wow, *nine* others!" she said, surprised, "but now that I think about it, that's about right, actually . . we planned something of a push today and tonight because tomorrow's the third and a lot of folks are leaving early for the holiday weekend, so there's less than half the regular number every day starting tomorrow until everyone goes back to work on the seventh . ."

"Do you trust any of the girls well enough to enlist their assistance in a diversionary tactic to separate him from his cellphone for two or three minutes? . ."

"There are one or two I'd trust with my *life*, Dudley . . don't forget who recruited these ladies . . I'm thinking about one in particular who'd sellout her sister if the price was right . . Smart as can be, too . .

She'd be glad to help—especially if she could have *fun* doing it!" grinned Barbara Sue. "Would you mind terribly if she enjoyed herself? . ."

But Dudley Thomas said nothing, preferring to sit comfortably in his chair with a blank expression while the gears inside his analytical brain fine-tuned the scheme to reveal a possible traitor in their midst. His heart and soul felt content: there was no known substitute for the security in the knowledge that, if his plan *worked*, surely he would have earned his money the old-fashioned way.

X.

Before crossing the Potomac late Thursday morning to catch his flight at Reagan National, Sidney Villary called Regina into his office, thus luring her into the grand conspiracy. She walked in to find him grinning like the little boy caught with his hand in the cookie jar, but he swore her to secrecy before she could ask what he was up to. He was sending along a little holiday cheer, he explained, and she was going to help him: without letting anyone else in the office know, she was to arrange to have two dozen long-stemmed red roses sent to Miss Charlotte Tillstrom at the British Embassy in Washington, with a note that read "Thinking of you the entire time I'm gone! Love, Sidney!" —and she'd have to move *fast*, because he wanted her to have them while he was still in the air between D.C. and Texas. Regina, in love with love, felt so thrilled to be a part of what had to be a white-hot love affair she fairly floated out of his office, tingling ecstatically from head to toe. Then he brought in Carmen by herself and issued identical instructions, the adjoining note with a different message, and then Julie—six dozen red roses in all. Of course, these didn't include the two dozen he'd sent to her condo that morning with a note which read "Forgive me for being such an insensitive *oaf!*"

Every mile on his ride to Reagan he reminded himself that, had he and she selected different clubs that evening in mid-May—or even the *same* club at different *times*—neither would be struggling with their present hardship. By the time the 757 entered Tennessee airspace his mind seemed transfixed by this most recent, deadly-serious case of the *'but for'* law: except *for* their physical attraction to each other, *nothing* . . would have happened. *But for* the fact that each made eye contact with the other and got the ball rolling, neither would be in this mess. *Were it not for* their subsequent actions after they first met, their lives wouldn't have changed one bit. The inescapable conclusion proved invariably the same: she was pregnant, he was the father, and it had all started because they made eye contact from opposite sides of the bar. *Jesus*, how was it possible to admire someone from a short distance and end-up with a child in the passing of a mere *evening?!* Why hadn't *someone, somewhere*, he reasoned . . had the presence of mind to provide some sort of protection to those who, through no fault of their own, found themselves in this sad state of existence? They were two bright, young adults with most of their lives ahead of them; they were careful to take precautions whenever possible—as they *had* that fateful evening—and still the powers that rule the universe had frowned upon them. *Why?!* It just didn't seem to make much sense. By the time the first plane landed and he'd hopped aboard another for the short jaunt to Preston Smith International in Lubbock, he'd jotted down a few notes in the form of questions; no passing fancy, these questions needed answers, and quick. Was it ethically or morally reprehensible to seek an abortion if precautions had been taken on the part of *both* partners to prevent a pregnancy, and both precautions *failed?* What laws were already on the books governing the concept and crime of entrapment, if any? In cases identical to theirs, if the child gains *person-hood* at the precise moment of conception, is it possible the child actually gains person-hood when the woman and man find they are attracted to each other at first meeting—*and* that initial attraction *directly results in pregnancy?* If not, *why* not? Finally—and perhaps most importantly—if a child *was*, indeed, the direct and natural result of a chance encounter between a man and woman, what protection was afforded the child *prior to conception?*

As the plane began its descent toward the longest runway a few minutes out of Lubbock, Sidney Villary still had only questions without answers . . but for the first time in over a week of intense, if intermittent, soul-searching, he felt reasonably buoyant. At least he had *questions*, and that was undeniable progress. By the time the plane's first tire touched the runway he'd constructed a list of people he wanted desperately to speak with: smart people, trusted people, familiar people . . *his* people! Answers would be forthcoming once he'd discussed matters with them. As he rose from his window seat in the plane's mid-section, the most negligible hint of a smile managed to purse his lips, and he realized at that exact moment that he could go forward into his heartland with renewed strength and vigor. After all, in about ninety short minutes Dow Pettigrew would have him seventy-five or eighty miles down highway 385 and *home*, at last!

He spotted his friend waiting for him just beyond and to the right of where the T.S.A. people were busy checking outbound passengers: *God*, it felt good to be alive and on the ground in the Lone Star state! After shaking hands and chasing-down his luggage they paused inside a handy bar for a quick bourbon and Scotch, then proceeded merrily toward the exits, a peculiar noise emanating from the area near the doors, which were still out of sight. A few moments later they knew what it was: a small group of Hare Krishnas, young men and women alike, had formed a circle inside the doorway and were busy chanting 'Hare Krishna, Hare Krishna, Krishna Krishna, Hare

Hare Hare Rama,' while a lone Krishna, hat in hand, stood close to one side to receive donations.

"Are you *kidding me?!*" roared Dow Pettigrew. "In Lubbock, Texas, of all places!? . . Small wonder this country's in so much hot water! . ."

"That's unbelievable!" echoed Villary, the chanting growing progressively louder with their approach. "I come home to Texas to stay in touch with the people and the first thing I see is a bunch of God-forsaken Hare Krishna *Muslins!? . .*"

Stepping at a brisker pace now, they'd almost passed the chanting youths when the young Krishna with the collection hat stepped in front of Sid, smiled and said "Hare Krishna?"

The beleaguered congressman stopped in his tracks, gave the bald-headed Krishna the once-over head to toe, shook his head at the white, lightweight flowing robes, and pointed at him with his free left index finger, saying "I personally don't *like* Krishnas—hairy, or otherwise!" He then turned back to D.P. and said "You better get me the hell outta' *here*, Mr. Pettigrew! . ."

The mood and atmosphere at the Highland Hills Country Club in the early evening of Thursday, July 3, was decidedly festive: the grand entrance was adorned with a huge red and white banner that read "Welcome <u>Home</u>, Congressman Villary!"—and the refreshing, unmistakable aroma of splendid west Texas barbecue wafted through the grounds from the golf course's sixth hole all the way to the front gate and beyond. The late-afternoon sun shone bright on those in the water and on the links, the tennis courts sitting directly behind the three-floor main complex on the east side primarily shaded now, the pools on the south side always shade-free. The crowd—members, guests, and a few select dignitaries—

completely savvy to the heady combination of barbecue and booze, the extended holiday weekend, and political overtones of later that evening, began trickling through the gates earlier than normal, the better to begin their Fourth-of-July celebrations with a resounding *bang*. The barbecue pits themselves—brick, stone, and cement monuments to what most west Texans considered one of their very finest religions—were located on the north end, but at the eastern side where a degree of shade could normally be found under the three elms. The shade just made good sense: whoever was tending the meat was the most important man on the country club's grounds and, according to the first club president, Ernest Cleveland, it simply wouldn't *do* "to have the barbecue master needlessly blinded in the execution of his sacred duties!"

A short forty-minute drive away, Sid and D.P. sat comfortably inside the den of the Pettigrew home, unceremoniously performing the mandatory critiquing of bourbon and single-malt, respectively. When he heard Velma pull into the driveway a few minutes before six—almost a half-hour *earlier* than he'd mistakenly anticipated—a terrified D.P. sprinted to hide his single-malt inside a lower door of the entertainment rack, his promise not to partake in spirits of any kind before their arrival at the club that evening having been solemnly given the night before. Velma, just departed from her hairdresser's, waltzed in decked in white shorts, dark-red top, and sandals; her tan already three months in the making, matched perfectly by her lustrous caramel hair, she was what some men generously refer to as a *vision*. A long, extended, exquisite hug and three or four very sweet kisses later, the congressman saw fit to suggest that D.P., rather than leave his house unattended, stay home that evening, as he was Velma's new escort for the barbecue *co-ed smoker*. Without hesitation she then walked to the proper door of the entertainment rack, extracted her husband's single-malt and returned it to his flustered hands, planting a Texas-sized smooch on his left cheek.

"That's for *not* drinking before you picked him up in Lubbock," she explained sweetly as she sidled out of the room. "Give me fifteen and I'll be ready for the road . ."

When they pulled through the country club entrance an hour later Sid grinned like a school-kid at first sight of the welcome-home banner. In the front passenger seat for the ride over, he swiveled round to face Velma sitting behind him and, holding her hand tenderly in his, brushed affectionate lips across her fingertips.

"I hope to see the same signage two years from now when I return home to campaign again . ."

"We'll all make sure you *do* . ."

The scene inside the clubhouse seemed as familiar as his parents' living room: as if he'd never left home for the loftier halls of the nation's capital, they came to him singly and in pairs and groups, the women to get hugged and kissed by their standard-bearer, the men to shake his hand, high-school flames and childhood friends, business leaders, important and not-so-important donors . . all there to mingle with their elected champion. By seven-twenty his busy cheeks reflected every color of the rainbow, lipsticks of every subtlety and shade having found their mark; even the ladies old enough to be his mother enjoyed a kiss on the cheek from their handsome representative. They were his people, and he was one of *them*.

At 7:35, situated in the hallway between the theater and dining room to explain the intricacies of the spending bill being deliberated in the House to a group of supporters, four couples he'd known better than twelve years, a shrill, familiar, even peculiarly-frightening voice from far behind him cried out "Look—*there's* my precious little boy!"

Without spilling a drop of bourbon, a look of benign bewilderment washing across his features, he stopped talking and, eying his friends with a quick glance of mock-fear, said "Is it *me*, or does mother sound like she wants to spank me with a *belt?!*"

Seconds later he kissed his mother on the cheek, hugging her close while shaking hands with his tuxedo-clad father, the best-attired man in a country club filled with men in suits, leisure wear, golfing apparel, tennis outfits—even post-water sports gear.

"How's it feel to be home?" said the old man.

"It's where I need to be, sir!" he said, ever the politician, always respectful of his elders. "There're a few important things we need to discuss for my benefit over the weekend, dad . . Please let me know when it's convenient for you . ."

"Everything alright with you, my boy?" said mom, clearly elated to see her one and only but, like any mother, worried about her tiny tot—even when he'd already cleared *forty*.

"My flight down was a *working* flight—out of *necessity*, mother . . I know you like Denny and Evelyn Warrington—so do *I*, really—but I feel certain that this is an honest-to-God *fight* for my political survival, so I need to make the most of my visit home . . I'll do fund-raisers, dinners, speeches, whatever it takes to ride-out this storm, so I'll need your help! . ."

"Let's talk Sunday after church," his father suggested, mindful of the fact his son belonged to the community. "The dinners and speeches will be over with by then . . we'll have some time to ourselves, okay? . ."

In anticipation of the nine o'clock speech by the guest-of-honor and the not-so-secret Denny Warrington TV commercial trial-run, to be telecast in tandem on closed-circuit TV, the main clubhouse began filling with invitees, members, donors, and friends a few minutes after eight. By half past the hour even a few local media, alerted the week prior about the congressman's visit home, arrived to witness the festivities, interview the area's favorite-son, enjoy the breezy club atmosphere, and snap a few pictures. Two representatives from the morning paper, a writer and photographer, gainfully employed by a friend of the Villarys, were immediately granted an interview with Sid in a private room adjacent to the kitchen where he'd been holding court with high school chums and team members of the football squad, class of '89. When queried about the possible contents of his opponent's as-yet-unseen television spot, D.P. interceded and claimed the Villary campaign had information "on *good* authority" that Denny's first spot would concentrate on Warrington's accomplishments as a state senator, his Texas background and roots, his family values, and the objectives he meant to achieve once elected. Just the usual *positive* introduction any candidate might use, according to Pettigrew. With Sid Villary, a man of principle, defender of the faith, and a true-blue Texas conservative, as the incumbent, the 'high' road would be assumed at all times—any mud-slinging, back-stabbing, ditch-diving, and throat-cutting would have to wait for the general election against Consuela Garcia. Denny Warrington, D.P. gladly reminded anyone within earshot, had himself been a Villary supporter in the last election and was therefore considered a *friend*—and friends didn't mess with each other in the great state of Texas. After giving the photographer four

209

or five poses—right or wrong, Sid had always believed his left side was the more-photogenic—the congressman settled in with the writer and quickly elucidated his vision for Texas and America. What the country urgently needed to turn itself around was the conversion of as many *blue* states to *red* as soon as possible—*forty* red states would be a good, round, *workable* number—with a commensurate number of conservative governors taking over state houses . . for the good of every citizen, naturally. Oh, *no*, nobody wanted any obstructionists in the House under *any* conditions: it was of *paramount* importance to ensure that an ongoing dialogue between rival factions keep the lines of communication open at all times . . just in case the two sides, at some nebulous point in the future, could agree on something more significant than what brand of toilet paper should be installed in the ladies congressional bathroom. Sidney Villary could point to himself when it came time to identify "movers and shakers" on questions of abortion rights, tax reform, immigration, military spending, Second Amendment rights, health care, and the ever-increasing size and power of the federal government. Tolerance and compassion, he pointed out, should rule any negotiations on matters of substance in the U.S. House.

The darling of the occasion continued to shake hands with late arrivals, perfect strangers he hoped to favorably impress, and important donors who arrived for the sole purpose of being present during his evening address. He hugged his pediatrician, newly retired after practicing her skills in excess of forty-two years, thanked her for having taken such wonderful care of him, and made a solemn promise to push tort-liability reform in the next congress. By a quarter 'til nine he finished his fourth bourbon and water, excused himself

210

from a circle of high school friends, and dashed into the club kitchen to grab a quick barbecue sandwich and bottle of water for his time on stage. D.P. arrived as Sid shoved the last bite of potato salad down his gullet, grasping a tall glass of pale-brown, slightly gold-tinged liquid his resident adviser brought.

"What's this?" he grinned, eying the color with a critically-piercing, if unscientific, evaluation.

"That's from your buddy, Adkins . . he poured this from a flask and mixed it with water—said you knew a quality bourbon from a bad one, just like him . ."

"True enough," he readily admitted, and with that the tall glass met his lips, the pale-brown liquid vanishing down his throat in large gulps, followed immediately by the patented Villary 'belly-tap,' indicating satisfaction. "Would you mind giving me a quick run-down on how everything's sitting right now? . ."

"Well, boss, it would appear my tragedy is presently unfolding," began D.P., referring to his Scotch and soda which, being a commercial, 'light' Scotch instead of a single-malt, had him nursing the beast. "But *these* people couldn't be happier to see you, so I'm telling you now . . by the time this is all over, you'll have them eating out of your *hand!* . ."

Clinking glasses triumphantly, they laughed at the absurdity of Denny Warrington attempting to unseat a popular incumbent, then proceeded toward the club theater for a bit of old-fashioned, Texas-style politicking, a hefty measure of glad-handing unofficially *de rigueur*. The closer they stepped to the club's grand entrance the more stops they encountered as old friends and acquaintances continued to express their delight at his arrival home, shaking hands, patting him on the back, kisses on the cheek (and other venues)

211

offered and graciously accepted. Yes, he reflected at length, thank *God* there was a place called 'Texas,' and wasn't it a *relief* to once again be rubbing shoulders with those who loved him and everything he stood for!

As they stood in the theater's entryway commiserating with three old college chums, the interior lighting suddenly began to dim, continuing intermittently for about a quarter-minute until the amount of light in the theater itself had been reduced by half. Ignoring the sudden change until the last moment of expanding darkness, Sid gave his pals a look tantamount to an unspoken "Okayyy . . and what in the hell is *this* supposed to be?!" — to which they shrugged their mutual ignorance of the proceedings. D.P. glanced at his watch and said "It's just about nine . ."

"Better grab a seat for the show, Sid," said one.

Everyone scattering quickly, they took their seats in the front row on either side of Velma who, like both her companions, expressed surprise at the unexpected commencement of festivities in an altered schedule. The lights dimmed to practically nothing as the first strains of *America the Beautiful* poured forth through the theater, a slightly more than life-size Denny Warrington on the giant screen at the rear of the stage standing to the right and slightly in front of his wife and daughters, who were situated on a public park bench in what D.P. guessed was San Antonio. Nothing fancy, he mused, but well-done, anyway.

"I always figured Denny for a *Battle Hymn of the Republic* kinda' guy," he whispered, tongue-in-cheek, "but he seems to like this one better . ."

"Good evening, friends, I'm state senator Denny Warrington and I'm running for congress from the state's thirty-eighth congressional district in west Texas," he began. Sid, the consummate proponent of all things G.Q., noticed Denny's outfit first: cowboy hat, sand-colored leisure suit with matching tie, light-blue business shirt, and authentic-looking cowboy boots—a genuine Texan, through and through—and not just any Texan, but a *west*-Texan—and looking the part was certainly important. I'll bet even money, he told himself, that if someone were to dig just a little bit . . they'd discover Denny's 'cowboy boots' were actually manufactured in Paris, *France*. Then he noticed the three girls: all dressed accordingly, tastefully and without pretensions or snootiness, probably the handiwork of Dudley Thomas, who had his grudging respect. It occurred to him that Evelyn Warrington, to no one's surprise, would probably have looked just as good attired in the filthiest of rags, or perhaps a potato sack. "This is my wife of fourteen years, Evelyn, and these are my daughters, Farrah and Phyllis, and we *love* our state of Texas! My wife and I were both *born and raised* in Texas by parents who were themselves born and raised in Texas. Our respective parents raised both of us with good, solid, conservative, *family* values and instructed us early-on to keep one idea foremost in our hearts and minds: be good to '*everyone*,' they told us, like our lord and savior would want us to.'

"My wife and I aren't quite sure we *have* that kind of representation today, but we *need* that fair-handed, unbiased representation for *everyone* more than ever," Denny explained candidly.

The images on the screen suddenly vanished as quickly as they'd appeared, Denny and family cut-out entirely by the editor's skilled handiwork in favor of a remarkably different sort of picture on the giant screen, the focus of which had changed from a perspective of perhaps twenty feet to something in the range of two *thousand* feet, and maybe more.

213

Gone were the mother, her daughters, and the park bench, replaced by the tranquil waters of what appeared to be a vaguely-familiar lake or river extending away from the shoreline in haphazard fashion. As the camera now panned slowly right a massive earthen embankment came into view, rising steadily from the waterline in the distance to a point where the packed earth stopped and reinforced concrete assumed control in the form of sixteen individual spillways of a gigantic dam, its height uncertain but easily a few hundred feet plus. Sid eyed first Velma, then D.P., but his administrative assistant sat dumbfounded, his mouth agape in querulous wonder at the visions set before him, which were constantly being altered in the camera's continuous pan to the right as Denny's steady pitch maintained its rhythm and velocity.

"We are now engaged in a tremendous struggle with immigration reform," Warrington told the now-rapt audience, "but we must look at our Hispanic population *not* as the enemy, but as good and decent people who would give *anything* to become American citizens . ."

"Oh, my *God!*" D.P. wailed quietly, his right hand clutching Velma's left arm in panic, "what in the hell is *this*, for Chrissakes?! . ."

As Pettigrew's anxiety level increased exponentially, the scenario abruptly changed: the viewer was presented with the archaic sight of three immense, wooden catapults sitting idly on the flat, rocky surface of cliffs probably no higher than thirty-five or forty feet above the surface of the water below. They appeared to be exactly what they, in fact, *were*: contraptions designed and built for the singular purpose of being used in a Hollywood production of war scenes involving Roman soldiers warding-off the Mongol hordes, or

214

perhaps a slave-uprising or battle with Carthaginians. But any notions anyone in the theater audience held about its being a gladiator-inspired production disappeared instantly with first sight of a few dozen men in shorts, tee-shirts, and tennis shoes milling about the antiquated war machines. And who should then appear on-screen in blue jeans, Armani shirt left un-tucked, and high-dollar Italian loafers, waving merrily at the camera with a Texas-sized smile in the hot summer sun, but their political hero and champion, Sidney H. Villary!

Velma, stupefied as everyone else in the theater, grabbed his arm and whispered "Sid?!"

"Oh, son-of-a-*bitch!*" he swore under his breath, finally recognizing the landscape. "It's Amistad Dam from Labor Day weekend last year! . ."

Sid and another man, probably ten or twelve years his senior, appeared in the next shot that hit the screen, arms around one another in cheerful camaraderie, the other man saying in a quiet, subdued voice "Well, folks, we think we've finally developed a workable, *alternative* immigration-reform plan, you might call it, here in southwest Texas that combines sportsmanship and the laws of nature, namely, that what goes up, *must* come down—we're gonna' send 'em back the way they *came!*"

The camera now panned to the first catapult, which had an undeniably-Hispanic gentleman laying inside the contraption's cup in the fetal position, its human ammunition, sombrero in place atop his head, his expression of catatonic terror very much in evidence as he quietly muttered *"Jesu, Maria, y Jose!"* while four men with rifles at the ready prevented his dismounting the primitive machine. Someone off-camera yelled *"Pull!"* and the catapult launched him up into the air, his stubby arms flailing desperately for something, anything, to grab hold of that simply wasn't there as he flew out over the water a hundred feet or further, splashing like a cannonball into the blue water feet-first. It was first-rate, high-quality camera work, for the lens followed his flight-path start to finish, the human *ammo* reaching a height of sixty-five or seventy feet before falling into the water, the sound of giggles and laughter off-screen erupting conspicuously at the point of contact, man and liquid, the lonely sombrero floating down onto the water's surface a few seconds later.

"These people are our friends, our co-workers, and our neighbors," Denny's voice said over the events on the screen, "and they deserve our kindness and respect . ."

The camera panned right again to the second catapult, Sid's older friend now standing on the edge of a cliff overlooking the clear, blue water below with what appeared to be a scatter-gun in his hands, a mischievous smirk on his cruel face. Situated somewhere off-camera, several men engaging in idle chit-chat provided an indistinct background noise. After a short wait of perhaps eight or ten seconds Sid's buddy looked at someone else off-camera, the scatter-gun resting on his right shoulder.

"Almost ready?" he grinned.

"We're almost there," said another voice off-camera from somewhere behind him.

Sid's friend then looked straight into the camera and said "Well-now . . we've shown you how the *nature* part works, where an object airborne cannot *stay* airborne for very long before falling to the water . . Now we're gonna' show you the *sportsmanship* part, as the boys and I are gonna' shoot a little *skeet!* . . we call this particular activity the *wash-a-shoot* because just after we shoot, the pigeon gets a free *wash!* . . Are we ready now, fellas'? . ."

216

The camera panned further right again to include the men holding rifles as they observed their new target, an uncomfortable-looking Hispanic man with short legs lying face-up in the catapult's cup, his multi-colored *serape* dangling loosely from his chest and shoulders. A swarthy man with scraggly beard and droopy mustache, he was barefoot, ill-kempt, and chubby, eyes shifting sadly to the camera as he muttered "Eeiii, *chihuahua!*" several times. The voice of Sid's friend returned from its position out-of-sight left.

"Jose? . . you swam over here not long ago and made it okay . . now, you can swim back—*if* you get lucky and I *miss!* . ."

"*Ready*, Jim Bob!" yelled someone from way off-camera, the swarthy little man atop the catapult crossing himself in muted fear and desperation, eyes closed in lethal fright.

"*Pull!*"

The camera followed the little man's flight-path perfectly, the catapult flinging him up and out high over the water, his frantic little arms desperately swimming the air long after his serape fell away toward the water some eighty feet below, his ear-piercing scream losing volume the further away he flew until the resounding explosion of the scatter-gun silenced him completely, all bodily movement arrested immediately, his corpse falling harmlessly into the water legs-first from 'Jim Bob's' precision shot. At the sight of the little man's movement being snuffed with the terrific report of the scatter-gun, an audible gasp erupted from the theater audience, a collective groan of dismay from the ladies in attendance easily heard when the body met the water. On-screen, however, wild cheering erupted from the ranks of those gathered round Jim Bob at his skillful shot, the images on the screen taken from a little further back now.

"I think you're right, Jim Bob!" remarked one young man on-screen. "It looked to me like that one went both *higher* and *further* than the first one did! . ."

Sid leaned forward again, glared at D.P. with fire in his eyes and said "So *this* is the introduction to Denny Warrington and his family, eh?! . ."

Velma, herself now mesmerized into a semi-paralytic state, stared at Sid in astonishment, literally unable to comprehend the immensity of the evil she'd watched with her own eyes.

"Sidney?! . . Please tell me that what I'm watching *didn't* really happen!? . ."

"No, it didn't happen the way it *looks!*" he said hurriedly, his eyes glancing furtively left and right as he sank further into his seat. "Actually, nobody got hurt at all, Velma, please believe me . . I'll explain the whole thing when this is over! . ."

"It's our responsibility as Texans to make sure our Hispanic citizens understand our way of life, our priorities, our work ethic, and *yes*, even our *values*," continued the voice of Denny Warrington, louder than the voices emanating from on-screen images, "because when we as Texans have done a good job explaining and demonstrating what it means to be good Texans, *they* are no longer Hispanic citizens—then, they are *Texans!* . ."

The camera, focused on the triumphant Jim Bob, his scatter gun, and another dozen men standing within ten or fifteen feet of him near cliff's edge, panned slowly right again to the catapult sitting furthest away, a group of four men busy preparing it for action.

"Hey, Sid!" shouted Jim Bob. "I believe it's your turn now, sir . ."

Congressman Villary, hiding from the state of Texas by crouching in the front row where everyone could plainly see

218

him, watched himself walk over to his friend, Jim Bob, who gave him the scatter-gun then escorted him to the last catapult, whereupon the third test-pilot was brought forward and placed unceremoniously onto the cup. Like the first two, he was distinctly Hispanic, but was also quite a large man who appeared to be mid-thirties, had no mustache or beard, and wore a highly-stylish gray suit and nice leather shoes fit for a businessman. As Sid cowered low in his seat, head drooping with a hand over his eyes, more than a few audience members felt as though the third man somehow seemed more familiar than not, and some of the women thought they recognized him as a performer of some kind, though no one said a word about recognition. The face seemed a hard one to peg. Even Velma thought there was something that seemed strangely *satisfactory* about him, though it was nothing she could put her finger on. Through slightly-separated fingers Villary took a precautionary peek at the on-screen proceedings from ten months before.

By the time Sid stood at cliff's edge with the scatter-gun in tow, the victorious Jim Bob just a few feet away lighting up a cigar, the 'loading' crew had hung a white sign around the soon-to-be-airborne man's neck with neither lettering nor numbers of any kind on it. Sid watched himself ask Jim Bob what the sign with no message was for—what a bizarre sensation to remember having done something long ago, then watch yourself do it *again* from an entirely different perspective—at which point Jim Bob said "Hey, *guys?* . . How 'bout the sign, huh? . ." The large, well-dressed man inside the catapult's cup, tired of waiting, turned toward his left and flipped it over himself, revealing the crudely-written **ADIOS, AMIGOS!** someone had written in bright-blue paint. From his seat in the theater's front row Sid then heard several audience members scattered here and there snickering "Adios!" in gleeful response, and when the man sitting behind him asked if the tossing of Hispanics into the Rio Grande would be part of his election platform, without turning around he whispered, "Certainly *not!*"

Moments later when the on-screen version of their congressman shouted "*Pull!*" and the large Hispanic "illegal" became a human bomb, hurled by an antiquated mechanism built for purposes only a few select individuals could absolutely swear to, the six-foot-plus *missile* took off with his back to the water, his glare of mock-surprise greeting the firing crew as he took off. Climbing rapidly to an acme of about seventy-five feet, the live missile turned round in mid-air and grabbed his heart upon seeing the flash of light from the scatter-gun's barrels, Sid pulling the trigger at just the right moment for maximum effect, and gracefully went headfirst into the water to a stunned-silent audience.

"Is *this* what you would call 'respect,' ladies and gentlemen?" asked Denny, his image returned to the screen in living color, his family seated on the bench behind him once again. "Is *this* the way you want to be treated yourself? . . Is *this* the best congressman Villary has to offer? . . I want to represent *all* Texans—not merely a select *few!* . . I'm Denny Warrington, and I approve this message because Hispanics are here to stay, they're decent, hard-working people, and *they* want good, solid, conservative representation, *too*—not mistreatment at the hands of an elected official! . ."

He sat with one hand covering his face in the still-darkened theater, pondering the ramifications of west Texans everywhere seeing such a gross, distorted misrepresentation of their hero in such a conspicuously-misleading setting. Velma's comforting hand on his left arm didn't improve a thing; his knowledge that the entire show had been staged using professional performers—at least for the time-being—wouldn't help either. He'd still be trying to explain this one away a month down the road, two   months, even *three* months! And *how* in the name of all that was holy had Denny and his band of child-molesters gotten their hands on it in the first place?! The theater was quiet as a morgue. Velma's presence of mind, and especially her alternate take on the situation, averting a potential disaster in the making, he would fondly recall years later when relating the story of how she'd saved him that night.

"Well, if nothing else, it *is* historical!" she whispered in his ear, an infectious smile creeping across her lovely features. "*Extremely* entertaining, too . . but I think it'd be a terrific idea to stand up and try to explain things . ."

With that Sid sprang to his feet, vaulted onto the stage in surprisingly easy fashion and turned round to face his supporters: he wanted to tell them that what they'd just watched was a staged event with stunt men and a well-known stuntman-turned-singer, all paid handsomely to help pull-off the elaborate sight-gag the year before. Once the light hit him he managed to say only "Now *folks*, you shouldn't believe everything you----!" before the country club theater burst forth with cheering so thunderous the lights flickered on and off a few times, everyone on their feet in spontaneous approval of their hero's actions, screaming, smiling faces wherever he looked, the hand-clapping and foot-stomping rising and falling in terrifying crescendos of sound unlike any heard that evening. After acknowledging their admiration by stepping down off the stage, the next five minutes was consumed by men shaking his bewildered hands, the women kissing his cheeks, his lips, or whatever they could reach, the pats on his back so numerous he found it near-impossible to keep pace with them until, at last, D.P. and Velma helped push him slowly toward the rear and the exits. Half way to the back Dow's cellphone chimed. Sliding into a vacant row of seats to accomplish a remote semblance of privacy, he plucked the phone from his shirt pocket to read the message, carefully checking the number first: it was from none other than Dudley Thomas. The text-message was as acid to his eyes: "By the way, Dow . . . Denny plays *HARD-BALL!!*"

"You savage *prick!*" he cried out-loud in the mixed company of the theater, the shock of his personal reversal rendering him oblivious to his surroundings until Velma grabbed his hand and led him straight toward the exits as he closed his phone and threw it angrily back into his shirt pocket.

Half-crazy by the time he reached the club lobby, Pettigrew couldn't locate Sid because a half-dozen supporters, delighted with the surprising film footage on Denny's commercial, surrounded Villary and whisked him away to a private bar in the club president's office. Then he tried to call Tommy Burke and *nothing* happened: it was as though the number never existed. He tried three more times in the space of five minutes . . with the same result. Terrified to the point of physically shaking, the enormity of his miscalculations still unknown, Velma possessed the presence-of-mind to procure a quick Scotch and soda to ease his shattered nerves before he made himself sick. They stood in a corner of the lobby watching the theater crowd disperse itself to other parts of the club; a waiter cruised by with flutes of pink champagne on a silver tray—one flute *less* after he passed Velma.

"I'm a goner for *sure,*" he told her, like he'd already been cut loose. He drank half his Scotch and soda in two huge gulps to help fill the massive hole in his belly. "And if I were in his shoes, I'd do the same damn thing! . ."

"He's *not* going to fire you, Dow," she said calmly. He was too upset with himself to notice the fact that every other man in the lobby, in pairs or groups, was enjoying the sight of Velma either by taking quick, furtive glimpses or inadvertently staring, neither of which affected her. "He may very well be *upset* with you for being so unutterably fooled by the Warrington crowd, but he also realizes there's a problem that needs to be dealt with, and *you*, my love, are the one who'll have to deal with it . . Sid *needs* you, darling—now more than ever—and both of you have a better notion of what you're up against because Denny and his gang have already played their trump! . . So unless I miss my guess, when he's had time to think about everyone's cards being thrown onto the table, he'll realize it was *fortunate—not* the other way around—and he'll go about his business a wiser and better man . ."

As they stood out of everyone's way, waiting for the victorious Sidney H. Villary to materialize, a club employee, a youngish man, probably moonlighting while school was in summer recess, approached Pettigrew, introduced himself, then whispered something private in his ear. D.P. listened intently for a moment, then suddenly pulled back.

"A package has arrived for *me?!*—here at the *club?!*" he said suspiciously, for who on earth, outside of those present, knew he was inside Highland Hills?

"It arrived by special courier from Midland a few minutes before nine, Mister Pettigrew . . It has no obvious markings on it except for your name—no return address either, and the guy who brought it said he was instructed to inform whoever signed for it that no one was to open it except for Dow Pettigrew himself—no one else! . ."

"No one but me, huh? . . Okay, go grab it and I'll take a look . ."

"I'll be right back with it, Mr. Pettigrew!"

"What's this all about?" said Velma as she gracefully snagged another flute of bubbly as a hoisted tray passed her by. "Did Cas send you something from D.C.? . ."

"I wish I knew—but my guess is it's *not* from a friend, it's *not* anything I'll want to see, it arrived by special courier, addressed to me and me *only*, here at the country club, and that's *way too many* damned coincidences for me to believe it's business-as-usual! . ."

Peering left down the hallway toward the kitchen and main dining room, he finally caught sight of Sid shaking hands with a small group of men a good hundred feet away. As the guest-of-honor turned to leave them a tallish redhead of about thirty intercepted him, a friendly meeting between old acquaintances, for when she hugged him he wrapped his arms around her and planted an affectionate smooch on her cheek before they parted. He got almost halfway to them before someone else stopped him for a handshake and momentary chat, Sid still grinning and politicking when they parted company. Only when he got to within twenty or thirty feet away did they notice the tumbler of golden-brown liquid in his left hand, which D.P. prayed had managed to help alleviate his boss's somewhat ruffled feathers. But when Sid stopped in front of him the smile was gone.

"Go ahead, let me have it," said D.P., resigned to his inevitable fate.

"I don't have time to tell you *exactly* what I think of Mr. Warrington's innocent little *family*-type introduction to west Texas," he said calmly enough, his frustration and anger at least temporarily cast aside, "but I can tell you *this*: we have a

224

mountain of work to do—a *mountain*, you understand—because a disaster of this magnitude isn't easily overcome, and since you were instrumental in putting us there, *you* can be just as instrumental in getting us back *out!* . . Tomorrow morning's papers will give us a rough idea of the damage done, so I want you at my folks' house by half-past ten . . I'll get on the horn to Cas and Lynch later on tonight to share the good news because, *one*, I'd rather they hear it from me instead of some newscaster and, *two*, they're both pretty good operators in the clutch—so put your thinking-cap *on* and help us figure out where we go from here . ."

"It was *not* a complete disaster, Sid," D.P. reasoned hopefully, frantic. "These people *love* you, inside and out! . ."

"I love them, too—but the *rest* of west Texas—and I'm tossing-in a *dozen* or so Hispanics here, *as well*—might *not* have thought it was very funny! . ."

"Mr. Pettigrew?"

The young club employee handed him the mystery package, took a lingering, pleasant assessment of Velma's more apparent attributes, shook hands with Sid, and quickly walked away. D.P. trundled over to an end table by a lobby sofa and set it down; already upset to distraction, his high blood pressure exacerbated by Scotch-and-anything, a *second* nasty, unexpected surprise like the first one, Velma quickly surmised, *might* tip him over the edge. She scooted diagonally toward the sofa and end table, just in case, and no one seemed to notice. D.P. stood over the package for a moment, contemplating its mysterious contents, while Sid, who'd slowly followed both of them, stood aside to stare down at it, though he had no idea why.

"So what's in the funny-looking box?" he said finally.

"We're about to find out," said D.P., eyes still on the bundle.

225

He picked it up to let it rest in his right palm, guessing its weight at roughly five or six ounces. Its very plainness, its more or less rectangular shape, bound by brown wrapping paper and bright-blue twine, belied its bizarre delivery method and acceptance instructions, so very exacting and deliberate. No more than eight inches wide, four inches high and about as deep, it was wholly unspectacular, but D.P. thought it unwise to just rip into it. "Baby? . . have you got your little pen-knife inside your purse tonight? . ."

The blade procured after a short dig into her pocketbook, he sliced the twine in two places and let it fall away, then carefully followed a raised seam of strapping tape over brown paper with the sharp, thin edge, a modicum of pressure sufficient to create a two-inch gash in the paper. The container beneath the paper and tape was merely cheap cardboard, non-corrugated, perfectly flat, and easily ruined by liquid of any sort, sealed only with transparent tape of dubious quality, which D.P. loosened by slipping his thumbnail beneath it. Inside the cheap exterior was a completely different matter: the contents, still a bit of a mystery through the translucent plastic, appeared to be of a dark-grayish tone with colorful highlights in highly-irregular patterns. The knife-edge again carefully sliced through the relatively-thin, light-gray plastic on one end, which allowed D.P. to pull the contents out into the open, revealing a neatly-wrapped stack of Sunday comics, folded and re-folded several times, made more compact by having been soaked in water. More than a little befuddled by such peculiar contents, all three exchanged puzzled glances with the small crowd of eight or ten who'd stopped to see what all the fuss was about, D.P. stepping back for a moment's reprieve before pressing on.

Sliding the pen-knife beneath a conspicuous fold, he very

deliberately unwrapped one side, then its opposite, then the remaining two to reveal the exact same packaging inside: the Sunday comics, neatly folded and almost dripping-wet, like an oversized moist-towelette. Again he used the pen-knife to help unwrap the watery folds, the fourth and last fold revealing the actual contents: he saw a standard-looking, black cellphone charger and a piece of white plastic with a series of numbers on it laying atop single-serve packets of vinegar and tartar sauce, the sort one might receive at a drive-through seafood restaurant. One look at the numbers told D.P. everything he needed to know: no *wonder* he'd had so much trouble reaching Tommy Burke by phone! Thoroughly disgusted, jaws wrenched shut like steel traps, he dropped the worthless contents, glaring at his companions through slit-thin eyes.

"What in hell is *that* crap?!" said the startled congressman.

"*That* . ." said D.P. through clenched teeth, "is Dudley Thomas—or maybe Denny, I don't know—trying to be funny, or maybe dramatic—whichever one it is, it *isn't* working! . . the cellphone charger belonged to my agent inside the Warrington campaign . ."

"But mini-packs of tartar sauce and vinegar?!" Velma said suspiciously. "What in the world does it *mean*? . ."

"All I can do is tell you what it's *supposed* to mean, in the Warrington campaign's sick little mindset . . It means that my boy Tommy's cellphone is swimming . . *with the fishes!*"

XI.

Joan Villary, scrip-sunglasses shielding her tender eyes from the glare of the morning sun, sat at her breakfast table drinking coffee, left shoulder holding her cellphone to her ear, gleefully listening to the sultry voice on the other end while Sid and his father sat grim-faced, poring over three separate morning editions, none of which raised their already gloomy spirits.

"Yes, my dear, I will *most* assuredly be there tonight," she promised happily. "Yes, it begins at seven P.M., but we'll arrive earlier, of course . . Why, *yes*, he can hardly wait to *see* you, dear . . alright, then . . alright . . yes, we'll see you there! . . Bye-bye!"

Mission accomplished, she closed her cellphone and laid it satisfactorily on the table: in the life of every mother who longed to someday become a grandmother, even when they had to wait what seemed an *eternity* for the grand event to finally occur, there was invariably *something* to be grateful for. Today Mrs. Villary felt grateful for the splendid life and, *yes*, the future happiness of a simply lovely young lady from west Texas.

"Darling, Sabrina Adkins will be waiting for you at the civic center tonight when you arrive . . She got in late last night from Paris! . ."

"I thought you said she's living in London now . ."

"Oh, she *is* . . but most of her friends are in Paris . ."

A smidgen distracted by idle banter when occupied with

something important, Sid looked away from the news stories momentarily, his focus on nothing in particular, and muttered "the God-damned *French* .."

'I *wish* you wouldn't speak like that," she said, her shoulders visibly shuddering. "It just sounds so .. *vulgar* .."

"No, mother, it's not vulgar .. only *profane* .. But I'm too busy worrying to argue with you, so I'll defer to your better judgment and refrain from speaking in such a *profane* manner .."

"Thank you, my dear .. And what might Sabrina think if she heard such talk? .."

He kept reading a few seconds longer then, suddenly realizing he'd missed something, noticed his mother was sitting with an expectant look on her face, waiting patiently.

"I'm sorry," he said, "what would *who* think about *what*? .."

"*Sabrina*, Sidney, *Sabrina Adkins!* .. what would she think of your profanity? .."

"If she's lived in a scum-hole like Paris she's already heard everything I could *ever* say, plus several more I could only *guess* at! .. Personally, I think it speaks well of her that she had a chance to move to London and took it, if for no other reason than it got her the hell *out* of Paris .. but I have to wonder at her returning there because most of her *friends* live there?! .. Living in London sounds so very *healthy* somehow .. Just visiting Paris is like taking a guided tour of a city's sewer-system! .."

"*Sidney!*"

"Well, there it is, like it or not, and I'm not the only one who feels that way .. Most of my house colleagues who've had the misfortune of visiting tell me it physically *stinks*, and for a number of reasons .. Apparently there are metal walls a few feet off the sidewalk one can step behind and relieve himself ..

Ah, what a divine fragrance that must be on a warm day! . . It doesn't matter though, mother . . . I'll give Sabrina my official autograph, ask her when she's going back, pat her on the ass, and send her on her merry way—*if* that'll make you happy, of course! . ."

She threw the last of her coffee down her throat in a huff, sat quietly observing her bachelor-son through eyes grown cynically impatient with the inexorable passing of time, then took a deep breath.

"Now listen to *me*, sonny-boy," she said in equal parts exasperation and menace. The two men, from past experience, instantly recognized the implicit threat in her tone and wisely lowered their newspapers to their laps, their undivided attention now riveted on the lady of the house. "You're my son, and I love you more than you can possibly know. I'm also extremely proud of you for all your accomplishments, and they are *many* so, wisely or unwisely, I indulge your whims and behaviors as best I can. Sometimes I think I let you get away with more than *anyone* should get away with, and right now I think *this* . . is one of those times! I can hardly expect you to propose marriage to Sabrina Adkins tonight, sight-unseen for all these years, but she's a *lovely* woman who expresses a genuine desire to see you again, and I can't think of a single reason why you can't be courteous, attentive, and charming—*unless*, of course, it's your objective to be as colossal a *scum-hole* as Paris! Now, I surely realize that after last night's little surprise by the Warrington campaign, you and your team have some work to do . . but imagine how it would look if the papers one day next week were to discover that congressman Villary's parents had chosen to *disown* him for the simple reason that he refuses under any and all circumstances to have a child, married *or* . . out of wedlock?! . .

230

At this point we don't really care *which!* . ."

"That's *blackmail!* . ."

"Call it what you *like*, my dear," she said sweetly, rising from her chair. "If you were *gay* it might be different, but you're not, and everybody knows it—including your mother and father! . . Oh, and happy Fourth-of-July! . ."

And with that she sauntered out of the room and disappeared down a hallway, her message sent and received loud and clear by Sidney H. Villary, who sat alone with his father in the dining room. The old man cast his son a wary eye.

"I'm afraid she means it this time, my boy," he warned him. "I, of course, understand you not having found the right girl yet, but if I were *you*, I'd give your mom a wide berth . . Also, I don't think it would hurt matters if you went out-of-your-way to be nice and charming to Sabrina this evening . . at least if your mom saw you in that light, it would keep her off your *back* long enough for you and Cas and Dow to figure-out what you're going to do about the back-stabbing Mr. Warrington . ."

"Alright, father, I will," he said respectfully.

He dutifully attempted yet again to envision what young Miss Adkins had become in the eighteen or twenty-odd years since he'd seen her, but the imposing, delightful visage of Charlotte Tillstrom, fresh in his mind, managed to intercede at every turn. For the briefest moment, in a temporary lapse of sanity, he seriously considered telling his mother about his new acquaintance, but in the next moment had to ask himself if he'd completely lost his mind overnight. It wasn't so much a risk of the *wrong* people learning of Charlotte through his mother; Joan Villary, if cajoled and humored and amused properly—in conjunction with a threat of serious bodily harm—could be fairly-well trusted to keep a secret. It was really a greater risk of literally everyone on the face of the

231

planet ending-up privy to the news, in which case what relatively little privacy he had remaining would also vanish, a prospect he was loathe to allow. He had a demented vision of a homeless person—probably a man, a pan-handler by trade, living on the mean streets of Milwaukee where dinner was *not* served every evening at eight sharp—but a hustler, nonetheless, who managed to eat a few meals a day and could at least afford a cheap cellphone. An accomplished pan-handler, he has a friend in San Diego, a grifter, whom he's speaking with on his cell as congressman Villary happens to pass by on foot while in town conducting the infamous *extra-sharp* cheddar cheese price-hike scandal. The congressman happens by just as the pan-handler tells his buddy in San Diego "Hey, Murph?! . . Guess who some hot-shot Texas congressman named Sid *Villary* managed to leave with-*child* on a one-nighter in D.C. last May?! . . *Yeah*, and get a load o' *this*: she's *British!* . ." Congressman Villary, in this particular nightmare, isn't the sort of man to become easily flustered and immediately begins to emulate mild-mannered Clark Kent, an investigative reporter for the Daily Planet in Gotham City, a relatively large suburb north of Milwaukee. After a ten to fifteen-minute interview with this well-informed, incentive-driven pan-handler, who after much prompting and negotiating will only admit his real name is Hector of Troy, Kent/Villary weans enough information to return to the office to begin his online investigation. Two days and nights later the exhausted reporter has narrowed the field of suspects down to three—or possibly *two*—likely candidates who conceivably leaked the vicious rumor about the Texas congressman. It's either a young lady living in a remote village west of Helsinki, Finland; an elderly gentleman of 92, a self-described "gamer" from Sydney, Australia; or a woman in

232

her early 60's with a chip on her shoulder . . *somewhere* in west Texas. *No,* telling his mother anything *at all* concerning the existence of a female whose company he actually *enjoyed* . . was simply out of the question. He began to peruse the morning's ghastly news in the San Leandro <u>Examiner</u>, the second paper that might have provided commentary on the night before, but stopped short on nothing more than a whim.

"Dad? . . Can I ask you a hypothetical? . ."

Mr. Villary dropped the newspaper into his lap and stared blankly at his beleaguered son: Sidney *despised* operating under "possible scenarios" and "what-ifs." *Hated* it. What on *earth? . . .*

"I suppose so . . if you like . ."

"I'm just curious to know how you'd react," he began in a hushed voice, almost as though his mother stood right next to him, "if I brought home a beautiful woman and told you we had no plans to get married, *but* . . that she was going to have my child anyway . ."

"You mind if I grab another cup of coffee while we discuss this?" said his father, a silly half-grin betraying his pique. He jumped up from his seat and strutted into the kitchen with a purpose, poured himself another cup, added turbinado and creamer and returned to the table, utterly disposed to the game. "*How* beautiful is she? . ."

"*Dad!* . . this is only hypothetical, okay? . ."

"Yeah, I know . . but you said the woman you were bringing home is beautiful, right? . . I'm just wondering what kind of scale you're using to judge her by, that's all . . Are we talking about a simply attractive female here—or is she really *gorgeous? . .*"

Sid thought it over for a minute before saying "Who's that singer you and mom used to rave about? . . . You told me he was from New Jersey and was the greatest singer who ever sang a note—you used to listen to him sing all the time? . ."

"You mean Frank Sinatra," said his father. *Jesus,* young people didn't know *shit*—why couldn't they at least know about people worth knowing about? "And we not only *used* to listen to him—we still *do* . . . But . . Frank's a *guy!* . ."

"That's him, yeah . . well . . You once told me he was quite the lady's man . . but what I remember best is your description of one of his wives, or girlfriends—I'm pretty sure you used the word *stunning* to describe her—any idea who I'm referring to? . ."

"You're talking about Ava Gardner, his second wife," the old man said enthusiastically, a twinkle in his eye, "and that *pretty*-well describes her, yes . ."

"Okay, then . . *That's* the kind of woman I'm talking about bringing home in this make-believe scenario . ."

"She's going to have your child, but neither of you plan to marry, right? . ."

"Yes, sir."

The old man pondered this information for a moment or two, then slowly nodded, saying "To be perfectly honest, son, I'd be disappointed in your arrangement simply because it's not how I was brought-up to behave—and neither were *you,* by the way . . The ministers and Bible-thumpers are always telling us how very difficult it is to comprehend God's plan for us—our own Reverend Malone has said it *many* times—and I confess there are thoughts and actions today's young people accept and even *embrace* that utterly baffle me—their tendency to believe that all history began on the day each of them was born being the most notable—but everything changes over time, I suppose . . Still, I'd be rather frustrated in your handling of the situation . .'

234

"On the other hand . . if you were to bring home someone as beautiful as Ava Gardner and told us she was pregnant with your child—and our *grandchild*, of course—I'd be obliged to welcome her into the family *and* hope and pray I'd get to hug and kiss her at least once in a while . . I'd also hope that someday you and she would find it in your hearts to accept the fact that you love one another and tie the knot accordingly . ."

"Let me give you another hypothetical then . ."

The old man stopped to take a nice, long look at the man seated across the table from him before saying "Are you feeling alright, son? . . it's just not like you to think in hypothetical terms, and even *less* like you to discuss anything having to do with women . . Here you sit across from me at the same table you grew-up with and I'm thinking I don't know the man I'm speaking with—but it *is* you—I may be over the hill, but I'm *not* blind—and I'm wondering if last night's experience at the club has thrown a monkey wrench into your gears or something . . Do you mind telling me what this is all about? . ."

"Nothing, really," said Sid, shrugging it off. He checked his watch: ten after ten. D.P. was due in twenty minutes. "I've been thinking about a number of matters lately, but nothing unusual . . Immigration, taxes, abortion questions, spending, the size of government—the standard arguments of the day— but I've been trying to at least consider them in a different light, from a distinctly *fresh* angle, and I find myself grappling with issues of *person-hood* as much as any other . . Would you mind if I ask you a few personal questions about you and mom? . ."

The old man's eyes narrowed measurably when he said "No, I suppose not . . as long as they're not *too* personal . ."

"No, father . . nothing too personal, I promise . . When you *first* met mom, was it attraction at-first-sight? . ."

"Don't you mean *love* at-first-sight? . ."

"Not necessarily, no . . what I'm wondering is *this*: was there any kind of *chemistry* between you when you first met, the kind of attraction that immediately told you mom was, if not *the* woman of your dreams, at least someone worth getting to know better? . ."

Mr. Villary sipped his coffee and leaned back in his chair to relax, the memory of that time long ago as fresh as if it had been the day before, his smile as wide as the Rio Grande itself.

"I knew the first time I met her that if I couldn't marry her I'd never be happy again . . LBJ had just announced he wouldn't be running for president again, so it was both a sad and happy time—sad that a Texan would no longer be in the White House, but happy that the next man to occupy it might be a Republican—so there we sat commiserating in that Poli-Sci class, but your mother was only vaguely interested that I was interested, so . . nothing happened for the longest time, but we slowly became friends, and then we became . . *more* than friends, I guess you could say," the old man smiled. "She was dating this over-achiever from Wichita Falls—Thurman Cox was his name—the sort of guy who, if you told him you had a friend who existed in a perpetual state of unrest, he'd wanna' know what the capital city of Unrest was?—and when I humbly suggested she could do better she flew into a rage— told me she never wanted to see me again, *ever*!—but she told me later she was mad because I'd hit the nail right on the head, and she didn't like that—so for me you could say it was love at-first-sight, but for her I was what you might call a 'project'—she's always been able to explain me away as an *acquired taste* . . at least, that's what she tells her friends who,

236

for whatever reason, find me less than agreeable . ."

Sid patiently absorbed his father's words like a six-foot-plus sponge and said "Do you suppose love at-first-sight is actually *possible?* . . The reason I ask is because I can't think of a single couple I know who just fell head-over-heels in love on their first date, but it seems like I'm always hearing about this man or that woman who dated someone all the way through high school, got married, and lived happily ever after—that maybe without any reason at all both just instinctively *knew* they'd met the right one, and that was that . ."

"I've known one or two couples like that," the old man said reflectively, "but I've known *more* who fell head-over-heels for each other—couldn't get *enough* of each other—who ended-up divorced five or six years later. Yes, sir, they were crazy about one another, and the operative word there is *crazy!* . . By the way, if you brought a woman home to introduce us to—and she was as gorgeous as Ava Gardner, but you *didn't* want to marry her—I'd wonder if you weren't a little crazy, too! . ."

"Really? . . Crazy?! . . How do you mean, exactly? . ."

"How do you *think* I mean, son? . . Let me give *you* a hypothetical . . Suppose a young man of, say, eleven or twelve happens upon a nudist camp and spots a place along the stone wall surrounding the camp he thinks he can climb successfully to get a look inside, but then for no apparent reason at all decides *not* to try it—he's not interested in what's going on inside! Now, what do you think of this young man? . ."

Sid paused for a long moment to carefully choose the most appropriate words before saying "*That* . . is what I'd call a very fine, a very *conscientious* young man . ."

"Don't hand me that *crap!*" cried the old man. "If he didn't want to see what's happening inside a nudist camp, *then* I'd

237

think something was wrong with him, son . . that's just human nature . ."

"I see your point, dad . . but what does that have to do with me bringing home a woman who's irresistibly beautiful and *not* wanting to marry her? . . I've brought home a bunch of pretty women—you said so *yourself*—but I didn't want to marry any of *them* . ."

"I've wondered about that, too," the old man confessed, "but I figured you knew what you were doing, so I let it go. But there are times I worry that, like *most* American men, you suffer from a case of P.W.S., and although I taught you *better* than that—plus the fact you've never given me cause to distrust you—*none* of us is perfect . . We all have weak moments, we all make mistakes . . but the fact is, *that* particular malady, like jazz music, is an American original, and it's certainly nothing to be proud of . ."

"You'll have to help me out here, dad." he said, for he had no notion of what his father was talking about. "I'm sure you've explained it to me at some point in the past, but I honestly can't even remember what P.W.S. stands for . ."

"It's what makes so many American men—even *successful* ones—such abysmal *losers*, son . . if it wasn't for Psychotic Womanizer Syndrome, everyone in this country would be *so* much better-off! It manifests itself in startling ways, too, *not* just the more obvious, routinely-embarrassing ways so many American men have adopted and subsequently perfected. I see it all the time and wonder how we came to *this*! . . Of course, I completely understand the male drive for conquest and seduction—done it a few times *myself*—but that in no way excuses the man from his responsibilities towards the female. And understand *this*: I'm not talking about what God or men-of-the-cloth instruct us as to proper behavior—I'm talking

238

about men who go about the hunt, locate and select their prey, seduce their intended partner, then *abandon* them when the least little thing goes awry! To their way of thinking, *if* unfortunate consequences arise from their tryst, it then automatically becomes the woman's responsibility to *handle* it! This, of course, assumes the man had *nothing* to do with the matter in the first place—the reality being the precise *opposite!* . .'

"The other most-common symptom of P.W.S. is the man who sets a date with a woman but scans the horizon for something better—a woman more voluptuous, a woman who's better in the sack, a prettier woman, a more striking-looking woman, a male *trophy*, as it were—and he searches for her while he's in the company of the first woman! What on earth could possibly be more degrading, more *humiliating* than to be with a man like that?! These men have a lot of class, too—but all of it is *low*, son—they are *low-class*, and no self-respecting woman would be caught dead with someone like that! There are other manifestations of the disease, naturally, and some are more subtle, some not—and I hope you can see I'm not moralizing here—we must all choose our ground as we see fit, individually and collectively, and men are free to behave as they like—I'm merely stating a *fact*, namely that American men, to a great extent, have their priorities *ass-backwards!* . . And here's another tip for you: the more women become like men, the more reprehensible *their* behavior becomes . .'

"The point I'm making, in a very roundabout way, is that if you are allowed the honor and privilege of spending time with someone as beautiful as Ava Gardner was, you wouldn't *want* to be with anyone else! So what's the trick? The trick, my boy, is finding the right woman to spend your life with, and it

239

doesn't so much depend on what's *outside* as it does on what's found *within*—*that's* the true test! . . And when you find her, she may *not* be as bright as the sun, she may *not* have movie-star looks, and she may *not* be the one your friends prefer for you, much less her *parents*—but she's the only one for *you*, anyway . ."

"Then may I assume for the moment that you actually *do* believe in love at first-sight? . ."

"I'll just say I think it's possible, but I don't think it's very likely . . I'd guess it actually occurs in maybe one in a thousand cases—and that may be too generous . ."

"Alright then, let's say you're right, dad—in fact, let's say it happens only once in every *ten* thousand cases," he suggested bravely, "and that it's the picture-perfect situation for both of them . . except that something goes terribly wrong and it's *not* the fault of *either* of them . ."

"How so? . . Is one of them terminally-ill or something, and not know it? . ."

"No, nothing as bad as that . . but I want you to bear with me while I attempt to explain this purely hypothetical scenario, because there are one or two questions I want answered myself, and I want you to know *up-front* that this particular issue is important enough to me to perhaps stake my political future on, okay? . ."

"Good *lord*, son," the old man muttered under his breath. "*Which* issue are we talking about here? . ."

"Specifically? . . *Person-hood!* . . And the questions I need answered are honest and sincere and, above all, *legitimate* . . Can you help me? . ."

"All I can do is try," his father said at length.

"Okay, here we go . . A man and woman happen to be in the same place one night and are almost immediately attracted to

240

each other from a short distance, and when they see and speak with one another in close quarters they find the attraction is even stronger . . The woman invites him to her house for the specific purpose of sleeping with him, and that's *precisely* what happens: they make mad, incredibly-passionate love repeatedly, which convinces both they were right all along in their initial assessments of the other. Now . . the *kicker* in this scenario is that both male *and* female use dependable protection, not just one or the other, but *both*, okay? . . and for reasons neither of them will ever really know or comprehend, *both* protective systems suffer catastrophic failures, resulting in a pregnancy . ."

"Excuse me for a second," the old man interrupted, "but who's the *aggressor* here? . ."

"Is that important?. ."

"Maybe . . or, maybe not, it depends . . I was just thinking of the possibility that either the man or woman has ulterior motives, that's all . . perhaps *both* do, who knows? . ."

"In that case, let's say it was the woman who exercised a little initiative and made the first *move*, but it could just as easily have been the man, okay? . . However, for our purposes here, there's no evidence to suggest either party had anything other than an intense attraction to their partner as a reason for spending the night together in bed . ."

"Interesting," mused the old man as he finished-off his coffee. "Okay, go ahead . ."

"There's no way in the world the female could've known her birth-control pills would malfunction until it's too late to take other preventive measures, so now she's actually about six, maybe seven weeks into the pregnancy before she experiences her first morning-sickness and finally discovers what might be considered a *growing* problem? . . But both

241

partners are mystified by the fact that each played by the rules, each did what they were *supposed* to do to prevent the possibility of—*how* did you put it?—'unfortunate consequences?'—and still the odds turned on them like a knuckle-ball thrown from deep left-field! . . So there it is, father: they did *everything* right . . and *still* got snake-bit! . .'

"Now . . I've laid-down the conditions and circumstances of the situation as best I know how, and I haven't left out anything important, so my first question is . . Precisely *when* is this future human being granted *person-hood?* . ."

"*That* . . is a huge bone of contention in this country," his father chuckled regretfully, "and I'm stunned you're asking me, because it's the legislator's duty to decide issues like that by determining laws that govern such issues. I know what most *liberals* consider person-hood to be, and I know what most *conservatives* consider it to be, and they're not the same— *that* much I can say for certain. That especially-emotional issue will neither go away in our lifetimes, nor will it ever, *ever* be decided definitively to the satisfaction of all parties, so to answer your question is a virtual impossibility . . As a conservative, of course, I can understand terminating the pregnancy *only if* . . it's a case of rape or incest, or if the mother's life is in real danger of being compromised, but these are purely *medical* issues and nothing else. Speaking as a human being, naturally I think they should've exercised *more* care and caution and been *less* spontaneous, but in a situation like the one you describe, one can't really expect that to be the case . . I think it's a crying shame it happened the way it did, but now the bottom line has changed from it being a discussion of two people . . to a new discussion of *three* . ."

"So in speaking as a conservative, you grant the future baby person-hood at the moment of *conception*, not at the child's natural birth . . is that correct? . ."

"That is correct, and I make no apologies for it. Can anyone logically *deny* there is a third life in the mother's womb when a licensed physician declares it to be so? . . Pregnancy is a cut-and-dried concept, and therefore requires no discussion . ."

"What about the case of my two hypothetical lovers?" he said, re-focusing the discussion without actually re-focusing it.

"Okay . . what about them? . ."

"When does their theoretical child receive person-hood? . ."

"At the moment of conception, the same as a real child would . ."

"But it's *not* a real child—only a *theoretical* baby, a make-believe life inside the fantasy womb of someone's imagination . ."

"Then it would be appropriately granted *theoretical person-hood* at the time of conception—how else could it come to pass? . ."

"But father . . why grant it person-hood so very *late?*" he said emphatically.

"You lost me there, son," said the old man, head shaking in bewildered amusement. "How the granting of person-hood to a baby at the time of conception could be considered *late*—by anyone's standards—has got to be one of the most entertaining notions I've heard in a *while* . ."

"Okay, let's put it in *real* terms then . . Though it may have taken you longer than you wanted, there came a time when you and mom were attracted to each other strongly enough to get married and have children . . Most couples I know agree on the number of kids they want, what their future holds, and a dozen other things *before* they tie the knot, and I strongly suspect you and mother had that very discussion, too . . am I right? . ."

"You better believe it . ."

"Then I should have been granted person-hood the same evening you and mother looked at each other with that *gleam* in your eyes because, technically speaking, without that attraction and subsequent activity, I wouldn't be sitting here talking with you, *would I?! . .*"

The old man sat with his arms folded on the coffee table, wholly perplexed: was his only son's idea a stroke of *genius* or a devil-notion, a flash of *brilliance* or a flash-in-the-*pan?* If nothing else, it was a unique approach to an old problem. Suddenly he burst-out laughing, the vision of himself and his wife ignoring one another at first meeting in a college classroom as fresh as the day before.

"That strikes me as a remarkable *stretch* of the facts, son . ."

"But if that's so, what about the two people who meet and are immediately so taken with each other they jump into bed together that very night and accidentally conceive a child —*but for* their initial attraction to each other, no child would *ever* have been conceived! So granting person-hood at the moment of first attraction doesn't seem like much of a stretch! . ."

"I hope you don't mind my saying this, son, *but* . . I seriously doubt you'll ever find *anyone* willing to go along with the idea that person-hood begins with the initial attraction a man and woman have for each other — too much happens in between times, and the interim can be a few minutes or hours, or a few *days* . . or, like in the case of your mother and me, even a few *months!* But I say this because I've no idea where you're headed with person-hood issues, and believe me when I say those issues are very, very complex indeed . . so I fear the worst, but wish you the best . ."

"Now wait a minute, father, please hear me out," he said as respectfully as possible. "I'm not saying a single word in reference to men and women who meet, get along well and fall in love, then eventually get married and have kids, because I'm not interested with them as a *group* at all. I'm thinking more along the lines of those men who willingly violate the *first* set of circumstances you described in your explanation of P.W.S.—you know, the ones who stalk their prey, seduce their victims, then *desert* them at the first sign of difficulty? . . Seems to me the only way to deal with such men—and occasionally women, too, I suppose—is to enact legislation that drives to the very *heart* of the problem—that being that the individual who refuses to accept his fair share of responsibility for the creation of another human being is faced with the dilemma of either *taking* responsibility for his actions—and in this day and age, *that's* easy enough to prove beyond a doubt—or being fined, put in jail, and being *forced* to do what he should've done in the first place . . Men and women meet in bars and clubs all the time these days and spend the night together—it's been like that thirty or forty *years*, at least, and no one seems to mind at all—it's become an American tradition and probably happens a few million times every Friday and Saturday night . ."

"I understand what you're saying, and I think it's a noble endeavor," said the old man, "but I think it's a fool's errand, too . . I see a couple of potential roadblocks in your plan, and it's not so much that I'm playing devil's advocate . . I just see problems, that's all—the first being that you'll never convince anyone with half a brain that person-hood begins with a sparkle in somebody's *eye!* I think the idea—even with your reasonable qualifications—has serious flaws, one of which is the fact that it borders on the *absurd*—but that's just my opinion, for whatever it's worth . . The second hit—and the far more *serious* roadblock of the two—is the miserable history of

245

proposed 'societal' shifts in our country, like Prohibition, which failed utterly because of two primary flaws. The first mistake was the assumption that since drinking alcohol suddenly became illegal, no one would drink, which was patently, wholly *ridiculous*—and the second was the arbitrary *singling-out* of anyone who wanted to drink being denied that opportunity by another group with a different agenda who thought otherwise. It was doomed to failure from the first *day!* Your proposal—no matter how well-*intended*—is really much *worse*, you see: you would place an artificial deterrent to consenting adults making *whoopee* by ruining their fun before it even *begins*, son! *Worse*, your idea actually punishes *both* partners for following their own natural instincts! . . Why would a man, *any* man—and especially one who's taken appropriate precautions—bother to pursue a woman if he has loss of freedom and money staring him in the face in case something goes wrong? And the poor female can no longer be seen as anything other than a bold conspirator attempting to seduce her victim for now-*legal* monetary gain—which is nothing more than a form of state-sanctioned prostitution! Why, young people all over this country would burn you in effigy, son! You'd be the guest-of-honor at weenie-roasts in all fifty states! . . now . . I'm not suggesting you walk away from this notion, my boy . . If I were you, I'd run like *hell!* . ."

Sid Villary, the picture of calm the entire length of the figurative butt-chewing from his old man, laughed out-loud at mention of running away and said *"Father?!* . . I'm not suggesting the two sexes ignore each other—nor am I trying to impede anybody's right to fool-around, sleep with whomever they please, or anything of the sort. *All* I'm suggesting is that someone—preferably *me*—should 'push' the proverbial envelope a bit, the end-result being that, *hopefully*, people are at least made aware that a problem exists. More specifically, it's my honest, forthright opinion that to merely *introduce* said legislation would suit my purposes splendidly—it would be a sort of calling-card to those careless, mindless, morally-vacant types that someone is, indeed, observing them and is subsequently totally aware of their shortcomings—but I've no plans to pursue bringing any of it to a vote . . After all, it was *you* who taught me morality shouldn't be legislated . . I remember *everything* you taught me, dad, and I'll be damned if I'll ever forget even the first—"

The sudden re-appearance of his mother breezing back into the dining room brought his discourse to an abrupt halt. On her way to the kitchen freezer now, her morning nightgown, robe, and house slippers had been traded-in for canary tank-top, navy-blue shorts, and sandals, the west Texas sun having worked its inevitable magic on her copper skin.

"Thurman Cox wasn't as stupid as your father makes him out to be," she said in passing, the old man hiding behind his newspaper now like it was a kryptonite shield. "Actually, he wasn't any brighter than a twenty-watt bulb . ."

At the first chime of the doorbell a perplexed Sidney Villary rose from the table, saying "What on *earth* possessed Dow to ring at *front* instead of just coming in through the back-gate?! . ."

But when he opened the front door the answer was right in front of him: there stood D.P., fittingly attired in comfy holiday shorts and shirt, but looking a might sheepish, strangely undone from the previous evening. On the street behind him sat two cars parked close to one another with a pair of occupants each, the congressman divining their assignment in the time it takes to blink.

"I kind of figured you didn't know they were out here, but

thought you'd want to know . ."

Sid's parents had never seen the modest side of Dow Pettigrew, suspecting for years that particular part of him simply didn't exist . . but he stood humble and contrite in their presence before the two politicos vanished into the family study for consultations. The Villarys seemed quietly amused when he promised there would never be a repeat of the night before—unless, of course, he were to become intentionally suicidal: one never could tell in the world of politics.

"Do you remember the very *first* thing L.W. advised us to do a month and a half ago? . . We were plotting campaign strategy . . remember?" asked Sid after they plopped into their respective chairs. D.P. could only stare ahead, his silence as thunder. "He said he made it a habit to *never* underestimate an opponent, and that it had never let him down? . . Well, by *God*, that's good advice—so I've cooked-up a little something *special* for tonight's appearance at the Civic Center, my friend—and I think it's gonna' get us off the proverbial hook . ."

"Talk to me!" managed D.P., a semblance of life suddenly rising from within.

But before he could begin to explain precisely what surprises lurked in the background that evening, the study swelled with the pleasant sound of music being piped into every room, courtesy of the family sound system. Without thinking he reached across his father's desk to turn it off, but stopped with his finger on the switch to listen: was it a flute or a clarinet, or maybe an oboe? A trombone? Whatever it was, it sounded *great*: the rhythm and arrangement sounded upbeat and *jazzy* . . which was another great American success story, like himself. A smooth, seemingly-effortless voice suddenly poured forth into the room, the perfect complement to the upbeat sound:

"I've got you . . . /   under my skin . . .
I've got you . . ./   deep in the heart of me . . ."

"I'll be right back, D.P." he said, mind ablaze with music
and Charlotte and Sabrina Adkins and beautiful singing
voices, and a thousand other trivialities. Compelling him out
into the hall, then back into the dining room where his parents
still enjoyed the morning, his dad looked-up when Sid strode
through the doorway.

"Music bothering you, son? . ."

"No, not at all . . just the opposite, in fact . . It sounds
terrific! . . I've heard you play this before,

too . . So *who* is that, anyway? . ."

"You *like* that, huh?" said his mother, peeking out from
behind her newspaper. "We like it, too . . that's Frank
Sinatra . ."

"*Really?!*" he said, smiling down at them both: no wonder
they were fans! Swiveling round to return to the study, he still
grinned as he said "Frank Sinatra! . . God-*damn*, that sounds
good!"

"*Son?!*" his mother called after him, "I really *do* wish you
wouldn't talk like that . ."

XII.

In his ten years as a city employee, Grey Stanbridge had seen a few crowds gathered in the Civic Center. The turnout for The Perditious Flesh-Eaters had been the *rowdiest* throng he'd seen: when the heavy-metal outfit announced tongue-in-cheek at the concert's beginning that their master plan involved taking a hundred hostages at show's conclusion, the crowd rushed the stage, hapless would-be volunteers at its front, and seven policemen had been hospitalized, trampled underfoot. The assemblage for the Reverend Guy Gabel had been the most *devout*: no one had professed anything less than total, complete satisfaction with his words of encouragement and love because, as Christian Tarpley, the Center's executive manager, had expressed it, "a *lot* of money" changed hands. The circus, of course, had been the biggest kid's draw, with nine thousand screaming angels laughing and howling at the feats of strength, skill, and talent. But Stanbridge decided at length that this Fourth-of-July appearance by Congressman Sidney H. Villary had drawn the single most *dedicated* group of followers of any he'd seen, an additional three hundred folding chairs brought in to provide enough seating. The general noise-level approached the intensity of the young people screaming for the Flesh-Eaters' show to begin, but this evening's crowd consisted almost entirely of adults of every conceivable age, from about twenty to ninety-five. When Stanbridge sauntered his slew-footed way out to the waiting podium, mobile microphone in hand to introduce the evening's guest, the spotlight following his every step, the applause was deafening, if short-lived, the crowd quick to realize the man speaking wasn't their home-grown hero . . *yet*.

"Good evening, ladies and gentlemen, and welcome to a special Fourth-of-July address by your friend and mine, our *three*-term congressman, Sidney H. Villary! Congressman Villary is appearing here tonight courtesy of The Committee to Re-Elect Sidney Villary, Hume Corlew, Chairman. This is the official kick-off of the re-election campaign and should be considered his first official campaign stop—and what better place to begin than his home, the same west Texas town his parents proudly call *home*, and the county seat of Paiute County, Texas! My name is Grey Stanbridge, and I'm *honored* to be the Master-of-Ceremonies for this evening's get-together!"

Eyes scanning the overflow crowd while they rendered him a more-polite, measured round of applause, his vision ultimately fell on a tall shadow standing in the dark a good sixty feet away, hidden from the recessed lighting of the Civic Center, ready to take that triumphant journey into the spotlight where the podium and mic waited for him, and him alone. The evening sun, barely squeezing through the narrow space between the west-facing front windows and the parapet in the Center's rear, lent a soft, natural glow to the auditorium's vast interior. The four chairs situated directly behind the podium were occupied by the mayor, the vice-mayor, the president of the city council, and the pastor of the largest Baptist church in town, all friends of the family and long-time supporters of their esteemed congressional representative.

"And *now* . . without further *ado*," Stanbridge dramatically announced, "it is my *honor* and *privilege* to present to *you* . . our great and valued friend, trusted ally, and glorious soldier

251

in our nation's capital, Mr. Sidney H. . . VILLARY!!"

He strolled out from the right side—he'd made it a point to refuse any sort of entrance involving the *left*—with his handsome grin, the casual gait some took for swagger, the dark hair perfectly prepared, the black suit and tie, pale-green shirt—and shook their hands one by one, stopping to speak with each and pose with him, the camera lights flashing, hundreds per second, until at last he stood next to the podium and humbly acknowledged their adoration, waving and smiling, returning their love and affection by blowing kisses to the thousands risen to their feet in welcome. Loud and sustained, the cheering reached new heights whenever he waved to a select group of friends or supporters, or pointed a friendly finger in the general direction of a selected area, his parents clearly visible in the fourth row right, seated with a woman crowned with vivacious blonde hair and smashing make-up. Retreating a few steps, he extended his left arm in recognition of the esteemed personalities sharing the stage with him, which only brought another deafening round of cheering and clapping . . just as he had intended. Finally, audience members began retaking their seats, ready to hear the avalanche of good news straight from the horse's mouth.

"Thank you, *thank you so much!*" he cried humbly, "and may our blessed lord and savior, Jesus Christ, bless each and every one of *you* this evening, and always! . ."

And then, like the seasoned veteran he was, he shut-up, thus allowing the assembled multitude to give themselves a round of applause: who but a true *Christian* could commit a sin so unutterably awful, so extremely heinous, that it passes mere borderline-criminality like a speeding train, and then ask for and receive—oh, *yes*, always, everyone, no exceptions— forgiveness by such a kind and understanding savior? *And,*

252

(the best part of *all*) not even have to wait for an answer? His temporary silence afforded them the opportunity to pay homage to each other for maintaining such strict faith, devoutness, and piety. Of course, in the midst of their applause he half-turned to the Reverend Hudson, smiled and said "No, *sir*, I am *not* trying to steal your *thunder!* Perish the thought!"

"*Gee*, it's great to be back home with friends and loved ones!" he began again, facing the crowd once more, his heartfelt, honest message ready to deliver, a smattering of cheering and hooting rising here and there from the multitude. "First things *first*, right? . . I'd like to thank you for coming out on a holiday evening, first and foremost, and I promise not to keep you any longer than necessary! That said, I'd like nothing better than to spend more time *here*, and less time *there*, so I could have me some o' that good ol' Texas barbecue anytime I want it . . but I've been a little *busy* doing my constituents' work a few miles east o' here, near the Chesapeake Bay! . .'

"And speaking of *work* . . did anyone here notice the latest piece of *work* coming from the other side of the aisle?! . . My liberal friends—and I use that term *loosely*, ladies and gentlemen—let's just say my friends on the *other* side propose an immigration-reform bill that, over an extended period of months and years, grants citizenship to illegals who have learned *our* language, have adopted *our* way of life, have chosen freely to learn exactly how *our* government functions, and have worked hard to gain *our* trust . . And I stand in front of you right *now* and tell you that my conservative allies in the House think *all* of those ideas are fundamentally *good* ideas . ." He stood facing the audience to his left, but executed an abrupt about-face to his right in one smooth motion, stopping to place his right hand on the podium for support, his smile never leaving his face. "Shoot, folks!—*I myself* think those are good ideas, *yes*, I absolutely *agree* with my conservative friends—if an illegal keeps his nose clean and meets every single one of our requirements, demonstrating beyond *any doubt* that he can become a tax-paying, law-abiding citizen of our great country—then he's *earned* the right to become a U.S. citizen and should be granted full citizenship—but you notice I said 'earned'—*not* 'given!' . ." At this point he nodded his head in complete sympathy with the hundreds in the audience nodding their approval of his emphasis on the word earned. "That's right, folks: the conservatives and liberals *agree* on these points, *but* . . it's the *other* parts of the bill that I—and more than a *few* of my colleagues—have a problem with, and here's *why* . .'

"The other side says, in an act of good faith, that it has *increased* the number of Border Patrol agents protecting us at the Rio Grande by several thousand—and to their everlasting credit, they *have!* . . But when we look them dead in the eye and tell them 'Thank you very *much*—but they're *still* getting across!' . . they look at us like we've got one great big *eye* in the center of our forehead!—like we have no way of knowing whether or not they're swimming the river, when we have photographic evidence of it! . . And the problem is really two-fold, ladies and gentlemen . . and it's what we've been saying all along: we need even *more* Border Patrol agents, and we need to build the stupid, dang *wall* a little higher and deeper, and we need to build it from Brownsville to the Pacific Ocean, *period!* . .'

"Now, our brothers and sisters to the north of us . . don't *see* what all the fuss is about, but you know *what?* . . They don't have 1250 miles of border with *Mexico* to worry about like Texas does either! . . *They* think it's a good idea to keep the number of Border Patrol agents where it is *now*—so they can do what *little* they can with what *little* they've got, I suppose—and if there's no wall there to keep them out, *well*, that's okay, too—with our already high unemployment, what's another few *million* illegals? . . I wonder what those other states would think if Texas decided to send each of them a couple hundred *thousand* illegals and said 'Alright, fellas' . . put 'em to *work? . .'

"And tell me *this:* if we open our borders and let folks pour into the country at will, what about the good citizens who are already *here? . .* Where is *your* protection? . .In Washington, D.C.?! . . We already know we can't depend on Washington to do the right thing, so I don't know why we even bother to think they might change! . . Well, I'll tell you where your protection is: *your* protection is standing right in front of you, because Sid Villary would rather *die* than sign-on to any bill that grants citizenship to illegals *without* closing the border first to protect the good people of Texas who obey the law, work hard, and strive daily to make Texas the greatest state in the union! . ."

He heard the first clapping behind him when he spoke the words "rather die," and the cheering became so incredibly volatile by the time he got to "closing the border" the Norse god of the skies might have laid down his hammer to cheer, too. Holding up his left hand to quell the fanatic response, head nodding in affirmation of their righteousness and power to see the light, his smile had now become a smirk of sympathy with their values. A full minute passed before he ventured to expand his message.

"And do you know what gets *lost* in this debate, folks? . . Do you realize what it is that no one wants to *mention?* . . Well, *I'll* mention it, then: who protects the jobs held by illegals already living inside our fair state? . . Let me put it another way: if we

255

open the border and let people dash across, what protection does *anyone* have for their job or security? . . That's *right*, young man back there in the rear, I heard you!" he grinned, his index finger pointing the way. "If we open the border, *no one's job is safe!* . . so I'm already thinking of *everyone's* job security when I make my stand! . .'

"*Now* . . my friend and worthy opponent in the upcoming primary, state senator Warrington, ran an advertisement last night that I'm sure most of west Texas was able to see simply by having their TV turned-on . . And in this particular advertisement you could plainly see *yours truly* taking pot-shots at illegals as these antique contraptions hurled them into the waters of our own Rio Grande down at our beautiful Amistad Reservoir—although the Warrington people were very careful *not* to tell you it was filmed inside Texas—in fact, they didn't *explain* much at all, because then they would've had to say it was a *staged event*, instead of the *misleading* film of me with a shotgun in my hands shooting an innocent man! . ."

A scattered round of whoops and cat-calls greeted his admission that it *was*, in fact, their champion and hero in the commercial, but the caterwauling didn't come across as derisive; rather, it was the sort of noise-making that told everyone present they were *proud* of their representative for having joined-in the fun, for partaking in an activity that every native-born Texan likely *wished* he could do himself, but could really only *dream* about. Most red-blooded Texas men, at one time or another, imagined themselves taking part in the battle of San Jacinto, fighting for Sam Houston, in April of 1836, and anyone who studied Texas history knew why. Mexican general Antonio Santa Anna's forces had killed every single Texan inside the Alamo in San Antonio in early March, 1836, when the Army of Mexico outnumbered the Alamo's defenders by at least twenty-to-one. Six and a half weeks later the tables were turned: Sam Houston's forces attacked the Mexicans at San Jacinto and drove them out of Texas in a resounding military victory. Re-joining the fight in the twenty-first century—like tossing illegals into the Rio Grande with catapults—was also something most could only dream about.

"Ladies and gentlemen, since the Warrington people *refused* to explain or honestly portray what was happening there near the water, I'll let you all in on the *secret* . . You see, that was Jim Bob Simpson of Ft. Worth running that particular show last September . . Now, I don't know how many of you know who Jim Bob *is*, but let me just say he's a businessman and a personal friend and supporter of mine who decided to have a little Labor Day *fun*, that's all . . *Yes*, those were real men getting thrown through the air into the water! . . *Yes*, every one of them was Hispanic! . . and *yes*, that was *me* with the shotgun in my hands!—an unequivocal *Yes* to all those particular questions! . ." The congressman was now pacing back and forth fifteen or twenty steps in either direction, but his eyes stayed riveted on the audience. "But did Denny Warrington's commercial mention the fact that these men are all professional *stuntmen* who work each day in the motion-picture industry? . . *No!* . . Did Denny's commercial mention the fact that they were being *paid handsomely* for their work that day? . . *No!* . . Did his commercial ever say a single *word* about every stuntman there being a native *Texan*? . . *No!* . . And was *any* mention made about the fact that that big fellow thrown into the water—you know, the one that I supposedly *shot*—and I *did* shoot him, too—with *blank* cartridges!—was our very own Medal-of-Honor winner from Sherman, Texas, Diego Manuel Sepulvida?! . . No, I didn't *think* so! . . So they can say what they *like* about the way I mistreat our fellow

257

Hispanics—but it's not true, because the *facts* say something entirely different! . ."

When the ensuing cheers and whistles finally began to diminish, Sid turned to the Reverend Hudson and quietly said "You might want to be up here with me when I finish my next subject, Reverend!" —at which point the sixty-something minister of the gospel nodded and said "Just let me know *when*, my friend . ."

Turning once again to his flock, safely nestled in the seats of the Civic Center, Congressman Villary allowed his smile to fade away before saying "Now it's time to discuss something which, to my way of thinking, is not only extremely important to all Texans, but also dear to my heart . . and that subject is the very contentious issue of *abortions!* . . This is *not* an easy subject to discuss either, for emotions tend to run high when any conversation concerning the murder of the unborn is called into question, but the very seriousness of the issue requires substantial thought and deliberation . . I've struggled with this issue for longer than I care to think about and, despite the remarkable progress we've made in ridding ourselves of this vicious curse, I've always felt—and still feel— like there is real progress attainable, so I pursue *any* and *every* pathway to the ultimate eradication of abortion in this great land of ours . .'

"Most of you know where I stand: I've *never* been a friend of so-called abortion *rights*—in fact, quite the opposite—and I never will be! . . It would suit me just *fine* to see legal, highly-available, and in some cases even government-*funded* abortions go the way of the dinosaur, and there is a sacred movement not only in Texas but across our great country to see that abortions become a thing of the *past!* . . Our own state legislature is in the process of restricting access to abortions to

258

a very fewlocations—*and* under the strictest supervision of highly-qualified medical personnel for purposes of *safety* to the females compromised by carelessness and unscrupulous men of their acquaintance . . There are, of course, safe-havens for abortion services in various parts of the country, and there is little or nothing we can do about those desperate and misguided souls, save for praying for their ultimate salvation when it comes time to meet their maker! . . *That* . . is something I'd rather *not* have to worry about! . . and so I take it upon myself, as the protector of *all* Texans, to do what I can to discourage the wanton destruction of life, but to also *encourage* the protection of life whenever possible! . .'

"This requires a seemingly *constant* evaluation and subsequent *re*-evaluation of the struggle, the better to stay current with not only state-wide but *national* trends in this most holy conflict, and were I to *ignore* or otherwise *overlook* some aspect of this issue—then I've failed not only myself and family, but I've failed *you*, as well . . And therefore I must ultimately face the universal truth of *change*: a friend and adviser of mine—someone I'd *gladly* trust with my life—once advised me that *change* is the one thing all of us can absolutely, one hundred percent depend on . . *Everything* . . will change, he told me and, as usual, he's correct . . I've never known him to be wrong about anything, so I got to thinking about how much our society has changed in general, and then I thought about how some of the changes have been for the better and some not-so-much for the better . . We all know and recognize the changes for the better, and they're mostly the result of the conservative elements of our society: tolerance, concern for the working-man, universal health-care for some, education reform, race relations, and second amendment rights . . But we typically tend to overlook the changes in our social fabric because those alterations are so very *gradual* as to be invisible to the naked eye . . Our elderly citizens, for instance, see our young people kissing each other everywhere — in public, in the supermarket, in our schools, in our *churches*, for pity's sake, and various places in between — and wonder how in the name of all that's holy such mindless permissiveness ever came to *pass?* . . They shake their heads in wonder, remember that they would never have *dared* do anything so brazen and tasteless in *private*, much less in *public* — and they chalk it up to the inevitable forces of *change* — but is this change for the *better?* . . I think *not*, ladies and gentlemen . . so I began to think about the ways our social rules have been altered over time, and after an extended period of consideration I surmised that several changes have actually *harmed* a substantial portion of our citizenry, and I'm not talking about a *few* of us — I'm talking about *millions* of us! . . I'd like nothing better than to stand in front of you and be able to tell you with a straight face that everything we as a people have done over the last forty or fifty years has advanced the cause of humanity . . I'd *like* to, but I *can't*, because it's not true! . . I would like to remind you that there are states that *lead* . . and, there are states that *follow* . . In this instance I can say Texas will *lead*, as usual, and I can only hope and pray others will see the light and follow, for what I'm about to propose seems at first glance like an unnecessary hindrance to the exercise of free will . . But, I can assure you, it *isn't*, my friends, so hear me out and judge for yourselves . .'

"There is a problem in this country today that has existed for as long as men and women have been attracted to one another, and the fact that we are dependent upon each other for the survival of the species makes the problem all the more crucial to our way of life. To say that the problem is the domain of men *only* . . is a blatant over-simplification of the issue, but I'm comfortable in saying that men are the *primary* culprit in this particular instance . . What I'm talking about is the tendency of men—and I don't mean *all* men—but I speak of *too many* men—who successfully seduce a female, and a female who more than likely is willing to allow herself to be seduced, to carve a notch into their erotic belt-of-love in much the same manner a fighter pilot might keep a roster of enemy planes he's successfully shot out of the sky—then leaves and pretends like *nothing* ever happened between them! . . But there are so many potential *problems* to consider now! How could any right-thinking, red-blooded American male *delude* himself into thinking something as *beautiful* and as *magnificent* as making love to a woman . . never even *happened? . ."* Now he rested his right arm atop the podium in support and spoke to the assembly as though they were all gathered into someone's living room for coffee-cake and drinks— just a few close friends and someone to stir the conversation. "The female has several options here—whether she's pregnant or *not*—and some of these are fairly recent developments in the medical world, or so I'm told . . The first option is that she do absolutely *nothing*: she goes on about her business of day-to-day living as though everything is fine—and, *indeed*, that may very well be the case—and then six to eight weeks later, after a bout or two of morning sickness, she discovers she's going to be a mother in another seven months . . *This* is where the trouble usually begins—if there's going to *be* trouble, that is . . The poor, dear girl looks around for the support and encouragement she needs and deserves—*yes*, for the support she's rightfully *entitled* to—and I do not use *that* expression lightly—and the man she slept with . . her partner in the creation of this wondrous *gift* God has given them . . is *nowhere*

261

to be found! . . Panic-stricken, she feels the pressure of loneliness and abandonment and makes the arbitrary decision to end her pregnancy by obtaining an abortion—a crime *against* nature, because the creation of life is a *natural* act—and we're left to wonder what that life lost might have produced, what *joy* might have been known . . had the man simply been a man and taken responsibility for his actions! . .'

"Now then . . some folks might suggest that she should have taken the so-called 'morning-*after*' pill and ruined any chance of bringing God's creation to full-term, and maybe they're *right*—and the woman might never actually *know* if she was pregnant or not—but God's work has *still* been destroyed, don't you see? . . If life really *does* commence at conception, as I and millions of others believe, *that* life is destroyed!—*that* life is *taken!*—by the morning-after pill, and there's *no* getting around it, folks! . . So whether the child is murdered the day *after*, or a couple of months *later* . . is really immaterial, isn't it? . . . What difference does it make *when?*. . *When* . . has no significance in this case, I'm afraid . . It's the *what* that becomes so very bothersome here . . But shouldn't we take a look at the *who*, as well? . . Doesn't the *who* play a critical role here in the destruction of a life and the condemnation of a female—just because she happened to be gullible enough to sleep with someone she mistakenly put her faith in? . . Does the mother have a degree of *culpability* here? *Yes*, but let me repeat what I said earlier: the *women* are, for the most part, *not* the culprits here—*not!*—and deserve our respect and support regardless of other circumstances! . . Why should the female be forced to shoulder all the responsibility? . . This habit of men going from woman to woman, sleeping with as many as possible, only to *disappear* in the night—this is a national *disgrace* and it must be dealt with effectively or the situation will only

262

worsen! . .'

"Now, I *know* what some of you are thinking . . Actually, it's two different, yet *related* items we're discussing here, but I see the doubt and confusion in some of your eyes and I want to put those specific fears to rest right *now*, okay? . . Some of you are thinking that Sidney Villary of the thirty-eighth congressional district in west Texas is telling you *how* to run your life!—that he's *moralizing* and instructing you how to behave towards the opposite sex! . . But I say to you right this minute 'No, I'm *not!*' . . I have no problem whatsoever with men and women going out and having a good time as *they* see fit! . . It's a free country, folks: adults are allowed to do whatever they like in public . . as long as it's not illegal! And in *private?!* . . Folks, that's the business of the two adults involved, and it's their business *alone!* . . People should just leave other people alone and let 'em do what they *like!* . . It's called 'the pursuit of *happiness*,' and *danged* if I can find anything *wrong* with it! . . And, some of you are thinking *this*: 'Now *why* . . would Congressman Villary give a hootin'-holler about a man who soils a woman's reputation and leaves her well-being compromised? . . After all, there are laws on the books about fathering children out-of-wedlock, and child-support, and deadbeat-dads, and the whole nine yards *already!*' . . Well, *yes*, there are, and several of those laws have been passed in our beloved state of Texas . . but my colleagues in the state-house tell me there are still problems, and since that's the case . . do you *really* think I'm gonna' stick my head in the sand like an ostrich and *hope* things get better? . . *C'mon*, y'all! . . You know me better than that! . . I can't have any direct effect on statutory developments here in our great state, but I'll tell you what I *can* do: in Washington I can begin speaking with my fellow congressmen about this very issue and see what kind of

263

situations they face in *their* districts! . . This problem concerning irresponsible grown men *not* manning-*up* to their duties as fathers and providers doesn't belong to Texas *alone*, I promise you—this is a national problem, and it requires a *national* solution! . .'

"And let me address those who think I'm attacking young people and young people *only*: if you believe that, you'd also believe young people are the *only* ones having children these days! . . You better take a look around, young 'uns, because men and women are waiting longer to marry, have children, and raise a family than they *ever* were, and there's a *bunch* of women in their mid-to-late thirties and early *forties* who are having children for the first time!'

"*Now* . . One last thing before I present my proposal to you . . Let me see a show of hands to indicate how many of you know and understand what the letters *W.W.J.D.* stand for! .   ."

He raised his left arm as virtually everyone seated in the Civic Center, knowing smiles of inclusion radiating their personal warmth and righteousness, extended their arm upward like their congressman, a chuckle of mutual recognition rumbling through the audience as friends grinned at each other in Christian solidarity. It was as near a unanimous response as any that evening.

"That's what I *thought!*" he said with evident satisfaction. "We *all* know that WWJD stands not for 'a' question, but 'the' question: '*What* . . would Jesus do?' . .'

"Please, *please* believe me when I tell you that is *precisely* what I asked myself when I first began considering this problem . . What *would* Jesus do? . . What should be foremost in our minds when we ask this most serious, most *consequential* question is . . 'Do the people involved have a

264

choice?' . . I think Jesus would tell us that the man or woman who has *no* choice—the human being who is backed into a corner and has no way to escape—can no longer function as a human being, but only as a caged animal might function—as a caged animal *without* choice! It is what separates us from the beasts: our capacity to reason, so we must maintain our freedom of choice *always* . . Men and women are free to choose as they like, *but* . . when the choice of one *injures* the other, I reserve the right to take corrective steps in order to *protect* the injured party . . and too often the injured party seems to be the *single mother* . . Therefore . .'

"It is my intention to at least begin the journey towards repairing the damage done . . This will be a long and painfully-slow process—and any progress noted or statistically-recorded will doubtless be a point of contention by either the A.C.L.U., liberal elements, attorneys-at-law—or maybe *all* of the aforementioned! . . But bring the struggle I *will*, because the struggle has to start somewhere, and I can't think of a better or a more appropriate place than the state of Texas . .'

"And so . . as soon as the details can be worked-out . . I intend to introduce legislation that will establish *person-hood* at the first moment a mature female and mature male are attracted to each other, when . . *when* . . that attraction results in the subsequent pregnancy of the female as a direct result of that initial attraction . . after it becomes obvious the pregnancy resulted from the physical joining of these mature adults, especially in the event the joining occurred that *first* night!" he said emphatically, his left index finger working overtime, bobbing through the stillness of the air to augment the force of his conviction. "In addition, to further prevent the scourge of abortion, my legislation shall make the rights and privileges of

265

said *person-hood* retroactive to the same day the male and female *met* and *consummated* their relationship . . In other words, the male shall become responsible for his part in the pregnancy *retroactively* to the moment of conception—*not* at the time of birth, *not* when the courts have decided anything, *not* three months into the pregnancy, *not* six months into the pregnancy!—but right *then!* . . Only in this way can the male assume his rightful duties as the father, as he *should* . . but so often fails to do! . . Now, he can either assume his duties *willingly*, or through friendly *persuasion*, but the fact is that if both parents are involved in the welfare of the child, chances of an abortion occurring drop to about *zero!* . . That is my goal, ladies and gentlemen, and I want to spread the good news from coast-to-coast across our great land and rid our country of the *scourge* of abortion once and for all! . ." He turned to Reverend Hudson and invited him forward with a simple tilt of his head, the minister rising gracefully from his seat to join him at the podium. "The good reverend and I are convinced that our proposal is truly *God's work*—it is what Jesus *would* do! . . And so you may well remember this moment, because the movement back to where we belong starts *now*, it starts *here*, and Texas was meant to *lead*, and lead we *shall!* . . God bless each of you, and may God bless the United States of America! Thank you, my friends, *thank you!!*"

The first applause had begun when Reverend Hudson joined him at the podium, the hesitant masses evidently confused as to the true import of his message, the weight of his words falling on timid ears unaccustomed to hearing sophisticated wizardry the likes of which their elected champion had just given. Those who first lauded the congressman's pronouncements won over the hesitant remainder as women in the audience initially jumped-up screaming their approval, then rose in small clusters to cheer and clap as the import of his message became clearer, the men dutifully, if a bit late, standing to acknowledge the holy mission of their leader.

"I wish you the very best, Sidney!" smiled Reverend Hudson as they shook hands and waved to the multitude. "At the very least, it's a gutsy call, and Imelda and I, Hugh Beauchamp, and Isaac Winton and dozens of others will give you all the support we can!"

The standing ovation extended itself into its second full minute, the Civic Center's subdued interior lighting slowly rising again, as the exuberant congressman stole a furtive glance at his parents: they were on their feet like the rest, his mother cheering happily next to Sabrina Adkins, who seemed taken aback by the entire evening, but applauded nonetheless. His father chatted amiably with three other men, one of whom he thought was Sabrina's father, Albert, bourbon connoisseur extraordinaire, though he couldn't be sure in the half-light of the spacious hall. The adulation proved genuine: no one moved from their seat until a full three minutes passed. When he again shook hands with Hudson and the three city officials sharing the stage he thanked them for their support and cooperation, promising to keep the crop damage from the rainless summer in mind. The mayor himself went out of his way to express his personal appreciation for the wonderful infusion of government cash into the district, the majority of which had managed to stay within the city limits, extending a dinner invitation for the following week on his cotton farm. The mayor, Sid knew, could never decide which bourbon tasted best, but hedged his bets by keeping six or eight to sample on hand at all times. Sid immediately accepted the invite.

Dow Pettigrew, still mortified by the debacle of the night before and more than a little concerned about job security, intercepted him before he could get a better look at Sabrina Adkins. Her appearance from afar seemed tantalizing but, having been picked-up at his parents' house by the mayor and his wife, Sid still hadn't had a clear shot at the prodigal daughter. Another difficulty, more sinister and far more threatening, surfaced whenever he ventured to look in her direction and, unable to either dodge or ignore it, it had managed to creep under his skin. He found himself thinking about Charlotte Tillstrom, which in turn brought their personal turmoil to mind, her medical condition a cause for concern but, so far, no viable reason for worry. He understood better than most how beautiful women could easily lead men astray: had it not happened to *him?* Still, there was just something undeniably *wonderful* about her: she didn't smell like other women, she didn't feel like other women. She certainly didn't *taste* like other women and D.P., sensing some sort of invisible intrusion into his boss's realm, hastily decided some sort of *deflection* was called for—and what better distraction existed than the *political?*

"Sid . . we ran *out* of bumper-stickers and yard-signs a few minutes after you finished . . and Velma thinks our gambit will both garner votes *and* piss-off the Warrington crew . ."

The congressman looked right at him, grinned and said "So . . what the hell *is it* about beautiful brunette women anyway, D.P.? . ."

The misplaced notion that his mother might stay in bed until noon, which ran headlong into every rule and tradition of her sleeping habits, first occurred to the beleaguered congressman about ten after nine Saturday morning while he meticulously examined the morning paper. His desperate need to see as many editorials as possible was certainly no thoughtless whim: after the debacle of Highland Hills and its surprising conclusion, his performance at the Civic Center the night before felt even more crucial. To a shallow degree, the hometown newspaper provided what he sought. His picture on the front page, taken during a moment when his hands and body were busy placing emphasis on his stoic, unexpected message, looked "pretty damn *good!*" in the words of Dow Pettigrew. The adjoining storyline he found to be 'refreshingly objective,' which meant that his dad's friends in the newsroom fell all over themselves praising their brave congressman's accomplishments and plans for the future—even if not many people understood them. More than anything, he needed time to search-out and gauge objective reaction to his earth-shaking proposal; on the other hand, he did *not* need to recount every move and counter-move made by himself and Sabrina over dinner at the country club . . but the play-by-play is what his mother would surely expect. Alone with his father at the breakfast table at a quarter-after, five minutes later she strolled through the doorway in her nightgown and slippers and headed straight for the coffee, winking at her sweet little boy as she passed by.

"Let me grab a cup and a bun, then you can tell me *all about* last night with the adorable Miss Adkins, my handsome boy! .."

Father and son exchanged familiar expressions of quiet desperation, resigned to the inevitable, then returned to their respective papers. Joan Villary was relatively tall and slim. Would Charlotte still be thin like his mother when *she* hit sixty-four? Would they be able to wear the same kind of clothes, since both were roughly the same height? Could his mother, a natural blonde herself, ever find enough room in her heart to accept a redhead as her daughter-in-law? A brunette? The fact that her blonde had turned mostly gray never seemed to bother his mother in the slightest—maybe because light-gray and blonde weren't so different in appearance—but what about dark-haired women whose gray inroads clashed so violently with their darker strands? What about *them?* With an increasing sense of guilt and shame he realized he'd done it again: he'd been sidetracked by thoughts of Charlotte and hair-color and everything he wanted to *ignore* while he pursued reaction to his Friday-night speech and bombshell statement-of-intentions. What in the hell is wrong with you anyway?, he asked himself. For Chrissakes, *focus!*

As he watched his mother set her coffee and Danish on the table, he decided a preemptive strike was perhaps his best strategy.

"I've seen Sabrina Adkins up-close, and she in no way resembles Ava Gardner . ."

"Well, of course not," she agreed, taking her seat, "Sabrina's a blonde and Ava was a brunette . . but what does *that* have to do with anything? . ."

"Sabrina and I decided it would be in our own selfish best-interests if we *didn't* get married, have children, and raise a family . . It just wouldn't work out because our respective interests and situations are so dissimilar—that and the fact that we both have so many disparate loves in our lives, it would be nearly impossible to alter ourselves so radically and deceive ourselves into thinking that, at some point down the road, we wouldn't want to tear each other to shreds . ."

"*Disparate* loves?! . . son, I don't even know what that *means!* Would you mind telling me what you're rambling-on about in language I can understand? . ."

"Mother, I knew I was in trouble when we sat at the club

and ordered our meals," he said with an edge in his tone, "because not only was there a *very* limited selection of French wines available, my date actually *frowned* when I ordered the wine I wanted with my steak . . When our waiter presented her with the club's wine menu she looked at it, saw the French wines at a glance, then looked-up at him and said 'Are you *kidding?*' . . By the way, did you know the French now have the fastest train on the planet? . ."

"Who cares about the train?—tell me about dinner and wine and the rest of it . ."

"Needless to say, she wasn't too impressed with *anything* the club had to offer . . She finally settled for a—I think she said it was from Bordeaux, an '03, and it had a fine, reddish color . . and unless I'm greatly mistaken, I think she said it was something called a *claret*—I remarked that her choice sounded more like a musical instrument than a wine, and she didn't appreciate *that* either . . Then I ordered my wine, and you'd have thought someone slapped her in the face with a dead mackerel! . ."

Mrs. Villary's face turned sour with the breadth of the catastrophe.

"You didn't order *white wine* with your steak, did you, son?! . ."

"Of course not, it was a red, too, just like hers—I may *seem* like a hayseed from west Texas, but I'm *not,*" he said proudly. "Mine was a Chateau *Leg-Opener* '98, from the Napa Valley . ."

The old man dropped his newspaper and burst into laughter, at which point Mrs. Villary dubiously eyed first her husband, then her son before saying "I can't believe I'm sitting at my own breakfast table on a Saturday morning, and you two *deviates* are my company . ."

"Would you believe she got a root-canal done for a hundred

and a *quarter*—and then the government *returned* over eighty-five of it to her?! . ."

"Who told you *that?!* . ."

"*She* did, mother! . . By the way, the 'adorable' Miss Adkins *loves* all things French—and that includes a remarkable list of items too numerous for the likes of a country-boy like myself to remember—about the only one I can recall is that France is roughly the one-hundred-thirtieth-*fattest* country on earth—that, and the fact that, according to the divine Sabrina, France is generally considered to have the best health-care system of anyone anywhere—including the Brits and Canadians, who the French look *down* on because their systems are so comparatively *inferior* . ."

"But isn't Sabrina a lovely girl, son? . . That blonde hair of hers is *hers*, if you follow my meaning," she said, tearing-off a bite of Danish. "*Nothing* fake there, my boy: *real* hair, *real* looks, *real* smarts! . . And a very nice grip on reality . . She'll make someone a *wonderful* wife, and I wish it was you . . but I suppose her fondness for all things French would eventually rub you and your house-colleagues the wrong way, so perhaps it's better you not become entangled . ."

{'If you only *knew* about me and entanglements with women, mother!' thought he.}

"I don't suppose there's anyone in Washington you're not telling your poor mother about, is there? . ."

Sid set his newspaper aside to pay closer attention: ever since Denny Warrington's "surprise" television commercial literally took his breath away, his antennae had shifted into world-wide-alert mode. If he had his way—and, of course, he *would*—there would be no more surprises from anyone, friend or foe. *Not* that his mother would ever intentionally sabotage his chances . . but being careful with everyone, family *included*,

272

was merely wise. So, too, both parents had known Denny and his family for many years, Evelyn being the niece of one of his mother's long-time pals. His folks knew literally *everyone*: they even knew L.W. Shaw's *wife!* Better to be safe . . than *sorry*.

"I hope you haven't been talking with the Warringtons lately, mother . . It's difficult enough having to face a Marxist like Consuela Garcia in the general election, but for Denny to come at me from the *right* in the primary next month? . . With friends like that, who needs *enemas?* . ."

"Son, *please* . ."

"And *another* thing, mother . . your lovely Miss Adkins doesn't want children because, as worldly-wise and pragmatic as she is about any number of subjects, she's too concerned with maintaining her youthful *figure* to give serious consideration to ruining it with two or three ripe, attention-absorbing, weight-gaining crumb-snatchers to tend to . . She went so far as to tell me she might *consider* adopting sometime in the future—but she didn't sound too enthusiastic about that prospect, either, so I'm thinking that if you *ever* want grandchildren, *maybe* Sabrina Adkins shouldn't be placed behind door number-*one* in the Future-Wife-of-Sid-Villary Sweepstakes . . she told me all this right after she *groped* me in the car on the way to the club . ."

"*Really*, son" she said ironically without looking up from her coffee and Danish.

"Naturally, I was shocked and dismayed by her clumsy, prurient advances . ."

"Shocked and dismayed," the old man repeated softly, "shocked and dismayed . ."

"I'm convinced we got off on the wrong foot when I told her I'd quit eating French fries four or five years ago," he said. "She's very high on the French, you know . ."

Sid grabbed the newspaper and began reading again of events from the night before. The paper's political writer described the decision to make "person-hood" retroactive to a couple's beginning awareness of their mutual attraction—in case of a resultant pregnancy, naturally—"absolutely ground-breaking" in terms of assuming responsibility for one's actions, with the ulterior motive of thwarting abortions actually sounding more like a benign, desirable side-effect.

"Maybe Sabrina considered it undiplomatic of me to remind her that the French kicked us out of France in the 1950's for no reason whatsoever," he said, his face still inside the newspaper.

A few minutes later he set his paper down on the tabletop, remembered his coffee cup was empty, noticed there was still nearly a half-pot in the carafe, and rose to chase-down another cupful, sauntering into the kitchen carefree and light of foot.

"Maybe it put Sabrina *off* a little bit when I happened to mention that Charles de Gaulle always reminded me . . . of a large, erect penis—with *arms* . ."

"*Sidney!*"

XIII.

Dow Pettigrew, cellphone to ear, half-listened to the angry voice on the other end, the venomous, caustic accusations being hurled as poisonous spears into his right ear, only to exit through his left a nanosecond later, the intended toxins corrupting nothing once they mixed with thin air. Sour grapes always sounded so much like . . *sour grapes*. Every minute or two he managed to inject an impromptu "Sure!" or "Yeah!" or even a satisfactory "We'll *see!*" . . but he knew from experience it was never easy to get in a word edgewise with Dudley Thomas—especially when his counterpart was upset. D.P. grinned at his co-conspirator, Sid Villary, congressman from the thirty-eighth district in west Texas, who sat behind the wheel of the metallic-blue Camry, driving with but one hand to the local television station for his Monday morning interview, to be aired that evening on the 6 o'clock news, courtesy of the Rex News Service.

Someone in New York City, reputed to be the arch-liberal, slightly-left-of-Joe-Stalin Caruthers F. Stanfill at the <u>Victory</u>, had gotten hold of the Friday-night speech at the Civic Center, performed an editorial critique (which the old man caustically referred to as a "hatchet-job, par-*excellent*"), and published it in the Sunday edition, ripping it to shreds philosophically, politically, humanistically, and socio-economically, regretting the fact that he could think of no other method of destroying it. Then the "Rexers" seized the opportunity and asked why *anyone* would line himself up against a measure meant to help curtail single-motherhood, a notorious and vexing problem in more cities and states than could usually be listed in a regular newscast. By Monday morning, July 7, the Villary proposal was being discussed on the morning talk shows, most of the commentary ranging from mildly uncomplimentary to overtly hostile. The general consensus seemed to be: *proper* objective, *wrong* method—yet everyone seemed to enjoy being included in the discussion itself.

This development, naturally, enraged Dudley Thomas, who wasted little time in communicating his extreme displeasure to D.P. who, after listening to a nearly ten-minute rant, suddenly said in a calm, clear voice "We have nothing but the highest respect for you and your campaign, *too*, Dudley! Take it easy, huh?.." He closed his cellphone.

"Dudley says 'Hi, how are ya'?' and sends his very best.."

"You're not scared to tell me what he *really* said, are you?.."

"Of course not . . I'm just not sure I can keep a straight face.."

"Do your best then.."

"The honorable Mr. Thomas claims you're a shameless panderer who received his code of ethics from a child-molester, who shall either remain nameless—or be named at a later time, in accordance with the rules of major-league baseball.."

"What else?.."

"The usual shit—you're not really serious about *any* of it, you just want the votes.. Seems so unusual that a man with *no* family of his own is 'suddenly' enamored with the welfare of the family . . Even if you someday find the masculine gametes to introduce the bill, it'll never pass muster . . Your newfound concern for the young moms and dads of America is nothing more than the fear that some*how*, some*where* . .

some*body* is having a good time, and you feel left out . . The whole damn mess is just a ridiculous ploy—a desperate gamble!—on the part of someone who needs the publicity, but already knows he's whipped . . And, because you already know you won't be returning to D.C. in January for a fourth term in office, you're busy angling for a position at Planned Parenthood . . you know—the usual *shit* . ."

"The sorry bastard's upset because my little surprise is so damn much *better* than his little surprise was—mine is causing *national* reactions, and the publicity is killing him, Denny, *and* their campaign . .They have nothing to counter it with," laughed Sid. "If Denny's stupid enough to come out now with an identical or even *similar* plan, he'll just look like the chump and copycat that he *is* . . He's stupid, but I don't think he's *that* stupid . . and if he ignores it and pretends like it either *didn't* happen or *won't* happen . . the Christian vote comes to me lock, stock, and barrel—which is what I wanted to happen in the first place . . And should he bewilder every *one* of us and ultimately take the 'high' road, it's just tacit acknowledgment I was onto something bold and necessary and did what I was supposed to do, namely, *lead* when it was time for someone to step forward and lead . ."

"What about your interview this morning?"

"What about it?"

"Devin Godchaux can be a pretty tough interviewer when he wants to be . . What'll you say if he asks you a specific question about this pending legislation and it's not something you've sat down to consider yet? . . Hell, there's parts of the program you and I haven't even discussed yet! . ."

"I'll just tell him we're still in the 'R and D' phase of planning, that it'll take more time to get it *just* right, that's all . . I mean, what can he really say to hurt me? That I should have worked out all the kinks *before* presenting the solution to the problem?! . . If that were true, no one would ever get *anything* done, for Chrissakes! . . I'm interviewing straight from the heart this morning—like I *always* do—and if Devin or Dudley, or even Mr. Warrington himself, doesn't *like* it, they can *blow me!* . . Did your pal Dudley say anything about my public rebuttal of their piece-of-*crap*, entirely-*misleading* TV commercial from Lake Amistad? . ."

"No, he was surprisingly quiet about that one . . not a word about it, in fact . ."

Sid steered onto the WICU lot and parked, 'REX NEWS' emblazoned on the side of the old three-story brick building in gigantic white letters. The thirty-ish receptionist, who evoked a smile and handshake from her congressman when he spotted her "Re-elect Villary" button lying next to her computer, told him she wasn't allowed to *wear* it at work—but no one had said she couldn't have it with her. She rang someone inside and a half-minute later a technician named Ted opened the massive steel doors leading back to the studios and ushered them in with a handshake and unexpected apology. They'd arrived on time at eight minutes before eleven.

"Devin's on his way back from Odessa and won't arrive before about ten *after*," explained Ted, a balding man of early middle-age Sid guessed was from somewhere other than Texas, "so we can either *wait* a little while for his arrival *or*, if you're pressed for time—which I imagine you *are*, in view of the fact that everyone on earth is talking about you—we can have you interview with Andy Koontz as soon as he's done with Reverend Wolfe, which should only be a few minutes away . . *Your* choice completely, congressman . ."

"Malcolm Wolfe is *here*, being interviewed?"

"That's right, sir . . being interviewed in direct conjunction with your sweeping proposal, in fact . . he and Andy should be finished in another four or five minutes, so if you've no objection, Andy's agreed to do your interview . . said he'd be *honored*, actually . ."

One glance at D. P.'s beaming face told Sid all he needed to know.

"I'm sure Mr. Koontz will do just *fine*, thanks . . I don't suppose there's any way we could watch the interview he's conducting now, is there? . ."

"I think that can be arranged . . please follow me, gentlemen," he said, and he pushed through a doorway further inside, then another, and led them down a fairly-narrow hallway of considerable length before turning right. Another fifteen feet and Ted stopped by a huge window on their left, his attention now focused on two men inside a chamber. Sid noticed a female off to the far right wearing headsets, monitoring the proceedings, while the cameraman stood with his equipment beyond the two men and slightly left, his right eye flush against the rolling camera's lens. Another camera and operator stood far to the left. Neither Sid nor D.P. could hear a word being said inside the studio, though the two men's lips were moving: he immediately recognized the Reverend Wolfe, pastor of the First United Church in Christ's Name, an old friend and supporter, the semi-white hair adding to his distinguished visage. Andy Koontz, probably thirty years younger, had the sort of face that could smile without smiling, with light-brown, wavy hair brushed back, what D.P. thought of as a '*preppie*' appearance; even Sid wondered if Baltimore might be Andy's hometown. The lady wearing headsets wore her ash-blonde hair pulled-up in back, her youthful skin and green eyes allowing few to guess her true age, all seventy inches of her lithe and nicely-toned. The sort of woman Cas Turley would surely appreciate by calling her *handsome.*

"That's our producer, Karin Beecher . . No one in there can see you through the glass . . *too* distracting," Ted explained. He placed his right hand on a button a few feet below a wall-mounted speaker and said "Here . . let's listen-in on their conversation . ." He pressed the button and the speaker instantly came to life.

"--has been laid at the congressman's feet, most of it negative," Andy Koontz was saying, "but it's *your* contention, Reverend Wolfe, that that very criticism is coming from those quarters one might expect them to come from . . Would you care to explain that, sir? . ."

"Well . . I don't think it's any secret that the more permissive elements of our society object to what Congressman Villary is trying to accomplish," said Malcolm Wolfe in his west Texas drawl. "The fact is that what's acceptable in the northeast and in California . . what many urban locales consider to be '*normal*' isn't necessarily what folks in Texas and the southeast and many areas of the western United States consider 'normal' . . I'm sure there are millions of otherwise decent folks who erroneously think it's okay to do whatever they like and, if something goes wrong, don't mind someone *else* footing the bill to correct it . . And I'm not saying this doesn't happen in Texas, too—I'm quite sure it *does*—but no one said they're *exempt*, either . ."

"Can you then tell me why Congressman Villary, Reverend? . ."

"As opposed to *another* lawmaker, you mean? . ."

"Yes, sir . . exactly."

"I'll *tell* you why . . I've known Sidney Villary for many

years, and in that time I've never known him to be anything but a respectful, hard-working, decent, God-*fearing* man who tries to accomplish not only what he and his colleagues think is best for America, but also what his lord and savior would think best for America . . It's his *personal* relationship with God-almighty that allows him to tackle the toughest problems we face with an open mind and welcoming heart . . He is the friend of the poor, he is the champion of women's issues, he is the *protector* of the unborn—he fights for those who cannot fight for themselves! . . He is a genuine American hero, and this country needs him in Washington, D.C. to do his best for his people and savior . ."

"Many people from several quarters claim Congressman Villary's notion to make person-hood a reality before a particular person is, *in fact*, a reality, is better-suited to Disney World, or maybe the lost continent of Atlantis, with an early-winter trip to the North Pole. Someone even suggested he might want to consider seeking professional help before pursuing his plans to introduce this legislation to a rational, logical, decision-making process . . any comments, sir? . ."

"In this respect it is my considered opinion that Congressman Villary has only taken the fight to completely outlaw abortion one logical step *further* by recognizing that, when a woman and a man are initially attracted to one another and that attraction leads to a physical consummation of their feelings for each other—the *result* of which is the creation of a human life—it is in the best interests of *all* concerned to recognize that, had it not been for the initial attraction, *nothing at all* would have happened! Therefore, because we *now* know the outcome of the attraction, we simply acknowledge that life began when the attraction first occurred, a perfectly *rational* take on normal relations between

281

men and women. This also extends rights and privileges to the life of the child that didn't before exist, making *both* adults jointly responsible for the well-being of their child from the first moment. Jesus Christ *himself* would applaud such a righteous and right-thinking facilitation to a member of his flock!"

"So I guess it's safe to say you're a Villary supporter? . ."

"I'd have to be a complete fool *not* to be!" drawled Reverend Wolfe. "Sid Villary remains the right man at the right time doing the right thing, and a Christian would have to be crazy not to support him. *Also*, Mr. Koontz, he has the right idea when it comes to the immigration problem, he is a tireless supporter of our military—which protects our right to worship as each of us sees fit—and he is a loyal advocate of second-amendment rights. I happen to *know* that in only a few short months he will be traveling to eastern Europe on a fact-finding mission to see what those godless criminals are up to, and we can count on *this* particular Texan to spread the good word while he's there . ."

"Inspirational words, Reverend Wolfe . . Thanks so much for being our guest today. This is Andy Koontz at WICU," he said directly into the camera. "So long for now . ."

D.P. pulled a handkerchief from his coat pocket and gave it to his boss, who stood with tears welling-up in the corners of his eyes; it had been such a heartfelt outpouring of respect and support Sid pursed his already thin lips to avoid a good, robust cry. They watched as the producer, interviewer, and cameramen shook the reverend's hand in a distinctly respectful manner.

"*Sid?*" whispered D.P., his voice so light as to be barely audible.

"What is it, D.P.? . ."

"We .. have got it *made!*"

Fiona Rodland stood in the lobby of the British Embassy peering out the front doorway onto Massachusetts Avenue, North-West, a sunny Monday morning after the holiday weekend, and wished desperately she could step outside for a cigarette. It had been five long weeks since she'd laid-down the pack of Dunhill's and refused to smoke anymore. There had been no 'gradual reduction' in her urge to light-up over three or four weeks' time, as some had promised; no gum to chew that would provide the nicotine alternative—*minus* the nasty side-effects, of course; no pills, no "patch," no *anything* to help soften the blow, not even the odd gallon-container of water to sip from, the single most benign, yet effective assistance known. It had been cold-turkey then, and it was cold-turkey *now*. But when in the name of Arthur Wellington at Waterloo did the *desire* for a cigarette, the unimaginably hot urge for tar and nicotine, finally go away? What did it *take*? "Don't worry, baby!" her American boyfriend, Bert, a smoker like herself, said when she quit. "You'll be past the worst of it in a week or two, I promise!" But, she was *not* past it a month and a week later; she was only past Bert, whom she sent packing when he insisted on lighting-up in front of her three weeks post-Dunhill. Half-crazy for a smoke, *any* smoke, she saw the FTD van pull into an unloading zone at the embassy's front; watched closely as the delivery man showed his delivery ticket to Sergeant Potts of security; carefully observed the driver open the back of the van to locate the proper bundle; then resigned herself to waiting for his arrival in the hope the bulge in his shirt pocket was a pack of anything legal.

She'd known as soon as he was within two or three feet, of course; smokers never realize how very noxious their habit is when around others who partake . . but someone who's been away from it for a while? Naturally, her accent would get her a free *fag*, especially if her target was a white American male. It *never* seemed to fail: when she opened her mouth and her exquisite King's English poured forth into the world, the target Caucasian male, completely undone by her unexpected speech-pattern and enchanting black radiance, was invariably willing to part with whatever it happened to be she desired at the time. That she was a visual delight never seemed to hurt either.

The delivery man, uniformed, reasonably buff, and under thirty, two dozen of the most beautiful long-stemmed red roses anyone ever saw gripped in his powerful hands, bounded effortlessly up the embassy steps two at a time, boom, boom, boom, and entered the building through a door held open by what he deemed to be an extremely good-looking black woman who actually grinned at him when he stopped in front of her.

"These are for a Miss . . Charlotte *Tillstrom?* . ."

"If you'll share one of those fabulous smokes of yours . . *Les*," she cooed sweetly in perfect English, noticing his blue embroidered name-tag, "I'll point you in the right direction, luv! . ."

"Just as soon as I get these out of my hands!" he said, yet another immediate admirer in an extended parade of admirers past and present.

"See that first door over there past the mini-Trafalgar Square?" she said with a nod toward the south hallway.

"I sure do . ."

"Well, don't go in *there*—you'll *never* find her! . . Go through the second door and stop when you see a young lady who strongly resembles a Roman *goddesse*—but come back to *me!* . ."

"Don't go away," said Les as he and the roses moved hastily toward the hallway. "Les . . will be right back to see *you!*"

Charlotte, the recipient of more flowers in the past week than she could recall being given in her entire life, every delightful bloom her favorite fragrance in the world, was forced to create a place for the latest shipment. Four dozen long-stemmed blossoms already adorned her desk, extra chair, filing cabinet, and bookcase, her office easily the most "olfactory-*friendly*" in the embassy, according to Miss Marigold Godwin. Even Francis Dill-Finchum, the Deputy-Attache, an ornithologist and, by most everyone's reckoning, the most unforgivable *punster* in the nation's capital, upon entering her office the previous Thursday casually remarked that several dozen roses scattered about the place "just made good *scents!*" — at which time the quick-witted Charlotte ordered him out, threatening bodily harm if he didn't curb his verbal lechering.

As soon as 'Les' settled the expensive porcelain vases on the carpet and wooden-wheeled cart holding the fax machine, then abruptly departed, his new quarry waiting patiently by the embassy's front entrance, she took enough time to absorb the ethereal fragrance of all twenty-four individual blossoms. The card read "Thinking of You *Always* . . Can Hardly Wait to See You Sunday Night!" And what a pleasant surprise he'd turned out to *be*: more gorgeous flowers than she knew what to do with, phone calls when she knew how incredibly busy he was with campaigning, any and *all* unpaid medical bills sent to his home address in Herndon — it was almost like being *in love*. Would she ever find anyone more thoughtful or considerate? Was it possible Sid Villary — she got a kick out of calling him *"Sidney"* and getting away with it — really *was* exceptional? And how best to describe her feelings for this

285

man: was it just *desire,* or fondness, or perhaps tender affection? What did real *love* feel like, anyway? How did genuine love manifest itself? When love finally came round, after having lived into her mid-thirties and *not* finding it, would she recognize it? As she returned to her desk and chair the familiar rat-a-tat-tat on her door announced her colleague's arrival, Fiona nudging her smiling face through the half-open door.

"May I, Charlotte? . ."

"Come on in," she beamed happily, "and take a few *deep* breaths! . ."

Fiona stepped inside and froze: the tantalizing spectacle of sixty red roses in vases placed here and there looked sweet indeed, but paled in comparison when she closed her eyes to inhale, slow, deliberate breaths bringing her to full appreciation.

"If we had a few bowls of strawberries and cream . . it would be just like spending the afternoon at the All-England Club! . ."

"You're looking *aw-fully* chipper there, too, Fi! . . Is there by any chance a little *romance* in the offing for the embassy's favorite executive-secretary? . ."

"It would seem your recent flower bonanza has benefited me, too, Charlotte!" beamed Fiona as she settled her back against the wall next to the door. "He *begged* for my cell-number, so I let him 'ave it—*after* he kissed my hand so softly it *tickled!* . ."

She glanced up from her keyboard and said "I *wondered* why he was so crazy to get out of here—well, that explains *that* . . Score one for you, Fi! . ." Then it was right back to work.

"And to *what* does the enticing Miss Tillstrom owe her sunny countenance in this cauldron of utter decadence we like to call the *colonies* this fine, sticky day? . ."

"I began a good book yesterday . . kept me away from the telly all day and night," she said without taking her eyes from the keyboard. "A Yank in Dublin, trying to study law . ."

"Come *on*, Charlotte—you can do better than *that* . ."

"What?" she said, finally abandoning the computer for a moment. "Better than *what*? . ."

"Charlotte . . tell me about the glow, please . ."

"The *glow*?! . ."

"Charlotte?! . . You are positively *radiant* today! . ." Fiona pulled her back from the wall and turned into the doorway to leave, then stopped and said "Yes, there's a definite glow about you today—enough for *two* people, I believe! . ."

Still secure in her secret, she sat quietly and exulted in Fiona's description long after the executive secretary left her office, her parting words--"enough for two people"—substantially more accurate than anyone in the embassy could possibly know. Only three people in the whole wide world knew of her so-called *condition*—the baby's father, her internist, and now her obstetrician—lord, she hadn't e-mailed her best friend or parents yet!—and not a soul in the embassy had any idea. Best of all, since she was still a little shy of being two full months *gone*, her desert-flat tummy certainly hadn't given anyone the first clue. As she keyed-in June's preliminary financial report she found herself working as efficiently as she knew how, laughing simultaneously at absolutely nothing . . except that her quality-of-life—and life itself!—were so irrevocably altered in less than a sixty-day period. By mid-May it had been literally months since she'd met a man she found even vaguely interesting—*months!*—and then she'd dropped-in at an out-of-the-way tavern that happened to have a neon-lit "GUINNESS" sign in a front window and, lo and behold, there he *was*, handsome without being arrogantly so, genuinely interested in what *she* had to say, comfortable in his own skin, intelligently-curious about a number of subjects, well-connected, single, and a virtual kettle of *lava* in the sack. Yes, really *hot* in bed, very warm and affectionate, ready to cuddle anytime—and *potent* too, apparently, as now there *were* two instead of one to consider. But would it stay that way? Was there *no way* to convince him that having a child together was the right move for them *both*, regardless of their future status as single or coupled . . or *whatever*? What would it take to change the opinion of someone so utterly resolute, so overpoweringly single-minded? She gave her flattened tummy—and her first child—an affectionate pat of her hand and continued her absurdly-contented workday.

As holiday weekends went, it had unquestionably been an abysmally *un*-festive three-day period for young Tommy Burke—and not just because he suddenly found himself unemployed or incapable of fully comprehending how such a sweet, *sweet* deal had so completely and unexpectedly turned sour. That was plenty bad enough, no doubt. The deeper, more profound questions troubled him relentlessly—troubled him to the extent that, every time his memory replayed the last five or six days of his miserable life in a fruitless attempt to construct a rational, chronological chain-of-events to help explain how and where everything had first begun to turn to *shit*, he drew the same inexplicable blank. It just didn't make any sense, and *damned* if that was the kind of deal *anybody* could forgive and forget. He'd get to the bottom of it if it was the *last* thing he ever did, no doubt.

Over and over and *over* again his mind replayed the same time periods, day-by-day, hour-by-hour, in the sad hope that *something* would trigger his memory into snatching even the slightest little ripple of *deceit* or *betrayal*, or even *carelessness*, thus lending him a plausible cause-and-effect. It still hadn't happened, though, and here it was, the Monday *after* the holiday, and he didn't have the first glimmer of hope. He lounged purposelessly on his mother's genuine, simulated-leather sofa, sipping a Texas-style sarsaparilla through a straw, pondering life's larger, more difficult, more *complex* questions: barefoot, or shoes; premium channel, or ESPN; canned spaghetti, or peanut butter and jelly? *God*, and things had been going so *wonderfully* up until the holiday grew close!

He'd reported for volunteer work at Warrington headquarters on time—fifteen minutes *early*, in fact—and had taken his place at the phones with the girls, *all* of whom he got along well with. He'd raised over fifteen *hundred* dollars by eight o'clock and, seeing the sun dip below the horizon about ten-after while making a bathroom trip in the building's rear, he knew the time was right for a quick smoke-break outside. But who should be waiting for him outside the men's room but Emma Schliessel, one of his fellow volunteers, who wanted to join him outside . . even though she didn't smoke. Emma, in the words of his good buddy and partner, 'T.C.' Levesque, was "unbelievably *hot!*" and Tommy, no stranger to women and possessed of a good pair of eyes, agreed, so outside they went, ostensibly for a quick smoke—at least as far as Tommy had been concerned, it was—but Emma had other ideas.

Before he even had a chance to light-up, he found himself engaged with a tasty pair of gloss-covered lips—Emma apparently being highly-skilled at gesticulating her upper and lower mandibles—a mass of dark-brown hair worn long and straight, two nicely-shaped breasts pressed firmly into his

289

chest, and a hand round his neck, the other hand playing with the button on his Levi's. Her perfume, he correctly surmised, was Pristine's *"Rock-On,"* which Tommy adored, so his nicotine urge was temporarily placed on the back-burner as he and Emma leaned against the building, two as one, to find out how far they could stick their respective tongues down each other's throat. After that, everything became hazy and confused: Emma inexplicably pulled-away from their clinch and whispered "I get to *taste* you on our next break!" as she turned and disappeared through the same door they'd exited from only a minute earlier, winking as she left.

Tommy, about as flustered and frustrated as a young man can be, first noticed his cellphone missing when he sat down at his work-station, assumed he'd set it down in the men's room but, not finding it there either, stepped outside to see if he'd dropped it. Nothing. None of the girls knew anything of its whereabouts either, so it was a deeply bewildered Mr. Burke who worked his campaign speech over the land-line as best he could until the police arrived a few minutes before nine. Two of the city's finest entered the building and were met by Dudley Thomas, who'd just returned from dinner and seemed as surprised to see them as everyone else. The campaign manager spoke with them for less than a minute before every ear in the place heard him say "Tommy Burke? . . Why, *yes*, he's one of our volunteers . . he's right over here . ."

Escorted from the premises by the men in blue, Emma and the other young ladies watching the bizarre event unfold, a terrified Tommy Burke felt too scared to realize how very peculiar the last hour of his life had become. That, of course, would come later.

"We're *not* arresting you, Mr. Burke," the taller officer told him once they had him outside on the sidewalk, "but there's been a complaint filed against you and you cannot remain on these premises . . Nor can you *return* to these premises for any reason—in fact, if you come within two hundred feet of the building, you can be forcibly detained and prosecuted for trespassing and malicious mischief . . Do you understand what I'm telling you? . ."

An enormously-relieved Tommy Burke, elated at *not* being busted for possession or something worse, still shaking in his socks and in desperate need of a change of underwear, still felt as unutterably bewildered the next morning as the night before, the late-night six-pack providing only a temporary respite from the surreal chain of events. How on *earth* had he been drummed-out? ! How could anyone possibly have found out his real purpose for being there? And where the *fuck* was his cellphone?! With two minor exceptions, his god-awful experience had seemed like something straight out of a grade-B horror-movie: it was all too *real*, and it was happening to *him!* At noon the following day, he hit rock-bottom when his girlfriend called him on his mother's land-line: Amber, a bona-fide Warrington supporter, had received a call from someone at campaign headquarters—*who*, exactly, was of "no importance"—informing her that her beau had been escorted from the building by the police. Rumor had it that a Villary "spy" had been uncovered inside campaign headquarters and that, although nothing strictly *illegal* occurred, only the worst kind of sleaze-bag would stoop to something so contemptible. They were, of course, *through*: no more weed, no more blow-jobs, no more romps 'in the hay.'

The humiliation had been comparable to being clubbed in the side of the head by a two-by-four: even when medical treatment was administered in such cases, the throbbing assuaged by modern-day pain-killers, the residual effects of blunt-trauma were debilitating. It was all he could do to pull himself out of bed before noon, stumble into the kitchen for coffee and whatever looked easy inside the fridge, and park himself on the sofa for sports shows and his favorite soaps. He foolishly checked the mailbox no fewer than *five* times before his addlepated brain finally remembered it was a national holiday and zero mail would be delivered, but the embarrassment of his forgetful-Friday was *nothing* compared to the Saturday morning surprise.

Cleverly waiting until he actually *saw* the mail truck drive onto his street, stop at his mailbox to deposit its rightful load, then go on about its business, the small package addressed to him came as a complete shock. With almost six months to Christmas and over nine to his next birthday, *any* package would have been unexpected, but considering the overt weirdness of the past several days he wondered about the odds of his unwrapping the small box only to have it explode in his hand, or something else just as sweet. One astounding look at his lost cellphone sitting atop the layers of cut and taped wrapping paper might have sent him over the edge, but his joy at seeing it laying in his palm precluded anything crazy or vindictive. The phone itself was *fine*: it hadn't been tampered with, no one had squandered his air time, there was no physical damage whatsoever—it was still *charged.* He smiled a weak, mournful grin, the phone's familiar weight and dimensions so very comfortable in his palm and shirt pocket: naked to the world no more, now he was *whole* again.

His buddy and cohort in political espionage, T.C., just returned from a holiday break in Vegas, called to check on available work and a fresh campaign status, understandably in the 'dark' about their reversal of fortune and its unknown cause. Tommy gave him a quick earful and suggested they speak alone in a secure environment as soon as possible.

"Is your place *safe?*" said T.C.

"Safe enough . . and we can run the sound system to provide background noise while we chat . ."

"Tommy-boy, you were *impossible* to get hold of while I was in Vegas . . seems like every time I tried your number, your phone decided it didn't wanna' work or somethin' . ."

"It's over and done with," Tommy told him angrily when T.C. stepped inside a little while later. The place was a mess: empty beer cans littered the rec-room carpet, dirty clothes lay everywhere, and the recently-unemployed host wore only boxers and T-shirt, an old pair of sandals at the ready by the sofa. "I'd be glad to tell you what happened while you were gone—except that I have *no idea* what happened while you were gone! . ."

"The cops escorted you *out* of the building?! . ."

"One on either side of me . . told me I'd better not come back, too . . Sounded like good advice, so I took it . . My contact with the Villary campaign hasn't called me for a *while*, so I suppose our cash supply is gone for good, too . . You know, I wouldn't feel so bad if I knew *how* those assholes got onto us, but I never gave anything away—not one *damn* thing—and would you believe I actually raised over nineteen *thousand* dollars for the Warrington campaign?! . . if there's a lesson here, maybe it's to stay the hell away from politics! . ."

"Seems like some o' that nineteen grand should go to you . . and maybe a dollar or two to *me*, too—just for G.P., you know? . ."

Suddenly Tommy froze in his couch-potato position, then sat bolt upright on his sofa, glancing eerily around the room, head cocked to one side as though an invisible spirit had entered his space to frighten him, T.C. now motionless as a corpse in his chair. The volume on the TV still loud enough to smother their voices, he grabbed the remote and hit *mute*, then cocked his head the other way, his left hand lifted palm-out to maintain quiet. He frowned.

"What *is* that?! . ."

"What is *what?!*'" T.C. said suspiciously, "I don't hear a thing . ."

Just as suddenly as he'd sat-up straight he cried "That's my damn *cellphone* ringing! . ."

Then he was up and moving like a man possessed, first right, then left, then behind him, chasing the tiny chime until he began digging into the sofa cushions, his phone lodged next to the sofa-frame on the right side. Scooping it up he read the numbers, eyes squinting in disdain.

"You're fucking kidding me!" he cried angrily before flipping it open to say *"Yeah? . ."*

For the next two or three minutes T.C. sat and smoked, buffeted by the curious sight of Tommy Burke standing with his cellphone to his ear—*listening*, for the most part—only an occasional "Yeah" or "Okay" offered in response to whoever was on the other end. His eyes suddenly grew round as half-dollars when he cried *"Really!?"*—his frown melting into a smirk. "I dunno' . . but I'll find out . . hold on a sec . ." Covering the receiver, he eyeballed T.C. with luminous, conspiratorial eyes and whispered "My man, you free around seven this evening?" With young Levesque's nod he removed his hand and said "Where do you want to meet? . . Okay, sir, at seven *sharp! . ."*

Tommy snapped his phone shut and stood pensively, gazing through the front window at nothing in particular, seeing his overgrown front-yard and his street and his neighbors' homes without really seeing them. Was it possible?

Was he on the level? Or was he being played like a piano again?

"Whassup?!" said the curious T.C. Levesque.

"That was Dudley Thomas from the Warrington campaign . . He wants to meet me at seven at The Copper Clapper at Midland Park Mall—and he wants *you* to come with me . ."

"No *way!* . . He doesn't even know me! . ."

"No, he doesn't—but he knows *of* you because of what we did for the Villary campaign," explained Tommy. "What he *said* was 'Bring along your copying expert, unless he has a problem with being paid in *cash!*' . . This is a *gig*, man—a paying *gig!* . . Let's *burn* one, baby! . ."

"Doddy gave me a copy of today's gazette because he had another copy someone gave *him*," explained Marigold Godwin, "so I'm giving it to you, my dear. I shan't be a moment finishing the 'International' page . . You might want to read an article about David Niven and how the show was stolen out from under his nose while they filmed The Pink Panther . . but he'd already been around twenty-five or thirty years and had a simply *wonderful* career. It's a good article . . mentions his friends from Hollywood, too, if you're into that sort of thing . . Errol Flynn, Tyrone Power, Charles Boyer, Dick Powell . . Deborah *Kerr*, too . ."

Charlotte, diligently working on reports at half past four, had taken her time finding a comfort-zone with Marigold occasionally "dropping-*in*" to check on her—though she was really doing nothing of the sort. Miss Godwin was merely taking advantage of that *perc* to which she was entitled, effectively hiding from late-afternoon duties someone else could accomplish just as easily.

"Who," said Charlotte, eyes still with the computer, "is

David *Niven? . ."*

"Oh, *dear* . . you *are* young, aren't you? . . David Niven was the quintessential English *gentleman* of the motion-picture industry for the better part of forty years—his only discernible flaw being that he had several *American* friends," lamented Marigold. The consummate British snob, she denied it vehemently, secure in the knowledge that British society, while perhaps not the *only* civilization on earth, certainly had to be the *greatest*. That the 'Yanks' had been descended from the British had to be some sort of historical *blunder*—perhaps they'd been sent to the island of Borneo *first*, then were allowed to emigrate and somehow managed to stumble upon the Land of Plenty. "Niven was the sort of person who could light-up a room just by walking through the doorway . ."

"Sounds like some sort of glorified *electrical* worker . ."

"You sound so *provincial* sometimes, Charlotte . . but I know better. Inside that pretty head of yours lurks a mind as sharp as glass and, though you profess this twisted sort of . . tolerance for these Cretins we call the *colonists*, deep-down you realize they're just as boorish as the Germans and French . . I *do* wish you'd find at least a semi-literate chap and enjoy a measure of his company . . but, I suppose, that's not as easy a task in this god-forsaken country as back home, what? . ."

"Oh, I *have* found him . . it's Hugh Billingham, the newsman on the BBC every evening at six—*he's* semi-literate! . . It's the perfect relationship, you see—he's in London, and I'm stuck here three thousand miles away—so we don't have to worry about being *late*, or what to *wear*, or any of that rot, because we never see each other . . Besides . . he doesn't even know I'm alive—so his expectations of yours truly always seem so very *reasonable* . ."

Her eyes moved away from her work just long enough to give Marigold Godwin the faintest of grins. Undaunted, the grand dame of the embassy bravely pressed on.

"*Fine* . . have it your way, my dear . . but your biological clock *is* ticking away as we speak, and try as I might I can't think of a single reason why the embassy would want *two* old maids rambling round her halls . . *Neither* of us is in our early twenties any more, you see—I've crossed my fingers for you, my dear, because I happen to know you want a career and family—complete with someone to love and care for, and I can't help but think the husband and family portion of your life's dream will never materialize unless you re-post somewhere in Europe . ."

"Marigold, what if the Thames flooded *all* London, an earthquake formed an impassable chain of mountains on the Scottish border, the president of France declared his country the newest and closest colony of Great Britain, and I fell head-over-heels in *love* with the coarsest, most hideously-*vulgar* American male possible—the sort of chap who, should I bring him home to have him meet my m. and p. . . would cause their *immediate* breakdown? . ."

"Oh, *Charlotte!* . . How can you *suggest* such a thing?!" cried Marigold, rising horror-stricken, the gazette splashing to the floor. Had the poor young thing been pushed over the edge? Straightening the tabloid, she set it on the desk and declared "Why, the very idea! . . I suddenly feel desperate for a large cup of *tea!* . ."

After the door closed she worked another few minutes on her reports, then backed her chair away, smiling with smug satisfaction at having so easily reinstated her privacy. If only you knew, Marigold . . if only you *knew.* I've already found him, you see, and he is, as you say, a bit of a boorish Cretin,

297

with more flaws than I can name—and probably many more I haven't even discovered yet—but I've found him, nonetheless. And . . I have *hope*: I hope that, since he doesn't seem to have quite found *me* yet, I hope someday soon he will. Maybe then, if I'm lucky . . .

She grabbed the slim section of newspaper sitting atop the small pile to the left, courtesy of Marigold via Doddy Kenworthy, and scanned the front page: Washington society bulletins, of which she knew nothing and cared even less. *Fascinating*. She grabbed another: the arts and entertainment forum, her favorite—perfect for the Friday before the weekend, not the Monday *after*. The next portion? Business—and where could one find a more captivating, a more *mystifying* interpretation of the eternally-stupefying puzzle called 'buying wholesale and re-selling for profit?' Finally, she came across a segment marked with a simple capital "A." How very fortunate it seemed, indeed, to be working on foreign soil where the two countries were forever divided "by a *common* language," as Marigold loved to put it. The headline read "CLASHES KILL DOZENS IN MIDEAST!"—and it occurred to her that *that* particular headline could have been the headline every day for the past *month*. When would some *real* news arrive for everyone to become nauseous by? If not informative, why couldn't newspapers be at least surreptitiously entertaining? Why couldn't fiction writers be assigned journalistic duties one or two days a week, just to add extra spice to the normal, mundane stories everyone had come to expect? Who wrote the law saying newspaper reporting had to be *boring*, and what reasons were given for making it so?

Unconvinced she'd find anything worthwhile on the front page's top half, she flipped it over and noticed a picture of the

Washington monument completely surrounded by scaffolding, prepared for its grand makeover, on the right side. Glancing left, she saw no additional pictures and started to reach inside, but stopped suddenly at the sight of block letters in a smaller headline towards bottom that read "VILLARY DEFENDS PROPOSAL."

"Well, well . . what have we *here*, my dearest?" she murmured to no one and, adjusting her posture, set the section onto her desk for a better look. Was it possible the man she was more or less *reluctantly* falling-in-love with was actually providing a newsworthy bit of information? Was it worth her time? Or was the paper so desperate for news of substance it would print promises from the campaign trail of a conservative congressman from west Texas? To say the afternoon gazette was a more-conservative newspaper than most D.C. dailies screamed of understatement, its staff never apologizing for its anti-liberal stance on all matters political. Charlotte simply couldn't know: contrasting British and American conservatism was beyond her scope—but not because of naivete or inability; it was more unfamiliarity with the American version.

"Congressman Sidney H. Villary (R-Texas), in a follow-up to his Fourth of July bombshell outlining his proposal to expand the concept of person-hood to limits never before heard or seen in this country, told a reporter from WKIA in Texas his proposal is merely a logical extension of conservative views regarding birth control and abortion rights, coupled with what he terms a 'Responsibility Factor.' Mr. Villary, in his first-ever primary-election struggle, has been accused by his opponent, Texas state

Senator Denny Warrington, of being a 'publicity-seeking, Christian-pandering, right-wing demagogue' more interested in being re-elected than accomplishing any legislative objectives.'

"In a related story, the West Texas Council of Ministers, headquartered in Odessa with a large office in El Paso, has endorsed congressman Villary's re-election bid, stating that he is obviously the proper legislator to further the pro-Christian stances adopted in their last conference held in San Angelo in February of this year. Earlier concerns about Mr. Villary's mistreatment of Hispanics, as reported by the Warrington campaign, in collusion with ethics violations, were found to be baseless and without merit."

She kept reading. The article ran to the bottom of the front page where "see VILLARY, A3" was written. The article, she quickly discovered, contained direct quotes from her midnight caller, her lover, the father of her child, the first few of which she found only mildly irritating because she was bright enough to realize different statements might be made while campaigning in correlation to what might be said between them in private. The explanation given about responsibility of parties to the creation of a child she found rather puzzling — the establishment of person-hood before the future mother and father had even enjoyed their first kiss seemed *especially* perplexing to her sense of perspective and decency. Halfway down page three she felt herself becoming inextricably annoyed at the tilt the article seemed to pursue, its insistence that Mr. Villary's stances on immigration, personal responsibility, and protection of the unborn were not only proper, but the actions of a true *pioneer*. Was *this* the man she'd come to know so well? To have such intimate feelings for? The next-to-last paragraph contained a direct quote from Sid Villary in response to a direct question about abortion and its availability. "I will *not* rest," said the west Texas congressman, "until the availability and the need and the *right* to all abortions has been completely eliminated from the countryside. Abortion is a scourge on our society and our families, it is a clear and present danger to *all* women, and it has no place in the greatestcivilization on earth." First thinking she'd misread the quote, or perhaps just misunderstood what he was saying, she read the quote again—with the same result. Reading it a third time, just to ensure against committing a preventable, yet enormous mistake, the quote's content was now really *quite* unmistakable: the same man who *championed* her to abort their child, who repeatedly mentioned his desire *not* to become a father every time they spoke—had now publicly renounced abortion as a scourge and danger to women. *Really!?* She read the remaining paragraphs, but couldn't see them clearly. She re-read different sections of the article, trying to gain a clearer picture of what she was facing, but experienced trouble seeing them, too.

She sat motionless in her chair, hoping something incredibly heavy would fall on her. Numb from head to toe, too appalled with herself to decide anything, she couldn't see his handsome face without the accompaniment of disgust and loathing. Her first instinct told her to never speak with him again, to hire an attorney to work out the legal details of her fatherless child's early to mid-February birth, and be done with it—and *him*—once and for all. Now it might also be advisable to speak with a reputable person from the American media—though she couldn't be sure there *was* one—to enlighten the public as to the congressman's true 'colors,' which were mostly chicken-shit *yellow* and *blackest*-black—to match his heart. Then she told herself she was being too vengeful, that she hadn't given him a chance to properly explain himself. And if she refused to take his long-distance calls for the better part of another week? Then he'd already *know* something dreadful awaited his return—and he'd know it way, *way* before he ever boarded a plane for the flight back to Reagan—*and*, she might never have a chance to tell him how she felt in person, which she wanted desperately to do. An all-out *fight* with a well-connected American congressman? *No*, she was angry, no question there . . but she wasn't feeling particularly *stupid*, and to pick a public fight with an elected official on *his* home turf would be nothing less than suicidal, and in so many ways. Any embarrassment she might cause would be returned ten-fold by a government official out to get even by any means: thanks, but *no* thanks. What she positively, unequivocally *knew* . . was that she'd get her chance to confront him *privately*, and that now there was *no* chance—*zero* possibility—of artificially terminating the pregnancy. She would be friendly, even intimate, on the phone . . but only from necessity, until she had him situated exactly where she wanted him—or inside her four walls, face-to-face. Then, one of two events would occur. She could either tell him good-bye, dictating terms pertaining to joint responsibilities towards their child, *or* . . she could finally receive some answers to the questions now troubling her—like how he managed to catch himself in the mirror without throwing-up, and what it felt like to be raised as anyone else might be brought along to adulthood . . only to turn into a ball of hateful *shite* by the age of forty.

Then . . . she could say good-bye.

The Copper Clapper Bar and Grill, by normal standards, seemed dead. A Monday night was typically slow, but the week following a holiday weekend had historically proven to be even worse, so the crew of fifteen or twenty bouncy young waiters and waitresses, servers, and bartender, plus the management crew of three, had been whittled-down to a skeleton crew of eight when Dudley Thomas arrived at 6:50. Thomas, who could stomach practically anything, started with ouzo-on-the-rocks as he sat with an unobstructed view of the front entrance, the better to get a good, solid look at Tommy's cohort when they walked in; it had to be someone other than their traitorous Mr. Burke performing the technical work because Tommy simply wasn't the button-pushing type. But he needed technical expertise to accomplish what he deemed absolutely necessary to achieve—*tactically* speaking—so you "bring along your pal, Tommy, so's we can have ourselves a little convo, *okay?*"

When the two younger men sidled into the Clapper at one minute after, the alleged northern- California sinsemilla having primed them for magic on their ride to the mall, their focus extended all the way to their fingertips. The hostess, instantly sizing them up, advised them to turn around, as Dudley Thomas sat directly behind them not five feet away.

When the two youngsters slid into the booth's other side Dudley said "What'll it be, men? . ."

"Lone Star, please!" they said in bizarre unison, and Thomas nodded at the hostess to go ahead.

"Who's your friend, Tommy? . ."

"Mr. Thomas, this is my good friend, Karl Levesque—but we call him 'T.C.' for short! . ."

The two shook hands, Dudley Thomas surprised by the

younger man's iron grip, T.C. shocked at what the older man appeared to be drinking.

"I don't know how you do it, Mr. Thomas," remarked T.C., his eyes transfixed on the white liquid in Dudley's glass. "I haven't had a glass of milk in over ten *years* myself! . ."

"Oh, it's not milk, I assure you . . Here . . take a whiff of my . . *milk* . ."

He shoved his glass a few feet across the table, barely grinning at all. T.C. brought it to within an inch or two of his nose, immediately recoiled at the caustic aroma, and set it back down close to Dudley's fingertips, Tommy Burke maintaining a keen eye on the proceedings. The older man enjoyed a quiet laugh: it didn't take a genius to figure out how the eyes of his temporary companions had become so bloodshot.

"I take it you don't especially care for licorice . ."

"Not like *that*, I don't!" frowned T.C. "No offense, but that's fucking *sickening* . ."

"Most people consider it an acquired taste," said Dudley Thomas, the two youngsters smiling as their beer was set in front of them. "What's the 'T.C.' stand for, if you don't mind my asking? . ."

"Top *Cat!*" Tommy Burke cried proudly, a gleam in his eye. "We've been calling him 'T.C.' since the first grade! . ."

"I understand you're a first-rate technocrat, T.C. . . . is that true? . ."

Unsure of the older man's intent, Levesque stayed quiet for a moment, finally saying "If you mean, can I make things happen with advanced technical devices, including computer-related skills a lot of people *don't* have? . . the answer is *yes*, that's pretty-much true . ."

"*Good!* . . You may very well be the man I'm looking for to provide a service—the kind of service neither myself nor my friends and business associates are in a position to do *ourselves*, due to the nature of our work . . I'm sure your friend Tommy here has filled you in on who *I* am and who I work for, so there's no surprises *there*—but I want you to understand this work I need done is being done for *my* purposes and no one else. State Senator Warrington doesn't even *know* about it, which is much safer for *his* purposes—and he need not find out! In other words, this is strictly between *you* and *me* . . So my question to you, T.C., is: *are* you interested in doing a little public-relations work for me? . ."

"Before I commit to something like this there are two things I *have* to know," he said, speaking now from the experience of having been burned once or twice in the past. "One . . is what I'll be required to do illegal enough to land me in the slammer, or *worse?*—and two . . if and when I pursue this *work*, as you call it, what are the chances someone—or even some *group*—will want to harm me by either shooting, stabbing, poisoning, hanging, or otherwise attempting to ensure I spend the rest of my life in a *wheelchair? . .*"

"Ordinarily I'd say those are reasonable questions that deserve, or even *demand* . . honest answers," Dudley Thomas smiled as he let a hefty swallow of his milky-white concoction slide perilously down his throat. "Your first question is really more of a semantical nature than practical, the second being more concrete, in its way, but hardly worth discussing in such an ominous manner, because this work—and it really *is* public-relations work—is neither illegal *nor* dangerous. If you asked me if it was *ethical* work?—well, we all have our ethics, don't we? . . I feel sure that when I tell you exactly what it is I want you to do, you'll agree neither of you has the first thing to worry about—you can't be caught because there's nothing

305

to *catch*—all I really want you to do is *find* something for me—and then spread the word to your friends in your approximate age-group that you found it." He stopped briefly to let his words sink in before continuing. "Care to hear more?"

"I'm all ears," said T.C., utterly intrigued.

"Well, as I'm sure you both know by now, congressman Villary has proposed legislation of a rather *bizarre* character which allows the state, or more likely the federal government, to stick its nosy fingers into the personal relationships of young people by declaring that any pregnancy resulting from a one-night-stand, so to speak, establishes *person-hood* for the child yet-to-come at the moment the young man and woman first find themselves attracted to each other—not only *that*, but his proposal renders the male responsible *retroactively* for his so-called 'share' of the child from that same moment! Now, it's been brought to our—"

"*Hold it!*" Tommy Burke almost screamed, his face an odd mix of terror and astonishment, "hold *everything!* . . Could you please let us have that one more time? . ."

"This is some kind of sick joke, right?" added T.C. "For a second there, I thought you said it might end-up costing me money if I *look* at a woman and find her attractive? . ."

"That's *exactly* what I said, men . . If you were to go out and raise hell on a Friday or Saturday night, *by yourself* . . and run into a woman you find attractive who also finds *you* . . attractive—*and,* you happen to hit a bed at the same time and she becomes pregnant—you're on the hook from the first time you laid eyes on the future *mother* . ."

"But that's *crazy!*" protested Tommy, his fingers wrapped tightly around his beer in a choke-hold of masculine anxiety. "I'm *supposed* to go out and find an attractive woman to spend time with! . . I'm *supposed* to try to charm her into the sack! . .

I'm *supposed* to show her a good time—and if *I* don't do it, somebody else *will!*"

Dudley Thomas rested his arms on the table, his case for action accepted at face-value.

"Then you understand your predicament . . *perfectly* . ."

"But what if you just go *out* with a particular female," said T.C., trying his damnedest to come to grips with the intricacies of the issue, "and you have a really great time—including a romp on the sheets—but *nothing* happens? . ."

"Well, good for you—you had a great time and nothing happened, which is how it usually works . . but what if something were to go *wrong?* . . What if your protection *fails* you, for whatever reason?—condoms have been known to break—and the female has *no* protection? . . What if *her* protection fails, men? . . Diaphragms, IUD's, birth-control pills—none of *them* is fool-proof either . . What if you *both* have protection?—*both of you,* mind!—and everything *still* turns to shit, heaven forbid?! . . What *then?!* . . Well, then, I'll tell you: *tough-shit,* that's what! . . Do the letters 'S-O-L' ring any bells, gentlemen? . ."

He sat back comfortably in the booth, his argument presented to his complete satisfaction, the desired result practically assured: the young men sat hopelessly brooding over the seemingly endless possibilities of their future evenings, now turned forever bitter. Quickly downing their suds in a rush of anxiety, more beer was ordered. Dudley smiled: *fait accompli!*

"But if what you're saying is *true,*" Tommy said suddenly, "*why* aren't young people all over Texas raisin' unholy-*hell* about it?! . ."

"Oh, they *are!*" Dudley said sympathetically, "everyone's mad as can be, but what can you do? . . He's a congressman . .

you can't just send him a poison-pen-letter, or threaten him, or have him beaten-up, or anything of the sort—they'd lock your ass up and toss the key! . . About the only thing you can do is let him know how you *feel* about his zany ideas, but that's risky, too—you can't send *vulgar* or profanity-laced e-mails to his congressional e-mail address either without running the risk of it being traced back to you—in which case you end-up in jail, so *that's* out, as well . ." He let them stew over their unfortunate circumstances for a long moment or two, heads hung in hapless, bewildered astonishment, faces turned to stone, before he ventured to say "You know, fellas'? . . it just doesn't seem *fair*, does it? . ."

"You're *goddamned right*, it doesn't!" cried T.C., the rest of his entire life ruined in the space of ten short minutes. "Who does that son-of-a-*bitch* think he *is*, anyway?! . ."

After giving them another minute or two of quiet reflection Dudley Thomas said "*Well* . . there is *one* thing you can do, T.C. . ."

"*Name* it! . ."

"You can hack into his *personal* e-mail account and say whatever you'd like to say using any kind of language you feel appropriate—vulgar or *otherwise*—then *spread* that address to all the young people who'd like to let him know how they feel! . . Of course, you still *can't* threaten him in any way—*that's* illegal as hell!—but on his personal e-mail, if you wanna' call him a stupid *bastard* . . you can call him a stupid bastard! . . If you wanna' call him a moronic son-of-a-*bitch* . . you can call him a moronic son-of-a-bitch! . . Truth is, on his *personal* e-mail . . you can call him anything you *like!*—*Comprende?!*"

"Loud and clear!" cried a suddenly-energized T.C. Levesque, that elusive ray of sunshine so desperately longed-for finally materializing out of thin air, giving him a speck of hope. "And we'd be doing this as a *favor?. .*"

"As a favor to *me*, yes," said Thomas. He reached inside his jacket pocket and pulled out a roll of bills secured with a fancy, expensive-looking sterling-silver-and-turquoise fastener. "I want you and your pal Tommy here to hack into that personal e-mail account of the congressman's . . Then I want you to get the good word out to friends and acquaintances—and young people everywhere—that want to share their feelings with congressman Villary in their *own* way . . Why, you can send him a message *yourselves*, if you like, and let him know how *pleased* you are with his new ideas . . *Now* then, my young friends . if you're willing to do this favor for *me*, I'm willing to do a favor or two for *you* . ."

He unhooked the fastener securing the roll of bills and flattened them in his left palm, older bills rather than new and crisp, a stack about a half-inch thick, the familiar green backs face-up before he flipped them over, revealing their multi-colored front sides. The young men had no trouble recognizing Benjamin Franklin and U.S. Grant. T.C. smiled.

"How big a favor are we talking about here? . ."

"You're the technician, so *you* get the lion's share: a thousand for you, five hundred for your partner—half up-front, the other half when the job's finished . . How 'bout it? . ."

Tommy Burke tapped his buddy on the right arm, smiled a redemptive smile and said *"See?* . . I *told* you we could trust this guy! . ."

T.C., his shattered faith in the future of mankind restored somewhat, grinned at their elderbenefactor and said "Mr. Thomas, I want you to know I've always thought of Benjamin Franklin as one of the very *greatest* American presidents!"

XIV.

The non-stop from Dallas-Ft.Worth International to Reagan National slowly swooped around the southern edge of Alexandria and followed the twinkling lights along the Potomac to the waiting runway, landing smoothly only a few minutes late at 10:22 P.M. It had been a surprisingly relaxing flight. His parents, reluctant to part with anything jazzy or classical from their music collection, had been badgered to the point of exhaustion, finally surrendering but a single Frank Sinatra CD, which Sid listened to blissfully all the way from Texas to northern Virginia. Exhausted himself from the grueling schedule of campaign stops, speeches, road-trips in the dead of night, and interviews granted as tactfully as possible, it was now back to the capital for two weeks of what he hoped would be relative *calm* after the stormy visit home to spar with Denny Warrington. It had been *bloody*, to be sure . . but it had also been *good*.

So far, the public had been generally tolerant toward his views on person-hood—*tolerant* in that no one—young, old, or in-between—had tried to kill him. *Yes*, of course the opposing camp had denounced his so-called "decision" as a cheap grab at headlines, a shameful attempt to minimize the damage done when their first TV commercial revealed congressman Villary partaking in the seemingly cruel hurling of Hispanics into the Amistad Reservoir to swim for their lives . . or *worse*. *Yes*, of course the opposing camp dismissed his "retroactive-responsibility" tenet as a *smaller* part of "a *larger* mistake," and predicted that any attempt to introduce such a ridiculous bill into consideration would result in public ridicule the likes of which hadn't been seen since the Susan B. Anthony dollar. *Yes,* of course the Warrington camp made a public spectacle of ignoring polls showing congressman Villary ahead in the Christian-conservative ranks by an unspeakable margin of 72% to 26%, claiming funding for any poll that indicated such ridiculous results had to be Villary-financed. And, *yes,* of course the enemy camp gloried in its claims that *independent* polling placed Denny Warrington a full *seven* percentage points ahead of the west Texas incumbent, though no one across the aisle—or even fellow conservatives, for that matter—seemed to know the origin or source of these "polls." Even Consuela Garcia, the liberal-opponent-in-waiting, expressed bemused skepticism when first informed of Villary's stance in defense of women during a live interview in Lubbock on Tuesday, July 8. A portly woman by most standards—a conservative pundit from Houston had actually once referred to her as "well-*fed*"—when told of Sid's dashing proposal, Garcia looked at the reporter, Di Callahan, burst into laughter and said "Oh, be *serious!*" When Villary's idea was repeated, the challenger looked straight into Callahan's eyes and, laughing no more, said "Was he *drunk?*"

But everything thrown at the incumbent had melted away almost as quickly as it hit him. The "Amistad Debacle," as the Texas press dubbed it, hadn't crippled Sidney H. Villary as planned: when it was discovered the Hispanics hurled into the water by the archaic catapults really *were* Hollywood stuntmen who hailed from the Lone Star state—and that they were being paid a small *fortune* for the make-believe "cruelties" Jim Bob and his pals were heaping on them—several Hispanic leaders pointed to them as success-stories other Hispanics

311

might very well want to emulate, winning Sid a fair amount of business votes. The seemingly-fabricated "issue" of premature *person-hood*, rather than alienating his fellow conservatives, had received many more press announcements from House and Senate leaders than anyone expected—most of them favorable. Comments generally ranged from *"long* overdue" and *"truly* thought-provoking" to more formal declarations of support and sympathy, like "I *wondered* how long it would take for someone with vision and courage to say what needed to be *said!"* and "It seems history will be made by yet *another* Christian conservative from Texas!"—that spoken by none other than the Speaker of the House, a Louisiana native. As for the Warrington camp's claims of Villary-financed *'funding'* for any poll showing the incumbent with a colossal lead among Christian conservatives, it was discovered by investigative reporters from Ft. Worth that not only was there *zero* evidence supporting the claim—the margin had also increased to 74% to 24%! The "independent" polls showing Denny with an overall seven percentage-point *lead* were found to be entirely independent—*so* independent, in fact, that no one anywhere possessed reliable knowledge about the phantoms allegedly conducting the polls. The bottom-line seemed to be that perhaps the Warrington folks had done their homework—they just hadn't done their homework particularly *well.*

Everything, but *everything,* seemed to be going Villary's way . . with the possible exception of Charlotte Tillstrom: their trouble, or whatever else it might be, was certainly nothing of substance, for he'd spoken with her every single evening he was away—and, strangely enough, it hadn't been for *her* benefit. Eternally hopeful he could wear her down over time and persuade her to, if not simply terminate their creation of her own volition, at least convince her that rearing a child by herself might embitter her toward the child—and perhaps everyone else who crossed her path, as well—the result of which could be devastating for all concerned: at least he'd tried. So every evening before he hit the sack he called northern Virginia, always courteous to a fault when conversing with her and ever mindful of the time-zone difference, as she rose early for the drive into the District. Less than a week after flying to Texas, he first noticed a change in her treatment toward him, a change so slight and subtle as to be practically imperceptible. It began as a thought he only *imagined* the variation—it seemed she wasn't as receptive to his entreaties as before, not as willing to consider *his* outlook on the future—though he appreciated the fact that their respective visions were in no way identical . . and very probably never would be. Early on he suspected the potential turmoil sprang from his stated intention to eradicate abortion—how very different were his professional and personal stances on major issues!—but she'd not mentioned a single word of it during their late-night conversations; on the contrary, he'd received nothing but warmth and affection over the phone. And now, *finally*, it was Sunday the 13th and he was back! He grabbed his luggage and headed for his car for the drive to her condo, the Sinatra CD playing the entire drive, love songs that, under the circumstances, he found wholly appropriate. Did absence *really* make the heart grow fonder? For his purposes it *did*: he could hardly wait to see her, to hold her in his arms, to kiss her as many times as she'd let him—to tell her he'd missed her and wished she'd been in Texas with him. He hoped and prayed she'd missed him, too.

Hearing him park outside her back gate next to her car, her rear door was already thrown open when he wearily climbed-out and sauntered through the lot, her still-perfect silhouette easily discernible through her sheer nightgown as she stood in the doorway, a vision of loveliness. Her smiling visage met his tired eyes as he strode through her open gate and cried "I've *missed* you, baby!"

Then they were in each other's arms, his kisses warm and fast on her neck and ears, on her forehead and cheeks, on her chin and nose, and a long, lingering kiss on her world-class lips as he hugged her tight, then tighter as he lifted her affectionately a few inches off the ground, her laughter and happiness all that mattered, Texas a million miles away, stuck in another time.

"Let me *look* at you!" he whispered, setting her gently on the floor. "I haven't seen your lovely face in two weeks—and I miss seeing it more than you could possibly know . ."

"You really missed me?!" she said in the accent he'd come to know and love, the slightest hint of surprise—surprise, and something else un-nameable—in her tone. Planting a tender kiss on his left cheek as he pulled her close once again, her soothing fingers caressed his back when she said "but you'd have to feel regret or sorrow at my absence to *miss* me . . *congressman* . ."

He held her softly at arm's length, searching for some tell-tale sign: it was the same face of ethereal beauty he'd found so enchanting upon first sighting, the same refined features any man would admire from a distance or up-close, the same softness of skin and eyes, without malice.

"What's that supposed to mean? . ."

"I've a flagon of your favorite spirit," she said in her empirical way, "and a small glass of red wine for myself as we sit and catch-up on important matters in the drawing room . ."

Then he knew. As it turned out, he hadn't imagined anything at all: as he watched her enter the kitchen to chase down drinks, the only question left unanswered wasn't whether or not there was some sort of disturbance brewing. *Now* it was a question of just how painful it would be and to what extent changes would have to be made. His heart sank steadily into his midsection as he meandered slowly into the living room, the celestial scent of eight dozen long-stemmed red roses scattered about the furniture much stronger now than when he'd entered through the rear door. It made him sad to think that maybe this night would be the end of something: there was so much they didn't know about one another, and if she found him to be wanting in some way, as he suspected, neither would ever have the chance to find out. As it was they didn't know each other well; why couldn't they work out some sort of arrangement whereby they could remain friends? Then he remembered, of course: what they had between them was already more complicated than any friendship, and of the dozens of women he'd spent time with—perhaps a hundred in all, he couldn't be sure—there was still only the one he could count on as a true *friend*—and she was married to his in-state head-honcho, Dow Pettigrew. He reminded himself that he was a gentleman from Texas and that anything Charlotte decided to do—and *might* decide to do at some point in the future—would be done not as a move *against* him, but as a move that would *assist* her. He'd never been able to convince himself of the merits of criticizing anyone, friend or foe, for being smart enough to look out for number-*one*—couldn't and wouldn't: he'd done it himself for as long as he could remember, and it had yet to fail him. He hoped she'd be kind, that she'd remember he had *tried* to be good to her . . even if he'd failed. Besides . . he was too damned tired to fight anyone or anything right now: it was late, it had been a very long week-and-a-half in Texas, and he'd come to her place to relax, not to quarrel. The red roses were just as lovely as fragrant; how would a stunning-looking woman like Charlotte look in *red?* he wondered. Hell, she looked fabulous in everything else!

"You look exhausted," she said when she entered with drinks, setting his bourbon-rocks on the coffee table in front of him, her red wine in a crystal goblet.

"I *am* exhausted . . the campaign trail is a time-consuming, hour-munching, energy-sapping *monster,* and I can never seem to acclimate myself to the accelerated pace required to run again, until the last two or three weeks—at which point I'm so energized I can work twenty-one or two hours a day, get a few hours' sleep, then get up and do it all over again! . . How about you? . ."

"I have some concerns," was all she said.

"I know you do," he said. "So let's talk . ."

"Yes, let's talk . ."

"And I hope you won't throw anything hard or sharp at me . ."

"No, nothing like that," she smiled warmly. " . . but I wanted to! . ."

"You talk then, and I'll listen . ."

"I've decided to have this baby, Sidney," she said simply. "And *not* to spite you, or in any way embarrass you, or anything of the sort . . I'm going to give birth to this child because I *want* to, and for no other reason . . And while it may be true that my *biological clock*—whatever that really may be— is surely *ticking,* that's not any part of the reason either . . The truth is, I'm ready to have a child, my doctors tell me everything is fine with the pregnancy at two months, and I'm looking forward to raising the child to the best of my ability . . I'm *not* returning home to have it, although I *could,* but I

316

thought staying here would be easier for everyone concerned—my work's here, too, and that won't be any kind of problem for me . . My parents are predictably *elated* . . Of course, they'd prefer I was married, but they also realize times change, and people change, so that's not as great a concern as it was a generation or two ago . . they're still grieving over Princess Di, so they've neither the time nor inclination to grieve over something I might or might not do . . At any rate, *that's* my decision, and I'll have to live with it as best I can . ."

"I suppose I'll have to live with it, too," he said, a quiet smile the best he could muster given the circumstances, the import of her decision certainly not lost on his sense of purpose, despite his weakened spirits. At least the suspense was over and he could breathe again. "Although I don't agree with it, I respect your decision and promise to do everything I can to help, of course . ."

"That's *another* decision I had to make, Sidney—and it was even *more* difficult than the decision to have the child," she said, and for the first time in the two months he'd known her he thought he saw anguish and pain in her splendor. An overwhelming sense of dread suddenly gripped his stomach in apprehension of greater alienation between them, though the gorge he'd helped create felt miles-wide already. "A week ago I'd have been overjoyed to have you spend time with our child, to be as large a part of its life as you wanted, and the more the better . . But I've since done an *enormous* amount of thinking on this very subject—I've even discussed the situation with my doctors, so it's nothing I've taken lightly— and I think it would be better if you stayed out of the picture *completely* . ."

"Completely!?" he repeated, the soothing brown liquid chilling his throat as it went down. "I don't understand,

Charlotte . . when you say *completely*, do you mean you'd rather I just give monetary support and stay away, or is it more a matter—"

"I mean it would be better if you stayed out of the picture in every way possible . . I don't want your money, and I don't want your sympathy or your help, and I certainly don't want you to think my mistake should tie you down—you have *your* life, and I have *mine*—and I think it best if we leave it that way . ."

"Charlotte, please . . *please* think about what you're saying," he begged, an unfamiliar sense of panic welling in his gut. "You don't *really* want to give birth to a bastard-child, do you?! . ."

"Oh, I haven't made final decisions on *everything* yet . . It may well be the child's last name is *Villary* . . but I'm content for it to be *Tillstrom*, too, just in case . ."

"I hope you'll tell me *why* I've been so callously cut-out of our child's future . . And what do you mean when you say 'your *mistake?!'* . . Please don't say this is all just a mistake, *please* don't! . . This isn't some sort of miscalculation or crazy bet that didn't pan-out, this is something entirely different and infinitely more serious, Charlotte—and the truth is, I'm already looking forward to the hour I can spend more time with you *and* the baby—please don't do this, I'm *begging* you! . ."

She took a long, deliberate sip of her red and looked him dead in the eye, saying "You want to spend more time with both of us, do you? . . And just *when* do you think that would *be*, Sidney? After your primary is over? . . Or might it be after the general election is finished in November? . . You could wait until Thanksgiving or Christmas, I suppose, but you don't *really* want to ruin the holidays, now do you? . . Of

318

course not, so I imagine sometime after New Year's would be the best time, eh? . . But of which *year?* . . It must be such an *inconvenience* for you to have to stop and think about myself and your child once or twice a day—especially during a re-election campaign when you're required to be even *more* egocentric than usual . . if that's even *possible!* . . Is there *no way* you can just hire a surrogate-someone to think about us here in northern Virginia? . . You know—*pay* someone to take an interest in our welfare oftener than when it intrudes upon your bathroom visit, or some bitter coffee someone brewed in error—someone who has *nothing* to do with your politics, or your lobbyist friends, or even the fact that you live in the Washington area—oh, c'mon, you *know*—like a *human being!* . . *Ah*, but wait! I *forgot!* . . You . . are . . *exceptional!* . . No one on *earth* can force you to be human because you're a politician, and . . unlike the politicians from the era of George the Third—you know, the ones who had a *pair?*—today's politicians are only interested in the betterment of a very, very *select* group of people: *themselves!* . . *Well*, then . . you're off the hook!'

"But let me tell you something, Sidney, before you raise your hand in protest a *third* time: you'll never get a better deal as long as you live! You could never find another woman who loves you *more* or *better* than I do—that's right, *loves* you, *Sherlock*, because I *do*, with all my heart, and that's what makes this so very difficult for me! I can see it in your eyes—you had *no* idea my feelings for you were so honest or intense!—but then, that would require you to think about someone other than *yourself* and your equally precious re-election, and since *that's* not likely to happen in our lifetimes, where does that leave us? . . So you see, I was *right*: I have *my* life, and you have *yours*—such as it is . ."

319

Feeling himself—and his position—growing weaker with each passing moment, and for the most selfish reasons imaginable not wanting to say anything she'd find even more upsetting—her mood not so much *vengeful* as remedial—he said "Charlotte, you don't know what you're talking about here . . American politics and British politics are similar in ways, but in terms of *methods* as different as—"

"I know *precisely* what I'm talking about, and it doesn't have much to do with *politics!*" she said, cutting him off in mid-sentence, her normally-tranquil eyes aflame. "What I'm referring to is the fact that your foresight extends all the way to the end of your *nose*, and no further! . . What I'm most upset about is the fact that your heart doesn't have room for the elements of existence that make life worth living! . . You seem to think you can compartmentalize your life into neat little *boxes*, with your political friends in one, your lobbyist friends in another, your family in what I'm convinced has to be the *smallest* box of all . . and all you have to do to get along in this life is let them *out* every once in a while for a bit of air before returning them to their friendly little cubicles to wait for the next occasion you need them . .'

"I've been reading a great deal about you and your friends in the government as of late—my reading-time has seen vast improvement since I have no significant-other to help get re-elected, you see!—and it seems to me your sense of accomplishment is realized by accomplishing *nothing*—and history takes a dim view of those who see a duty and *ignore* it! . . And at one point in my reading the most *glaring*, the most *insidious* question seemed to be . . that with all the pain and suffering there is *already* . . *why* are you and your colleagues so obsessed with creating *more?* . . When I read about your '*ground*-breaking' proposal to make person-hood retroactive to

320

the very moment the mother and father of a child *meet* for the first time, I—and *most* of my embassy colleagues—had a good snicker at the sheer *absurdity* of such a rampantly *myopic* vision! . . But when I read your quote saying abortion should be not only discouraged, but completely *eliminated* from the landscape—and this the *very* next day after having urged *me*—your *lover*, and the mother of your *child*—to end my pregnancy—to *end* it!—for the sake of congressman Villary's *convenience* . . it convinced me you weren't any kind of lover—or *man*—at all! . . Ever since, whenever I think of you . . but am *then* reminded of your reasons for doing virtually *anything* . . I'm forced to think of you as some sort of daft *prick!* . .'

"And just when I think matters couldn't possibly become any more *ridiculous* than they are already . . . I see that your friends and colleagues actually think your proposals on person-hood and abortion are *good!*—that as *laughable* as they are, they actually have *merit!*—and I have to wonder if your law-making body doesn't have some form of *brain-cancer* to contend with? . . Oh, *Sidney*—yours must be a *cold* existence without anything to covet which comes from our humanity—the things *you* covet are just *things* pulled from the air—you covet your *majority* when it's the proper time to be re-elected—you covet your *seat* in the House, the same one your majority gave you—you covet your colleagues' *opinion* of you, and covet the *notion* that it's favorable—and you covet—no, *worship*—the idea the work you do is heaven-sent . . Have you never felt a sense of loss about *anything?!* . . Have you not *yet* realized that life isn't concerned with a voting record, or a college transcript, or a retirement nest-egg? . . *Life*, my darling congressman, is about *loss*: the family members, the loved ones, the people you know and admire personally, the ones who make you *happy*—even the ones who make you *sad*—

321

losing them is the flip side of having held them *dear*, and *missing* them is the act of still holding them in your heart after they're *gone* . . And that is as human as it gets, believe me . . I suppose that's what upsets me *most* about you, my love: I cannot *imagine* how anyone forty years old lived so long, and not only does *not* hold dear anything worth holding dear—but somehow also failed to figure-out *what's worth holding dear!* . . By now you've probably grasped the fact that I'm not an overly-religious person . . but I shall *pray* for you and your salvation . ."

"Please *do*," he said, his empty tumbler of bourbon tipped in her direction, "because as tired as I am . . and as thoroughly unprepared as I am to quarrel with you, and as unwilling as I am to fight with you about anything tonight . . *that* . . is the most complete beating I've suffered in many a year . . In fact, it strikes me as awfully *peculiar* that you can sit there on your sofa and euphemistically cut me to shreds—then call me *darling* and tell me you love me in the same breath . . Perhaps it's just the mix of bourbon and exhaustion, I don't know . ."

"No, I don't think so . . It's just that, like any good woman, I can give you an honest, up-front critique of what I perceive to be your shortcomings and simultaneously appreciate why you've turned out to be the love of my life, which—like it or not—you *are!* . . All of us have our flaws, my darling—you just haven't thought about me long enough or seriously enough to recognize mine—perhaps you never *will*, for that would take time, and time is a very precious commodity! . . Would you care for another bourbon? . ."

"I know where the kitchen is, " he smiled sweetly.

He stood at the kitchen sink pouring the dark-amber liquid into the tumbler and spotted a small, rectangular calendar attached with a thumbtack to the side of the upper cabinet to

322

his right. Grabbing a handful of ice from the freezer-top he dropped it into the bourbon, but kept his eyes riveted to the calendar: a simple paper calendar of no special attraction or significance, it seemed a little out of kilter, like the congressman himself, as the days of the week and their corresponding dates seemed as if from another era. Then he saw the misconception and immediately felt better, however clumsy his mind from fatigue: right year, *wrong* month! It was *May* of that year, and Wednesday the 14th was circled with a black fountain pen.

"That day marked on your calendar in the kitchen from a few months ago . . is it important for something I might want to be aware of, too?" he said when he re-entered the drawing room and sat again, the weariness on his shoulders too heavy to measure. He sipped slowly and fixed her with an admiring stare, the better to enjoy the enchanting vision. "Whenever I think of you, Charlotte, the notion of mid-May somehow enters the picture . . but I was never sure of the exact date . ."

"That was the night I met my true love, yes," she said, blue eyes sparkling in the dim light.

"And that's *another* thing . . *How* is it that I've become the love of your *life?*—and all we've really done is meet and grow fonder of each other's company?! . ."

But before he finished he realized that, through her fluttering eyelashes and startled expression, he'd managed to say the wrong thing . . *again.*

"*Sidney?!* . . Do you know *nothing* of people?! . . Can you not *see* why?! *Really?!* . . Well, for starters, you're the father of this child, and as much as that appalling fact makes you a bit leery of me—and every *other* woman you've ever met, I suspect— you'll always be this child's father! Even if I were to someday have another child, or children, with someone else, you'll still be the father of my *first* child, and mothers invariably reserve a special place in their hearts for number one, or so I'm told — so you're elected, ex post facto . .'

"But there are other reasons, too . . I hope what I'm about to tell you won't necessitate your running away to purchase a larger *hat*, but . . you're the *only* man I've ever known who was better in bed than I thought you'd be — *not* that it matters especially — and *not* that I've been with many, because I *haven't*, you see . . Sidney? . . *Sidney?* . ."

He sat with his eyes closed, fast asleep, the tumbler of bourbon wedged loosely between his knees, his right hand still holding on. She gently removed the tumbler from his grasp and first kissed his forehead, then his eyelids, then his lips.

"Good-night, my exhausted boy . . if *only* you could see your way to those who love you, my darling . . maybe you could love *them*, too . ."

Then the lights went out and darkness ruled the night.

Carmen spotted her second-favorite man in the world stopped cold in the hallway outside his office to shake hands with four colleagues, all evidently glad to be pounding the flesh, though everyone seemed to be in a rush to be somewhere else as quickly as possible. Striding through the door with a sense of purpose, he stopped cold when confronted with her indeterminate stare.

"Oh, god . . *What?!*"

"Come *here*, handsome" she squealed with delight, jumping out of her chair. Away from her desk in a flash, she wrapped loving arms around him before he could drop his briefcase, hugging him close before resting her chin on his chest, the easier for him to give her a long-awaited peck on her expectant glossies.

"Wow! If you missed me *that* much . . perhaps I should leave D.C. more often! . ."

"It's not that *this* time, oh my hero and champion—though we *did* miss you!" she grinned, her left arm still round his neck as he managed to blow kisses to Regina and Julie. "*These* hugs and kisses are for the man who finally called-out the mindless American *assholes*—I mean, the mindless American *men*—who see themselves as sacred gifts to the women of America as they breeze *into* their lives, give them something to think about until the day they die—*abuse*, usually—and breeze *out* again, never to be seen or heard from because they're too busy with their *next* victim! *So* . . thank you so much, from all of us! . ."

She placed both arms round his neck again and planted a colossal smooch on his right cheek, grinning like a child when she said "*And* . . welcome back!"

"Wait 'til you see your *e-mail!*" cried Julie, her hugs and kisses as heartfelt as Carmen's. "You've never, *ever* received as much *positive* feedback on any single piece of legislation since we've been here, and I counted over six *hundred* messages myself! We've been *inundated* with requests for buttons and bumper-stickers and flags and—*oh*, and your campaign contributions have risen an average of 27% *per-gift*, with an overall increase of something in excess of four hundred *thousand*—but we're sure you already know how *energized* your constituents have become since you made the announcement! . . *Still* . . I can't wait for you to see your mail: it's *un*-believable! . ."

"And speaking of *mail* . ." said Regina Watts, leaning as far as she could across the top of her desk to receive her great-to-be-back kiss from the boss, "Friday morning, *this* was delivered by special courier in anticipation of your triumphant return from Texas this morning . ."

She handed him a familiar-looking envelope of palest lavender with **Sidney Villary** written on the front in a distinctive, elegant longhand, her eyes meeting his with a pleasant glow. He ran his fingers across the silky texture of the Brazilian stationery—but the real joy lay in receiving a personal message from one held in highest esteem, its mere existence more than compensating for the hard work and rigors of the campaign.

"Thank you *so* much," he said humbly. "I've got a thousand and one things to do before I fly back home on the 29th, so I'll be busy with my e-mail for a little while before heading over to the floor for consults with Mack, Jeremy, and the boys . . I've missed you all so much, words can't really express how truly happy I am to be back with you . ."

"Lynch didn't miss you as much as we did," grinned Carmen, "so he warned us Friday he'd be late coming in today—that way he wouldn't have to see us get-teary-eyed at having you back . ."

"I love Mr. B anyway," he said as he headed through the doorway toward his office, "but *you* guys have a special place in *this* congressman's heart! . ."

Dropping his briefcase onto the carpet behind his desk, he almost dove into the welcoming comfort and security of the Yellow Rose, his bulk settling nicely into the soft luxury of the velvet upholstery. God, it felt so *good* to be back! He sat for a while thinking about Texas and what a turbulent whirlwind active campaigning had been this time around: how gratifying the crowds had been, how very supportive the Christian ministers of his acquaintance had proven to be, how grateful people of his generation and the one before seemed to be. He thought of his office staff and how much he loved and appreciated the girls, of Lynch Bohannon and his blustery manner, Cas Turley and his grounded counsel, Dow Pettigrew and Velma, the latter of whom he still felt a genuine affection for. At last—and most significantly—he thought of his friend and mentor, L.W. Shaw, and the lavender envelope sent by special dispatch, waiting for him to open, which he would save for last because of its origin and the deep, almost God-like respect he felt for his most illustrious ally and adviser.

And despite his intentions to the contrary, whereby any feelings of an intensely personal nature tended to render one weak and ineffective, thoughts of the extraordinary Miss Tillstrom couldn't seem to stay away for any measurable amount of time. What an incredible assortment of contradictions she was! She was now determined to have the baby, to raise the child as a single mother, and wanted no help or interference from the father of any kind—in fact, didn't want the child to necessarily know who its father *was*. And if *that* particular slap-in-the-face was deemed insufficient, she didn't think enough of his moral character to ever spend any more time with him—she simply didn't approve of anyone who said *one* thing, and then turned around and did *another!* It was as though a congressman was there to tell the truth! Did she not *want* to understand? Of course, all this animosity, or whatever it was, was more than offset by her admission that she loved him—loved him *now*, and would love him *always*— as the father of her first, and perhaps *only*, child. He was, in *her* words, the love of her *life!* When he awakened that morning from the first full night's sleep he'd had in a week— in one of her living room chairs, of all places—she'd been as loving and affectionate as he could ever remember, her hugs and kisses of farewell as warm and enticing as could be. *God,*

327

what a woman!

He eyed the bronzed heads of Ronald Reagan and Audie Murphy sitting atop stacks of loose papers on his desk, first one, then the other, thoughtfully considered their lives and what each had brought to *his* life, their inspirations and strengths, their collective greatness.

"Dutch? . . I love ya' like a brother, but I *must* defer to my friend, Audie, on this one, I'm afraid . . Audie-baby, I know for a *fact* that while you were fighting your way across Europe during the *big* one you had to have run into some Italian, French, and German *stunners*—maybe even an *English* stunner or two—but you never ran into *anything* like Charlotte Tillstrom! . . and neither have *I!* . . Now, I count on my buddy there, good ol' Dutch, to point me in the right direction on questions of policy, politics, and economics—but on questions of gallantry and courage and valor—you know, doing the right thing, the *brave* thing, even when it might work against you?—*you're* my man, Audie-baby! . . So . . what's it going to be, hmm? . . Send me a sign, Audie-baby, send me a *sign!* . . What can I do about this woman I don't want to have to think about—that I seem *always* to be thinking about?! . . You were in Hollywood for a while, too, Audie—you must've been tempted once or twice making those westerns, right?! . ."

He languished in the Yellow Rose, pondering life's intangibles and grotesques, for what seemed to him a short eternity: Carmen, Denny, Velma, Texas, D.C., Lynch, elections, Cas, Julie, mom and pop, L.W., Dr. Milner, Dow, primaries, Consuela Garcia—*Charlotte!*—only to discover he'd existed "in a state" for something less than ten minutes. Oh . . my . . *God!* Charlotte!

"Let me know something ASAP, Audie-baby!" he said finally, his trusting eyes on the little man he considered the very greatest Texan of them all. "I'm countin' on ya' . ."

He triumphantly entered his government ID and password on his desktop, grinned inexplicably like an idiot when he saw there were 1,192 messages in his mailbox—*joy* was such a fleeting commodity when one found himself working inside the Federal Government and was, thus, part of the problem—then glanced hurriedly at his watch and gave himself an hour and fifteen minutes to read as many messages as humanly possible, pen and paper at the ready in case his girls needed to post *personal* replies, which they invariably *did*, to some extent—all part of the greater pleasure of working inside the District. It could also be enormous fun to hear from someone he knew and recognized, either from the return address or the closing of the message.

He scrolled-down thirty or forty entries without recognizing a single name or handle, stopping at random on a line marked with the name 'Mal Miller.' He quickly clicked and read: "Dear Congress-man Villary . . My wife and I thank God fer you ever day! Only a true-believer could call upon his Lord and Master to help straighten-out the mess we find ourselves in, what with kids going crazy finding love on the internet and running-oft with people they don't really no. There is so much personal tragedy in our little town of El Paso it hardly lets a day go bye without hearing of some young woman being abandoned whose in the 'family' way. The Mrs. and I never thought we'd see the end of the abuse—and we still haven't—but at least someone's trying to do something about these crazy young people getting together, in never seeing each other again. Our oldest little girl, Jeannie, has been victimized this way and no one seems to know what happened with her boyfriend, Ricardo. We heard tell he'd returned to Mexico, but he's to smart too do that. We wish you the best and want you to know that you'll always have *our* votes. You are a gift from God and Jesus himself. Sincerely, Mal and Trudy Miller"

He stopped next on a line that read 'Cindy Roby,' which he clicked and read: "Mister Sidney Villary . . . I'm a single mother of two who tries her best to take care of her two young children when their worthless father ain't around, which is always. No one I know, and no one my *family* knows, seems to know what has happened to him. He could be dead, for all I know, but it wouldn't really matter, would it? He didn't work when he was around, but he always made sure *I* got to work on time! He's a sweet guy, but he's a little confused about some things—like how to be good to people. There are a lot of women like me out here, Mr. Villary, a whole *lot!* I'm not religious at all, but I sure want you to know how much me and some of my girlfriends like you and appreciate what you're trying to do! We're all voting for you, too, so keep up the good work! Bye! Cindy Roby"

Scanning down the seemingly endless list of names, he'd passed-by perhaps a dozen before catching a glimpse of something familiar: the name read 'Big-Dog Blue,' but on second look he realized it was an old buddy, Randy Ballew, from northeast Texas. He smiled, clicked, and read: "Sid-ley, man . . How-you-R, me amigo? I was just reading about what you're up to this time around and knew you'd appreciate a little news from the Mt. Pleasant area . . Most folks here think you're *crazy*—like a FOX! I don't know where or how you came up with such a devious method of keeping the wolves away from your door, but it sure looks like you've got Denny and his compadres running for the outhouse! Well-done, my friend, and drink a shot or two for me! Kudos, and Big-Dog Hugs, R.B. P.S.: Is it okay to consider bourbon *health-food?!*"

'Big-Dog,' he replied, punching the keys with surprising agility, 'Bourbon was the *first* health-food!' . . . your pal, Sid.

Scanning again, he stopped on a line marked 'That's Right, Rev!' and clicked to read: "Congressman Villary: I'm sure I speak not only for myself but my entire congregation when I say to you how very pleased we are with your announcement(s) of July 4th. It's refreshing to know someone in government has gumption enough to tackle a subject that, frankly, two weeks ago no one was even willing to mention, much less discuss—when the truth is we should have been talking about these same problems years ago. As a minister and youth counselor, I see problems with young people most all the time because they are by and large a trusting sort, but their trust, and *faith*, is compromised by those lacking any form of moral compass. So many young men and women simply cannot tell right from wrong, so it falls to people like you and me to set things on an even keel. You must be a disciple sent from God and Jesus to assist us in this holy endeavor; rest assured you have our undying support in your work, and may you stay where you are until your cause is achieved and your work done. *Vaya con dios!* Reverend Paul S. Graham, The Apostles Church of Santa Maria."

His pen moved swiftly across a piece of scratch-paper plucked from underneath Audie-baby: 'Send autographed 8 X 10 to the Apostles Church of Santa Maria, with *personal* signature and frame!'

His next stop read 'Elizabeth Davis,' chosen at random like the others. He clicked to read: "Thank God for *you*, congressman Villary! I'm a twenty-year-old student pursuing a degree in Electrical Engineering and have the misfortune of running into college boys every day of my miserable life, and I mean BOYS! I was runner-up in last fall's Homecoming Queen

331

court, so I'm physically blessed and receive more than my share of attention from the guys. But it's the *wrong kind* of attention! None of them—not a single one—could care less that I'm smart, spiritually alive and active, have a relationship with God, and am assured of a bright future! They don't *care!* They just want in my pants! My friends and I, in *their* eyes, are just here for entertainment purposes (one young jerk from Waco actually told me he wanted to wake-up with me 'nude, screwed, and tattooed!'). My parents are long-time Villary supporters, and now my friends and I are, too! We'll pray for your continued success and vote in both the primary and general elections, as several of us are from the San Remos area. May God bless and keep you, congressman; if college girls are being mistreated, can it be any better for working girls? Your friend and new supporter, Beth!"

"Converts and young supporters are always welcome," he mumbled to no one while he resumed his search with a smile of grim satisfaction. " . . A very warm welcome to my sacred world, Beth . ."

'Ralph Beilaoviecz,' which he had no idea how to pronounce, caught his eye, so he stopped and clicked: "The good lord truly works in mysterious ways, does he not? The Mrs. and I never really gave you much thought one way or the other until this *parent-hood* hubbub came up. Our daughter, Madelaine, got involved with a young fellow we liked and thought well-of, until she turned-up with child, and he then disappeared. Only *then* did we find out he introduced her to unspeakable acts with toys and what-not that made her feel wonderful physically but, alas, robbed her of her soul. As the scriptures say, he has been a lamp unto my feet: the young fellow, fearing your swift reprisal, has now returned to 'face the music,' so to speak, and they are to be married in two

332

weeks. We are hopeful, of course, and eternally grateful to you. And, we *vote!* God bless you, Mr. Villary! Ralph and Mildred B."

"Glad to oblige!" he grinned, his pen working overtime to the familiar tune of 'Letter with Personal Creed, 3 X 5, and envelope for remuneration. *Personal* signature!'

He scrolled down the row of messages nearly seventy spots before stopping on one marked 'Judith Searcy,' which included an adorable little devil with tiny trident in hand next to her name. He clicked and read: "My hero! I'm glad my husband and I have separate e-mails, not that it matters, but I like my privacy, *comprendez?* Our daughter and only child has been compromised by a young man of dubious character (wish we'd known about him earlier!) and I'm not sure what to do about it—at least, I *didn't* know, but with your help, I do *now!* My husband still doesn't know, congressman; he's a 'forgive and forget' Christian? *I,* on the other hand, am an 'eye-for-an-eye' Christian! Sally Sue is going to have the baby, we're all going to pitch-in and raise the child properly, and the first chance I get I'll grab Rory by the throat and collar and cut his nuts off! Hallelujah, my brother! In *his* name, *Saint* Jude"

"Bless her *heart!*" he whispered, a tear forming in the corner of his eye. "We could've used you on 9-1-1, darlin'! . ."

The next stop, forty or so lines further down, folks identified themselves as Cecil and Ramona Wing. Pausing momentarily for no special reason, he stared at the last name, mystified, rubbed his chin with his left thumb and index finger, then clicked on it: "Boy, howdy! My husband claims you're doing this 'retroactive-responsibility' crusade because it will provide the attorneys of the Lone Star state a measure of badly-needed revenue, things being what they are with people unemployed so much and unable to pay their legal fees from jail. 'Course, Cecil never *was* the brightest bulb on Broadway. Anyway, I say you're doing it because it's *God's* work, and the Lord, Jesus Christ, saw fit to make you his vessel of deliverance. Don't you think this 'payback-is-a-sumbitch' concept is a little *late?* Way back when, my daddy had to track-down Cecil all the way to the forests of Oregon to make him own-up to some *humma-humma* with yours truly—*gosh*, the good a sawed-off shotgun is capable of!—so it ain't like this problem is something new, you know? Cecil claims you just want all them lawyer-buddies of your'n to give you as much money as they can, legally or otherwise, 'cause political shit's so damned expensive, but *I* say what you're doing comes from the heart (and maybe the *loins*, too, LOL). Anyway, our pastor got in a bit of a fix several months ago with a young lady from our church, and it took an attorney from Midland to make him 'see the light,' so to speak, so maybe my old man isn't a *complete* muscle-head, but I still say Cecil's elevator never could seem to locate the penthouse, if you follow me— *I'm* the smart one—but he says he's voting for Denny. Now, don't worry, okay? He has a tendency to get contrary from time to time, but if he doesn't change his ways, I'll cut his ass completely *off!* I *mean* it: he'll think *pussy* is a million-dollar, one-time traveling show—and that he missed the *train!* I *know* for a fact you remember me: a couple years ago we ran into each other at a honky-tonk in San Angelo, and Cecil was passed-out at the table? You liked what you saw—and vice versa—and we had some fun with each other below the table-top? You said I was *tasty* and you wished we could spend more time together, then I did you a little favor outside in your car? *Remember?* You told me if I was ever in the Washington area to look you up? Well, this is the *next*-best thing, getting to send you a personal message you and no one else will see! You just keep running for congress, and I'll keep voting for you, honey-bunch, okay? And don't worry about Cecil; that motor never *did* get-up to full speed! XOXO! Your baby-doll, Ramona Wing!"

"Oh, my *God*, what a tiny world it *is!*" he exclaimed, his memory of that night a little bit hazy on specifics . . but the place, time, and woman herself as clear as glass. *Pretty* girl. Delightfully cold beer. Good music on the jukebox. Hotter than *hell* outside. Dow and Velma had been there, too, but left early for a midnight swim in their pool, probably in their birthday suits. No *wonder* that name had rung such a thunderous bell: for days afterward, he told acquaintances he'd just 'Winged-it!' that night, then smiled and gone about his business.

With something approaching religious veneration he carefully opened the pale-lavender envelope, his letter-opener slicing through the pleasant material with ease, a single sheet of the same soft paper perfectly folded inside: it was time for the official verdict on his progress, *aux* L.W. Shaw. Heart in his throat, he opened the paper and read:

Hey, kiddo!

When faced with the gathering storm, the weak among us search frantically for refuge, accept what we find and rarely come out. The tumult, other-worldly, seems just that, and lost ground remains lost forever. Such is the lot of the weak. The strong, of course, remain resourceful and meet the challenge head-on, for it is *not* the best way—it is the *only* way. The strong really *do* survive, and emerge better than

335

ever to facilitate prosperity, which is rightfully theirs. They find a way where and when it seems all paths are blocked. They *triumph*.

Kudos, my young friend! *Superlative* triumph! I'm right proud, too.

L.W.

He read the message a second time, then a third, savoring each word. It was almost as wonderful as receiving a message from Jesus Christ himself, or Abe Lincoln, and better than anything anyone *else* might send his way. *God*, it felt terrific! He drew-in a massive lungful of air and slowly exhaled: he could *breathe* again.

XV.

His rental house in Herndon, so warm and comforting as seen from the street, seemed the loneliest place imaginable when he entered the kitchen from the garage, another sensation with which he was wholly unfamiliar, the vision of Theresa wrapping her happy arms around Lynch as he walked through *his* door intruding itself upon his already disquieting arrival home. No matter, he thought, ignoring the anxiety of self-imposed solitude: I can have a bourbon or two, change into something comfy, and get some work done. Checking his cell merely as an afterthought—a rare occurrence in his habit of answering every call (unless sleeping), at half-past seven he saw the message from D.P. and took a quick look. 'Dudley Thomas furious at your support from other House members, including friends inside Texas! LOL! Also, T.S.! Velma sends her love! We already miss you! Can't wait to see you on 29th! Bourbon **FOREVER**! The Dow-ster ...' He closed the phone, content with his world.

Meditating on life, work, and friendships as he enjoyed his first bourbon and water, the soothing voice of Sinatra serenading the premises with his rendition of *You Make Me Feel So Young*, he smiled in spite of himself at the thought of so many friends being happy with their lives. Wasn't that what his work was *really* all about? How many times had the old man looked him in the eye and said "No matter *what*, all I want is for you to be happy!"? He understood the reasons Dow and Velma complemented each other so beautifully, why they seemed such a perfect match; her passion and his efficiency, taken separately a contradiction of potential catastrophe, fit together like pieces of an intricate puzzle. The Bohannons seemed like a good fit, too: the roar and fury dominating Lynch's persona had long been tempered by Theresa's un-ruffled feathers, her influence serving to calm his instability, especially with matters political. Cas Turley and marriage, for whatever reasons, just hadn't been a good fit. Already the wise Mr. Turley had made plans for a *rendez-vous* with an unspeakably lovely Italian lady on the *Cote d'Azur* once the primary season was concluded, to be followed by a week in the Bernese Oberland with a female acquaintance from Finland. L.W. Shaw had been married to the same woman for nigh forty years, and Sid didn't envy any of them the first ounce of their well-deserved contentedness. The inescapable conclusion that he might never be with one woman for any measurable amount of time, a situation born more from necessity than some nameless, virtually non-existent desire to be left alone, hadn't bothered him in twenty years of adulthood. Since discovering she was pregnant with his child the notion that, if Charlotte Tillstrom couldn't win his unceasing love and affection then *no one* could, had increasingly come to dominate his non-political life. He saw her face in everything he did, every place he went, every activity in which he partook. She accompanied him at meals and in the shower, in his offices at work, at his desk in the House itself. She tenderly tucked him into bed at night, kissed him affectionately, then slid underneath the sheets to sleep the night away in his arms. When they appeared together in public, he was more than content to see it was *she* who garnered all the attention, and why not? Women of her caliber *always* found the limelight! She did all this and more . .

338

without him being within ten miles of her! The most *puzzling* aspect of their non-relationship? She stayed in the forefront of his thoughts . . when no other woman he'd ever so much as *hugged* could be recalled a week after they'd stopped seeing each other! By the time he poured his second drink he'd become concurrently bemused and annoyed: he had *work* to get done, period, and here he was obsessed with a woman who adored him, yet found him so contemptibly undesirable as a fellow human being that she'd turned her back on him. The frustrated congressman slipped into shorts and football jersey and took a seat at his desk, his laptop awaiting its master. Perhaps—ah, *perhaps*—the delectable Miss Tillstrom had e-mailed a message to come and see her . . ASAP!

"Come *on!*" he chided himself miserably. "Come on—*snap out of it! . .*"

ID and password entered, he clicked again and cast a cursory glance at the *"MESSAGES"* box, fully

aware that after being out of town for nearly two weeks there were more than likely thirty or forty entries waiting for his response. 'YOU HAVE {8,357} MESSAGES, EL SID!' it read. He burst into nervous laughter as his eyes examined each of the four numbers singly, then altogether, then each individual number again. He instinctively clicked-out, unequivocally bewildered at such a ridiculous aggregate: after all, no more than twenty-five or thirty people on *Earth* had his *personal* e-mail address! He re-entered ID and password, clicked once more and read: 'YOU HAVE {8,360} MESSAGES, EL SID!'

"Now wait just a minute!" he cried reassuringly. "*Those* aren't the same numbers that were there before . ."

He wrote "8360" on the back of an envelope and clicked-out again, threw down the last of his drink, then headed to the kitchen for another, his self-imposed limit of two cocktails having suddenly fallen by the wayside. When he returned, drink in hand, he stared suspiciously at his laptop: if computers were capable of instigating a viable *conspiracy* against a sitting member of the United States Congress . . . then maybe there *was* a problem! Never taking his eyes from the screen, he dropped slowly, carefully into his desk chair, timidly entered his ID and Password a third time, and clicked into the system, a full four-and-a-half-minute interval having passed: 'YOU HAVE {8,374} MESSAGES, EL SID!'—another fourteen entries having arrived in the interim.

"Oh, my God," he mumbled, heart wedged securely in his throat. "Oh, my *GOD!*"

Was it even *possible* to hold that many messages? Would his computer *explode* when it hit 10,000 ? *15,000?* If not, *when?* 25,000? Would his house blow-up when he tried to read the first note? The second? Would his parents, safe and secure in west Texas, be notified the next morning their only son had died in a massive fireball, causes unknown, in northern Virginia? He remembered reading many years before of an unfortunate glitch in an accounting and billing system on the web: the system, *unfortunately*, had inadvertently omitted the *decimal point* in its configuration one disastrous night in October, the result of which had been predictably chaotic. Millions and *millions* of people had awakened one Tuesday morning that month to find *astronomical* charges on their credit cards and, infinitely worse, their check-cards, from the past weekend: a $300.00 hotel charge had become a *$30,000* hotel charge without the little "dot," a $500.00 shopping-spree converted to a *$50,000* shopping-spree! Unsuspecting people had actually been saddled with thirty and forty-*thousand-dollar* charges above and beyond their credit limits, with catastrophic results: bills paid with debit-cards were rendered worthless, and mothers couldn't buy their children a container of milk! Maybe this was just another computer-glitch, he hoped . . but in e-mail, of all things?!

He tentatively clicked on the first message. It was from someone called *kiki/in/ketchikan*, and in retrospect turned-out to be one of the nicer, *less*-volatile notes: "Hey, *Shit*-for-Brains!: My girlfriends and I appreciate your kind thoughts and concerns for our general health and welfare—*really*, we do! That's why it's so incredibly *easy* for us to return a 'kind thought' your way, and pray it will benefit you the same way you've benefited *us!* We want you to reach way, way down—*that's it*, reach *way* down there—then place your hands firmly on your shoulders, and pull your head out of your *ass*, you moron! XOXOXOXO!! Your palz, the Luvly Ladiez of Alazka!"

For a fleeting second he considered deleting every message in the system, actually banishing fifteen or twenty entries to e-mail-cyberspace-hell before reconsidering, his second stop-to-read from *rawMeat4Marcie*: "Wow! Marcie here, in El Paso! What's *wrong* with you, motherfucker, did someone drop you on your empty head?! My friend, Estelita, is here with me and thinks you need some *panocha* worse than any human being who ever *lived!* We graded *your* comments and gave you a great big *El Fail-o!* How 'bout movin' your ass to Peru so you can search for your *dick?!* Adios! Wee-uns!"

This time he scrolled-down a hundred places and clicked on the first entry he saw, *Wiz-uh-duh-West*: "I gotta hand it to U, pahd-nuh.......U cood eat nuthin but shit from now 'til 4-evuh, and it wooden be neer enuff! U nock-in down 6 figgers!, in the best U kin du is make-it hah-duh 4 us 2 fin duh ladeez? Y not go uh-way in nut come bak!? U gots sumpin ginst *pussee?!* Da Wiz-uh-duh-West sez good-bye and EF OH!!"

Searching for an English entry, he scrolled-down another

hundred or so places and stopped on an entry marked *ClarkCindy1992*: "Congress-*man*: Inasmuch as your latest maneuvers labeled '*Person-hood*' and '*Retroactive Responsibility*' are just transparent attempts to disguise the fact that you and your imbecilic friends want to deny women everywhere the opportunity and, yes, the *right* to end the life of an unwanted child, I'd like very much to discuss *your* last pregnancy. No, no, congress-man: *not your mother's* last pregnancy (we *all* know how badly that one turned-out, don't we?). No, no, congress-man, a thousand times . . *NO!* Not your *wife's* or your *girlfriend's* last pregnancy. *NO! Your* . . last pregnancy, congress-man! What's that you say?! *Can't* get pregnant?! Isn't it enough that men are at least partly responsible for the mistake (if not *completely?*)? Why can't women be allowed to *correct* your mistake? The next time you find yourself pregnant, try letting a complete stranger tell *you* what to do with *your* body and see how *you* like it, you arrogant *bastard!* And don't forget to have yourself a nice day!"

Utterly convinced there had to be at least one or two messages of support *somewhere* inside so many thousand disapprovals—how on earth could they possibly be all *bad?*—he clicked on the very next one, a fine American known in *e*-circles as *bobSeahawksfan6,3,89* and prepared for the worst. The message was short and sweet: "Dear congressman Villary: *Blow me!* Respectfully yours, *bob*"

Again he moved down a single entry, his faith in young people as strong as ever—though it *did* seem like several had some sort of ax to grind. He clicked on *stan7cardwithU* and read: "Sid, baby? You've got me in a bit of a hard spot here, man........My main-squeeze told me that you and your honchos telling women what to do with their bodies is like her and her friends telling *you* and your friends which NFL teams to root-for and which ones to hate! Unfortunately, I told her that telling *anybody* which football teams to love or hate was none of her fucking business, and she told me that what she and her pals do with *their* bodies is none of *your* fucking business! Then Phoebe Ann—that's my main squeeze—gave *me* the business: she's cut me *off*, Sid, baby! Told me if I didn't vote for some Hispanic split-tail come November it was all over between us, and I *dearly* love Phoebe Ann *and* her delicious cooter, so I'm in a bit of a situation here, man.........Yes, Amarillo has a million pretty women and, *yes*, I could probably go out bar-hopping and locate a little *strange*, but I don't want to, and you know what? I shouldn't *have* to! I'm with you, Sid, baby—men need to step-it-up and be *men*—but I can't be going three or four months *without* that sweet stuff, so help me out here, how 'bout it? Take it all back, or *something*, fuck! This is killing me, hoss! Stan's in a bad way, a *really* bad way, so send some relief my way, tell her you were just *kidding*, tell her anything, for fuck's-sake, but *please* get her off my back! Right-*on*, brother! Stan, the Man!"

"Je-sus H. Christ!" he swore under his breath. "How'd I get mixed-up in *that?!* . ."

He clicked on REPLY and tapped the keys: "Stan: I hear you, buddy! Tell Phoebe Ann my bill has almost zero chance of ever becoming law, and that she has my personal guarantee she can do whatever she likes with her body, including sharing it with *you* in any manner she sees fit! I appreciate your vote, Stan! Sidney H. Villary, Congressman, 38th District, Texas!" then he hit the SEND button and it was gone forever.

Risking everything on a hunch, just after returning to his desk with cocktail number four, he moved the cursor but a solitary space below, where *smithml0916Ynot?* waited for his eyes only. Really, how much *worse* could it get? He reluctantly clicked on it and read: "Good morning. Over the past several years I've become convinced that all the needless gun-violence stems from mental-health issues—or, at the very least, a *hefty* portion of it. Is there *anyone* I could speak with concerning *congressional* . . mental-health issues? Since you are evidently the patron saint of the Committee on Nut-Cases, Southwest Edition, can you help me? Is there any way you can tell me about when it was you lost your *last* marble? Is it true your proposal will be presented as the *Lobotomy* Amendment? The reason I ask is that my boyfriend and I think you've lost your fucking mind and don't even know where to *look* for it! BTW, this is Maddy and Greg!"

He moved the cursor down one notch. *milehighMarielLeo* had seen fit to communicate with him, and Sid could hardly wait to sample the approaching toxins: "Greetings from the Centennial State, asshole! People tell me I'm confrontational; I prefer to think of myself as *honest*. Any complaints, dickhead? I didn't think so! I'd like to apologize first for not being in Texas to vote for someone *else—anyone* else, actually. FYI, I'll goddamn good and well screw whoever I want to, whenever I like, OK? I'll take care of me; you take care of you, alright? I hear they're looking for pricks in Paraguay—you might want to go check it out for yourself! *You* . . could earn *top*-dollar! XO Take it easy."

His faith in his fellow man as strong and firm as ever—and nearly as strong and firm in women—he moved the cursor down *two* spaces to *iluvmy69vetteGDit* and clicked on it, ready for whatever it was headed his way: "high-school grad here. Metal shop and combustion engines. Not impressed with college types. *Still* looking for the blown head-gasket *app*. Stone-*fox* came in yesterday. Over-heating problem. Fixed it. Asked her out tomorrow night. She said '*Yeah!*' If we have a good time but don't kiss, are her future children with somebody else *my* fault? LMK *quick!*......Jimmy P"

"That wasn't so bad," he said. He keyed-in the hoped-for negative response, then keyed-in 'Vote *Villary*,' and followed it with a 'Thanks, Jimmy!'

Had he finally stumbled across the magic interval? *Skip* every-other message and read the good ones . . the ones where nobody wanted his blood spilled? Fifty-fifty seemed an acceptable percentage for such an emotional controversy. He skipped over the next entry, letting the cursor stop on a message from *KatQueenNQuerque*: "Hello again, my love. I remember well when we locked eyes the first time on your visit here three years ago: *Sensational* vibe. I'll never forget our first touch: *electric-Fantasyland*. Then, in a span of less than ten short months, our first flowery kiss: *Spectacular* two-lips. And then, *finally*, the world-class, blue-ribbon, gold-medal seduction: *Tres-magnifique!* — and I haven't been the same since. Neither have our two children: where's the child-support, jock-o? Please contact my attorney @ 1-800-328-7448 (1-800-EAT-SHIT). Farewell, my love. P.S. — R U still a *lousy* fuck? Just wondered.............."

Undaunted, he then skipped-over two entries, stopping on the *third* message, the old tried-and-true '*shotgun*' approach, as viable now as any time prior. *alfredRexIIIA&M* beckoned. Ignoring the last three symbols as best he could, he clicked on it and crossed his fingers: "Well, well. *Congressman* Villary — or should I say, soon-to-be *ex*-congressman Villary? You have really done it this time, Kid-Sid: pulled it *way* out from whence it came, spread it on the ground like a starving piece of twine, and trod upon it with reckless abandon, rendering it useless in the future for any and all females under the age of six! But then, since you haven't had *it* since *it* had *you*, you

345

shan't miss it, what? We're proud of you,*ma'am!* Toodles!"

He lowered the cursor *four* slots, then took it down one more in honor of his fifth cocktail and stopped. Were high-school graduates the only ones smart-enough to see what a monstrous favor he was doing for Americans everywhere? Were college types universally set against him now? There had to be an improvement in the quality of messages—*had* to be—hadn't there? How long would it take to come across the more-favorable reviews? He clicked on *GLAD2EATU2* and read: "Hey-hey.....Que *passo?* The boys and I here in San Angelo—or is it Odessa?—maybe it's *Lubbock!*—anyway, the boys and I here in the *western* U.S.A. don't think you've gone far enough. Man, if only you could put some *realistic* laws into effect governing the behavior of early 20-somethings like ourselves?!.............How about no women *over*-40 eligible to partake in a quality gang-bang? (the 'key' word is *quality!*)......How about no sex *whatsoever* for anybody—except for Thursday through Wednesday in Oklahoma, and Saturday through Friday in Texas?.........How about no women sucking cock unless they can *prove* their ability to suck a tennis ball up through a garden hose?..........We think all our ideas deserve at least a second look, and we'd like your opinion, as well. Denny Warrington thought we deserved an answer, too! Ur *amigos* in crime, Patrick, Ricardo, Stephen, Jonathan, and Pauly!"

"Smart-asses!" he muttered, letting the cursor scroll-down a full sixty or seventy slots. How was it possible that thousands of people now had his personal e-mail address, all of them were upset over the same issue, and no one was interested in listening to an alternative proposal? *How* was that possible?! The next message, he willfully decided, would be a more-subdued, rational, highly-cerebral treatise giving serious

346

consideration to the merits of his views on person-hood and abortion—it was a foregone conclusion, as far as he was concerned. The cursor stopped on an entry marked *lori73Really?* And he began reading yet again: "Where I am couldn't matter less, but I'm about your age, give or take a year or two. I'm responding to your proposals concerning rights of the unborn and adult American men . . . but, I repeat myself. How did you come-up with *this* one? Did you discuss these ideas with the men in the white coats at Happy Farms . . or the *inmates?* I'd like to know exactly what *time* . . you were born last *Thursday!* Ah, *here's* a stumper for you: if this country is *not* being led by narrow-minded, wholly pathetic, insensitive, pandering, bought-and-paid-for adolescents like yourself, why is no one surprised at both the idiocy of your aspirations and the degree of support you've received? Please beware of anyone who refers to you and your ilk as *imbeciles:* in a world *filled* with them—yes, I'm afraid they've been discovered on *every* continent, usually with small penises and a shocking percentage of diminutive *testicles*—these genuine, run-of-the-mill-imbeciles would be understandably upset at being placed in the same class with the elusive *congressional-*imbecile which, as I'm sure you're well-aware, is in a class by *itself.* Do you really think women so thick-headed, so inept and clumsy, so short-sighted—in short, so very *manly*—that they somehow missed your intentions? Do you *really* believe we are so insensitive that we can be clubbed over the head by some pea-brained, twat-deprived shithead (like *you,* congressman) and *not* know we've been clubbed over the head? If you believe that, then you're even dumber than you think I think you are, times ten, with the expectation of exponential growth! Here's the long and short of it, *ace*: if you don't want an abortion, *don't have one!* If you don't want to have any

347

children, *don't have any* (I notice you're neither married nor a father, so the next time I'm feeling singularly *masochistic*, I'll have you explain to me how abortion has *anything* in the whole wide *world* to do with the likes of *you!*)! One more clarifying, ridiculously-easy, *tiny* question, and then I've got to go: have you any idea what *hell* looks like? For someone like yourself, destined to visit there for an extended period of time, I'd at least *try* to do a little checking! It's been fabulous, my friend: Sieg *Heil!*"

"Don't you people know a *ruse* when you see it!" he screamed, exasperated.

The numbers punched-in on his cellphone, he sat patiently and waited.

"You by yourself? . ."

"Yeah, no company tonight," said Cas. "What's up?"

"I need you to come over and take a look at this shit on my computer . ."

"*What* shit are you referring to, Sid? . ."

"I've got over eight *thousand* messages in my e-mail, Cas, from all *over* the damn place, and these people are more than a *little* upset at my person-hood and abortion stances—I mean, these kids want *blood*, for Chrissakes! . ."

"Somebody just hacked your account, Sid . . happens all the time . ."

"But *why* would anyone wanna' do that—and *who* would it be?! . ."

"They'd just do it to spook you . . and I've got a pretty good idea who's behind it, too . ."

"Who in hell would *do* something like this? . ."

"Who do you *think?*" said Cas, a little exasperated. "You got plenty o' bourbon? . ."

"Enough, I guess . ."

348

"I'm on my way . ."

Forty-five short minutes later Cas Turley, riled from a tranquil evening at home, took his seat in front of Sid's laptop, bourbon-rocks in a highball glass emblazoned '*DON'T MESS . . WITH TEXAS!*' in dark-orange lettering in his left hand. Sid, his righteousness aroused to fever-pitch, sat comfortably in a   hoop-chair facing away from his desk, cocktail in his lap: he'd seen more than enough of his desk and computer already.

"*Wow!*" said Cas, the first indications of a grin appearing on his rugged features. "Impressive! . . Over eighty-four *hundred* messages from fine, upstanding American boys and girls, upset that anyone would have nerve-enough to try to curb their over-active glands! . ."

"Yeah, over eight thousand . . and climbing every minute . ."

"I see here you've looked at quite a few of 'em . . *Lord*, it'd take forever to read 'em all! . ."

"I've read enough of them to get the picture, I can tell you . ."

Turley scrolled through the first few hundred entries, head shaking from side to side in sheer admiration of the *bulk* of messages when he muttered "Ol' Dudley sure knows how to get on a body's *nerves*, don't he? . ."

"Next time I see *that* sumbitch," vowed Sid, suddenly animated at the sound of his tormenter's name, "I'm gonna' have somethin' for his *ass!* . ."

The congressman's immigration-policy guru stopped the cursor at random on an entry from someone identified as *86MannyBNawlins* and read carefully, bursting into laughter when he finished.

"These young kids sure are creative!" he said admiringly, and he scrolled-down again to his next stop, a message from *ICUcanUCme2?*. He clicked on it and read for a few short seconds, then stopped. "Some of these are really short and sweet, aren't they? . ."

"Short, yes," Sid agreed. "I'm not so sure about the 'sweet' part . ."

A minute later Cas was consumed by laughter so physically violent he had to set his drink down to keep it from spilling, rocking back and forth in the chair with his eyes closed, the back of his left hand covering his mouth to help conceal the noise. Sid sat stoically with cocktail number seven.

"Hey, Sid . . get a load of *this* one!" he finally managed, wiping a tear away with his shirt-sleeve. "It's from *cowgirl89nPA* . . it's not especially *short*—but it *is* sweet! . . 'My darling Sid: How could I ever logically explain the phenomenon that is *you?!* I wondered what all the noise was about, so I looked you up on the web and can now honestly say I was physically attracted to you the first moment I laid eyes on you! How could I have known *then* that you'd find me so attractive, too? Your dilatation and curettage was unquestionably superior to anything in my experience! Your first kiss was *heaven*, the first neck-nibble joy *supreme*, the first ear-bite a pleasure reserved for *queens!* And then . . *then*, you touched me *there*, and in mere seconds I was *sopping!* When you began nipple-nibbling I thought I'd *explode*, but nothing prepared me for your performance while you ate dinner at the *why'* . . and she spelled that w-h-y, too, Sid . . 'Oh. *Oh.* OH. *OH!* Your grand entrance was nothing less than a master-*stroke*— *hundreds* of them!—as we had our *steak*, and ate it, too! I'd never known such ecstasy, such charisma—such *bratwurst!* We both stretched way out—*wayyyy out!*—oh, oh, oh, oh, Oh, Oh, Oh, OH, OH, OH, OOOOOHH MMYYYYY GGOODDDDD!!!!'

Pausing for effect, a moment later a much quieter Cas

350

Turley read the end of the message: "I'll let you know how everything turned-out about the first of next *April!* . . Mmmmmm-*Wah!* me."

For Sid, only the taste of good bourbon—coupled with Sinatra's golden voice—gave pleasure as he leisurely pointed out "Cas?! . . you're *not* helping! . ."

XVI.

Tuesday morning, 29 July, the west Texas sun brought the temperature up to 89 by 8:30 A.M. Congressman Sidney H. Villary, a mere three weeks away from his primary-election challenge, flew into Texas a few days earlier than planned, accomplishing two unrelated objectives. It sent shivers down the backs of Denny Warrington and his crew, and Dudley Thomas—already shaken by the loss of Christian support through 'person-hood' publicity—felt helpless to stem the tide. And with no pending legislation in either the House or Senate, there was no legitimate reason for hanging around: D.P. and Velma picked him up at El Paso International mid-afternoon on Sunday the 27th, took him to grab a bite at Cielo Vista, then headed east on I-10, flying low through far-west Texas 160 miles before branching left onto I-20. At eight that evening he met with a group of young people in a school gymnasium to hear their grievances, just as he promised he would, the biggest surprise of which—as far as the young people were concerned, anyway—was the fact that he arrived *at all*. More than one juvenile had gumption-enough to tell Sid he'd been convinced the youth-beleaguered congressman would be a gigantic *no-show*—but there he was in full living color, despite the obvious misgivings of more than half the assembled crowd: it was a decidedly pro-Warrington group—at least, it was when the meeting *began*. When he finished, the once-suspicious multitude gave him a standing ovation; he merely familiarized the young people gathered with several harsh realities, most of which were geared toward *their* protection. His immigration policies protected those already in Texas, *not* those who still wanted to come. He was traveling to eastern Europe in September looking for trade and industrial ties, and would be happy to help anyone in the crowd travel there, too, to work or study: all they had to do was call his office! No one was going to move Fort Hood away from Texas—*or* to any other location inside Texas, if he had anything to say about it. The mere *notion* was absurd. Finally, he didn't want to see anyone involved in a so-called "shotgun" wedding, where a mistake or miscalculation had been made by the young man or young lady, or possibly both parties; these marriages rarely, if ever, proved successful, typically ending with hard feelings and divorce, or worse. Young people needed to follow the same common-sense ideas, now and in the foreseeable future, he'd espoused all along: be good to one another, be respectful to one another, and always, *always* operate using caution and *precaution*—if one was careful, almost any problem could be prevented, and prevention was the *key*. He wasn't trying to ruin anybody's *fun*; he was only trying to make sure they could have fun without any unexpected   surprises ruining everything. When one young man tried to hamstring him on a technicality, Sid reminded everyone present that there were already laws on the books: he was merely attempting to protect those who couldn't protect themselves because, unlike just about everyone else present, he'd taken an oath of office. A few still seemed bewildered when the meeting ended, but most admitted they felt better about a host of issues, including person-hood and a woman's right to an abortion—which he reluctantly admitted was *still* the law of the land.

That Monday he'd made appearances in Jacksville, Steele, Tarleton, and Lyman with solid crowds bordering raucousness at every stop, D.P. accompanying him the whole long way. At six that afternoon the optimistic Mr. Pettigrew felt a growing sense that the worst danger had now passed them by, that Warrington and his forces had made as many inroads as they were capable of, and were now headed in the opposite direction. They met Velma at seven for dinner at El Jefe in Odessa, then retired to the Pettigrew spread for swimming and cocktails, Sid persuading D.P. at length to play some jazz-type Sinatra while they swam. Tuesday would be another full day as Dow had scheduled visits to Tallulah, Maribone, Park City, and Cinnamon Springs, a round-trip of well-over 300 miles. At about half-past ten Sid felt a sudden, wholly-inexplicable premonition of disaster, literally the polar opposite of the excitement D.P. felt earlier about their primary opponent, but was slowly persuaded out from beneath it by the illustrious cooing of Velma, who insisted he was worried about nothing. Logic told him she was right: it had been an extremely-productive day, she accurately pointed-out—and, Lord have *mercy*, it was a *Monday!* How bad could the rest of the week be? He finally laughed it off—even allowed himself another small bourbon-rocks—swimming around every inch of the pool to the happy strains of Frank at his jazzy best, returning to his drink every few minutes, his appreciative eyes very much stuck on Velma, who looked incredible in her orange two-piece.

So when Tuesday morning he awoke at seven inside the Pettigrew guest-room, the sun just rearing its bright and shiny face, he dove back under the quilt and stayed there until 8:30 when the temperature   outside hit 89 . . and an extraordinarily low-key, very subdued, almost apologetic Dow Pettigrew knocked on the door.

"I'm up, I'm up, I'm up," he lied as he lay on his right side facing the window.

"*Sid?* . . your mom's on the land-line in the rec-room, man . ."

"Tell her I'll call her back after my shower, okay? . ."

"*Sid?* . . You need to talk to your mom . ."

"It can't wait fifteen or twenty? . ."

There followed a short pause before D.P., his voice filled with sad regret, said "I'm afraid *this* one can't wait . ."

When the mildly-curious, still sleepy-eyed Sid entered the rec-room in shorts and T-shirt a minute later he found the surroundings—indeed, the rest of the house—strangely quiet, almost gloomy, despite the sunny day outside with the usual bustle of morning traffic and insect chatter. He grabbed the waiting phone and said "Good morning, mother! . ."

"Good morning, son," came her familiar voice, but even with the fog of the early hour he couldn't miss the shade of melancholy in her tone. "I hate to wake you so early, you being so busy and all, but some things are better confronted when they happen . ."

"What is it, mother? . ."

"I'm afraid I have some bad news for you, son . ."

"Is dad okay?!" he said, suddenly tuned-in to the unthinkable. "Is he all right? . ."

"Yes, he's right here, and he's fine . . I just don't quite know *how* to tell you, is all . ."

The glare of the morning sunlight overpowering the room, he turned round and spotted D.P. and Velma standing together in the kitchen, D.P.'s arms wrapped tenderly around his wife in a protective embrace. Her head rested on his chest, tears streaming down her face. Sid froze in muted terror.

"For God's sake, what's *happened*, mother? . ."

"Honey . . L.W. Shaw is *dead* . ."

He couldn't breathe. He felt the air being knocked out of

him, sucked-out by the cruel delivery of a few words. He'd been gut-shot over a telephone line: there was obviously some sort of *mistake*, or *mis-communication*, that's all. His friend and mentor, the man he held in greater esteem than anyone, the man he trusted with his very *life* . . wouldn't *dream* of leaving without saying good-bye.

"*What* did you say, mother? . ."

"Cas called a few minutes ago, thinking you were here, of course . . I wanted to tell you myself . . He had a massive coronary late last night and died a little after midnight in Georgetown . . they *tried*, but the trauma doctors couldn't save him . . Cas is extremely upset, of course, just like we are . . Lord, everyone is simply devastated, son—we've known L.W. for over forty years, and we never met a nicer, more benevolent, kinder man in our lives . . Your father's taking it pretty hard, of course, what with having known him in college and all . . I haven't spoken with Leslie Lee or any of the kids yet . . I'm quite sure she's got more than enough on *her* plate, poor thing . . Cas said it's too early to think about funeral arrangements, but if a memorial service is held in D.C., your father and I will absolutely be there, naturally . . Are you all right, son? . ."

"Hell, *no*, I'm not all right! . . I'm *numb* from head to toe, mother, I can't even *think!* . ."

"I'm sorry, son, I know how you feel about L.W.—we all do—and I realize how very excruciating this must be for you," she said, heartbroken at having brought the news. "Of course, this couldn't happen at a *worse* time, with all of us *here* and all of them *there*—and right in the middle of your fight with Denny . . Of course, there's *never* a good time for this sort of thing . ."

He stood holding the phone, a thousand emotions

356

contending with a thousand fleeting, conflicted thoughts, rendering him catatonically unfit to function. One look at Velma, her eyes puffy from tears gushing as from some kind of bottomless well, explained more than ten thousand words spoken in anguish, D.P.'s somber stare into the kitchen floor screaming their collective sorrow. Through the opaque curtain of uncertainties suddenly thrust into their midst— occasioned by journeys begun but temporarily halted without desired conclusions, ignited by fires which burnt brightly— the solitary thought that shot through the morass of shock and abject sadness was . . everything stops *now!* Denny Warrington could do as he liked—but the Villary camp, even with only three weeks remaining until election-day, would postpone the entire campaign to pay homage to a great American.

"What can I do to help, son?" said his mother. "Is there anyone you want me to contact that you and Dow might not have time for? . ."

"We'll take care of campaign-stop cancellations," he said meekly. He shook his head violently for a long moment in an attempt to chase the cobwebs away: think, damn it, *think!* "When Lynch calls, tell him I'll fly-in sometime tomorrow and ask him if he's heard anything about the schedule-of-events with services—*that* is the single most-important event in my life until this is over and done-with—and if you get a chance, please call the airlines and see if you can get me on something fairly early tomorrow morning back to D.C. . . Looks like I'll be there through the weekend, but I don't care . . You and dad gonna' wait to book flights until we find out about visitation and services? . ."

"Yes, but we don't want to be any later getting there than tomorrow night in case Leslie needs something from us . . If we end-up spending one or two hapless nights unnecessarily in D.C. it surely doesn't matter in the long run . . we just want to be there for her . ."

"Yes, of course," he said, his wits beginning their molasses-slow return from exile. "You still have keys to my place, so make yourselves comfortable in the guest room when you land . . Can you and dad remember how to get there from the airport? . ."

"We'll be just *fine,* thanks . . will you be headed this way anytime soon? . ."

"I'll see you in a few hours . . I should be there by noon, anyway . ."

"I'm so sorry, my precious boy . . be careful when you head this way . ."

"Bye, for now . ."

He dropped the receiver into its cradle and stood motionless, eyes closed in the struggle to find safe harbor in the storm, another victimless victim of the inevitable currents of life, crushed beneath the oppressive heaviness of *being.* His life and career, his future plans . . his friends, all changed forever—for the worse. He glanced toward the kitchen again: Velma, still in tears, fumbling with the coffee-pot with one hand, the other tissue-filled, struggling to see, D.P. too numb to do anything worth mentioning, his sense of well-being shattered.

"I'll make some breakfast," she announced bravely through teary eyes.

"Not a *chance,*" said the sobered congressman, whereupon he was finally moving again, away from the rec-room into the kitchen where he walked right to her, gathering her into his arms as much for his benefit as hers. He gently rocked her from side to side, her joy of the night before drowned in tears. "Sweetheart, none of us is in any shape to do anything except try to *recover* from this . . let's all get dressed and go, then I'll get everyone's breakfast . . *then*, we can start thinking about the long, hard trip to the east . ."

Wednesday afternoon the nor'easter blown asunder from the Mississippi Valley pushed its way through the nation's capital just after lunch, its squall-line gusting the frightened air across the Potomac at sixty miles an hour, temperatures dropping twenty degrees and more until the sun returned at half past two to ignite the resting rainwater, steam rising from roadways in sultry waves of comfort. The jumbo-jet transporting Mr. and Mrs. Villary left Dallas-Ft. Worth easily enough, its crew fully aware they'd likely encounter the front about the time it crossed the Rapidan or Rappahannock southwest of the District; the storm's ever-increasing velocity had the lion's share of the wind causing havoc at the Orioles' game in Baltimore as the jet's wheels first touched-down. Sid had thought politicians the unquestioned masters of euphemisms—but his congressional brethren could learn something from flight-attendants, he decided at length. Three different ladies, nattily-attired in American Airlines' best, gave the exact same answer when queried about storm developments in northern Virginia: "Looks like there's some *weather* up there!" Well . . . thank you so *much*.

Still wet but beginning to clear-off when they landed, his parents quickly grabbed their rental car and fled to Herndon to freshen-up before driving into Georgetown for a private commiseration with Leslie Lee who, like Jackie Kennedy before her, remained stoically courageous to the world, though devastated. An incredibly-strong woman, his mother described her, from the mountains of western Montana, where she might very well return once L.W. was mourned and memorialized. But what news of the now-belated arrangements? Sid avoided his office, the girls given time-off during the mourning period, like so many other congressional staffs, preferring Cas Turley's favorite bar on the Lee Highway in western Arlington, the two drinking alone together until D.P. and Velma flew-in a few minutes after five. The day before, every national news outlet featured the 'untimely death' of L. Wilson Shaw, "war hero, author, statesman, diplomat, professor, and adviser to no fewer than *five* presidents." 'And more than a few senators and congressmen, too,' Sid thought Tuesday evening, grateful that every single news channel he watched—even the ones who didn't necessarily agree with everything L.W. stood for—had been gracious about his undeniable contributions to the country he loved and served so honorably in so many ways.

Cas Turley was as grim-faced as Sid could remember, dark bags under his eyes from sleep deprivation—or maybe some new, unknown tart from Maryland—maybe both. When Sid walked-in he stopped fifteen feet away, assessed the other's appearance, and rendered the verdict.

"You must be the raw steak I ordered from the plane . ."

"Great to see you, too, buddy . ."

"Catch me up on things, my friend . . Turkey and water, rocks," he told the bartender as he dropped   onto the stool next to Cas and shook hands. He removed his suit-coat and carefully folded it across the bar-top next to his friend's windbreaker, still moist from the storm. "How long you been here? . ."

"Not long enough to get drunk," Cas said ruefully, "but *that's* what I need to do—get good and drunk—and I mean *hammered*—I tried to last night, but it just wasn't in me somehow, 'cause I couldn't get my arms round him being gone . . And things won't be set aright until what's left of me wakes-up one morning and I feel so rotten I can't remember my name, then spend the rest o' the day in bed trying my damnedest to recover from what I've done to myself . ."

Sid gave his henchman a sympathetic pat on the back, much the same as D.P. had given him the morning before as the emptiness, the finality of their collective loss began to settle-in. He noticed Cas's regular dark-as-night ale had been replaced by something stronger and decidedly more-concentrated . . though lighter in hue. Such was the lot of the bereaved: this was no time for any damned kid-stuff, and he'd adjusted accordingly. Sid allowed himself a minute to give the premises the once-over: a young couple sat at the bar opposite them, talking quietly; the booth situated closest to the door had a middle-aged toper hard at work on some sort of business invoices; a booth further back and away from the bar, better-suited to privacy, had a young man of perhaps twenty-five enjoying cocktails with a well-dressed, attractive woman at least twice his age, who seemed to be enjoying the younger man's attention immensely; and a thirty-something man in the farthest booth, busy with matters Sid couldn't perceive, focused on paperwork resting on the table, rarely glancing-up to check on bar activity. When he turned round he noticed another, more-seasoned couple had entered and taken seats at the bar to his left and down, tourists in D.C. to take-in the historical sights, he figured, searching for a late lunch. The bar's interior walls were adorned with posters of movies and political figures from a bygone era, stars and public servants long dead and buried, memories for an older set like his parents and their friends . . like L.W. Shaw. At least the bar's open side faced northeast, away from the afternoon sun, foiling the blinding rays. He grabbed his first drink and held it a few inches above the bar-top.

"I'd like to toast my friend and comrade, L.W.," he said solemnly, the drink lifted higher now in respectful salute. Cas grabbed his glass and brought it up within a few inches of Sid's until they met in crystal harmony. "To my friend and compatriot, L.W. Shaw . . *the* greatest counsel any politician ever had . . a genuine, bona-fide American hero of my parents' generation . . King of the one-per-centers, and a man whose memory I'll hold dear to my dying day . . My *hero!* . ."

"Amen, brother!"

They clinked glasses again, taking long, melancholy swallows, the better to affirm their sorrow and unabashed affection for the man who was no more.

"There's visitation at the funeral home tomorrow afternoon from two to four-thirty, which I imagine will be pretty-well attended, Sid . . L.W. had a ton o' friends from all walks—not just military and political, mind you, but statesmen and diplomats, kings and queens, Jesus—everybody under the sun, really . . The service itself is scheduled for eleven at National Cathedral on Friday, with the bishop of the Archdiocese of Washington performing the ceremony—God only knows who'll show-up for that one!—then the body will be transported by train to his final resting place in Mountain Home, Idaho, where he grew-up . . it leaves Saturday morning . ."

"I almost wish I could make the trip home with him . ."

"And with the president in the Far East and not due back until early next week, I'm wondering who the ranking politician attending might be when Thursday morning rolls around . . not that it matters much, but I'm giving odds the V.P.'ll be there—and not a few justices from court . ."

Sid stared into the bottom of his drink: not even choice,

quality bourbon, one of Kentucky's very best, tasted as good today as it usually did. Then again, nothing else seemed right either.

"I don't know what the hell I'm gonna' do now, Cas . . how do you replace someone who's utterly irreplaceable?! . . I might as well piss up a rope as try to find another one like that, so why try? . . My folks knew him a lot longer than I did—my dad knew him in school, and mom met him at their wedding reception—he was still active-duty then and flew home for the ceremony, which he attended in his dress-blues—God-*damn*, he looked good in uniform!—they're headed over to see Leslie Lee in a little while, and I understand the youngest son is flying-in this afternoon from Afghanistan . . You know something, Cas? . ."

"What's that?"

"The thought crossed my mind that I'm over-reacting to his passing," he said quietly. He set his empty on the bar and nodded for another, pointing at Cas's for a double refresher. "But everybody I know—and I mean *everybody*—absolutely loved the guy! . . when we parted ways yesterday, Velma was *still* crying . . D.P. wasn't in much better shape, truth be told . . Have you seen or talked with Lynch yet? . ."

"*Shit*, if you think I'm in bad shape, you oughta' see *him*," he murmured, the faintest hint of a smile curling his upper lip at the corners. "I called him last night about nine—you know, just checking-in—and *Theresa* picked-up—this is Lynch's *cell* I called, mind you—and Lynch is in bed, passed-out! . . Seems he left your office, grabbed a fifth on his way outta' D.C., and decided drinking straight from the bottle on his way home was a *great* idea! The very *last* person on God's green earth that should be drinking *any* damned thing with alcohol in it is doing *eighty* down the freeway—drinking straight rum! But that's not the weirdest part: he actually makes it home without *killing* anyone—*then* passes-out in the shower, blubbering like a kid with a bee-sting! . . Poor Theresa . . Lynch chugged the whole fifth on his way home, save a swallow or two, which he promptly dispatched in the shower just before sliding-down the wall, landing like a sperm-whale with a thud so loud it brought her running into the bathroom, and *that's* how she found him! . . You've heard of being 'Drunk on your ass?' . . Well, that's what he was—drunk on his *ass*, literally! She had to drag him out of the shower and into their bedroom, dry him off, blow-dry his *hair* so he wouldn't catch pneumonia, then hoist the big lummox into bed so he could sleep it off . . And you know, the more I think about what he put her through, the   more convinced I become she deserves canonization—and *not* for being such a sweetheart, although she is certainly *that*—but for taking such exquisite care of a grown man who is, in so many ways, little more than an overgrown *kid* . .'

"I spoke with her this morning about ten . . Lynch was still in bed, but you can imagine what kinda' shape he was in when he finally woke-up . . whatever time *that* was . . and I'd give odds that, not only did he *not* make it into work today— he's still in bed a little after two-thirty the next day, categorically mystified as to what hit him! . ."

"Can't say as I blame him," Villary said sympathetically, reflecting on the sad events of the past day or two. "Here I sit, and I'm not in very good shape myself . . When I spoke with Regina yesterday morning she was in tears, too . . She had to tell Julie and Carmen when they came in, and that couldn't have been much fun, either . . She told me Carmen sat there at her computer, working the morning away, tears streaming down her face, so I told her to send everyone home, lock-up and be outta' there by three herself . . I hope to God she left, too . ."

"Back in a minute," said Cas, jumping off his stool.

Sid reached for his suit-jacket, but spotted a strip of thin, off-white paper peeking-out from beneath Cas's windbreaker: *ahh*, the <u>Washington</u> <u>Standard</u> from that morning! The story he sought ran on the front page, lower-right section, with a picture of a grinning, young L.W. in his fatigues, circa 1970, his second tour in Vietnam, taken just days after his most heroic exploit. The 7/16-inch headline read 'Major Shaw Remembered as Reluctant Hero.' He slowly sipped his bourbon and wished he'd been there at the end, just to render a well-earned salute. He read quickly:

'L. Wilson Shaw, awarded the Distinguished Service Cross for gallantry-in-action in the Viet Nam of 1970, and a well-known deal-maker in political circles in the nation's capital for thirty years, died early Tuesday morning, July 29, in a Georgetown hospital. He was 67.

Major Shaw, as he was best-remembered by several colleagues, never relished his hero's mantle, even after attaining notoriety as a politician, statesman, and trusted adviser to presidents. A four-term congressman from Idaho, he championed increased funding for military families, advanced weapons systems, and battlefield innovations in medicine, but found time to emphasize diplomatic solutions to political problems first in eastern Europe, then the Middle East. Presidents from both parties sought and received his counsel regarding

365

coalitions. He served as Special Advisor to NATO, both as counsel to existing members and east-European countries seeking admission after the fall of the so-called "Iron-Curtain" countries and the former Soviet Union.'

The same-old, same-old he'd heard repeatedly on the news networks the evening before. Nothing new. Why could journalists never interview friends and acquaintances in trying times like these? As a sitting congressman, he gave interviews as a matter of routine; why not *now*, when he could personally attest to the largesse of the deceased, his distinctly-austere benevolence, his monumental acumen and gifts of counsel— his overwhelming desire to merely *serve?* No, the average American would never realize what an extraordinary patriot it had lost. But Sid and politicians like him, public servants and, yes, even heads-of-state, would mourn his passing as they would a family member. When he stopped to recall how very helpful L.W. had been, how truly kind he was when Sid arrived in the District for the first time, the son of an old friend, and how very *wise* his advice had always proven to be—then realized it was all gone now, never to return—the tidal-wave of feeling deep within Sidney Villary, sensations such as he'd never before experienced, suddenly revealed the horror, the sheer torture of irrevocable *loss*—an extremely challenging emotion to digest as a forty-year-old novice.

Sprinting through section after section of the paper, he searched frantically for obituaries, his last chance to see the names of L.W. and Leslie Lee's children in black-and-white in order to ultimately commit them to memory. Were any or all of them ever in need of his services, and he was still in a position to assist in any way, it would be done, no questions asked; he owed him that much and a great deal more. He found a section marked 'All About Town' and opened it: the death notices began on page 4, and L.W.'s write-up consumed nearly an entire column, top to bottom. Hungry for information, he perused from the start, skimming rapidly line-by-line until encountering names, dates, and other niceties, at which time his reading slowed:

'**L. WILSON SHAW**, age 67, of Georgetown, died suddenly on July 29 at St. Matthews Hospital in Georgetown. He was born April 2, 1947 in Mountain Home, Idaho, to James Cooper and May Gunnerson Shaw. Mr. Shaw served with distinction in the United States Army. He is survived by his loving wife of 39 years, Leslie Lee Shaw. He leaves three children: his son, Joseph Shaw (Emiline) of London, U.K.; his daughter, Patricia Stallings (Jeremy Stallings) of Mesa, AZ; and his son, Thomas Shaw, United States Army, Signal Corps, stationed overseas. Mr. Shaw, whom many people referred to as 'L.W.' or 'Major,' won the Distinguished Service Cross while serving............'

'..............sent to Brussels, Belgium, in 1994 to assist with post-Soviet reconfiguration treaties with long-standing members of the North Atlantic Treaty Organization (NATO) and countries formerly comprising Yugoslavia (Bosnia, Croatia, Serbia, et al). While stationed in Brussels, Mr. Shaw was named Special Envoy to Ambassador Henry Watts in the Federal

Republic of Germany as part of the negotiating team to end the conflict in Croatia and Serbia...............'

'..............Visitation will be observed Thursday afternoon at Watauga Hills Funeral Home in Georgetown, from 2:00 P.M. to 4:30 P.M. High Mass and Celebration of Life Memorial Services will commence Friday morning at 11:00 A.M. at National Cathedral, Massachusetts Avenue at Wisconsin, in Northwest Washington D.C. His body will be laid to rest in Mountain Home, Idaho, after his final journey home by rail to join in calm repose his parents and other family members in the cemetery watched over by the mountains surrounding.............'

'...............Honorary pallbearers at the High Mass are: the Honorable Clancy Swift of Montana; the Honorable Daniel Pritchert of Oklahoma; Lieutenant-General Edward Loftis; the Honorable Robert Butterworth of Pennsylvania; the Honorable Sidney Villary of Texas; Major-General M.E. Carlson; the Honorable Pecton Manville of Arizona; and Vice-Admiral Everett Clayton.'

He very slowly, very deliberately read the names of the honorary pallbearers a second time, not so much to see his name *in lights* as to wonder at being included in such exalted company. So impressive was the list he didn't pause to observe that one of the pallbearers was a well-known liberal senator;

he simply didn't *care*. He was to be an honorary pallbearer at the funeral of the one man whose opinion he valued above all others; someone, perhaps L.W.'s wife, whom he'd never met, thought enough of him to count him amongst the most honored list of men he'd ever *seen*. It was simultaneously astonishing and magnificent—and overwhelmingly humbling—an odd combination for someone like himself who never had occasion to shed a tear for anything, but as he downed a healthy swallow of bourbon, then another, he felt the unique and wholly unfamiliar sensation of tears dropping from both eyes onto his cheeks. He felt fine; he just missed him. As he sat pondering how his life had been forever altered, Cas gave him a supportive pat on the back. Sid turned and looked at his friend, eyes moist, yet opened wide in bewildered sadness, unable to speak his heart.

"Go ahead, let it out . . I did . . it'll kill you if you don't . ."

The parking lot at Watauga Hills Funeral Home, normally more than large enough at 130 spaces, filled to capacity at 2:12 P.M. Thursday afternoon, sending visitors scrambling for impromptu parking arrangements, even though management staff had wisely placed a rustic-looking employee on-site to usher-in someone new as quickly as a space became available. L.W. wasn't the *only* guest in temporary residence, only the best-known, so funeral home management designated the Shenandoah Room for the Shaw family due to its larger-than-normal seating capacity and configuration close to the main entrance. In anticipation of a distinguished assemblage of visitors, a royal-red carpet was laid from the doorway of the Shenandoah to the gondola supporting the closed bronze casket, thirty-two additional chairs brought in to help with what they correctly assumed would develop into an overflow crowd. They didn't have long to wait: Corcoran Turner, minority leader of the U.S. Senate and certainly no champion of L.W.'s perceived political leanings, arrived with his wife a few minutes after two to extend their sympathies to Leslie Lee, a gracious gesture made even more poignant by Lauren Turner's tearful hug with the grieving widow.

Traditionally an early-riser, Sid arrived at his abandoned office a little after seven-thirty to check his government-sanctioned e-mail: he was *still* receiving notes of congratulations and general gratitude from not only his Christian constituents in west Texas, but from good, solidly-religious folks all over the country. Donations from outside Texas had quadrupled! These rampant successes had been somewhat tempered, of course, by the fact that he'd stopped checking his personal e-mail at home when the incredible tally of hostile messages reached fifteen *thousand* the week before. The messages he found on his office laptop, now numbering over two hundred due to his absence since the previous Friday, were more of the same: God and Jesus—not necessarily in that order—*loved* him and would see to it that he'd sweep past his opponents in *both* elections! He reluctantly recalled one of the last messages he'd read on his personal e-mail which, surprisingly enough, also had Jesus as its subject: a young lady, ostensibly from somewhere in southern California, suggested that if Jesus Christ had even the faintest notion of what the congressman was doing in the name of his Lord and Savior, the son of God would never get off the analyst's couch—or the commode! It had actually been the nicest message he'd seen on his home e-mail in *weeks*, the others ranging in tone and ugliness from "incredibly-*nasty*" to "dreadfully-*threatening*," .. like the first few hundred he'd slogged through.

The more-engrossed he became with his office e-mails the

more concerned he felt with the level of hostility certain of his House colleagues declared regarding the contentious spending bill everyone was so up-in-arms about. *Well*, thought he . . you guys can do what you like, but Sidney H. Villary isn't moving one *millimeter* from his previous position! So enamored with his single-minded sentiments he forgot to keep track of time, casually firing-off rebuttals to opponents and weak-kneed supporters bent on *"moving forward,"* it was almost 1:00 P.M. when he finally came up for air. Frightened into action, he locked his offices and left, stopping briefly to exchange a few words with two colleagues, both of whom were headed to lunch before embarking on the sad trek to Georgetown to pay their respects.   Angry for having worked too long, he grabbed a bite of lunch at an outdoor cafe a stone's throw from the famous Watergate complex, wishing he hadn't left his cellphone at home . . but how else would he ever get any work done? Now he wished desperately he could call Charlotte and, since she refused to discuss the two of them as anything but strangers, maybe she'd be willing to answer a few well-thought-out questions about the baby . . *just to hear her voice!* How he wished they were still on friendly terms! How he longed to hold her, to kiss her! How he *missed* gazing at her loveliness, being surrounded by her exquisite fragrance! How very impossible it all seemed: realizing his positions were incapable of being modified—and knowing her opinion of him as a hypocritical, thoughtless jack-ass wasn't likely to change—wishing and hoping was little more than an exercise in futility. Useless energy spent. Surrounded by people talking and sharing laughs with one another during his lunch, unfamiliar pangs of loneliness crept round him as he enjoyed his steak-and-blue-cheese sandwich.

When he drove to within a block of Watauga Hills at 2:35,

everything stopped: there was nowhere to go, nowhere to park, no visible means of escape—*nothing*, even though two D.C. policemen were now engaged in traffic-control, their whistles shattering long-abandoned notions of quiet respect. His car's congressional ID sticker *might* help him get inside the funeral parlor a bit quicker . . and, it might not; his car certainly wouldn't be the only one with government privileges today. Sensing movement to his right side as he sat motionless in the middle of the street, he peered in that direction just in time to see someone backing-out of a parking space barely ten feet ahead; noticing the military tag with two bright, silver stars, he wondered if he knew the occupant inside as the car pulled away, Sid taking the empty spot with a flourish, engine racing as though preparing for the big one at Daytona.

Before he completed the short walk to the funeral complex he stopped twice to shake hands and commiserate with other suit-clad clusters of men, the vast majority of whom stood solemnly grim-faced and respectful, invariably promising to see him again at the memorial service the next morning. Another dozen or so stood outside the main entrance talking quietly in the afternoon heat and Sid,   being acquainted with fully half of them, stopped again to shake hands, in full agreement that it was, indeed, good to see one another, but under the most unfortunate circumstances imaginable.

The Shenandoah Room proved to be all bustle and chat, the noise level about what one might expect with the better part of a hundred people present in various stages of arrival, departure, and why-not-stay-awhile. Sid stopped long enough to mentally catalog the names already found inside the Guest Book situated outside the doorway of the central hall, signing-in as he admired the signatures of the powerful and well-known, key figures from congress, some noted VIP's from the

Pentagon—even a few names he thought completely out-of-character for such an event. When he stepped inside, he first spotted his parents situated toward the right-front, sitting close to a well-dressed lady who had to be Leslie Lee Shaw, two young men stationed nearby with several young women in close proximity. Scanning the room right to left, it pleased him to see some familiar faces sitting or standing in clusters scattered about the chairs, most contenting themselves by standing off to either side or all the way to the front, another ten or fifteen just inside the door with him at the rear. Wanting to march directly to his fallen comrade, he stopped to kiss no fewer than seven women on the cheek, shaking hands with twice that many before arriving next to the casket, an impressive coffin of indeterminate materials but of obvious quality and workmanship. He said a solemn, silent prayer with eyes closed, carefully placing his fingertips through the luscious white blossoms he couldn't recognize; the smooth, expensive feel of the metal he found strangely soothing as he knew this was as close as he'd ever again be to his friend. Peg Sorenson, the wife of a House colleague from Maryland, kissed him on the cheek amidst a fond embrace when his eyes opened, his father standing patiently right behind her.

"Come on, son," he said calmly, "there're some people I'd like you to meet . ."

He was first introduced to the oldest son, Joseph, then Thomas, the army officer home from duty in Afghanistan. Then he met the daughter, Patricia, and her husband, and it then occurred to him that all three children bore a somewhat striking resemblance to their father, Patricia being merely a softer,   more-elegant version of the 'old man.' He shook hands with a startling-looking woman, Joseph's wife, Emiline, who hailed from Sri Lanka, and was then led, heart in his

373

throat, toward the lady he'd seen with his parents as he entered. From ten feet away he could see her perfectly: a deceptively-lovely woman of refined simplicity, she required no makeup to enhance her oval face, which seemed calm and peculiarly content considering the present circumstances. Brown-eyed, with fairly-voluptuous lips and delicate nose set below a high forehead, her light-brown hair pulled up and back, its richness cascading halfway down her back, he guessed her at about sixty, though she could easily have passed for mid-thirties with such unwrinkled, blemish-free skin. Tall and lithe, she was a *vision*: that L.W. had loved such a woman seemed unflinchingly appropriate.

"Son, this is L.W.'s wife, Leslie Lee," said his mother, who was now seated next to the widow. "Leslie, this is my son, Sidney . ."

"I'm pleased to meet you, Sidney, at long last," she said calmly, offering her right hand, which he took in both of his as graciously and gently as he knew how. His eyes fixed upon hers and remained.

"I'm honored and humbled to finally meet you in this, the blackest week of my life," he said mournfully. "I am so *very* sorry and upset at the loss of your husband, their father, and my dear friend that I can hardly say what I feel . . I am simply *overwhelmed* . ."

She turned to the gentleman sitting to her right, an older friend dressed in Madison Avenue finery, who rose and walked away in full comprehension of her wish.

"Please sit down so we can talk for a minute," she said, patting the chair's seat for him. He quickly obeyed as she said "L.W. was really very fond of you . . he told me you reminded him of himself when he served in congress . . He maintained high hopes for your future . ."

"I always tried to make him proud of me . . It was my fondest wish that I perform to the best of my ability and that he, hopefully, would be pleased by what I did . . I received a handwritten note from him several weeks ago when I returned from my first campaign-trip back home . . I keep it locked in my desk-drawer, safe and secure . ." He paused for a moment before continuing. "I've decided to have it framed and placed on my office wall . ."

"Oh, L.W. *was* proud of you, Sid," she said reassuringly. "You were one of a very select few he thought worthy of his time, but he didn't take you under his wing just because you're the son of one of his favorite college chums—although I'm sure that didn't hurt—he thought your potential unlimited because you stick to your guns and play the game as it should be played . . with *tenacity!* . ."

"Is there anything I can do—anything at *all?* . ."

"There's really nothing to be done, is there?" she said serenely, her gentle gaze falling lovingly upon the flower-draped casket. "There's nothing left to question or ponder . . only to accept. I have to accept the fact that he's gone from me physically—we'll never know that sublime happiness again—but he'll *never* leave me because we'll always have each other . . Sidney, L.W. and I were very happy, just as your mom and dad are happy, and we were incredibly lucky that way . . We were compatible in just about every way a couple is capable of . . Thankfully, our children have been lucky that way, too—well, not our Tommy yet, but he's still so young he's plenty of time—and L.W. always hoped you'd be lucky the same way, because at a fairly young age he instinctively came to understand how two-as-one was infinitely stronger than two-as-*two* . ."

"We never really talked about it because I've always been

375

single . ."

"Maybe you and he never talked about it," she said with a mischievous twinkle in her eye, "but *we* certainly did! . ."

Sensing he'd been set-up, he suddenly drew back a little and glared past Leslie Lee to his mother, who was busy speaking with the older gentleman who gave up his seat for Sid.

"*No,* your parents have nothing to do with this," she assured him, her complacent smile soothing his ruffled feathers. "Believe me, L.W. and I, being longtime friends with your folks, have always been keenly aware of their desire for you to marry and give them a grandchild or two—and between those two events, I've become more and more convinced they'd settle for grandchildren under *any* pretext— not just you being married first, *then* following suit . . But that's not what L.W. was really concerned about at *all* . ."

"*No?*" he said, his curiosity slowly being piqued. "What was it, then? . ."

"He always felt whether a man was single or married was a personal choice and should be left alone . . I *myself* was a good three or four years later than all my female friends when we married, so I've no room to talk—I just *knew* he was the right one the day we met, and I was right—so you see, there's no magic formula to follow or anything of the sort, just as there's no particular day you suddenly awake and discover you're but a single day too old to get married! . . What he was concerned with might not seem like much, but he was worried you'd reach your forties and, being by yourself with no outward desire for companionship, your sense of solitude might slowly morph into *loneliness,* which can become something more, and a potentially *dangerous* 'something more,' at that . ."

"He worried needlessly then . . I'm already forty—actually, I'm a little bit closer to forty-*one* now—and I'm better than ever," he said, forcing a smile to help betray the terrible weight of the occasion. "I enjoy my solitude now as much as I ever did—besides, it's not like I'm so incredibly busy I don't have time for friends, or even girlfriends—didn't you know I have my very own dating service, open for business twenty-four-seven—even *holidays?!* . ."

"*Really?*"

"Absolutely, yes," he said, and he leaned forward to whisper in her ear, a fresh conspirator readily-trusted with top-secret information, his voice but a whisper. "The 'Mr.-and-Mrs.-Villary-Would-*Kill*-For-A-Grandchild' dating service has been open for business for almost as long as I can remember—it's just that business has been a little *slow* . ."

"I *see!*" she grinned happily, half-turning to her left for a moment to ensure his mother hadn't heard his impromptu admission. The sensation, the mere sight of seeing L.W. Shaw's wife enjoying something he said, transformed his trip to the funeral home from one of grief to that of an unqualified success in the space of a few seconds, a glimmer of light in what had to be the darkest, most somber week of his life. "You know, Sidney . . it's both sad *and* funny, but there's more truth in your words than most would know—L.W. and I have both listened for years about how uncooperative you've been, and we've been sympathetic to their point-of-view, for the most part . . but I understand your position, too. My husband just didn't want you to be lonely for too long, is all . . *and*, he wanted someone near you in case anything happened to you . ."

"In case something *happened* to me?! . . Like what? . ."

"Oh, you know—if you were to fall off a ladder cleaning-out gutters or something, and broke your arm, or if you were to get really sick suddenly and needed to get somewhere *stat* . . that's all he meant . . you'd have someone there to help you, to drive you to the E.R., if need be . ."

"Not to worry," he smiled reassuringly. "I'm as healthy as a horse . ."

"Sure," she said agreeably, "right now you probably are . ." She turned her gentle gaze toward her husband's casket and gave it a long, lingering, mournful stare, the flowers, even the coffin itself, insufficient to shield her vision from the contents within. "L.W. was healthy, *too* . ."

Sid felt the tingly sensation of the hair on the nape of his neck bristling in shame: he'd somehow managed to worsen an already dreadful situation, grasping defeat from within the jaws of victory. The fact of its having been utterly unintended had no bearing. In quiet desperation, he stared mournfully at the coffin with her.

"They're simply beautiful," he ventured quietly.

"What's that?" she said finally, the spell dissolved, her attention returned his way.

"The flowers . . they're just *gorgeous* . . what are they? . ."

"White gardenias, his favorite . . for as long as I knew him he adored everything about them, with lilies and roses a close second. In fact, the night we met, L.W. had an enormous white blossom pinned   to his lapel . . he was always pleased with himself for that because you can't always find them . ."

She suddenly leaned-in toward him, a conspirator again, and spoke in a hushed voice.

"Can I tell you a little secret? . ."

"*Absolutely!*" he grinned, grateful for the distraction and, even more-so, her sacred trust. "Please do! . ."

Her voice a murmur to maintain the integrity of her

revelation, she said "Several years ago when Frank Sinatra died, L.W. somehow discovered white gardenias were *his* favorite, too—so he strutted around, proud as a peacock, saying 'Well . . of *course*, they were his favorite! . . Frank knew I loved them, *too!*' . . Would you believe he actually *shared* that with a few friends, as though it were true?! . . I tell you, the sheer audacity of the man was something to behold! . ."

"*Really!?*" It was a side of Wilson Shaw he'd never known existed, the result of which found Sid laughing out-loud in spite of himself: what *nerve!* "He actually *said* that!? . ."

"I'm afraid so . ." She leaned toward him again, ready for yet another quick revelation delivered in the same muted tone. "L.W. *never* said so . . but secretly? . . he was tickled *pink* he and Frank loved the same flower! . ."

"I'm not surprised . ."

He sat grinning at the coincidence, marveling at the workings of the world. What were the odds? The week prior, while chasing-down a can of shave-cream in a drugstore, he'd stumbled upon an old Sinatra CD, a 50's-vintage number he'd never heard of, and even though he recognized none of the song titles, he'd bought it anyway. He'd listened to it ever since: perhaps his parents, whom he'd never, ever considered *hip* in any way, weren't as naïve and out-of-touch as they seemed.

As his eyes scanned the space beyond where his mother sat talking and panned right, he caught the cheerless sight of Dow and Velma, or what was left of them, entering the Shenandoah Room clothed in their Sunday-finest, Dow in a well-cut three-piece and Velma decked in a svelte-looking black dress. Haggard and forlorn from their dreary set of circumstances, most of their wounds the self-inflicted type, their droopy, blood-shot eyes served as the perfect reflection of the immense strain they'd endured since Tuesday morning. Joining Cas and Sid at the bar in west Arlington after dropping-off luggage at their hotel, it had been a drunk for the ages: D.P., in rare form on the flight from El Paso through Denver to D.C., managed to destroy twice the amount of alcohol he might normally be expected to consume through sheer sympathy and finagling. Velma, never one to go out of her way to fly, drank if for no other reason than to soothe her frazzled nerves. All in all, the bar management had been truly kind to them, the first-assistant sending over food selected in a dual effort to keep them relatively sane and, hopefully, free from alcohol-poisoning. D.P. strolled through a fifth of Scotch, Velma opting for a slower, more pain-free descent into ruination by ordering Harvey Wall-bangers before surreptitiously siphoning-off her husband's seemingly endless parade of cocktails; Cas, for his part, achieved what he'd later refer to as "cognizant *nirvana.*" None of them could quite recall having left the bar, including Sid, who graciously covered the nearly three-hundred-dollar tab, so there was little question in his mind as to what *their* morning felt like when they at last came up for air, poor things. It hurt to see them.

Excusing himself, he barely negotiated the thirty or so feet to his friends before Velma grabbed him and held him close, hanging on for dear-life, a bewildered, "What-*hit*-me?!"-stare on what remained of D.P. Sid kissed her forehead and smiled down at her.

"You okay, sweetheart? . ."

"*Yes* . . but I drank too much, then slept too long, so I'm not feeling—or looking—my best by a long-shot—and I feel so *badly* for the family . . I only met him three times, but I feel like my brother died, and I *hate* feeling like this . . Where is she, Sid? . ."

He no sooner got them headed in the right direction than he felt a tap on his shoulder and, fully expecting to turn and face another colleague or his wife, eager for a hug and peck on the cheek, met his surprise of the week. There they stood, three of them in business suits, and a more unlikely threesome   he couldn't imagine. And what the hell were *they* doing there? Jake Steinberg, a congressman from New York City and avowed liberal, stood to the left; Benny Marsh, another liberal from Minnesota, stood front and center; and the biggest foe of all, Sean Weir, from San Francisco, who stood politically a few notches to the left of the Kremlin, stood right. Too stunned to speak, instantly suspicious of their motives for being there, he nevertheless shook hands and noticed no one was smiling.

"Come to *gloat?*" he said, only half-serious.

"Are you kidding?!" cried Marsh, an oldster like L.W., seemingly aghast at such invective. " Not on your life, buster . . We're here for the same reason *you* are . ."

"We came to honor our friend and fellow patriot," Weir, a man even younger than Sid, said with sincere respect. "He was one of the greatest Americans I *ever* knew, and I'm proud to say he was my friend and adviser . ."

Materializing as if from nowhere, an adorable-looking brunette of perhaps thirty, very pert and stylish in her midnight-blue and fuchsia outfit, sidled-up to Weir and put her arm round his back, at which point he returned the favor by kissing her on the cheek.

"Honey, this is Sid Villary from Texas, my House colleague . . Sid, this is my wife, Meg . ."

"How do you do, Meg," managed a still-bewildered Villary.

As they shook hands she suddenly said "*Oh!* . . You're the person-hood guru! . ."

"That's right," he said, though he wasn't quite sure what she meant.

"Honey, we were just talking about L.W. and what a friend he's been to all of us . ."

"We are completely *undone*," she said simply, her cheerful visage gone in an instant. "If it hadn't been for L.W., I don't know *how* Sean and I would've managed when we first got here . . He guided us to the best churches, restaurants, schools, told us where to have fun and what to avoid—*everything!* . . I love L.W. Shaw like my father! . ."

Sid could hardly believe his ears: here stood a group of men from way, *way* across the aisle—the gulf between them seemed as a veritable ocean—and they were singing L.W.'s *praises!* Suspicious by nature, and caught off-balance by ulterior motives he couldn't comprehend or identify, he first looked at Jake Steinberg, who hadn't said a word but nodded his accordance with the others. Then he eyed Benny Marsh who, smiling his famous "*Compassionate-Benny*" smile, seemed to divine his political enemy's uncertainty and doubt.

"I served with his unit," he said by way of explanation, "and though we disagreed about a great many things, I never knew a kinder, more-tolerant, more-accepting human being in my life . . We were friends for more than *forty* years, young man, and I wouldn't trade the experience of having known L.W. for anything. He was, in every way, a truly exceptional person, and I shall miss him . ."

"Sid, the three of us need to sit down with you and Cahill and Perkins and hammer-out this damn spending-bill mess!" Steinberg cried, finally coming to life, his two cohorts nodding their blessing to the proposal. "Maybe the rest of them can't see the light, but the six of us need to do it in memory of L.W.—*he'd* have found a way and gotten it done! . . Are you *in?* . ."

382

Before leaving the funeral home at half past four, the congressman from west Texas agreed to a top-secret, six-man meeting to help break the stalemate rotting on the House floor, again shaking hands with his three liberal co-conspirators, even hugging Meg Weir in full sympathy at having lost her dearly beloved L.W. . "I love him, *too*," he told her, and he meant every word of it. Careful to spend additional time with his parents, D.P. and Velma, the predictably-tardy Lynch Bohannon and Cas Turley, a dozen other friends and colleagues, and especially L.W.'s children, he saved a particularly gentle hug and kiss-on-the-cheek for Leslie Lee and Patricia. Before heading to his car he gave the widow Shaw both his e-mail addresses, his mailing address, and his cell-phone number, pleading with her to contact him immediately if there was anything in the world he could do for her, the children, or anyone they might need a helping-hand with. And just prior to heading through the doorway out of the Shenandoah Room he spoke privately with Tommy, the youngest son, promising to lend any required assistance with his military career if it was humanly possible. And as he made his way down the sidewalk toward his car, having stopped one last time at the coffin to say a private word or two with his fallen comrade, he wondered how it was possible to gain the trust of men he instinctively mistrusted—and to trust them in turn—and become working friends with a common goal through the sorrow of having suffered the loss of someone each man held close to his heart—how on earth could he possibly make an otherwise sensible woman—and such a vivacious, good-hearted, usually *kind*-hearted woman as Charlotte—see the light and come round to his way of thinking?

XVII.

"It's been . . *stressful* . ."

Had Sid Villary not been intricately involved himself with what had to be the most horrific week of that summer — or any summer, for that matter — D.P.'s three parting words likely wouldn't have carried half so much weight. But when he and Velma climbed aboard the plane late Friday afternoon at Dulles for the flight home, Sid's parents already safely in their seats and eager to leave, the congressman knew exactly what his friend was feeling. The untimeliness of their friend's early death had been too much; the hasty flight to D.C., under the worst of circumstances, had been too much; and the amount of Scotch he'd consumed that week, even for a seasoned veteran like Dow Pettigrew, had been *way* too much — all, indeed, had contributed to the unhealthy weight sitting on D.P.'s shoulders like a gigantic boulder with no place to go. Sid kissed his mother and Velma good-bye, promised to see them in Texas that Sunday afternoon, and hung around long enough to see the plane disappear into a near-cloudless sky. The main rigors of the week behind him at last, the short drive to Herndon energized him.

And what a superlative memorial service it had been: an appropriately grand send-off for one of the grandest gentlemen in all of Washington, D.C.! Sidney H. Villary occupied a place of honor, wedged between Pecton Manville and General Loftis, while no less a personage than the Vice-President, Edwin Jackson, delivered the eulogy. Easily the most humbling experience in his forty years, National Cathedral had been utterly, completely packed: nearly four hundred military from all branches turned-out in their dress uniforms to pay homage, another twelve or thirteen hundred mourners from all walks of life filling the splendid house of worship while four networks, their correspondents and film crews respectfully quiet, discretely recorded the event. At service's conclusion, Sid's mother secured a solemn promise from Leslie Lee to visit Texas before the year was done as the casket rolled out of the holy sanctuary, seemingly-endless rows of service members rendering crisp salutes to the fallen hero.

Now he drove east toward his house from the airport, heavy-hearted from the abysmal week, yet strangely roused now that formal activities had concluded—"loaded for *griz!*" as L.W. liked to put it. Mere blocks from his residence, he passed the right turn-off leading to his driveway and headed straight for the District, traveling quickly several miles before bearing-off right to go south in pursuit of his favorite watering-hole: after all, it was Friday night, his plane to Texas didn't leave until late Sunday morning and, as D.P. had so astutely observed, the week had been utterly *Borneo*.

The Friday-night crowd at Pandora's Box, typically boisterous and loud, filled every table and booth available; the rectangular bar, the true centerpiece of the Box, maintained stools on all four sides, but a quick check revealed only two empty seats, neither situated in a location that especially suited him. Resigned to the corner seat on the northwest side, his lines-of-sight to the ceiling-mounted big-screenswere hardly adequate, but he found solace nonetheless; six weeks down the road the Redskins would be playing, too, and by then finding a seat, *any* seat, would be a major undertaking.

He managed to spot the Nationals game being played-out in Phoenix without becoming a circus contortionist, but couldn't help notice a big-screen directly overhead four or five feet up and a foot behind him, which was *extra-special*: someone sitting across from him had a simply wonderful view! Encouraged by the sight of Max, the Box's main bartender/music-programmer, holding dominion over the Friday evening bar-action with an able assist from a long-time server named Calley, his outlook brightened: any *schmuck* could pour a bourbon or open a bottle of beer, but Max was both affable and efficient. Roughly Sid's age, the veteran mixologist grinned and waved at first cognizance of their well-known patron—good tippers, after all, *were* accorded certain privileges at the Box—and trundled over to Sid's corner, utterly prepared to begin the inevitable train of whiskey deliveries. Sid's eyes sparkled in anticipation.

"Let me have a Guinness, Max," he said without thinking, his eyes on the Nationals game spread across the screen twenty-five feet away, his focus spread from D.C. to El Paso. Max reached inside a cooler directly beneath him, grabbed a cold bottle of stout and opened it, and set it on the bar next to Sid's left hand, his expression an odd mix of humor and doubt. The congressman turned away from the game long enough to grab his drink, saw the brown bottle and frowned, then looked up at a clearly-perplexed Max.

"*Guinness?!*" he said—like someone else made a mistake.

"I wondered, too!" grinned Max, "but *that's* what you ordered . . so *that's* what I gave you . ."

"Son-of-a-*bitch!*" he muttered under his breath, shrugging it off. Too bad Cas wasn't there to enjoy the spoils. "But it's been a long, hard week, Max . . just put the 'Guinea' on my tab and give me the usual, please . ."

386

"Okay . . need a menu?"

"Not right now, thanks . . I had a dinner-sized lunch early afternoon I'm still feeling . . Maybe a bite or two later? . ."

"Just let me know . ."

By seven-thirty, the Nationals—D-backs contest knotted at 3-all in the top of the sixth, the announced crowd of over 21,000 basking in the glorious, arid 105-degree heat in downtown Phoenix, Sid was still warming-up to the tune of bourbon-and-water, rocks. The Box, only marginally less-crowded than an hour before, maintained its Friday-night noise level to the extent that, everyone keeping-up with the action, like the congressman, could only *watch* the action— unless, of course, they happened to be sitting within two or three feet of the screen. With two out in the top of the sixth and a runner on first, Sid watched triumphantly from a short distance away as someone in a red and blue-trimmed Nationals shirt hammered a 3-1 fastball into the left-field bleachers for a 5-3 lead, rousing cheers from a fair-sized portion of those present. As the hitter jogged around the bases Sid's eyes caught sight of a smaller-screened TV to his left and further down, a different 'game' being played-out on another network: it was footage of the magnificent service held earlier that day for L.W. Shaw. As the camera swung to the left he identified the area he and the other pallbearers had occupied, followed by the sight of hundreds upon hundreds of others, grim-faced and somber in their suits and uniforms, all gathered for the formal farewell. The church-footage suddenly vanished, replaced by a picture not of a young L.W. in his army togs, but of an older, more mature, more distinguished-looking Shaw in a suit, the new image of his friend reasonably close to the way he'd looked when last they met. He quickly slid-off his stool and stood proudly erect, hoisting his bourbon high in the air for a few seconds until L.W.'s picture faded from view, then finished-off the contents in two large gulps, re-taking his seat. Max, the bartender, perceptive by nature and known for not missing much, observed his favorite bourbon customer start-to-finish, immediately sending Calley with bourbon-and-water-rocks number five. Drifting Sid's way a moment later, he noticed the now-gloomy visage, instantly connecting the memorial service with his somber-faced friend.

"Did you know him? . ."

"I knew him *well*, yes . ."

"Were you there today? . ."

Taking a long, mournful belt of his drink he said "In a way, I feel like I'm still there . ."

When the game ended in a 6-4 victory a few minutes after nine, Pandora's Box had bid farewell to half its dining-room clients, most of the bar patrons long departed. Initially attracted to the Box four years prior, meeting colleagues there for dinner and drinks, Sid averaged a few stops a month for the very same, occasionally dropping-in on a whim for a drink or two; wisely, a salad or plate of hot-wings invariably accompanied his ride home. Being a semi-regular long enough to familiarize himself with the menu and, not necessarily a creature-of-habit where food was concerned, he knew the Box's offerings well enough to detect changes without being told, the addition or subtraction of a particular item perfunctorily noticed as a matter of routine. Encouraged by the Nationals' 6-3 lead headed into the bottom of the ninth, he ordered a celebratory chef's salad with bread-sticks, dispatching both by game's end when management cut sound to the TVs. There almost three hours now, he hadn't heard anything beyond the noisy crowd inside and a semblance of the game's color-commentators, delivering the play-by-play in bits and pieces. Now the background music came pouring through the system speakers, plainly audible but nowhere near screeching-loud. The robust tinkling of the jazz piano and catchy melodies provided a welcome contrast from the earlier din of chatter and nervous laughter, Sid clinging tenaciously to his sacred discipline of bourbon administered in small doses. It pleased him to think Max, situated behind the bar all evening long—save a short break around eight— seemed to have accomplished a reasonably-lucrative night, an attractive blonde sitting opposite, her full attention on the bearer of drinks, an enticing bonus.

"Max? . .Did you just start the music a little while ago? . ."

"Good lord, no," he grinned, setting Sid's number six in front of him. "I program the evening's sounds, so that's always the first thing I do when I come in at three . . the key is that I *have* to know if there's a game playing later on, because that affects *what* I play and *when* I play it—otherwise, there's something loud and lively running while the game's on, which tends to piss people off—mightily!—so I tend to play my hot-'n-heavy *early*, before half the town shows-up . . then I tone it down for two-and-a-half or three hours while the game's on, and—at least theoretically—after the game's over, I should be able to go hot 'n heavy again . . but, it rarely shakes-out that way . ."

"Oh? . . Why's that? . ."

"The late hour, mostly . . nobody much wants to crank it up in so small a space after nine, so instead of givin' 'em heavy metal or rock n' roll, I'll cruise-in with some blues or jazz— maybe even a little easy-listening—and that's the way it stays for the rest of the night . . just between you and me, if I thought I could get away with it? . . I'd put on classical and

389

never take it off . ."

"Classical?! . . You mean like . . like, ummm—"

"Like Beethoven, or Mozart, or Haydn—I could listen to "Jupiter," or the fabulous *Ninth* twenty-four-seven, and it wouldn't bother me at all . ."

Not recognizing any part of what the other was saying, he said "You're about my age, aren't you, Max—early forties? . ."

The bartender grinned and glanced down the bar at the blonde, who held him in her sights.

"Well . . the *forties*, anyway . . why?"

"You were already working here when I made this place my home-away-from-home—and that's been a while . . how long you been here? . ."

"It'll be seventeen years this October—and if you're wondering why I've stuck it out so long in one place—well, you can figure it out . . You're a smart guy . . Truth is, I don't work for just wages and tips—though I do alright there, too . . I've had a piece o' the action ever since I procured a bottle of '76 Rhine *Beerenauslese* for the boss's wife back in '02 . . They were in Europe for three weeks in July   of 2000 for their silver anniversary and didn't want to come home—and that'76 Rhine wasn't just *any* bottle of wine—so things have worked-out pretty well for me . . Excuse me a minute . ."

With that he sauntered away toward the blonde, her empty glass begging for attention, leaving Sid to ruminate on the week's events, the weariness he'd been saddled with, the ocean of priorities swirling madly through his head— campaigning, flying home, his parents . . and, the hole in his heart. For a few minutes he failed to realize the music had changed, the piano and saxophone gone now, the heady combination of bourbon and melting ice mellowing the unfamiliar feelings of regret and anxiety as the melodious, uniquely-smooth voice delivered an unwaveringly-upbeat Johnny Mercer tune. Suddenly, through the indigo haze of booze and fatigue, he recognized it—and only one man in the world could sing like *that*. He grinned proudly at having correctly identified the voice—and he hadn't had much to grin about all week.

"Hey, *thanks*, Max!" he cried across the bar, his mood uplifted literally in the blink of an eye. "That sounds great! . ."

"I didn't know you liked Frank . ." After setting a couple of beers on the bar for two youngsters to Sid's left, he sidled back over towards Villary, wiping the bar-top as he moved, dirty glasses and empty bottles disappearing in the process. "People our age—and young people in general—don't seem to know much about him, but I've been listening to him since I was fifteen . . In fact, he's the sole exception to the rule I mentioned a little while ago! . ."

The bourbon and fatigue having their inimitable way, Sid stared through empty, unseeing eyes.

"Exception? . ."

"I said I'd play classical music and nothing else if I had my way? . . I'd like to retract that statement in favor of Frank—listening to him is never a bad idea . . nice to know you like him, too . ."

"I owe that to my parents," he confessed, surprised at the realization. "They've been listening to him for as long as I can remember—and now I'm hooked, too . . What you're playing sounds as good as any I've heard . . what is it? . ."

"One of my personal favorites," said Max. "Hold on a sec . ."

Crossing the length of the bar, he reached down to open a cabinet door and revealed the sound system's electronic heart, the amplifying equipment lit-up in electric splendor. Searching briefly, he emerged a few seconds later with a translucent CD jacket and promptly carried it back to Sid's eager hands.

"It's from the early 60's . . I've always liked the numbers, and the arrangements are especially nice . . That's a commemorative copy there . ."

Mesmerized, he took his time admiring the artist's rendition of Sinatra's smiling face, taken from the right side, "*Sinatra and Swingin' Brass*" highlighted in three pastel colors proclaiming the work's title. Three song titles he instantly recognized.

"It's a commemorative copy, you say? . ."

"Yeah, they re-released it after his death in '98, like so much of his work . . That's easily one of the most memorable times we've ever had here at the 'Box,' what with our clientele—you know, the ladies being so sad and all—and the men?! . . Bless their hearts, we set sales records that weekend we won't break for a hundred years . ."

"Really?" said Villary, finally prying his eyes away from the song-list on the jacket's back side. "*Sales* records?! . . like what? . ."

"Well, we got word of his passing kind of late that night—too late to do anything special that evening—so the owners, who are *huge* Sinatra fans, decided to run a special on Frank's favorite, umm, '*elixir*' the following night, which was a Friday, too," said Max, grinning like a kid at his use of the euphemism. "At first they thought it'd be great to give a price-break to anyone with blue eyes—in *his* honor, of course—but then they thought about it and decided that was too exclusionary—so we knocked a dollar off the price of his favorite and ran it as the 'Sinatra-*Special*,' and *oh-man!*—we'd never seen anything like it!—haven't since, either . ."

"By the way, what *was* Frank's drink?" Sid inquired innocently.

"Jack-Black!—and we sold so much of it that night the owners had to run around to a couple, two-or-three package stores and buy the stuff *retail* because our back-stock was gone before sundown! . . . Man, I tell you, it was *crazy!*—women crying in their drinks at every toast, men tearing-up when they heard his voice on the sound system! . . And now, over fifteen years later, we've never come within five hundred dollars in sales of that particular drink on that particular night—and mind you, we were selling it *discounted*, too! . . and it's a pretty popular drink anyway, you know? . . We sell a fair amount o' Black every day . ."

"Burned in your memory, huh? . . I'm not surprised . ."

"Friday, May the 15ᵗʰ . . I'll never forget it," said Max as he set another bourbon and water-rocks on the bar and moved on, the quintessential bartender, always on the move.

Sid instinctively clutched his fresh drink and took a hefty draft, still meditating on the tasks awaiting him before flying-out Sunday morning, the music as balm to his emaciated soul, when he suddenly set his drink down, cocked his head to one side and said "Max? . Did you by any chance say that was May *15ᵗʰ*? . ."

"Yes, sir, that is affirmative . . a Friday night for the history books . ."

"But Frank actually died . . the day *before* . . isn't that what you   said?   .   .
"That's right . . he died on a Thursday evening in L.A.," said Max with a casual nod, "on the 14ᵗʰ . . I'm sure of it . ." He continued pouring an exotic concoction for a patron on the bar's left end, catty-corner from Sid, but noticing the congressman's puzzled expression then said "It's inside the CD case, if you wanna' take a look—his dates of birth and death, I mean—but I'm absolutely *sure* it was Thursday the

393

14th! . ."

Sid carefully opened the CD jacket and found what he wanted on the sleeve's left side at top: 'Francis Albert Sinatra – December 12, 1915 —May 14, 1998.' He sat and stared at the dates in much the same way he'd stared at L.W.'s coffin, seeing everything, yet seeing nothing, strangely aware of the ghastly immensity, the unspeakable cruelty of the event . . even through his 90-proof eyes. Over and over the date of death cast its spell: May 14, May 14, May 14! MAY *14!* He'd seen the exact same day circled on a calendar in a kitchen: May 14!

"I was right on the date, wasn't I?" Max nodded triumphantly from the bar's other end.

"Yes, Max," he said with a discernible silence, ". . you were right on the date . ."

He'd never felt so lonely as he did now, sitting on a bar-stool at his favorite haunt. But how was that possible? How could a third-term congressman with a direct-support staff of a half-dozen energetic, enthusiastic, loyal employees, dozens of friends and supporters from within the ranks of the U.S. House, and thousands upon *thousands* of advocates and admirers from his home state, ever begin to feel he was thrust out upon the proverbial branch, unloved and unprotected, to go it alone now and for the foreseeable future? He thought of Mr. and Mrs. L.W. Shaw: yes, his friend was gone, never to return—and he'd known his wife less than two days—but he knew he'd never see them in his mind as separate individuals, as distinct, unrelated adults, without any semblance of connection . . no, they would only be remembered as a *couple.* That's what they'd become, and that's how he would always see them. What *was* it Leslie Lee had told him the day before when they'd finally ceased being complete strangers? *How* . . had she put it exactly? ("L.W. just didn't want you to grow old and lonely!") And of utmost significance: how would L.W. view his various and sundry personal and professional dilemmas? How would his mentor react to the knowledge that, in the world of political mud-slinging and dirty tricks, the Villary camp had been the first to smudge the lens? That the same camp wantonly—even purposefully—neglected to consider entire segments of the population he served? And, worst of all—dear *God*—how would L.W. view the fact that Sidney H. Villary, congressman from Texas's thirty-eighth district, had fathered a child and sought to disengage himself from the milieu? That he'd been so vain in his ambition to protect himself he'd completely cast aside any concern for the mother and child? That he'd been so forthcoming in assuming his responsibilities that his child's mother, only two and a half months pregnant, now refused to let the illustrious congressman have anything at all to do with either her or the child? That he'd acted like millions of other American men by sleeping with the female, leaving her bed with a temporary thrill of conquest and satisfaction—not to mention something else less-thrilling, but much more permanent—and summarily disappeared from view? My, yes . . what *would* L.W. think about his young friend's behavior? Yay . . or *nay?*

He took a hefty mouthful of bourbon and, rather than send it quickly to its appointed destination, let it wallow on his tongue, pleasing his taste buds, numbing his mind. *Well*, Sid . . yay or nay?

Staring straight ahead at nothing in particular, his eyes absorbing a Pandora's Box table forty feet distant, utterly without recognizing it or anything else as mere inanimate objects in a world dependent upon human animation, he saw himself as a creature of vanity. A selfish bastard. Wholly consumed with *his* career, *his* future, *his* ambition. A complete and utter *fool*—the kind of fool who would gladly deny his parents what was rightfully *theirs*; who would plot and scheme without consideration or decency, just to prove a point; who would say one thing because it suited him . . then do the opposite merely because it amused him; worst of all, the kind of fool who would spurn the love of a woman of genuine grace and class. The brick wall, heavy in its power to destroy, priceless in its ability to motivate, crashed like thunder on his empty head: he was absolutely, positively head-over-heels-in-*love* with this delectable, sensual, affectionate woman! Regrettably, she'd seen him for that which he appeared to be: a boastful, arrogant, egocentric prick, one entirely unworthy of her time and effort. So that was it. Accurate right down to his world-class hubris. Lord, what have I done?

What . . have I *done*?!

There was no time to waste now, no time to pause and reflect, no time for regret and apprehension. *That* time was over: action was the only possible remedy, and it had to be *now*.

"What's my tab, Max?" he almost shouted, off the bar-stool, wallet in-hand.

A minute later Sidney H. Villary, congressman from the 38th District in west Texas, turned abruptly on his heel and walked a straight and narrow line—if a slightly wobbly one—to the front door of Pandora's Box, then vanished into the humid, starry night.

One-handing the steering wheel as he tore over the two-lane headed southeast toward Tyson's Corner, he punched-in the numbers on his cell and waited: *voice-mail!* Click! Uh-*uhhh* . . no messages left *tonight!* A mile further he tried again with the same result. *Damn!* And what were the odds she'd gone to bed

396

early . . on a Friday night?! With a sudden sense of dread, he imagined her hurt inside her condominium, stretched-out prostrate on her parlor floor, helpless: *no*, Sid, one of the most naturally-graceful women on earth would never allow herself to succumb to such clumsiness, transformed into a maladroit . . simply because you're desperate to see her! Mashing the brake like a teenager on his first night with a license, he turned right into her complex at the last possible moment, sparing a chunk of masonry protecting the water fountain cascading over the river-rock below. Reducing his speed to virtually nothing, he took his foot off the accelerator, idling past the darkened units until reaching building R, exhilarated at having arrived so quickly, yet apprehensive about a face-to-face meeting. *Yes, there's her car!* He parked and crossed the lot, soft light pouring through her downstairs windows: okay, Charlotte, are you in there or *not?* Ignoring the invisible gremlins screaming at him to stop wasting his time, he knocked lightly and waited, the translucent curtain over the backdoor glass revealing no interior movement. A few seconds later the door swung open and there she stood, resplendent and stunning in a cotton-print, orange-and-mauve sun dress, a comb and brush in mother-of-pearl adorning her glorious locks.

"*Charlotte?!*"

"Well . . *look* who it is!" she grinned through the screen-door, her Runnymede accent more evident than usual. "If it isn't the Honorable Congressman *Hypocrite*, of west Texas! How *art* thou, my lord and dual-tongued Janus? . ."

"You're here," he finally managed, heart in his throat.

"Evidently . ."

"You're here," he said softly, a pleasurable edge to his voice now. "May I come in? . .

"Do you know what *time* it is? . ."

He stood contentedly on her second doorstep, looking up at her from below, elated at breathing-in the sheer sweetness of her nature, delighted with the cosmetic-free loveliness, his silent pleasure more than satisfactory with their proximity.

"Yes, Charlotte . . I know *exactly* what time it is . ."

"Good *lord*, Sidney!" she cried in exasperation. "I just got out of the shower . . what is it you want?"

"I want to hug you and kiss you and tell you I *love* you," he grinned happily, "but I'd rather do it *inside*—where I can hug and kiss you . ."

When she stood staring at him, saying nothing, he immediately offered his premiere justification.

"It's so much more *fun* that way . ."

"Shall I *guess* how many cocktails the congressman has enjoyed this Friday evening? . ."

"You can guess if you like, but I'm willing to tell you—I want no secrets between us, Charlotte—*none!*—but I'd much rather tell you how many I've had once I'm *inside* . ."

Regarding him through narrowed eyes, her suspicious ears alerted to the sort of excrement one occasionally encounters when roaming through the pastures of rural England—true, he *did* seem to have a gift for pandering—he seemed perfectly fine right where he was: outside.

"Sidney, *please* . . it's really quite late . . now tell me what it is you want—and be *quick!* . ."

"I want to marry you . ."

"Then you've doubtless had *way* too much tonight and need to go home and sleep it off . . Now drive back to Herndon and get some rest, then call me next week . . wait a minute . . I'm working next week, so call me when it's more convenient for both of us—*Christmas* week would be good—or you could wait 'til the first week of the *new year*, when I'm home in

Surrey on vacation . ."

"I'm *not* drunk, Charlotte," he said evenly, even pleasantly. "Have I been drinking? . . Yes, quite a bit, actually . . Am I *drunk?* . . No, I'm not . . You don't see me standing out here struggling to maintain my equilibrium, do you? . . and, believe it or not, there's a *good* reason for that . . How am I ever going to apologize and beg your forgiveness if you don't let me apologize and beg your forgiveness . . . *inside?* . ."

"Let me make sure I've got this straight," she grinned, suddenly warming to the idea of desperation- without- subtlety. "*You*—Sidney Villary—want to beg forgiveness and apologize?! . . You know, that's so unlike you it's almost nauseating! . ."

"You're not going to let me inside, then? . ."

"No, I'm not . ."

"Then I'll have to tell you from out *here* . . Charlotte Tillstrom? . . I want to apologize for having been so incredibly blind as to doubt your intentions . . I'd also like to apologize for being so pig-headed and unwilling to see things any way but *my* way . . I beg your pardon, young lady, and solemnly swear never to do it again, *ever*—for as long as I live . . I also feel it's important for you to know that I *adore* you—that I am absolutely, positively, irrevocably *crazy* about you—I *love* you with all my heart, Charlotte Tillstrom, and I won't be happy, ever again, until you tell me you'll spend the rest of your life with me! . . Please say you'll marry me—*please!* . ."

"*See?!* . . Groveling isn't hard, is it? . . But tell me something, Sidney . ."

"Anything! . . Everything! . . *Whatever* your heart desires! . ."

"What on *earth* is wrong with you?! . . And why are you so very desperate to get *inside?!* . ."

Offering what he hoped was his most-ingratiating smile, he

said "Because I've been dying to get inside you ever since the *last* time I was inside you—*that's* why! . ."

"*Sidney!*"

"Can't we talk about this *inside*, please? . ."

"Talk about what?! . . There's nothing to talk about! . ."

"Go ahead then, turn me down, call me 'Sidney,' keep me out here on your steps, I don't care if you abuse me or not, all I want is to know for certain that you'll let me stay in your life and take care of you and our child for as long as you'll let me . . I *love* you, unequivocally and absolutely, and would blow away like dust if you didn't want me, because I love you *madly*—and it took me a while to realize it, but the fact is . . I've probably loved you since the first moment I saw you sitting across the bar at Pandora's Box . . I'm just sorry it took me so long to tell you . ."

She covered her heart with folded arms in a reflexive motion: how could he speak so many words in such a short space of time when he hadn't spoken that many since they'd first met? How could it be? Might he be in some sort of danger if he tried to drive home to Herndon in his condition? And how was it possible the father of her child could be such a well-known member of the American congress and still be such an out-and-out . . *flake?*

"Are you going to behave like this . . for a *while*, you think, Sidney?   ."

"I imagine so . . for the rest of my natural life, I think . ."

"You had better come in, then . . where you're less likely to get in trouble . ."

No sooner had she flipped the button-latch to open the screen-door a crack than he was inside, encircling her in his grateful arms, hugging her close to him in a warm embrace, effortlessly lifting her off the floor in triumphant celebration,

400

laughing, replete with joy.

"Are you some sort of maniacal, mechanical Sidney-*twin*," she said when he set her down, "who mysteriously managed to grow-up with *scruples?!* . ."

"Go ahead, make fun of me all you like," he said happily, "because the only thing I care about—*really* care about—is your happiness! . . And you know something? . . You're as happy and contented a person as I've ever known . . so I'll leave you alone and hope you stay that way . . And we can have as many children as you like—one or *ten*, it doesn't matter to me, however many you want—I just want to make sure you stay as happy as you can possibly be! . ."

She stopped to hold his face in her hands, to search his eyes for signs of what might be unrecognizable, yet undeniable evidence he was inebriated to some degree: well . . how about *that?!*

"Why, *Sidney!* . . you don't seem to be drunk at *all!* . ."

"I never felt more sober in my life, Charlotte—nor have I ever seen my future more clearly—I want to spend the rest of my life with you . . starting *now!*—Of course, I'm sure you realize you've only yourself to blame for this! . ."

"*Myself?!*"

"It was *you*, Charlotte Tillstrom, who told me I'd never find a woman who could love me more or better than yourself— and at this point I'm inclined to agree with you—and since I could never in a thousand years find anyone better to love and hold dear . . it would appear you're just going to have to become my wife! . ."

Tearing herself from his embrace, she backed away a step, fire in her smoldering eyes.

"I'm not going to marry *you!*" she vowed, unafraid to assert her vision of their future. "I told you I *love* you—not that I'd ever marry you, Sidney—they're *not* the same! . ."

"Then we can just live together," he continued, undaunted. "You and me and the kids . . and I'll build the house that *you* want, wherever you like, okay? . . I just want to be with you and love you, that's *all* . . so I'm willing to take you any way I can get you . . I will cherish you and hold you close to my heart to my dying day, Charlotte . ."

"*Sidney!?* . . Can you not realize how very difficult it is for me to believe you when you do a complete and utter *about-face!?* . .What you're telling me is in direct contradiction to *everything* you stand for! How can anyone take you seriously when you spew such *nonsense?* . ."

"Charlotte," he said calmly, her hands held snugly in his, "I've made a great many mistakes and been wrong about more than I'd ever care to admit . . but I'm *not* wrong about my feelings for you, nor about my intentions to love and care for you and our children for the rest of my life . . The sad truth is, I can't guarantee I'll even be alive to do it tomorrow . . but I can promise you *this*: no woman on earth will be loved more ardently or completely, or held more precious or dear, than *you—that* much I can absolutely guarantee—until I can no longer draw breath . ."

She felt herself soften as he pulled her towards him again, their lips nudging closer, then closer still until kisses came as gentle as snowflakes.

"I love you, Sidney—and I *want* to believe you," she said. "I just wish there was some way I could know for certain . ."

They stood facing each other for what seemed to each a short eternity, inextricably snared in an impasse of their own creation, a viable solution beyond their grasp, helpless. Suddenly his face became strangely animated, an unmitigated grin of pure delight overtaking his features, the gloom and doom of a moment before cast away like so much flotsam.

"*Charlotte!* . . I've got an idea! . ."

XVIII.

The early August, mid-afternoon sun in west Texas bore down cruelly on the parched earth, sending anyone eager to catch-up on their gardening back inside to await a more seasonal opportunity to improve their landscapes. Cecil, the Villary's beloved yard-man, a veteran of countless ground-cover-and-flower initiatives over the span of twenty-three years, threw in the towel just before 2:00 P.M. when the temperature hit 103, high humidity serving as the catalyst of misery, as usual. "Mr. V? . . a Saturday afternoon in west Texas in summer should be spent watching baseball on TV!" he said by way of explanation, Mr. Villary sending him on his way with a cupful of ice and a bottle of cola to help ward-off the very real prospect of heat-stroke. "Damned if I'd be out there either, Cecil!" he said before retreating inside to the cool comfort of the den, the sun drenching the house's west side with its poisonous rays. The structure's *position* had proven to be the home's initial attraction for prospective buyers: with the facade angled nearly due-west, the back side received the morning sunlight, which was admittedly warm, but nothing compared to the withering heat of the afternoon. The relatively-abundant percentage of glass in the structure's rear—sliding-doors leading out to the patio, with more glass separating the den from the forces of nature, plus two other glass doors and slightly-oversized windows—had been a concern at first but, in Mrs. Villary's portentous words, *"That's why God, in his wisdom, created drapes!"* And that had cinched it: three short weeks later they moved-in and hadn't budged since. Their spacious master bedroom sat in the rear northern end, fastidiously draped against even the tiniest sliver of sunlight, and had survived two rather violent tornadoes; the den—Mrs. Villary preferred to call it the "take-it-easy" room—received the bulk of time spent within the house, and when the sun slowly positioned itself directly overhead, the drapes were pulled back, revealing the gentle hills to the east. The remainder of the day, any and all occupants now shielded from direct sunlight, was spent with the drapes pulled to the side, the separate two-car garage on the home's south end visible only if one sat closer to the glass wall in the den's northern section. Neither the formal front door, which was rarely used and then only when they entertained, nor the formal living room itself, was visible from the den, owing to the immense interior wall running from the hallway due-south thirty-two feet to the formal dining room. One could easily see the driveway on the home's south side— *if* he happened to be standing in the dining room or kitchen: an asphalt parking area for dinner guests, wide enough to handle three vehicles, had been added directly to the home's front years earlier, with a departure-lane running west-northwest to the street. But the den, secluded from view from any angle—unless one happened to be standing on the patio— yet the most private room in the house, save for the bedrooms, granted two-way security: outsiders couldn't see *in*, and the den's occupants couldn't see much beyond the patio but grass and the fence.

When the old man began to doze in front of the TV at 3:50, Mrs. Villary on her cell-phone with the mayor's wife and the very latest country-club gossip, and the front doorbell rang unexpectedly, she looked at her husband and said "Are you

405

expecting someone? . ."

"No, not a soul," he said with a quick glance at his watch, "and Cecil's been gone almost two hours . . ."

"Mandy? . . Let me call you back in a bit, someone's ringing our *doorbell!* . ."

She switched-off and laid the phone on an end-table, but had just started to get to her feet when she heard "*Mom? . . Dad? . . I'm home!*" from the direction of the front door.

"*Sidney?! . .* Is that *you?!*" she cried, frozen in mid-step.

Suddenly, one of the most outrageously-beautiful brunettes she'd ever laid eyes on stepped through the doorway, her hand held by the congressman from Texas's thirty-eighth district, who stopped next to her and stood proudly in front of his parents.

"*Sidney!?*" his mother cried, clearly stunned.

"Hello," Charlotte Tillstrom said softly in greeting.

The old man, rousted out of his recliner, stood and stared transfixed at the vision of loveliness not ten feet away, quietly muttering "Ava . ."

Then he looked his son in the eye—he *had* to know.

"*Ava?*"

Sidney Villary grinned exultantly, edging closer to his beloved.

"Mother? . . Father? . . I'd like you to meet the woman I love . ."